AXPHERIAL

Axpherial

**AJ
KELLEY**

Self-Published

ISBN Number: 9781088219836
ISBN Ebook Number: 9781088219881

First edition

DEDICATION

I DEDICATE THIS BOOK TO ALL THOSE THAT BELIEVED IN ME. THANK YOU FOR YOUR FAITH IN MY CRAFT. I GIVE YOU ALL THE LOVE AND GRATITUDE.

Prologue

The quiet ecstasy of space cradled a resplendent sphere, encircled by a solitary ring of light. Within this planet, an array of vibrant landscapes and seas unfurled. The lands displayed hues of vivid red, blue, green, and yellow, while the oceans predominantly shimmered in shades of blue, occasionally interspersed with seas of green and pink. Delving deeper, one could spot a petite island, its dark green surface adorned with splotches of blue. Nestled at its heart lay the advanced city of Elmana, where flying vehicles crisscrossed the skies, forming four distinct traffic lanes.

The cityscape boasted towering structures, surpassing any on Earth, their peaks nearly brushing the heavens. One particular building stood out, with its sharp, ivory silhouette dominating the skyline. Known as "The Great Strength," it served as the paramount government building in their world.

Surrounding this central hub sprawled a variety of residences, shops, and the bustling vivacity of urban life, all leading toward the dark blue sea. These illuminated buildings were interspersed with lands that floated high above, cloaked in vibrant green or blue vegetation. These floating lands hosted a variety of homes, many of which exhibited square or spherical designs.

Near the coastline, an impressive theme park unfolded. The accompanying beach, graced by velvety golden sands and gentle lapping waves, exuded grandeur with its sheer size and a boardwalk lined with an assortment of games and rides. These rides were enchanting, with a Ferris wheel-like attraction hovering several feet above the ground, seemingly unsupported, and a scarlet roller coaster executing precise maneuvers on a vibrant red, seemingly holographic track. The riders on the roller coaster cars filled the air with their excited screams.

Furthermore, the park featured computer-generated mini-games, with various screens and holograms.

Cheers reverberated throughout the park, as visitors reveled in joy and entertainment. Suddenly, a piercing screech, akin to a scream, tore through the park, prompting individuals to rush either toward or away from the source—the Ferris wheel. Each of the wheel's cabins plummeted to the ground, leaving the passengers trapped inside, unable to escape.

| 1 |

Kam

"Jump already!" A voice called from below. Kam shifted his gaze to the base of the roaring waterfall. He squinted against the bright sunlight, his bronze, sun-kissed skin glowing healthily. His kinky, curly hair formed a tall high-top style and glistened with moisture. His deep violet eyes were clearly visible in the late afternoon sun. His appearance suggested someone in their late teens. Lost in thought, he was jolted back by the call from below and prepared himself for a graceful landing.

"Stiff or what?" A female voice called out from the bottom of the waterfall, the same voice from earlier. She was a young woman with bronze skin and emerald green eyes. Her lustrous, jet-black hair cascaded down her back in a braid, and she wore midnight-hued clothes that hugged her chest and hips. She beamed, her cheeks creasing into symmetrical dimples that amplified her smile's brilliance.

Beside her stood a strapping young man with cobalt eyes, dark brown skin, short curly hair, and bulging muscles. He nearly towered over her, wearing loose black shorts that reached above his knees. Talo confidently stated, "I think he's up there looking for his confidence after he saw what I did." Orna raised an eyebrow and curled one corner of his mouth in a disdainful smirk. "I didn't know we were having a contest, Talo," he remarked. "Don't kill the fun, Orna," Talo retorted. "Contests are more fun!" she added. "Yeah, and I know how much you like fun,"

3

Orna teased. "Yeah, and 'stiff' up there is ruining it," Talo complained. "Come on, Kam! Whenever you're ready to lose!" Talo cheered.

Kam heard her loud and clear, smirking as he stepped back onto the smooth gray rocks covered in red moss. He focused and then, with a swift motion, executed three flawless flips before plunging into the lake with perfect form. Orna smiled at the sight, and Talo attempted to hide her admiration. Kam swam to shallower waters, trudging forward with a tight-lipped smile. "Did you enjoy that?" he inquired, genuinely curious. "That was perfection, man!" Orna exclaimed.

Talo's lips curled up in a mischievous smirk as she shot a sideways glance at Kam. "The third flip was a bit awkward, but otherwise amazing," she said, trying to sound pleasant. "Awkward? Even your compliments carry a hint of sarcasm," Orna remarked. "Yeah, yeah, it was great," Talo replied, attempting to sound unimpressed. "Wow, she accepts defeat like a champ," Kam said, smiling. Orna's lips curved upward, emitting a soft chuckle. Talo smiled, unable to truly dampen her spirits about something so minor. "You know we enjoy testing your fire. Straighten up," Kam said, giving her a friendly pat on the shoulder.

She had to tilt her head back to meet his eyes; he loomed above her, a full head taller. Talo was almost ready to give up, but she wasn't finished. "I may not be the best at this, but at least I'm more equipped to handle a delfona!" Talo said. "Hey, I'm getting better!" Orna chimed in. "Let's not talk about that," Kam said, holding back a laugh, and Talo cracked a small smile. Orna's cheeks reddened, and he averted his gaze, doing his best to hide it. All three of them were learning to open portals to other dimensions and various places in their universe; a common practice with a delfona. The delfona resembled a watch with a circular, middling-sized glass screen that took up most of the average wrist. It had many more functions that were hard for anyone on Earth to comprehend.

They ended up losing themselves in their swim, something not unusual for them. Kam suggested they should head back as the sky had shifted to a deep blue hue. Three moons encircled the planet, two of them half illuminated, while the third was a crescent. Two moons were similar in size to Earth's, while the third was much closer, dominating a significant portion of the sky. The two smaller moons were Khalofa and Talpo. Moto loomed large in the night sky, overshadowing the others.

They exchanged glances before rising into the air. Though physically similar to humans, they possessed something unique. Inhabitants of Axpherial were blessed with extraordinary powers like telekinesis, flight, and accelerated healing. They could recover from injuries three times faster than earthly humans. Kam and his friends resided on Elmana Island, slightly larger than the Bahamas on Earth.

Axpherians were a peaceful race, dwelling on the fourth planet from their sun in a seven-planet solar system. Renowned for their stunning appearance, they had eyes of extraordinary hues—violet, gray, blue, orange, green, and even red. Crime was virtually unheard of, despite their 117 distinct territories and numerous languages. United by one government, they held their meetings at The Great Strength.

Emerging from the waterfall, they faced a vast expanse of tall, amethyst grass swaying in the wind. As they descended, their eyes landed on a humble wooden cottage with two circular windows and a doorknob-less entrance. Kam placed his hand on the door, and a red light flickered before it opened. Inside, a slim blue couch with a wooden table stood in the center, covered in blueprints of vehicles, buildings, and other designs on cream-colored paper. Upstairs, a small room held a twin bed and two giant black bean bags. This was Kam's second home; his secret hideaway.

Kam had dreamt of building his cabin for two Earth years before acting on his plans. He chose a minimalistic design, carefully studying every aspect of his blueprints. He constructed the walls and frame piece by piece, drawing inspiration from his father, who had let him help build their current home as a child. The memory of putting part of the door together still made him proud.

Some Axpherians had a unique way of building that didn't rely on physical materials. Instead, they used mental designs to construct buildings, sparing their planet's resources. They were called Okrias. Kam belonged to this special group. Axpherians shared abilities and possessed one unique power. It took Kam three weeks to put his cabin together, with Talo and Orna observing most of the process. Talo even offered help, eager to be involved.

There were no divisions of rich and poor, and everyone had the right to build their homes on whatever land they wanted. Currency did exist, but was mainly used for obtaining goods and luxuries. To own property, Axpherians had to reach the age of maturity, which was 16 in Earth years. Kam and his friends were each eighteen in Earth years, which was equivalent to 4.2 Axpherial years. It took Axpherial four years to rotate around their sun, and four years on Earth equated to one Axpherial year.

The door slammed shut as they entered the cabin. "That was thrilling," Talo remarked. "Thrilling to watch your pride crash and burn," Orna quipped, earning a smirk from Talo, tinged with annoyance. "You know," Talo said, "Quietude suits you. It looks cute on you." Amusement played on Orna's smile. "Aww, you called me cute. I feel like I might die from being charmed to death," he joked, eliciting chuckles from Kam and Talo. "Come on, let Captain here get us home," Talo said, guiding Orna upstairs.

Kam's eyes crinkled, a smile spreading as he watched them ascend. An excited "Home!" resonated as the house hummed with a low engine sound. Two bright blue lights at the base provided power, lifting the house off the ground and into the sky. Faster than any of them could fly, it passed through the thin white clouds in the night sky. Kam admired the scenery, savoring the moment. He was truly living for this breathtaking view. Kam changed clothes as the house neared its landing.

Kam watched as Talo and Orna descended from the stairs as the home softly landed in the middle of a mysterious forest. The trees surrounding them were decorated with bright red leaves and were covered in a vibrant green moss. A perfect square of land seemed to be specifically tailored for the home. Kam could not help but smile as they all stepped out, now wearing clothes.

Talo was dressed in a pristine white tank top and a pair of equally airy white pants, while Orna was sporting a snug, sky blue sleeveless shirt and black pants. Kam had on a loose white sleeveless shirt, loose black pants, and a long, shiny black beaded necklace with a blue pendant that glimmered under the cabin's white lights.

The inhabitants of Elmana had a distinctive fashion style with mostly handmade clothing with silk and wool like material, and futuristic accessories like illuminated hair bands, wristbands, and necklaces. They also valued crystals and many Axpherians wore crystal accessories that radiated high energy that you could feel through touch alone.

They embraced in a tight hug, and it was evident to any onlooker that they shared a unique bond. Kam and Orna had been best friends since childhood and encountered Talo during their freshman year at the training academy. At first, they thought she was very arrogant and discourteous, yet they eventually discovered her gentle and compassionate nature. Despite her inclination to be competitive, they also saw that she was loyal and protective of those she cared for.

Kam, Talo and Orna were all required to attend the academy for at least five earth years, which was equivalent to 1.1 Axpherian years. Their parents homeschooled them in their early years, after which they went to the academy to learn how to further use their abilities and to gain knowledge in other subjects such as mathematics, science and technology. At the start of their time at the academy, they had to choose their desired profession, although they were allowed to change their minds later. Furthermore, they attended classes tailored to their chosen profession in addition to receiving basic education.

They were all juniors, as the graduation age was 4.3. "Do you think we'll get into trouble for being out late?" Orna asked, voice laced with worry. Talo replied confidently, "My mom's pretty lenient about stuff like this, so I'm good." Kam then added, with a grin, "If I'm quiet enough, mine won't even notice." "Such a rebel," Orna remarked. "You said that like it's a bad thing," Talo retorted. "Yeah, rebels have more fun," Kam added. Orna then said, with a hint of anxiety, "My parents keep close tabs on me and my twenty siblings so can we hurry?" Talo laughed, "Look at the tremble in his voice. You're a little afraid. That's okay." Orna joked back, "I'm not afraid. Scared, but afraid? Nah." Talo and Kam shared a knowing glance, their eyes crinkling in amusement, before bursting into laughter.

Orna didn't really have twenty siblings, he actually had eight. He was the second oldest. His mother was of royal descent from Zobeth, a planet seven light years from Axpherial.

Orna was a combination of Axpherian and Zobeth, having access to both sets of supernatural abilities, something that Talo secretly envied. Talo was apart of the seers, an ability that included heightened intuition and visions. She still deep down wished she had Orna or Kam's abilities instead. The Zobethians had the power of animal shape-shifting, whereas Orna had access to both kinds of abilities.

Talo rolled her eyes as Kam opened the door, and she beckoned to Orna. "Come on, stiffy. I'll race you home," she said, as they stepped outside. The night was dark, illuminated only by the moons, and the trees seemed mysterious and beautifully terrifying in the darkness. "Don't break your arm again," Talo said with a hard grin. "I broke it racing you!" Orna exclaimed as they positioned themselves to take off. Orna smiled and waved back at Kam, cheerfully saying, "See you at training tomorrow, brother!" "Oma," Talo said as she was about to leave. "Oma," Kam replied, using the term which signified goodbye on their planet.

Orna waved, bowing his head and clasping his hands together in a prayer position. Kam smiled and nodded in acknowledgment. Then, they took off into the sky, Talo slightly ahead. Orna's form abruptly shifted, and before their eyes, he transformed into a petite bat, his wings stretching wide as Talo screamed, "cheater!" As they both began to laugh and joyfully scream as they flew through the air.

Kam gazed up at the sky, watching them disappear beyond the broken white clouds. He stayed there a moment, admiring the moons, before reality pulled him away and he quickly turned around, heading back into the cabin. Entering the living room, he paused to take in the array of vehicle designs spread across the table. Despite the urge to work on them, he succumbed to procrastination yet again and moved on. His hand touched the wall at the end of the shallow hallway behind the living room, and it glowed red. In response, the wall disappeared, and a staircase of wood appeared in its place. Making his way down the stairs, he noted that the wall had materialized again behind him.

He descended into the large, dimly lit basement, where yellow light was spread across the corners. His gaze met with the bulbs that lit up the room. Occupying the middle of the large space were three long rows of tables, filled with incomplete weapon designs and detailed blueprints. The southwest corner was accompanied by a small silver desk and a large rectangular computer that was 24 inches long. On the other side, in the northwest corner, was a door labeled "Training", and next to it was another nameless door.

Kam grinned as he stepped through the blank doorway and found himself in his armory. The walls were lined with an array of weapons: the left held a multitude of swords of similar shape but they were tucked inside different colored scabbards, and the right was stocked with guns of all shapes and sizes with unlimited laser ammo. In the center of the room was a worktable with blueprints spread on top, and a half-made sword with a thin black scabbard beside it. As Kam touched the sword, a mysterious blue light shimmered around the handle. It was a feature all his swords possessed - the ability to sharpen while being held.

Kam gingerly raised his hand across the sword, and a blue radiance illuminated from the tip. He paused to concentrate and used his creative ability to perfect the sword in his mind's eye. With his eyelids shut tight, he visualized the blade as though it were already finished. He opened his eyes to see his completed sword held tightly in his grasp. Satisfied, he took the sword into the cramped practice chamber. He situated himself in the center of the room, crossed his legs, and held the sword firmly in his grasp. Then, he began to meditate.

In a matter of minutes, the room changed from a small room to a dark field with swaying emerald grass. Taking up his sword, it glowed blue as it intensified in his hand. Three men in all-black attire came running towards him. Kam grinned and cut the first soldier's sword in two and amputated his arms. He then faced the two other men, sword clashing with them for a few seconds, before releasing a loud grunt and decapitating the second man. The last man, standing breathless, was met with the charge of Kam. They began to clash swords, but Kam suddenly became distracted as he pondered over returning home on time. The man in black took advantage of this and ran his blade through Kam's waist, causing him to cry out and shake himself out of his meditation. The tall, lush grasses of the field wilted away, the vibrant green now gone. The room felt bereft, its walls now barren and forgotten. Kam eyed the sword in his hand, pleased with his performance, yet craving to try again. With a smirk, he placed the sword in its scabbard and set it back on the table in the armory.

He kept his secret basement hidden from his friends, as he was hesitant to reveal his fascination with deadly weapons, for fear that it might drive them away. They were already aware of his various vehicle and home designs, but he kept this side of himself closely guarded. At times, he even felt apprehensive about his darker side, yet eventually he came to terms with it.

He admired the night sky one last time before closing his eyes and slowly ascending into the sky. With his home not far away, he was able to fly there easily without the need of a vehicle.

Kam drifted to a small land hovering several meters above the ground, surrounded by deep blue shrubs dangling from its sides. Kam arrived at a squared, two-story white home, with circular windows and a smooth black knobless door. He made his way to the left side of the second story and opened the large circular window with ease. He drifted through the window, letting it close silently behind him. He slipped silently under the bedsheets, praying that his late-night entrance had gone unnoticed. Soon enough, sleep overtook his body and he slept through the night, secure in the knowledge that he had evaded detection.

| 2 |

Kam

Kam awoke to the blaring sound of the alarm. He groaned and slowly arched his body, stretching it out. Finally, he let out an exasperated yell, "Stop!" His room was spacious, with a circular bed adorned with tan, brown, and white bedding taking up half the space. Realistic and beautiful drawings of planets, vehicles, and people decorated the walls. A shiny wooden desk stood to the left of the bed, and the tall wooden ceiling was just out of reach. Kam's eyelids fluttered open, and he groaned again as he sat up in bed, the sheets rustling beneath him. He ran a hand across his face, feeling the lingering fatigue in his body.

The door jolted as a loud knock reverberated from the other side. "Nooooo!" Kam exclaimed, sounding half-asleep. A young lady entered the room, a year and a half younger than him. She had shoulder-length kinky dark hair with violet tips and light brown skin, with freckles adorning her cheeks. Her violet eyes were strikingly similar to Kam's. She exuded an aura of purity and angelic charm. "Had fun?" she asked in a sweet, gentle voice. "Is it that obvious?" Kam replied, still sounding tired. "I heard you come in last night. You're not as quiet as you think," she said. Kam continued to rub the sleep from his eyes, disappointed that she had caught him.

Kam had the sudden urge to lie back down, but he remained sitting upright. "This bed turns me into an anchor," he said, attempting to

11

change the subject. "Anyway, I hope you don't sit in bed for too long. Mom made breakfast. And your cover is considered blown if you're not downstairs and smiling like last night didn't happen." Kam's brow furrowed and his fingers clenched together as he pondered her words, adrenaline coursing through his veins.

Suddenly feeling more awake, Kam reached for the wooden drawer to the right of the bed. He waved his hand, and the door opened without a handle. Shirtless, he rummaged through his clothes to find something decent. "Bliss, Kam! It's ready!" A sweet woman's voice called from down the stairs. "Will you cover for me if I need?" Kam asked, still searching. "Don't I always?" Bliss smiled. Kam's lips curled into a smirk as he paused, gazing at her. "See you downstairs, big bro. Awake. Or at least do a good job pretending," Bliss said, inching toward the door. Kam's lips curved upward into a gentle smile. "Don't I always?" he replied, his drowsiness fading. "You definitely do your best," Bliss said as she headed downstairs. Kam quickly put on a loose blue sleeveless shirt, and caught up with Bliss, tailgating her down the stairs.

At the bottom, they turned left and found themselves in a house with a familiar interior—resembling Kam's room, with wooden walls and ceilings, polished wooden floors, and a compact size. Skipping the living room, they entered the kitchen and took seats on two black bar stools at the breakfast bar. Although the house was small, it suited their four-person family well.

In the sunlight, the crystal-clear glass bar glistened. Only one more bar stool could fit, occupied by a man wearing a black leather jumpsuit. Three red stripes lit up on each sleeve. His skin tone resembled Bliss', and Kam noticed his emerald green eyes focused on his tablet. He typed calculations, the blue, red, and white figures visible from their perspective. His gaze was intense, his mouth a tight line.

Ala entered from the left entryway, a stunning woman with violet eyes and a glowing smile. Her jet black hair with white streaks fell to her chest. "I fixed the talpoz from Toah, mashed and mixed with berries," She said as Kam and Bliss scrutinized their plates. Though she was their mother, she and the man at the end of the table, their father, appeared only a little older than them. She was actually 129 years old and he was 133—equivalent to 32 and 33 in Axpherian years. Axpherians aged differently from humans, taking an average of 100 Earth years to age what would take a human only 10. Until 18-24, Axpherians aged like humans, then the process slowed significantly, explaining their youthful appearance.

Kam grabbed a two-toothed fork and shoveled some talpoz into his mouth. Talpoz was a peculiar green vegetable from Toah, one of Axpherial's moons. It constituted about a fourth of Axpherial's food supply. Toah's atmosphere was conducive to life, with familiar and unfamiliar animals but no intelligent species.

Kam's eyes lit up and he smiled as if the food were divine. But it was far from divine. The food was mediocre, with a lukewarm flavor and slightly overcooked texture. Ala smiled, pleased with the verdict. "Good as always," Kam said, awkwardly stirring the talpoz and mashed berries together. Bliss ate slowly, giving Ala a thumbs-up as a sign of approval.

Ala noticed her husband tapping away, ignoring them. "Meeka," she said softly. He jerked his head up, his attention suddenly on her. "Yes," he said, his tone abrupt. Meeka towered over Ala and Bliss, his broad shoulders and thick arms evidence of his considerable strength. At over six and a half feet, he was taller than Kam, who was also over six feet. His muscular frame and aura were intimidating.

Meeka continued to gaze at Ala, slightly disrupted. He recomposed his expression, displaying sympathy. "I'm sorry, love, but this task needs to be completed today. I need to submit these figures to the L.C.," he stated, attempting to sound both comforting and stern.

The Lead Commander, or L.C., was a term for a general in the army. Meeka was a scientist who worked on mathematical calculations for weapons, machinery, equipment, and tools. In this role, he had met Ala, also a scientist and mathematician, and they had shared common ground.

Ala's gaze remained fixed on the tablet screen as she inquired with a gentle, yet increasingly impatient, tone, "Is the food not satisfactory?"

Everyone in the room could tell that Ala usually wore a pleasant demeanor, but a darker side simmered beneath her placid smile. The room had witnessed her outbursts before, and it was never pretty. "I apologize," he said, "I'll eat it. And Tama." Meeka waved at Kam and Bliss, his voice reaching them from behind his tablet.

Tama was the standard greeting for "hello" on Axpherial. They smiled and waved back, their responses nonchalant as Meeka returned his focus to his work. Kam was nearly done with his meal, while Bliss's plate looked barely touched. Kam shoveled the final forkfuls of food into his mouth, barely pausing to chew. Afterwards, he thanked them with a satisfied smile as he exclaimed, "Thanks, Ma! As always."

Ala glanced at Kam worriedly as he sipped a light violet liquid from a short glass near his plate. He swallowed the liquid, savoring its sweetness. "I have training, Mom. See you later!" Kam exclaimed, rushing up the stairs. Ala watched him go, while Bliss picked at her food, uninterested in the bland flavors. Bliss was accustomed to Kam's antics; whenever he sneaked out, it was always hard for him to act rationally.

Bliss made a face, knowing exactly why Ala was scrutinizing Kam so intently. "Doesn't he seem a bit... I don't know," Ala said. "Long night working on vehicle designs. He needed assistance," Bliss said, sounding only slightly convincing. Ala's worried expression remained unchanged. "I thought you found designing unengaging," Meeka said, still typing on his tablet. "I do. A lot, actually. But he just needed a distraction as he finished up a design he'd been working on," Bliss said, her words becoming slightly rushed. Kam's sword design, shown to Bliss a few days ago, nearly slipped out. Meeka appeared unconvinced as he nodded, still immersed in his work. "He makes designing look festive," Ala said, still sounding worried. "He's jittery. Long nights like that have that effect. He'll be fine by the time we get to training," Bliss reassured. Ala bit her bottom lip, her brow furrowed in concern. "That's what I hope," Ala said. "I'm going to check on the walls to make sure he didn't bounce off them. See ya," Bliss said as she quickly left. "Not finishing?" Ala asked as Bliss disappeared. "Not hungry," Bliss called from upstairs, the heavy wooden door shutting behind her.

Ala paused, staring at the steps for a moment before turning her gaze to the two plates. One was still full of food, the other almost empty. "Well, at least sneaking out gives him a generous appetite," she said, sounding lightly discouraged. "Remember when that was you?" she asked, smirking. Meeka's lips curled up at the corners, a mischievous glint in his eye as he briefly reminisced. "We'll have to make a few things clear when he gets home though," Meeka stated, looking at Ala from his tablet. "Yeah, we should. But we've got bigger things to worry about," Ala replied. "Speaking of importance, take a look at this," Meeka said, showing her his calculations. Ala smiled, squinting at the tablet screen. "Impressive," she replied, furrowing her brow and scrutinizing the math with intense concentration. "You're almost done," she added, smirking. "Took a few sleepless nights, but I managed," Meeka stated, pausing for a beat. His eyes were filled with sorrow as he looked at Ala. He regretted overlooking her and the children earlier, allowing his obsessive work habits to take precedence.

"Look, Ala, I'm sorry for being inattentive. This just had to..."

"You're forgiven," Ala said, smiling.

"But I'm always forgiven. I really am sorry."

Meeka's eyes softened as he locked onto Ala's, his expression conveying genuine sincerity. "I like the long face. Your vulnerability is attractive," Ala said, her full smile lighting up her face. Meeka's expression shifted to seriousness. "But things are more critical now. More so than before. We have a planet to save. This could be our last chance," he said, urgency in his tone. Ala's lips thinned, her eyes dimming, the joy that had been brightening her face moments ago replaced by a gravity that matched his. She tilted her head slightly, a subtle gesture of agreement.

| 3 |

Maxine

Dozens of people stood in a single file, facing a colossal wall that towered stories above them. The city behind the wall appeared like any other, except for the military trucks driving through. Armed soldiers, wearing black uniforms and bulletproof vests, patrolled the openings of the walls, checking IDs and running handheld devices over faces. The devices whirred and chirped in a steady rhythm, emitting two beeps for each person that passed. The people, in general, looked trauma-tized. Many were injured, bandaged, or in wheelchairs; they seemed to have survived something horrific. Despite the bright blue of the early afternoon sky, no one paid attention to the scenery. They were all too exhausted and stressed. They'd been through hell and couldn't care less if they showed it.

"I have to take a piss," a young man muttered. Ahead of him, four people stood in the middle lane, their backs turned, waiting their turn. He had a short dark fade, skin the color of caramel, and mesmerizing eyes with large, dark pupils. The white tank top and tattered blue jeans he wore showcased his lean frame. "Kincade, shhh," a young lady said in front of him, trying not to giggle as she lightly tapped him on the shoulder. "I'm sorry Max, but I've been holding it since the shuttle," Kincade replied with a grin. Max, short for Maxine, had similar fea-tures and complexion. Her long, dark box braids fell to the small of her back, her hazel eyes sparkled, and she was wearing an oversized blue checkered shirt and black sweatpants. She was slender, though not as thin as Kincade. Kincade and Maxine were twins, with Kincade being the elder by just a few minutes. He was still often referred to as "big brother" by Maxine.

"Kincade, behave," came the stern admonition from the man in front of them. He was a couple of decades older, with a full beard and was significantly taller than Kincade and Maxine. Maxine was a little over 5'6", and Kincade just shy of 5'10". His thin glasses gave him a sophisticated look, and his black shirt fit snugly around his muscular frame. Kincade and Maxine's rich brown skin tones stood out in stark contrast to his dark brown complexion. He was quite a handsome man.

"Sorry Dad, but rapidly impending golden shower here," Kincade said, clutching his bladder. Maxine chuckled lightly. "Anyway, this viola thing seems lab orchestrated," he added out of nowhere. Both Maxine and their Dad glanced at him as if he were crazy.

The Viola virus initially emerged in infected pigeons a few years earlier, making its first jump to humans in Japan before spreading globally. Its lethality was staggering, claiming billions of lives in a mere matter of ten months. The odds of survival were bleak, although a fortunate few possessed immunity or had received the vaccine earlier that year. The remnants of civilization sought refuge primarily in United States and Mexico, where the majority of the world's population now resided.

Much of the world crumbled, reducing some to fear-driven submission. Prolonged and ineffective quarantines, coupled with the imposition of military law, fueled escalating tensions. A desperate craving for freedom gripped the world. However, these immunity cities were their sole refuge. Not many of them left, and they were capped at 2.5 million. Luckily, this metropolitan area was just under 2 million. They were entering Zeus City, the next immunity city over from the one that was mysteriously bombed.

"Hold off on the conspiracy theories, big bro," Maxine said, grinning. "Conspiracy facts, sis. Sleep is for the sheep, woke gives you hope." Maxine shook her head, suppressing a laugh. Their Dad averted his gaze to the city gates, ignoring him. "I hate you," Maxine quipped. "Wow, the black hole in my chest says thank you," he replied, smiling. "It's thanked," Maxine grinned.

Maxine, Kincade, and their father suddenly found themselves at the front of the line. Tobias Hewitt, their father, handed over his ID, which was somewhat damaged. His name and address were barely legible. The soldier scanned it twice, encountering some difficulty. He then ran the thin, squared device over Tobias' forehead, which beeped twice. He allowed Tobias to step to the side to wait for Kincade and Maxine.

Maxine extended her identification to the soldier. The device beeped. He held the scanner up to her forehead, and the machine emitted two short beeps in response. He nodded in approval, and she stepped aside, right next to Tobias.

Kincade handed over his ID with a blank expression, barely sparing a glance for the soldier. He then glanced toward Maxine and winked, receiving an approving thumbs up in response. The soldier ran the device over Kincade's forehead, and it emitted three loud beeps. Maxine's smile quickly disappeared, and the soldier's expression turned to one of worry. Kincade raised an eyebrow in confusion. "What's the issue?" Kincade asked. "You're positive," the soldier replied. He tapped the device to run the scan again, and the same three distinct beeps sounded once more.

The soldier's fingers fumbled as he yanked the walkie-talkie off his belt, his knuckles turning white as he tightened his grip. "Sargent, we have a 10-17, I need reinforcements at door A2," he commanded. "10-4, sending help," came the reply. With his rifle pointing directly at Kincade's head, the soldier ordered, "Keep your hands up and step aside." Kincade's hands trembled as he raised them, his eyes wide and his face drained of color. "I was tested before I got here!" he stammered, his voice quivering. "Just hold tight, kid, and step aside like I said," the soldier warned, unwavering in his stance.

Kincade stood as still as stone, unable to move. "Hey! Step aside now!" The soldier commanded, raising his voice, gun still trained on him. Kincade swallowed hard, his throat constricting as he backed away with evident reluctance. "You don't want this to get ugly, kid," The soldier warned, malice lacing his voice. Kincade's fists clenched, his jaw tightened, and his eyes narrowed, conveying a clear desire to punch the soldier in the face. "Hey, everyone back up! Suspected infected person!" He shouted, gesturing for the line of people behind Kincade to retreat. Three soldiers marched toward Kincade, each grabbing an arm to restrain him. Kincade glanced around, fear and confusion contorting his face. Tobias was in shock, while Maxine fought to keep her composure, bearly maintaining a fake poker face. The sergeant and the soldier spoke in hushed tones as the others stood guard.

Everyone seemed to know what would happen if you were infected. You would be expelled from the city and sent to a camp where they housed the infected. The camps were crowded, dirty, and filled with death. They were like horror houses, worse than death to most. But the camps were never discussed in the mainstream media. They claimed to take the infected to an abandoned football dome where they were housed, fed, and treated. Not like the death camp described through social media and word of mouth. All in all, the death camps were a theory. But the infected were never seen again after they were taken, fueling the rumors.

The sergeant approached Kincade. "Just relax, son. We need to make sure by scanning you one more time," He said, attempting a calm tone. "How fun," Kincade said, sarcastically. His heart rate accelerated, yet he was determined not to display his fear again, lest he encourage Maxine and Tobias to do the same. Maxine's mouth twisted into a tight line, her brow furrowed, and her eyes were wide and anxious. She forced a smile and tried to look composed. She did a good, though not great, job. Tobias, on the other hand, had taken on a more placid demeanor due to Kincade's unusual calmness.

The sergeant slowly raised his device to Kincade's head as Kincade stiffened. All the other lines came to a sudden halt, watching as if he were a spectacle. The device beeped twice, and the sergeant confidently announced, "He's clear." The soldier who previously scanned him looked puzzled, and the sergeant requested to see the scan. Reluctantly, the soldier handed it over.

The sergeant tapped the device a couple of times, then scanned another soldier. It beeped three times, causing him to tap his chin in contemplation. He scanned the soldier with his own device, which beeped twice. Declaring the other scanner defective, he handed the soldier a new one. He used it to scan Kincade, and it beeped twice, bringing relief to those nearby. The two soldiers holding him let go, and he looked down, shaken up. "You're free to go," The sergeant told Kincade, who attempted to look tough as he nodded. The crowd slowly resumed their entrance into the city. He glanced at Maxine, who winked, and he offered a nervous OK symbol with a smile.

Tobias's lips twitched upwards in a relieved smile as a wave of relief washed over him at the sight of Kincade. "That was close," Kincade said, attempting to sound composed. "No shit," Maxine said with a re-assuring smile. "Good job keeping your composure, son," Tobias said, smiling as he patted Kincade on the shoulder. "Well, my bladder is near imploding thanks to my near heart attack, so can we please move along before I soak my jeans?" He said, anxiously. "Don't you mean explode?" Maxine asked. "Imploding is internal, exploding is external," Kincade corrected. "Dude, you almost ended up at camp death, and you're still the vocab police," Maxine smiled. "Camp death doesn't exist," Tobias said as they exited the gates. "Dad, you're trippin'. Name one person you saw go to that so-called isolation arena downtown. Where else are they going?" Maxine asked. Tobias averted his gaze, lips pursed in silence. "I knew he would fold! Good job, little sis!" Kincade chuckled as he and Maxine high-fived each other. Tobias rolled his eyes as they walked to the rest of the crowd, waiting for the various shuttles that dropped everyone off at their homes.

****

The sun had sunk low in the sky, leaving behind a golden-orange hue. The shuttle stopped in front of their driveway, and they trudged up the path to their house. Exhaustion was evident in their expressions, and Kincade let out a faint yawn. The house was a faded white color, with an ancient oak tree still standing on the left. The grass was wildly unkempt, rising more than nine inches off the ground. The two-story home appeared mildly worn down from several decades of wear.

They approached the front door, their feet crunching on the gravel driveway. The door was a dull, rusted red color, with a tiny square window in the center. "Home, we missed you, buddy," Kincade said as Tobias rummaged for his key. "Ugh. Dude, I'm having the biggest nap craving of my life," Maxine said. "Me too, 'cause those hard hotel beds did a number on my ass," Kincade joked as Maxine laughed quietly. "You're my favorite idiot, you know that?" Maxine said as she finished her laugh.

"Look, an IQ test doesn't determine my worth, okay. It's long outdated. Stone Age outdated. Like your wardrobe outdated."

"Dude, shut up," Maxine said, her smile still intact.

Kincade raised his hand and gave her a quick, mischievous flick of the middle finger. "That's cute," she said, smirking. Tobias grinned as he tried not to laugh while opening the door.

The house looked much newer on the inside, full of life. Neat and renovated, its walls were painted in a light beige hue. The door opened to reveal glossy black stairs with a white wooden railing. The living room to the left boasted a long black couch facing a round glass table and a 64-inch flat-screen television, with a white furry carpet beneath the table. The walls were adorned with warm memories, each one captured in a framed family photo.

Above the fireplace, a black and white vase held the ashes of Maggie Hewitt, Tobias's mother, from whom he inherited the house. She had passed away a decade ago, leaving him the property through her will. This decision had stirred envy from his older brother and younger sister. Tobias had never been particularly close to his family members or many other people. He was naturally a quiet, introverted man, often subjected to bullying due to his small stature. However, puberty had brought a dramatic transformation. He quickly grew into his looks, developing early facial hair and a smooth, muscular frame.

A young lady, appearing to be in her late teens, was meditating on the couch with her legs crossed. Kincade quietly shut the door as she emerged from her trance-like state. "Well, if it isn't my favorite hipster," Kincade said, smiling. A hint of a smile tugged at the corners of the young lady's lips. "Punches are just rolling through the door, huh? And nice to see you too," she said with her small grin still intact. "How was the vacation? Was it nice?" she added.

Maxine shook her head. "Hey Ava, and no. It was nice as hell. Literally," Maxine said, sounding mildly serious. Ava squinted, furrowing her brows as she tried to make sense of what she had just heard. "Where is Mrs. Hewitt?" she asked. "In the hospital, Ava. She's in stable condition, but they still need to run a few tests," Tobias said. "Are you guys okay, Mr. Hewitt?" she asked, sounding genuinely worried. "I told you, you can call me Tobias," Tobias said, like it was the millionth time. "I know. Blame my subconscious programming. It's just manners that are permanently latched into my brain," Ava said casually. Ava was striking with her smooth caramel skin and two long, black braids that reached her chest. She wore a white midriff top that revealed her slim waist, and a clear quartz crystal hung from her neck on a black cord.

Tobias bowed his head slightly in acknowledgment. He secretly found her a little strange but kept her around for Maxine's sake. "You guys seem oddly calm about Mrs. Hewitt.... I meant Georgette being in the hospital," Ava pointed out. "We laugh to keep from... aww you know the cliché," Kincade said with a casual smile. He was right. That's exactly what they were doing. Keeping themselves distracted to not worry if their mom was going to survive. Survive the hell she and they had just gone through. "I'll explain later what happened, girl," Maxine assured her.

Kincade's eyes narrowed as he stared at Ava, a puzzled expression crossing his face. "Trying to stare into my soul or something?" Ava asked, sarcastically. "Manners? Is that right?" Kincade asked with a grin. "Kincade, your asshole is showing," Maxine said, mostly joking. "Figuratively or literally?" Kincade asked, this time with a harder grin. Maxine stood with her arms crossed, her mouth drawn into a tight line.

"Oh no, I want it all to hang out. It gives me an edge."

"How about you edge your fade, dude. It's looking a little seesaw-ish," Maxine said, waving her hand like an actual seesaw.

She and Ava shared a laugh. "Ha, ha, I'm having a complete laugh attack," Kincade said sarcastically, with little enthusiasm. "Dude, you're not supposed to laugh. You're the joke!" Maxine replied as she and Ava laughed again. Kincade let out a loud guffaw, his tongue poking out between his teeth as he attempted to imitate their laughter. "Okay, y'all, I'll be right back," Maxine said as she finished giggling.

Maxine crept down the hallway, her eyes locking onto a glossy white door. She took a deep breath and grabbed the door handle, pushing it open. The garage revealed itself—a red Kia Soul, a black Jeep Grand Cherokee from the late 2000s, and a sleek Harley motorcycle. Her gaze fell on the Kia, and her heart pounded in her chest. Her foot inched forward, her gaze flicking over the car. She paused by the driver's side door, her body tense as if the car might bite. Her eyes finally settled on the keyless fob tucked in the sun visor, and she swallowed hard.

She kept her gaze fixed, as anxiety began to swell inside her. Her pulse raced, and a wave of warmth flooded her chest. Her breathing became unsteady, her complexion paling. She seemed on the verge of collapse. "Conquering demons?" she heard from the left. She jolted at the sound of Kincade's voice. "Ummm, just admiring," she lied, putting on a forced smile. Her unease was still palpable, though she did her best to mask it. "It might as well still have the bow on top of it. Still haven't driven it yet," Kincade said. Maxine's hands shook as she rifled through her thoughts, searching for the perfect combination of phrases that would make her appear brave. However, her mind was blank.

The car had been gathering dust in the garage for over a year now, since her 18th birthday. She got the car, Kincade got the motorcycle. Sweat trickled down her face as she recalled the dizzying fear that had engulfed her during the panic attack. Her hands shook as she remembered the intensity of that day. She could still recall the sheer terror that had taken hold of her, so much so that an ambulance had been called. The paramedics examined her and determined that her symptoms weren't serious enough to require hospitalization, for which she was grateful. Afterwards, however, she went into her room and cried until her body ached and her eyes were too heavy to stay open. To make matters worse, her initial reaction had been caught on camera.

"Well, whenever you're ready to seal the deal. I'm in my bat cave upstairs," Kincade said with an encouraging smile. Maxine replied with a nervous grin. "Thanks big bro," She said, trying her best to sound calm. Kincade paused, his hand on the doorknob. A smile spread across his face, lingering for a few seconds before he shut the door. Maxine gazed at the car one last time before leaving the garage, feeling defeated. She hated looking weak. And weak is exactly what she felt. But she wasn't weak. Far from it. Especially after what she went through.

| 4 |

Kam

"Accuracy and concentration are essential for a successful execution. It is important to be aware of one's surroundings and to remain in the present moment, keeping one's sight set on the desired outcome," Uni said, his tone stern. Uni was an instructor at the training palace—Palace 111.

The palace was a sight to behold. It stood majestic in white, comprised of cube and rectangular buildings with large windows that sparkled brilliantly in the sunlight. The day was glorious; the sky stretched like a canvas of blue, adorned with only a few clouds dotting the horizon. The grass formed a lush blanket of deep violet, each blade cut with meticulous precision. This was one of three palaces on Elmana.

A group of students, all around eighteen in Earth years, stood in a straight line. They hailed from different races, wearing black suits with the number 111 stitched onto the left side. Kam stood at the end, exuding the most focus. Orna appeared on edge, as if about to break, while Talo seemed bored, as if she had heard this information countless times before.

"Spread your legs slightly and aim forward," Uni instructed, referring to the delfona devices attached to their wrists. They all followed the instructions, some slightly faster than others. "Remember, mindfulness," Uni reminded, moving down the line, his bright green eyes carefully scanning everyone's position. Standing at the front, he appeared dwarfed by the towering teenagers around him. He ran his fingers through his short black hair, gathering it into a sleek ponytail. Black tattoos of various art symbols adorned both his arms. He wore a black sleeveless shirt and gray pants cinched with a black rope.

Despite being significantly older, he only appeared a few years older than his pupils. He was 98 years old in Earth years. Approaching a girl, he corrected her stance by adjusting the width of her legs with his own. Her eyes remained fixed ahead, ignoring his presence. Kam's unwavering focus caught his attention as he approached; he was deeply impressed. He raised his head and nodded before moving to the back. "On my signal, fire!" Uni commanded, slowly lifting his hand while everyone held their positions. He counted backward from three, then shouted, "Fire!" as everyone shot forward.

Most left shoulders shifted slightly, except for Orna, who stumbled and fell to the ground with a loud grunt. A few students chuckled, some suppressing smiles behind cupped hands, while the majority remained silent. White beams emitted from the delfonas, forming dull white spheres about ten feet ahead of them. However, two students had red spheres. "Looks like most of you did well. But you two have the wrong moon," Uni remarked, pointing at the students in the middle. One of them was Talo, whose face reddened, a clear sign of her embarrassment. The other was a young woman with dark red eyes, ginger hair, and an ivory complexion. She also appeared somewhat ashamed.

The color of the sphere indicated the destination. This exercise tested their ability to reach Talpo, the largest moon in the sky. Talpo was an alluring planet, with snowflake white clouds eloping its atmosphere. Kahlofa, on the other hand was different; Its sky hung heavy and crimson, enveloped in a thick haze. "Red signifies the Kahlofa moon, not Talpo. Losing focus during transport can be perilous. And Talo, you usually excel at this. What's distracting you?" Uni inquired as the portals in front of them quickly shrank and dissipated.

Talo's shoulders slumped, her gaze fixed on the ground, her mouth downturned. "I thought you said Kahlofa," she murmured. "I repeated my instructions several times. You seemed hardly attentive. Perhaps something is diverting your focus." Talo had no response. She stood there, wearing what felt like the longest face in the world. "Sorry. It won't happen again," Talo admitted, disheartened. Uni's lips curved slightly, a smile spreading across his face. "Don't be too hard on yourself. You're an exceptional student. A stumble is forgivable. Don't let this break you; you're a warrior." Uni turned to face the group. "All of you are. Remember that." He looked back at Talo, offering an encouraging smile. Talo managed a feeble smile in return, unable to conceal her disappointment. "Alright, let's take a break," Uni announced, and the single file formation dispersed.

✴✴
✴✴✴✴✴✴✴✴✴✴✴✴✴✴✴

Kam, Talo, and Orna moved slowly across the glistening golden grains of the shoreline. The sun had set after their training session, and they were on their way back home. Their footsteps synchronized, producing a soft crunch on the sandy path—the only sound for miles around. A dense cloud of tension hung over them, making the air heavy and oppressive.

"I don't understand," Talo said, breaking the silence. The trio came to an abrupt halt, freezing in place. Kam and Orna leaned in, their eyes wide and eyebrows raised, focusing intently on Talo.

"I'm usually on point. I just lost focus for a split second."

Kam and Orna regarded her as if she might shatter at any moment. "You'll be okay," Orna said, trying to sound optimistic.

"Please save your sympathetic gratitude," Talo quipped, picking up on their overwhelming empathy.

"Just trying to help."

"I'm fine," she replied quickly, stopping Orna in his tracks.

Talo's face turned downward, as if she were trying to count the grains of sand. "I'm sorry," Talo said, realizing her harsh tone.

"It's okay. I know your pursuit of perfection is a winding path. With death traps," Orna added. Talo couldn't help but crack a smile. Kam quietly chuckled.

"Yeah, at least you managed to stay on your feet," Kam joked, nudging Orna as Talo laughed.

Orna's lips curled up in a smirk, and he looked nonchalantly into the distance, unaffected.

"At least my moon prediction was accurate!" Orna chimed in.

"Stop!" Talo said, still grinning.

"Well, he's not wrong. Red, though?" Kam said, his smile wide.

"You both give me a headache," Talo admitted, feeling better.

"But we're your headache!" Kam retorted. Talo chuckled quietly, shaking her head in amusement. "We enjoy teasing you. It's oddly satisfying," Orna said, giving her shoulder a gentle pat. "And exhilarating," He added with a heavy grin.

"Anyway, are you still planning to visit Earth?" Orna asked as they resumed walking.

Kam shifted his gaze away, avoiding eye contact, and stared at the ground—a nervous habit he had when feeling uncomfortable. "Yeah, unfortunately," he replied, unenthusiastically.

Talo appeared slightly puzzled. "I thought you liked Earth."

"I did, until they suddenly required us to get vaccinated before going. We all had to."

Orna's eyebrow arched in curiosity. "Hold on, what?"

"Yeah, there's some virus trouble on Earth. But that's all they told us," Kam explained.

Orna's eyes lit up. "So you mean that thing they call dis... um..."

"It's called diseases. And yes, it's everywhere," Kam filled in. "They made the announcement a while ago. Were your ears on vacation?" Talo asked as she turned her gaze to Orna.

Important announcements were regularly broadcasted on every monitor in Axpherial. Orna always seemed unusually distracted during such moments, lost in thought until Talo or someone else nudged him back to reality.

"Well, on Earth, they also keep animals on leashes," Orna commented, shifting the topic.

"And they eat them. Disgusting!" Talo cringed. "Imagine if we treated animals the way they do."

On Axpherial, owning animals for captivity, even as pets, was against the law. As a democracy, each territory's representatives voted on laws. A majority vote was considered 60/40. This specific law had been established many years ago and was voted on every 2 Akras—an Axpherial month, equivalent to 1 Earth year. The planet's light ring orbited in sync with the planet's rotation, completing one orbit per Arka.

They continued walking, Kam nodding in agreement with Talo. "True, but we have to visit Earth twice in an Arka. Our folks both work as scientists for the DAA," Kam explained. The DAA, or Defense Allegiance of Axpherial, represented one of the most powerful and advanced armies in their universe.

"So, you don't have a choice?" Talo inquired.

"No. They want to keep an eye on me and Bliss."

"Why?" Talo pressed.

"Because our idea of fun isn't very fun to them."

"But I love your kind of fun," Orna quipped.

"Do you? Because every time we try to have real fun, you're full of excuses," Talo remarked.

"You guys love playing with fire," Orna interjected.

"You can't fear the burn, man!" Kam exclaimed.

"I know, I'm just more cautious," Orna replied casually.

"Cautious, huh? Bum still sore?" Talo teased.

Orna blushed as he looked away, pressing his lips together. "We tease you too, you know," Talo said.

"Yeah, it's exhilarating," Kam added.

Orna chuckled, trying to mask his slight embarrassment. "I thought I was the comic relief in this group!" Orna exclaimed.

"You are. Now stop being such a loser, or I'll gladly take your spot," Talo said, suddenly halting as they realized they were above Kam's home.

"Well, as much as I'd love to chat, I've got to go. I have a date," Kam smirked.

"With who?" Orna inquired.

"My bed," Kam replied, as if he'd just delivered a punchline. Orna and Talo exchanged a knowing glance, their lips curling into faint smiles, though they made no sound of laughter.

"I see who's not taking my position," Orna quipped.

"I wasn't even trying," Kam retorted.

"Thank the gods for that," Talo added, with a touch of dramatic flair.

"Thanks a lot," Kam replied, seemingly unfazed.

Kam wrapped his arms around them both, eliciting broad grins from their faces. "Oma," he smiled, gently floating off the ground and soaring to the violet land above, his home. Talo and Orna watched as his figure disappeared among the floating vegetation.

"Isn't he the coolest square we've met?" Orna mused.

"He's alright," Talo responded. "But I still love him."

Orna felt Talo's sudden surge of energy, watching her eyes light up with excitement. He recognized the look and felt a sense of both anticipation and dread. "Race you home!" Talo exclaimed, quickly backing up and taking off into the sky. Orna, seeing this coming, backed up and yelled, "Cheater!" before quickly chasing after her, both soaring high into the sky.

| 5 |

Maxine

"He's not here, I'm sorry, Ma," Maxine said. She and Ava stood by Georgette's hospital bed. Georgette frowned. "What was the excuse?" After a brief pause, she added, "This time." Maxine scanned the room, as if the answer were hidden in the gleaming marble floor. It had been over a week since they returned to town.

Kincade, Tobias, Georgette, and Maxine had come from a city two hundred miles away, a city destroyed by bombing. The lights flickered before the bombs went off. Maxine's family had barely escaped. They had been in the city because Maxine's mother took a temporary nursing job there. Tragically, the hospital where she worked was one of the first targets. Georgette was among the few survivors, but she suffered severe injuries.

Maxine visited her nearly every day, Ava nearly as often, and Kincade at least three times. Tobias hadn't come at all. "He wasn't home to give one. He was already at work," Maxine explained. Tobias worked as a professional photographer, capturing images for local and online newspapers. He attended press conferences, particularly those related to the Viola virus.

"Have you driven the car yet?" Georgette changed the subject. Maxine bit her lip, her brows furrowing in hesitation, and glanced away. She silently shook her head. "You'll be ready someday, princess.

I know how strong you truly are." Maxine's shoulders slumped, her gaze fixed on the ground. She had grown tired of pretending, tired of projecting strength when all she felt was vulnerability masquerading as "strength."

Maxine forced a smile, her cheeks lifting in an attempt to mask the previous worry. "I'm strong, Mom," Maxine said, unconvinced. "A warrior since birth. Remember when you fell off the swing and refused to see the doctor, baby?" Maxine laughed lightly and nodded, lost in the memory. She felt a round of tears brimming, but she made sure to keep them down. "She's practically a superhuman, isn't she?" Ava chimed in. Georgette beamed. "It's good you think so. But I want her to believe it too," Georgette said, her gaze locked onto Maxine's eyes. Maxine nodded, uncertain of how she could transform into the "super-human" Ava spoke of. "By the way, what did the doc say? How's your condition?" Maxine asked.

Georgette let out a long sigh. "My spine might take time to heal. Severe burns on my chest, stomach, and back. They think I'll be here a few more weeks." Maxine's expression fell, her disappointment evident.

Georgette, a beautiful woman with hazel eyes like Maxine's, possessed a slightly fuller frame and impeccable bone structure. "I don't have any poems tonight, Mom. Severe writer's block," Maxine admitted.

"Don't worry about it, baby," Georgette reassured her. Maxine managed a faint smile, her suppressed tears creating a dull ache in her throat.

"You haven't been the same since your sister. You and Imani were quite the duo," Georgette said, her voice heavy with meaning. Maxine swallowed hard, unable to bear the emotions any longer. She needed an escape. "Alright, Mom, I need to catch the train," Maxine said, unable to stay mentally present any longer. The thought of her sister, Imani, threatened to engulf her. Imani had passed away two years earlier in a tragic accident. Memories of nights spent sobbing in the shower and weeks of refusing to eat or sleep still haunted Maxine. With support from Kincade and Georgette, she eventually returned to a semblance of normalcy, but she remained far from fully recovered. The events of that night still haunted her.

With her mother, Maxine saw only the vibrant Georgette—full of life, with her radiant smile, flowing brown hair, and boundless energy. That energy had been drained by her condition. She looked nothing like the Georgette that Maxine remembered. She was frail, scarred, and her once flowing hair was now only inches long. Maxine gently kissed her mother's forehead, offering a final smile before departing. "Goodbye, Mrs. Hewitt," Ava said, following Maxine out of the room. Georgette's lips curved into a pleased smile as she watched them leave. After they were gone, Georgette's expression shifted, a mix of joy and sorrow. Joy to see her daughter, and sorrow at witnessing her struggle so profoundly.

****
****

After what felt like the longest train ride ever, Maxine and Ava stepped through the door. Maxine appeared drained as she carefully hung her jean jacket on the coat rack and kicked off her shoes by the entrance. Ava followed suit, albeit more swiftly.

"Well, well, it's the girl who never goes home," Kincade's joking voice drifted from upstairs. "I'm baaack!" Ava chimed in, their paths crossing on the stairs.

Ava's fingers wrapped around the doorknob, and with a gentle twist, the door to the guest room clicked shut. Kincade descended the stairs, pausing midway upon spotting Maxine at the bottom. "Like seriously, go home, Roger," Kincade remarked playfully, eliciting a chuckle from Maxine. She glanced down and spotted a perfectly rolled joint in his right hand. "What's that?" she asked sarcastically. "Pain medicine. Meet me at headquarters," Kincade instructed, heading for the garage. Maxine beamed, following him.

"I thought Dad would be back by now," Maxine mentioned. "He tends to work late when he's avoiding something," Kincade commented, opening the garage door. He sprawled across Maxine's windshield, producing a lighter adorned with the Superman logo. Maxine offered a small smile as she reclined beside him. He flicked the lighter, holding the flame to the joint. The tip glowed red, and tendrils of smoke curled into the air.

"How's Mom holding up?" he asked.

"Holding on," Maxine replied.

"I'm sorry I didn't make it tonight," he said, completing the joint's ignition.

"At least you make the effort to visit," Maxine added, a trace of overt shade in her voice.

Kincade raised an eyebrow. "You taking a shot at Dad for not visiting?"

Maxine paused, not answering. Kincade took a puff. "Though I'm not exactly keen about the medical industry—a profiteering cash cow off the sick—and as much as I hate it, I put on a brave face and visit her. Dad? No bueno," he said, taking another drag. "Here, sis, come fly away with me," he offered, passing the joint to her.

A smile spread across her face as she inhaled. She took a deep drag, feeling the burn in her lungs without flinching. It was like she had done it countless times before. "I could smoke a hundred...thousand of these right now, dude," Maxine quipped, taking another puff.

"Amidst all the chaos, this is the least I can do," Kincade reflected. Maxine brought the joint to her lips, inhaling deeply before handing it back to him. He took a long drag. "Wanna take my baby Harley for a ride?" Kincade gestured towards the Harley tucked in the corner of the garage.

"If I weren't floating so high in the clouds, I might've considered it," Maxine said, grinning broadly.

Kincade took another drag. "No problem, lil sis," he acknowledged, exhaling smoke into the air.

He passed the joint back to Maxine, and she took a few puffs. "With Dad, I can't tell if it's cowardice or hurt. I'm torn," Maxine's filter slipped as the influence of marijuana took hold.

"I'd say he's a grade-A mixture of both," Kincade responded, inhaling again.

"But I do empathize with him," Maxine admitted.

"He and Mom always tell us how tough we are. I remember when he told me, 'Tears show fear, fear shows weakness,'" he mimicked, and Maxine passed him the joint.

"Preaching and practicing are different beasts," Kincade stated, exhaling after a drag. "Words are easy to come by. You can convince a pig to fly with words. But actions? Actions reveal your true colors like nothing else," Maxine said, a tinge of bitterness in her tone.

"Word, little sis," Kincade affirmed. He spoke in a hushed, gravelly tone, completely at ease and soaring on a high.

Their conversation continued for several minutes. They discussed the virus, Kincade's passion for comics and motorcycles, and Maxine's writer's block as they smoked the joint down to a roach. Kincade extinguished the joint in an old, dirty ashtray atop the broken freezer by the door. "I feel a lot better," Maxine said, as Kincade closed the main garage door.

Although she felt better in that moment, she'd rather feel nothing than face her emotions. Clenching her fists, she took a deep breath and slid off the car. "Marijuana sure gives me a Clark Kent complex," Kincade mused.

"Well, go fight crime or something productive then," Maxine replied, still on cloud nine.

Ava reached the door before Kincade and opened it before he could react. The potent scent of marijuana wafted from the garage. "What did I miss?" she asked.

"The fun part," Kincade answered, strolling past her with a wide grin.

"Hey, I wanted to join in on the fun too, asshole," Ava called after him. His footsteps echoed as he ascended the staircase, already upstairs. Maxine smiled contentedly, though a hint of guilt lingered. "Drink you upstairs!" Ava cheerfully called.

"What?" Maxine laughed as she and Ava headed to Maxine's room. "He had his fun; now I want mine," Ava declared as they reached the top of the stairs. That was Maxine—always striving to ensure everyone's happiness, everyone except herself.

| 6 |

Kam

Kam and his family's hovercar floated above the plain gravel in front of their Earth house. The old, boarded-up residence was a stark contrast to their petite yet beautiful Axpherian home. As they stepped out of the vehicle, wheels suddenly materialized along with door handles, reshaping the car into a Tesla-like form. Though lacking a steering wheel, the car was controlled through mind commands. The front bumper featured a discreetly hidden portal activator amidst the curves and swirls of its metalwork. On the dashboard sat a sleek square glass GPS display, flanked by a blue light shaped like a hand, mimicking a gear stick. The car's interior boasted luxurious black leather seats, accommodating five passengers individually.

Secluded and remote, a dirt road extended from the dilapidated house to the highway—an hour away from Zeus City, a major metropolitan in New Mexico. "Remember, minimal interaction," Meeka said. Kam rolled his eyes. "Three days here, don't forget," Meeka reminded, walking toward the boarded-up door. He placed his hand on it, prompting a red light to shimmer across. The wooden door responded to the touch sensor, sliding aside. "Do we really have to wear those ugly Earth wigs again?" Bliss grumbled, her annoyance evident.

An awkward silence hung, everyone's gaze fixed on Bliss. "Yes, my sweet one, those wigs," Ala affirmed. "Sweet one" was a common term

37

on Axpherial, akin to "honey" or "sweetie." "Well, I can wait then," Bliss said, rolling her eyes. "They itch like crazy," she complained, causing Kam to chuckle. "You're fortunate you don't have to endure that torture," she told Kam, her annoyance dissipating in humor. "But I still have to deal with the ugly black contacts," Kam quipped. "So do I, remember?" Bliss retorted, pointing at her violet eyes, stark against the sunlight. "Violet eyes aren't natural in this dimension," Ala explained.

In total, there were 7 realms. The first realm was Hades, filled with dark planets and damned souls. The somber realm featured worlds that were predominantly cruel and unforgiving, inhabited by various dangerous and exotic life forms. Darkness and corruption prevailed. Anarchy was home to Earth, relatively more peaceful but still marked by significant corruption on many planets. Tranquility, of course, was the home of Axpherial; a beautiful realm of super beings, magic, and beings who were often very unified. Eutopia was teeming with extravagant worlds ruled by demigods, fairies, and other powerful species. Guardians were considered gods, while Bliss represented heaven, with immortal worlds and peaceful souls.

"Let's not complain for all three days here. Different dimensions, different regulations and rules—it's part of the deal. You should all know better by now," Meeka admonished, his tone stern. They entered the house, revealing a stark contrast from its exterior. The facade was a mere holographic disguise, the interior an exquisite revelation.

Within the house, everything was pristine white, encompassing a spacious living room to the left. Two black couches formed an L-shape around an all-white fireplace. The polished wooden floors gleamed with a golden hue. The kitchen radiated elegance, with a glass dining table and a cream-white breakfast bar accompanied by black stools. A circular glass fridge, built into the wall, stood beside a stovetop without its usual covering. A 40-inch glass screen hung above it, displaying "Chef Variety" in large white letters against a sky-blue backdrop, with "version 322" in small black letters in the corner. A door adjacent to the fireplace led to a basement, and a hallway connected the living room to three distinct rooms. The master bedroom stood in the center, with

Kam's room on the left, and Bliss' room along with a full bathroom to the right.

"Stay here; your mother and I have pressing matters to attend to," Meeka instructed Ala, his urgency evident in his gaze. Ala's lips twitched slightly, and she took a deep breath, attempting to maintain her composure. "Can we fulfill a pressing matter, too?" Bliss inquired, already frustrated with boredom. "The only matter I wish for you to fulfill is to alter your attire to resemble Earth's style," Meeka declared.

Bliss wore a black tank top with long sleeves, showcasing a glowing red belly button piercing. Her hair was secured with a radiant blue hair tie, and she sported open-toed black shoes. Kam donned a dark blue sleeveless shirt tucked into loose black pants, adorned with his signature black beads around his neck. Meeka wore all black with black robes that reached the bottom of his pants, accented by tightly wrapped brown beads. Ala opted for a simple gray dress, her hair elegantly coiled into a bun.

"I'll assist you later, and I'll ensure it's painless," Ala promised, smiling reassuringly at Bliss. Bliss' lips curved upwards, though her eyes remained unresponsive. She was already weary of the trip. "And Kam?" Meeka directed his attention to him. "Yes?" Kam replied, sensing what was coming. "No antics this time," Meeka warned, his tone as unyielding as iron.

In their previous visit, they had snuck into the city, assuming the roles of street magicians. To conceal their identities, Bliss wore an awkward, straight wig, while Kam donned a comically small Afro wig with a blonde streak, both complemented by dark sunglasses and hoodies that concealed their faces. Their street magic act involved levitating small items like purses, a street performer's drumsticks, and a deck of playing cards. The video of their performance went viral, earning them a scolding from Meeka and Ala upon their return home. However, the two merely laughed about it in the privacy of their rooms, relishing the shocked expressions of the downtown crowd as they rewatched the video.

Kam bit his lip, his eyes narrowing in reluctant agreement. He knew he wouldn't follow through. "The same goes for you, Bliss." Bliss averted her gaze slowly, her brow furrowing in silence. "Let's go, Ala," Meeka said, guiding her toward the basement. As the door closed behind them, Bliss' gaze fixated on Kam, her lips curling into a mischievous smile. "Any bad ideas?" she teased, amusement in her voice. Kam merely grinned as he and Bliss stealthily slipped out the door.

****

Bliss and Kam walked outside, their eyes fixed on the beautiful blue sky above. An airplane could be seen flying in the distance, and they both tracked its movement with their gaze. "Score," Bliss exclaimed, a smile spreading across her face. Stepping back a few paces, they jumped and began to float upwards into the sky. The white clouds gradually closed in around them, wrapping them in a misty cocoon. The plane's nose dipped down, its engines roaring as it veered sharply and thundered straight towards them. "Ready?" Kam inquired, and Bliss eagerly responded, "Absolutely!"

They concealed themselves behind a thick cloud as the plane approached. The engine's deafening noise filled their ears as they swiftly seized hold of the left wing, gripping tightly as the plane soared through the sky. The engine's clamor was nearly unbearable, but they persevered beneath the wing. Adrenaline surged through them as they screamed and laughed in exhilaration. During the escapade, Bliss's hair became disheveled.

Kam felt his necklace graze his face and instinctively adjusted it, tucking it back beneath his shirt. Exchanging a knowing nod, they released their grip and began ascending through the clouds again, laughter bubbling up as they climbed higher and higher. Finally, they descended back toward the earth house, landing about 30 feet from it. Upon touching the ground, their laughter persisted, grounding them in the moment.

"This vacation just turned into an actual vacation," Bliss commented, attempting to fix her hair. "Yeah, antics sure are fun," Kam remarked, brushing off his shirt and adjusting his necklace. "Almost lost it," Bliss noted, referring to his necklace. "These are pure black crystals from Starla Mountain near my travel home. They radiate some of the strongest energy I've ever experienced; they're not going anywhere!" Kam affirmed, kissing the crystal blue pendant. Bliss smirked knowingly, arms crossed tightly. "What's on your mind?" He queried immediately. "I'm betting they're unaware," Bliss replied, referring to his travel home. Kam smiled knowingly, immediately catching on. "Do they ever really know anything?" He joked, grinning.

They started walking leisurely toward their home. "Do you think they'd be bothered if they learned?" Bliss pondered.

"Not necessarily bothered, just more controlling,"

"Yeah, and you and I both know how cringe control is."

"I'm approaching 5 lozas soon. I just want to find a bit of independence away from them. That's not asking for too much, right?" Kam asked.

Bliss didn't respond immediately. "Right?" He pressed, seeking reassurance. "No, not at all. Independence is important," she affirmed. Kam couldn't determine if she truly meant it, but he moved forward nonetheless. "I haven't even informed them I plan to move off the island after completing training," Kam disclosed.

They paused, the gravel crunching under their feet, standing about fifteen feet from the entrance. "Where to?" Bliss inquired, too intrigued to contain her excitement. "To Saymorna." "The massive territory right above us?" Bliss queried.

Their island was situated 650 miles from Saymorna, the largest landmass in Axpherial. It was comparable in size to Europe. "To Desty, the capital city," Kam revealed. Desty was sprawling and boasted a futuristic aesthetic akin to a perfected version of New York City. The streets teemed with people as far as the eye could see, an unending sea of humanity stretching for miles. However, their island city, Elmana, held a population of just over one million and covered less than half the area of Desty, even though their island fell within the same territory as Saymorna. If, for instance, Saymorna represented the United States, Elmana was analogous to the Bahamas.

Bliss tilted her head slightly and let out a soft hum of agreement. "I feel confined on the island. We occasionally visit Earth and a few other planets, but we've barely scratched the surface of Axpherial. It should bother you, too. Don't you also feel restricted?" Kam questioned. Bliss raised her shoulders slightly, then dropped them in an indifferent shrug.

"I mean..."

"Do you really need to think about it?" Kam inquired seriously.

"I mean, I have, but I like the island. It's my kind of boring, and I enjoy the simplicity," Bliss admitted hesitantly. "Speaking of Earth," Kam redirected the conversation. "Have you noticed Mom and Dad coming here more often? And isn't it odd that we needed shots before coming?" He probed. Bliss's shoulders moved up and down in a single, casual motion. "Whoa! Where did my little sister vanish to, the one who was right here?" He teased playfully. Bliss responded with a half-smile. "I'm not concerned. Probably boring DAA stuff," Bliss remarked, sounding apathetic. "Okay, not Bliss, why aren't you worried? You usually pick up on strange behavior like this," Bliss grinned, aware she was putting on a facade. "They've been unusually secretive about something. They're keeping us in the dark about Earth not being Earth lately," Bliss disclosed. "Apart from the pandemic situation?" Kam inquired, understandably perplexed. "I was just pulling your leg, it's not mundane DAA stuff. It's something significant. Something they're trying to talk about in codes. And yes, it's bigger than the pandemic."

Kam leaned forward, his eyes wide and alert, hanging on her every word, eager for more details. "What else do you know?" He prodded, hoping for a straightforward answer. "That's all, big bro. They isolate us in this field, and we venture into the city now and then, with or without permission. But we haven't been back to Earth in an Arka. I knew something was up. So, there you have it. Your sis is here, truly," Bliss said, a triumphant grin spreading across her face. "That's the confirmation I needed," Kam declared. "However, there's one more thing. Something I couldn't help but eavesdrop on," Bliss confessed, as if she'd been waiting her whole life to share it. "Well…" "Bliss, Kam!" Bliss was unable to finish as they looked to their left. Ala was at the door, beaming.

They jumped slightly, relieved that she didn't seem to suspect anything. "Let's get ready, my sweet ones," Ala said, her smile radiating warmth. "What were you two up to?" She asked. "I bet Bliss I could reach the other side of the field before her. I won," Kam claimed, while Bliss folded her arms and shot him an exasperated glance. Kam grinned and shrugged. "It did a number on your hair, though," Ala observed, referring to Bliss. Bliss ran her fingers through her hair, completely forgetting about it. She felt caught, even though Ala appeared oblivious to any peculiarities.

"We're going into the city tonight for dinner," Ala announced. "Earth food, Mom? Can we skip consuming another unfortunate animal?" Bliss requested. "Order something plant-based. Your father loves it," Ala advised. "Salad it is," Bliss responded, a hint of disappointment in her tone. "Come on, let's get ready," Ala urged, ushering them inside. "Yay," Bliss echoed, her enthusiasm feigned. Kam chuckled quietly as they entered the house. They headed to their respective rooms, and as Kam shut his door, he leaned against it. He needed answers, and he needed them promptly.

| 7 |

Maxine

The sky hung gray and gloomy as Maxine walked down the city street, flanked by various vintage-looking storefronts. The stores stood empty, and for the most part, the streets were as well. Since the virus outbreak, people had become reluctant to leave their homes. Still, a few individuals lingered, cars passed sporadically along with the usual off green military trucks every couple minutes. A handful of pedestrians ambled by, some sheltered beneath umbrellas, others exposed to the rain that poured ceaselessly, as if determined to turn the city into a river.

Maxine clutched a large black umbrella and wore an oversized black hoodie, given to her by Kincade that morning in anticipation of the looming storm. Despite the inclement weather, Maxine remained resolute in her determination to visit her mother, Georgette. The train platform lay half a mile away, and she was committed to her course, regardless of the rain. A nearby car beeped, startling her. She turned, noting the sound of an engine.

"Need a ride, dear?" a gentle female voice asked. Without hesitation, Maxine shook her head. The idea of getting into any car, especially after what she had experienced, was out of the question. A bus, a shuttle, a train—those were acceptable modes of transportation. A car, however, was not an option.

"I'm taking the train; I'll be fine," she replied, hoping that the occupants of the car would swiftly drive away. The windows were so heavily tinted that she couldn't make out the woman's face inside. Her pocket buzzed, and she retrieved her phone to find a text from Kincade: "Hey sis, train is no bueno. They're saying it'll be gud in a few hours. Try coming back when you can."

Maxine kept a neutral expression, concealing her frustration from the woman in the car. The chill in the air and the relentless rain, weren't deterring her desire to see Georgette. Perhaps she could take the train later when it was back in service. As absurd as it seemed, she began contemplating walking, despite the hospital's considerable distance. "Listen, young lady," a deep male voice resonated from the car. "It's not wise to brave these conditions to reach your destination. The most rational course of action is to accept a ride."

Her heart rate surged, and a surge of adrenaline coursed through her veins. Saying no was on the tip of her tongue, yet her yearning to see her mother prevailed over her trepidation. "We mean you no harm, I assure you," the woman inside the car added. Maxine nodded, her anxiety refusing to subside. The back passenger door swung open, and she hesitated as her gaze fell upon the interior. Two figures were seated there, yet the dim lighting made them hard to discern.

Her thoughts raced in an anxiety-fueled frenzy as Maxine cautiously entered the car, clutching her umbrella tightly. She fought to conceal any traces of her fear or unease, though her heart raced within her chest. She offered a faint smile as the door clicked shut. Glancing to the side, she caught sight of two striking individuals in their late teens, both with dark brown eyes, and both clad in black coats. The young man exuded a radiant grin, while the woman's hair framed her face with shoulder-length locks and bangs that appeared to be a wig— though Maxine pretended not to notice.

The young woman in the driver's seat glanced back at Maxine and asked, "Are you okay, sweet one?" Maxine's inner monologue reacted to the term 'sweet one.' Managing a smile while gripping the seat, she replied, "Thanks for the ride," striving to maintain a veneer of casualness. The car began to move, and though a tempest raged outside, an equally fierce storm of emotions swirled within Maxine. Anxiety raced through her veins as the car accelerated.

Yet, these weren't just any passengers—this was Kam, Ala, Bliss, and Meeka from Axpherial. Their combination of beauty and kindness caught Maxine off guard, creating a sense of relaxation in her presence. She inhaled deeply, shutting her eyes to combat the torrent of anxiety surging through her veins. She envisioned the train—its graffiti-covered walls, dim white lighting, wide windows, and off-blue seats that felt as uncomfortable as stones. Gradually, her heartbeat began to steady.

"Hey, what's your name?" Bliss asked. Maxine opened her eyes, her fantasy turning back into a storm. Her heart rate was going up again. Maxine smiled like normal. "Maxine," she said, sounding seemingly calm. "Left or right?" Ala asked, approaching a stoplight. "Keep going up and turn at Linda Drive, then keep going on that street. It's just a few more miles after that. Then turn on Michael Street and you'll see the Zeus City medical center. Just drop me off at the main entrance." Maxine said, maintaining her false calmness.

"Well, I'm Lisa, and this is my brother, Joey," Bliss said like it was the truth. "Joey" smiled and waved, as she waved back, quickly looking away. Earth names to disguise their Axpherial ones. Their family and planet were very protective over their identities when going to other planets and dimensions. "Hey Lisa, it's nice to meet you," she said calmly. She looked at Kam, as he smiled at her. She quickly noticed his smooth brown skin, perfect bone structure, and infectious smile. She felt another warmth in her body, but it wasn't anxiety. It was a warmth she didn't want to feel. Especially now. "Not too keen on cars," Maxine suddenly admitted without trying to. "How come?" Kam asked immediately. "Joey, that's enough," Meeka said from the passenger side. He stopped without contest. Maxine was glad. She didn't want to answer anyway.

Maxine started to feel a sense of calmness, until she jolted from the impact of a pothole. Her heart rate soared and the heat rushed back into her body. She felt a sharp pain in her chest, as if death was lurking nearby. She found it hard to breathe, her breaths coming in short and fast. "Is everything alright?" Ala questioned, her face full of fear. Maxine shook her head, Bliss and Kam stared at her with obvious concern.

Each breath felt like a battle to Maxine. "LET ME OUT! PLEASE! LET ME OUT!" She screamed, as her fingers tightly gripped the seat. "Hey, I'm here! I got you!" Bliss said, enveloping Maxine's hand in hers. Maxine felt herself fading, her anxiety slowly consuming her. "Focus on your breath. Mindfulness," Kam instructed, his calm demeanor seeming to help. "Breathe in for 5 seconds." Kam said. Maxine followed through, although it was still hard to breathe. "Hold for 5 and breathe out for 5," Kam said, looking as calm as he could manage. Maxine followed Kam's instructions the best she could. "Do it at least a few times. You'll be okay." He said as she closed her eyes and saw the train again.

First breath, Her heart rate going down again, and the pain in her chest eased up. Second breath, she felt her breaths become easier. Third breath, the tightness in her lungs disappeared. Fourth breath. Fifth breath. Sixth breath. Seventh Breath. She opened her eyes. "Better?" Bliss asked. Maxine nodded, still a little breathless but noticeably improved. "You got through it," Kam said, patting her shoulder as Bliss reached out in support. Maxine managed a weak smile, though the aftermath of her panic attack still weighed heavily upon her.

Maxine sat, attempting to relax, practicing her breathing quietly as the car pulled up to the hospital. She mustered a smile as she got out of the car. "Thank you," she said, gathering her umbrella. The door opened and she waved to Kam and Bliss, who waved back as the door shut. "Good luck with everything!" Ala said. Maxine nodded with appreciation.

She stood there, watching the car drive away in the heavy rain. A feeling of accomplishment welled up within her; for the first time in a year, she had successfully gotten into a car. Despite her apprehension, she was determined not to give up, yet part of her wished she'd never have to ride in a car again. With a sigh, she walked through the automatic doors, ready to face Georgette and the knowledge that her mother would be proud of her.

| 8 |

Maxine

"I always knew you would," Kincade said.

He lay on his bed, looking down at Maxine, who was sitting on the floor, leaning against an X-Men poster. His walls were adorned with Marvel and DC superheroes in full action – comic book front pages, cartoon posters, and live-action movie posters – along with a collection of souvenirs on a wooden dresser. A black shelf with a dimly lit lamp held three rows of comics beneath it.

"You kicked PTSD's ass. We should have a celebratory shot," Ava said, holding a bottle of vodka. She sat upright on the floor against the bed, looking slightly fatigued.

"Not sure if I'm in a drinking mood," Maxine replied calmly.

"Don't be a modest bitch, okay? Just one for me," Ava persisted.

"You drive a hard bargain. Whatever, dude. Give it to me," Maxine said, taking the bottle. She took a swig and cringed as she swallowed.

Kincade's grin stretched from ear to ear, revealing the mischievous glint in his eyes. "You're a terrible influence," he remarked to Ava.

"You're no better, garage boy," she retorted, her grin half-hearted.

"Marijuana has medical uses. It's a mood booster. It should be pre-scribed for depression, anxiety, bipolar disorder, and all the other 'dis's with orders in it," Kincade added, while Maxine chuckled. Ava's lips curled into a sly smirk.

"Right there are the devil's tears. That's why it feels so hot going down," Kincade quipped.

"Good. His misery, my blackouts. It works," Ava shrugged, taking another sip.

Maxine chuckled, feeling a bit cheerier after the car ride.

"I thought meditation was your steez," Kincade remarked.

"I like options," Ava replied, taking another shot. Kincade looked at her like he was confused. "What? I like to have my cake," Ava paused for a second before finishing, "And drink it too." Kincade couldn't help but crack a smile as Ava and Maxine shared a laugh.

"Here supergirl," Ava said as she handed Maxine the half full bottle of vodka. Maxine took another shot. "Edited for TV supergirl or comic book supergirl?" Kincade asked. "Here we go…." Ava said, rolling her eyes. "Can you say wasted potential? Stop referring to my sister as wasted potential," Kincade said with a sarcastic grin. "I've seen many dorks in my nineteen years, But never one as punishing as you," Ava said. "Are you flirting with me? Cause that was flattering," Kincade grinned as Ava gagged. "You should meditate with me sometime," Ava suggested to Maxine.

"Hmmm, I'll sleep on it," Maxine responded, showing little interest in her tone.

"No seriously, it'll help you not go into panic mode again. You'll love it, sweetie," Ava suggested, as Maxine handed her back the bottle.

"Want some tears?" Ava asked Kincade, offering him the vodka.

"Hard pass," he declined, as Ava shrugged and took another shot.

Kincade gave her a strange look suddenly. "Soul staring again?" she asked, bracing herself.

"Where is your home again?" he asked, genuinely curious. "You've been coming over the past nine months, and you're always here."

Ava looked down at the bottle, twirling it in her hands. Silent.

"Dude," Maxine interjected, not pleased with Kincade's question.

"It's a genuine question. Not trying to set fire to this 'fantastic' night, but at this point, I can't hide it anymore. You good?" he inquired, sounding genuinely concerned.

Ava finally looked up, her gaze first on Maxine, then Kincade, then the bottle again. "My parents are religious cliches. They found out I was bi last year," Ava paused, then continued, "It was here or the shelter. I've already aged out of the foster care system, so that's a bust. So yeah, Tobias doesn't know either. I don't see how he can't. I sleep in the guest room, I get my caffeine fix with Maxine in the mornings, meditate in the afternoon, and drink in the evening."

She looked at Kincade and formed a grin. "So yeah…I am home, geek." Kincade appeared as if he wanted to embrace her, expressing his empathy.

"That's heavy, but I figured something was going on," he said. "I'm sorry I said nothing, dude. I'll tell Dad when I can. But he probably already figured it out, too," Maxine said, trying to reassure him.

"Or not, as often as he's been flying out the door. Especially lately," Kincade added.

"So, you're not mad?" Ava asked Kincade.

"You're like a cold pool. An ice-cold pool. An ice-cold pool in Antarctica. But eventually, your body temperature adjusts to the excruciating pain. You are that pain, but I've adjusted," Kincade explained with a hard grin.

Ava laughed, feeling comforted from his words. "Welcome home, punk," he added, making Ava smile with relief.

"Like I said, I'll think about the meditating thing or whatever," Maxine said to Ava, considering the option after briefly experiencing its benefits earlier. She stood back as Kincade and Ava continued their spirited debate on various subjects, mostly about superheroes. Maxine got up, stretched, and felt the exhaustion creeping in. It was late, well past one in the morning.

"I suddenly feel heavy and a bit tipsy. I'm gonna go sleep it off," Maxine said, her voice sounding drained.

"Okay, supergirl, sleep tight," Ava replied, now leaning against the comic book collection. She knew exactly what she had done, finding Kincade's annoyance amusing.

Kincade grinned at Ava, expressing a mix of fondness and annoyance. "Don't even," she warned Kincade, a hint of seriousness in her tone.

Kincade just smiled, then rolled his eyes. "You know what, hand me the tears," he said, holding his hand out for the bottle.

"Magic word first," Ava teased.

"You make me sick," Kincade smirked.

"That's the spirit!" Ava said, handing him the bottle. He took a sip and scrunched his face, causing Ava to laugh.

Maxine left the room and headed to her own space, shutting the door behind her. Despite the darkness, she effortlessly flopped onto the bed and dozed off within a few minutes, grateful that the day was finally over.

| 9 |

Kam

It was a moonless evening in Elmana, the city illuminated by its radiant lights. The pointed white tower, dubbed the great strength, loomed over the surrounding tall buildings. Holographic screens flickered in the night, displaying various advertisements, and flying cars darted between them. Perched on the golden sandy shoreline was a glowing amusement park where Kam, Orna, and Talo were engrossed in a game.

Blue-glowing shotguns fired lasers at moving holographic targets. The game abruptly halted, and their scores were displayed in red at the top. Kam had scored 850, Orna had 777, and Talo held the highest score with 990. "A bit of real competition is all I ask," Talo said, grinning with confidence. "You had practice! Not fair!" Orna retorted, offering a smile with a hint of passive-aggressiveness. "I don't need practice for perfected skill!" Talo shot back. Their argument faded into the background as Kam's gaze drifted to the floating red Ferris wheel.

A sudden wave of terror coursed through Kam's veins, accompanied by an energetic buzz in his hands. It was a sensation he experienced only occasionally. "Hey, having a good time?" Bliss's voice brought him back. She stood to his right, her face lit up with a warm smile.

Kam composed himself and replied, "I don't know. There's this... I can't piece it together." Bliss looked puzzled. "Not catching your drift," she admitted, seeking clarity. Then, a spark of realization lit up her eyes. "She went on the ride alone, didn't she?" Kam nodded in response. "I had a strange feeling, but she insisted," he said. Bliss smirked knowingly. "Zina's always going to do what she feels," she remarked. "And when I explained why I felt that way, she told me not to entertain voices in my head, said they always lie," Kam shared, his gaze fixed on the ground. "I like her though; she definitely has a way of mellowing you out," Bliss said, offering him an encouraging smile. Kam did his best to return the gesture.

Talo and Orna soon joined them, forming a small circle.

"May we join the party?" Talo inquired with a playful grin.

Bliss raised an eyebrow at them.

"Just having a counseling session with my brother here, who's letting anxiety mess with his sanity," Bliss said, her grin aimed at Kam, radiating reassurance.

Orna placed his hand on Kam's shoulder. "You've got to drown out those voices, man!" he declared, his smile infectious. "Zina gave me a similar pep talk," Kam admitted, his voice trembling slightly.

Amidst their reassurances, a sudden deafening bang jolted them all. The surrounding chaos caught their attention—people were either running or flying away or towards the Ferris wheel. With each car that hit the ground, Kam's heart raced faster. He shouted Zina's name and, along with the others, sprinted towards the scene. The impact was jarring, and the ride attendant was frantically pressing on his glass screen displaying a red warning with the word "Error" in bold white letters. Kam's heart sank as he saw the terror in Zina's eyes as her car slammed into the ground.

However, Kam's abrupt awakening brought him back to his Earth home. Blinking in the semi-darkness, he murmured a sleepy "Lights," prompting the neon lights around him to flicker to life. His room was a far cry from his one on Axpherial—simpler, with a desk near the door, walls adorned with old sketches of vehicles, and a large black bean bag in the corner.

He climbed out of bed, donned a thick white sleeveless shirt and loose black pants resembling sweatpants, and slipped on black lace-less shoes that adjusted to his feet. He made his way down the hallway and knocked on Bliss's door. She opened it, rubbing the sleep from her eyes. "Tama," she mumbled, observing him.

Kam's expression was a mixture of distress and vulnerability. Bliss understood why he sought her company. She patted his shoulder and closed the door, dressing quickly. Her hair was gathered into a pony-tail with a blue illuminated hair clip, matching her black leather coat, pants, and plain black shoes. The shoes conformed to her feet perfectly. She opened the door, a smile playing on her lips, and led the way as Kam followed.

****
****

"I haven't had a dream about that in so long," Kam said, his eyes fixated on the ground. They were now on the rooftop, with a sky adorned by an array of stars. It was a new moon night, and the dark sky was mesmerizing. Kam stood at the rooftop's edge while Bliss sat against the worn chimney, her knees drawn close to her chest.

"I thought I was healed," Kam admitted, his voice tinged with sad-ness. He felt the oncoming of tears in his throat, a departure from his usual calm demeanor. Bliss sensed the weight of his trauma and the emotional turmoil he was going through. Kam stood still, hands in his pockets, lost in his thoughts.

"Healing doesn't have a strict timeline. It's more about..." Bliss paused, searching for the right words. Kam looked at her, hoping for some guidance. "It's hard to put into words without sounding too preachy....I want to be realistic yet hopeful," Bliss explained. Kam turned his gaze to the night sky, seeking solace in the scenery.

"She was the first person who truly understood me," Kam contin-ued, his voice trembling.

"Yes, and your endless curiosity. She had a tolerance made of steel for it," Bliss said with a slight smile, trying to lighten the mood. Kam managed a faint laugh. "Yeah, she really did," he acknowledged, wiping away a tear. "It knows no bounds, but I love you anyway," Bliss added, offering a reassuring grin.

Kam felt his eyes well up with tears, and he turned away, hoping to hide his emotions. But Bliss gently insisted, "No, turn around. You don't need to hide anything."

Unable to hold back any longer, Kam's emotions burst forth. He sobbed uncontrollably, crouching down, and Bliss immediately wrapped her arm around his shoulders. "I thought I could save her. Her face, before she... I can't get it out of my mind," Kam struggled to articulate, his voice breaking.

Bliss held him closer, her presence offering comfort as Kam let out his grief. "I got you, brother. I'm not going anywhere," Bliss reassured him firmly.

Kam looked at her through tear-filled eyes, his sorrow evident. "I failed, Bliss. I couldn't stop it when I had the chance. And I can't change it now..." he choked out between sobs.

"No one could have saved her. Stop blaming yourself for something so inevitable," Bliss's voice grew more resolute, trying to break through his guilt.

Kam's gaze met hers, and he nodded, absorbing her words. "You're right. I'll grieve, but I won't let guilt consume me," he agreed, his tears gradually subsiding.

"Moments like this make me appreciate having a sister," Kam said, wiping away the last traces of tears.

Sniffling, Kam regained his composure, though he still felt the weight of his emotions lingering. "How are you feeling now?" Bliss inquired gently.

"I'll manage. Thanks for always being there for me, even when I'm a handful," Kam said with a weak smile.

Bliss playfully responded, "Oh, you definitely are a handful."

Kam chuckled. "But seriously, thanks. Your patience means a lot."

Bliss grinned. "Well, I've grown accustomed, don't sweat it big bro."

As they gazed at the starry sky, the heaviness in Kam's heart seemed to lift. He turned to Bliss and asked, "So, what did you want to tell me earlier?"

Bliss hesitated, fully aware of what Kam was pressing about. "The shot we received earlier is meant to protect us from a virus called Viola," she admitted slowly.

Kam's gaze intensified, urging her to continue.

"Furthermore, several Axpherians have been hunted down. I'm not sure by whom, but..." Bliss's voice trailed off.

Kam's eyes never left hers, waiting for more information.

"Though Axpherians are naturally immune to death from the virus, it seems the virus has other effects. It can potentially block our abilities if we were infected," Bliss explained, struggling to recall what she'd overheard her parents discussing.

"Someone or some group is trying to eliminate us," she continued, her urgency palpable. "They bombed cities with immune survivors, and they're not done yet. I heard the folks theorize Zeus City might be next, and even Axpherial. They're a threat to both our worlds."

Kam absorbed the information, his mind racing. "That's...unsettling," he said, the gravity of the situation sinking in.

Bliss cautioned, "Don't put on your hero cape just yet, big bro. Whoever they are, they're too formidable to tackle alone."

Kam's eyes lit up, surprised that Bliss had read his intentions. "You know me too well."

Bliss laughed. "We can't take them on single-handedly. We should leave this to our folks and their fancy DAA connections." Kam nodded in agreement.

"Rest sounds like a good idea," Bliss suggested, rising to her feet and pulling Kam up with her. They hugged, their bond evident even in simple gestures.

"And yes, I'll sleep in your room tonight," Bliss mentioned, teasingly predicting Kam's reaction.

Kam looked puzzled. "You're scaring me."

Bliss grinned mischievously, and together they left the rooftop, their home awaiting them in the darkness.

| 10 |

Maxine

Maxine awaited the train that was moments from approaching. The expanded platform hosted two others standing near the edge. A tattered sign above her head faintly read "Michael Street." She wore white Bluetooth headphones, listening to soft R&B music, her favorite genre. Having recently visited Georgette, whose condition had improved but still kept her away from returning home, Maxine's mind was preoccupied.

A vivid image of Georgette's radiant smile flashed before her, a memory now overshadowed by the city's devastation that had shattered her image. She shook off the memories as the train rolled in. Glancing at her watch, it read 8:15 pm. She stepped into the second-to-last train car, which was sparsely occupied. Settling into her usual spot in the back corner, Maxine took in her surroundings.

The seats appeared aged, covered in a faded ashy dark blue with faint red swirling designs, remnants of their former vibrancy. Worn advertisements adorned various spaces, some marred by graffiti. Among the graffiti, a sign with bold red letters reading "444" caught her attention. It emitted a peculiar feeling, as if trying to convey a significant message. Dismissing the notion, she started the next song on her headphones. Pulling out her black and white college-ruled notebook, she poised her pen over the paper, but inspiration eluded her. Frustrated, she closed the notebook and gradually shut her eyes, allowing the music to lull her into a more relaxed state.

The train had already passed a few stops when Maxine jolted awake. Glancing around the now partially occupied train, she calmed her racing heart. Just as she was about to close her eyes again, a familiar baritone voice disrupted her solitude. "Hey, it's you." The voice was calm, with a hint of depth. Maxine paused her music and turned her gaze to her left. It was Kam. He occupied the corner seat across from her, his big eyes and gentle smile a comforting sight. Dressed in all black, from his jeans and shirt to his leather coat, he exuded a sense of enigmatic charm.

"Hey. How have you been?" she asked, her shyness showing. "I was worried about you. It's good to see you again," he said, his grin sincere. His gaze lingered on her notebook, raising an inquisitive eyebrow. "What's the notebook for?" he inquired. Maxine quipped with a playful smile, "My dark, fascinating secrets. If I tell you, I might kill you." Kam chuckled softly. "Gee sounds amusing," He said, attempting to sound suave but coming across a tad awkward. Maxine winced slightly, her honesty not sugarcoating her response. "I find your charm a bit clumsy, but oddly endearing," she said.

Kam blushed and grinned shyly. "Don't be too hard on me. I did say it was endearing," she reassured him. With a nod and a flustered grin, Kam seemed to accept the reassurance. Maxine tilted her head, studying him with curiosity. Her fascination was evident; he was like a puzzle she was eager to solve. Deciding to start with a simple question, she asked, "Where are you from?" Kam's eyes darted, caught off guard by the question. Maxine's expression turned puzzled. "You really need to think about it?" she inquired.

"If I reveal it, I might have to kill you," he quipped playfully. This time, his charm managed to charm her, albeit with a hint of clumsiness. "Hey, that's my line!" she exclaimed, grinning. "Are you a martian or something?" she prodded further, still seeking answers. "Martian? What? No," Kam replied quickly. Maxine's confusion grew. "All I can say is that I live fifty miles outside of the city." Maxine's eyes suddenly lit up. "Wait. Did you see the death camp?" Kam's face contorted, puzzled. "You seem lost," she said, her disappointment palpable.

"I saw a huge building surrounded by a barbed wire fence," he mentioned. "Yes, that was the death camp," Maxine confirmed. However, Kam still appeared baffled. "They take the infected there. At least that's the rumor," she explained. Kam's bewilderment persisted. "You've been hiding under a rock this whole time?" she asked incredulously, frustrated by his lack of awareness. "No, I've never heard of it," he admitted. Maxine was astonished. "You've definitely been under a rock, dude," she remarked with annoyance, surprised by his unfamiliarity.

"I suppose I have," Kam responded. "Wow, you're weird," Maxine commented, her tone colder than intended. She immediately regretted it. "I'm sorry, did I—" "No, my bad. I didn't mean to sound so rude. I'm just in mind-blown mode from your lack of knowledge. This pandemic has kept us over informed and isolated for over a year. We just came from a city that was bombed. My mom's a traveling nurse and a retired model, believe it or not. That's how she met my dad, who used to photograph her. But anyway, the bombings shook us all. My brother, Kincade, rambles on about it being an inside job. I'm not entirely sure I agree, but he's a firm believer that there's always an ulterior motive behind everything."

She looked at Kam as his curious eyes gazed at her intently. All ears. "You sure love it when tea is spilled but won't spill any yourself," she said, detecting his curiosity. "I'm gonna assume 'spilling tea' means telling on myself," he said. "Not necessarily telling," she rolled her eyes before continuing, "You make it sound like I'm interrogating you. I just want to get to know you, that's all. I don't bite. At least not often," She said with a charming grin. Kam beamed, happy to see her no longer so distant.

The train lights flickered again as it went over a bump. Both jolted in their seats as they went over it. "So, I have to ask, what happened in the car earlier?" Kam asked without a second thought. Maxine suddenly felt a flash of irritation, sensing that his questions seemed specific and uncomfortable, especially this one. But something about him seemed comforting, innocent even. She could tell it wasn't ill intent.

So she smiled and said, "That's classified info." She then added, "Maybe if we see each other again I just might let you know. But for now, I'd rather keep that to myself. If that's not too much to ask." Kam smiled to hide his nervous tension. "I can try and keep my foot out of my mouth for now," he said, suddenly self-aware of his invasiveness. "God, you're painfully adorable. Has anyone told you that?" she asked, genuinely curious. Kam furrowed his brow, appearing puzzled. "No, that's new actually," he said, feeling charmed all of a sudden. "It fits better than any puzzle piece ever could," she smiled. "Did you just compare me to a puzzle?" Kam asked, forming a grin. Maxine grinned too, no longer finding him eccentric.

The lights flickered once again as Kam felt a sudden sense of urgency. The feeling blindsided him. He immediately flashed back to the Ferris wheel as he felt his hands buzzing. Kam stood up, his heart suddenly pounding. Maxine looked confused once again. "You good there, tall and handsome?" She asked with a flirtatious smile. Kam frantically scanned the nearly empty train car. His breathing became rapid. Maxine looked at him, transitioning from confusion to concern. "What's wrong?" she asked. Kam said nothing as he continued surveying every corner of the car for a potential threat. The lights flickered again, making Kam jolt. He shook his head. "Déjà vu," is all he could manage to say as he swallowed hard.

His hands continued buzzing as he continued to gaze in every direction possible. His anxiety became infectious, as Maxine also started to look around, unsure of what exactly to be wary of. The light flickered again as the train screeched. Kam's heart raced faster, feeling like it could explode. He had to sit down, as his heart rate was too high for him to continue standing. He sat down and slowed his breathing. He suddenly got a grip, utilizing the breathing technique he had taught Maxine earlier in the car. His heartbeat finally subsided with each breath.

The train came to a sudden stop. "Now approaching, Meadows Avenue," the monotone male voice announced on the intercom. Kam felt better, but still sensed imminent danger was close. "Dude, you're okay?" Maxine asked, observing Kam with his head against the window, eyes shut as he continued his breathing technique. The train car opened, two occupants exited, leaving only them and a middle-aged lady reading a book in the middle aisle. Kam nodded. "Panic attack, I'm fine," he said nervously, his heart rate returning to normal. Maxine's empathy kicked in, as his anxiety reminded her of how she felt in the car.

A couple of stops later, Kam finally began to settle down. Kam and Maxine were in their own worlds, too shy to carry on a comfortable conversation. Maxine lay back as she began thinking about Tobias and his elusive behavior toward Georgette. She quickly pushed away this thought as memories of her deceased sister, Imani, suddenly haunted her. She could see her stunning features: her hazel eyes, freckles, shoulder-length black and brown dreads, and exceptional confidence. Confidence she envied. She began feeling emotional, then shut her eyes tightly to erase the memory. A few agonizing seconds passed. Each second felt like minutes.

Kam looked out the window and gazed at the city lights of downtown Zeus City in the distance. The city lights engulfed his vision as he took in the various structures. He felt at ease, hoping his panic attack was simply repressed memories resurfacing. He suddenly looked at Maxine, observing her thick long braids, polished brown skin, and her petite frame coiled against the corner of her seat. He felt something stirring within him—an urge to bring her closer. Not lust, but a genuine interest in getting to know her more intimately. Maxine turned around, catching his stare. He looked away, feeling caught.

Maxine smiled, unfazed by his response. "How are you?" she asked, her voice gentle and calming. Kam smirked. "I'm still a bit anxious, but I'm much better," he admitted. Maxine was growing more fond of him by the moment. Sensing an opportunity, she decided to make a subtle move. "I'm just one stop away," she mentioned, hoping he'd catch her drift. "Oh, okay. Well, I guess I'll see you around," he responded, completely unaware of her intention. Though disappointed, Maxine was determined to try again.

"It's getting late... and there's some nocturnal creeps lurking outside. Watch my back? I'll watch yours," she suggested with a grin. Kam's face lit up. He hadn't felt this level of excitement in a while, and it was making him a bit anxious. "Um, yeah, of course. I'll protect you with my life," he replied, hoping his words didn't come across as awkward. "So, you're basically volunteering to be my shield?" she playfully asked, charmed by his response. Kam prepared to say something else, but suddenly, a loud boom interrupted their conversation.

Kam felt a violent jolt, his head colliding forcefully with the window behind him. Maxine was thrown to the ground, shaken by the impact. Something had struck the train car ahead of them. The blaring train alarms added to the chaos. Kam quickly got to his feet, his head throbbing from where it had hit the window. He touched the back of his head, his fingers coming away sticky with blood. His heart raced, and a sense of urgency flooded him. He helped Maxine up, and they both crouched down, bewildered by the unexpected impact. Their eyes locked, each wearing a look of astonishment and disorientation.

The middle-aged woman in the center aisle struggled to her feet, clearly rattled by the situation. "What in the world was that?" she exclaimed in a strong southern accent. Kam glanced toward the window next to her and spotted a blazing fireball hurtling towards them. "Get down!" he screamed, but the woman seemed confused, unable to comprehend the danger. Suddenly, the fireball struck her, and Kam shielded Maxine just in time. The woman was engulfed in flames. Kam and Maxine stared in disbelief as flames consumed the top half of the train car.

"We need to move!" Kam shouted, reaching for Maxine's hand as he tried to lead her toward the back door that connected to the last car. Maxine hesitated, struggling to process the shock of the situation. "Come on!" he urged her. With shaky hands, she gripped his hand, and they ran, narrowly escaping as another fireball hit the car behind them, setting it ablaze. The force of the explosion behind them propelled them forward, and they tumbled to the ground.

Kam shielded Maxine as debris rained down on them. Once the chaos subsided, they attempted to pry open the exit doors, desperate to escape. However, the doors refused to budge. "Damn it!" Maxine exclaimed. "How do we get out of here..." Another explosion interrupted her words as yet another fireball struck the train car, engulfing the first half in flames. Kam and Maxine dropped to the ground once more. Kam landed heavily on his back against the back seats, while Maxine fell onto the floor face-first.

Suddenly, they felt a shift in gravity as the train car started to tilt and teeter off the tracks. "Hold onto the seat!" Kam yelled over the chaos. Maxine clung to the seat next to her as the car hung precariously, flames consuming three out of its five sections. Beneath them, a pool of fire blazed. Smoke filled the air, making it difficult to breathe and obscuring their vision. Through the haze, Kam saw Maxine struggling. "Hang in there!" he encouraged, his voice strained.

Maxine's coughs echoed in the smoky air as she fought to catch her breath. She sobbed as the weight of the situation bore down on her. Kam was dangling next to her, searching through the thick smoke for her. He reached out, hoping to find her hand. "Reach out!" he yelled above the roaring flames pooling beneath them. Maxine coughed, her lungs burning for air, and extended her hand into the smoky darkness. Kam's strong grip found hers. "Let go!" he shouted. Confused and apprehensive, Maxine hesitated for a moment. "What!?" she screamed in response.

"Trust me, just let go!" Kam's voice was urgent. Despite the apparent insanity of his request, Maxine closed her eyes and released her grip on the seat. She felt a rush of weightlessness, the cool night air brushing against her skin. She looked up, relieved to see Kam holding onto her. Together, they landed softly on the train platform. Kam shielded Maxine as they hit the ground, protecting her from the impact.

Amidst the chaos, they heard a thunderous boom; followed by an eruption of flames as the train crashed down below. As the fiery wreckage descended, Kam and Maxine looked at each other, their expressions shifting from shock and terror to a profound sense of relief. They were alive. "Wh...who are you?" Maxine managed to ask between labored breaths. Kam didn't realize that his contact had fallen, revealing his glowing violet left eye. Their breaths were heavy, and their faces were mere inches apart. Kam began to rise into the air, ascending above the billowing clouds of smoke that filled the sky. Maxine laid on the ground, her emotions a tumultuous mix of relief, trauma, and confusion as she watched Kam fly away. Who was responsible for this? Why had they been targeted? Questions lingered unanswered for both of them.

| 11 |

Maxine

Maxine had been sitting in the hospital room for over an hour, perched on the glossy blue hospital chair. Her left arm and forehead bore bandages, and small spots of blood stained her hoodie. Her head hung low, her body seemingly fragile, as if a mere touch could shatter her. Her thoughts were a tangled mess of questions, jumbled and confused.

"Who was that? Did he actually fly, or was that just my imagination from the shock? Why me? Why do I have to endure trauma again?" Her mind raced, and a slight tremor coursed through her. The hospital environment only added to her discomfort; her past experiences with hospitals had been overwhelmingly negative. Kincade's asthma attack, Georgette's condition, and her own previous ordeal replayed in her thoughts.

A doctor entered the room, glancing down at his tablet. His round glasses framed his dark brown eyes, which reflected Maxine's medical chart. He appeared to be around 35, with light caramel skin and short, wavy black hair. Focusing on her chart, he commented, "Your vitals are mostly stable. Your blood pressure is slightly elevated, likely due to anxiety." Maxine kept her gaze lowered, still struggling to process everything. Concerned, the doctor frowned and inquired, "Are you alright?" Without looking up, Maxine responded in a low voice, "Take a wild guess, doc."

"Your brother is on his way; he should be here soon. Can I get you some water? Maybe coffee?" The doctor's attempt to offer comfort was met with Maxine's silent indifference. He nodded understandingly and left the room, leaving Maxine alone with her thoughts.

Just a few minutes later, an older man with ivory complexion and snowflake-colored hair and dark blue eyes walked in. Not in a doctor's attire, he wore a dark blazer, dress slacks, and a sky-blue dress shirt with the top button undone. "I'm Detective Blake Landon," he introduced himself, flashing his badge to Maxine, who still had her gaze fixed downward. "I have a few questions about the train derailment earlier tonight. I need your cooperation, as there are certain aspects that struck me as quite peculiar. Do I have your consent?" His tone was firm.

Raising her head, Maxine's expression turned hostile as she glared at him. He pulled a white stool from the marble counter, sat across from her, and opened a mini black notepad, ready to take notes. "Just so you're aware, I'm wearing a wire, and this conversation is being recorded. Can we proceed?" He sought her agreement as a formality. Maxine gave a slow, reluctant nod. "To start, in your own words, can you explain how you managed to escape from the train?" Detective Landon inquired.

Struggling to find the right words, Maxine hesitated. "Umm," she began, her voice uncertain. "Someone helped me," she managed to say, her voice choked with emotion. She fought back tears, sniffling as she avoided eye contact. Detective Landon, sensing her distress, shifted his approach. "Could you provide more details?" he prompted, his tone softer now.

"I saw fire approaching the train. A woman died when it hit the car. A fellow passenger..." Maxine's voice trailed off, her throat constricting as the memories resurfaced. "Was this passenger someone you were acquainted with?" Detective Landon interrupted, his pen poised to write.

Frustrated by the interruption, Maxine continued, her voice mono-tone and weary. "No, I met them tonight. They pulled me towards the back when more fire struck. After that, I blacked out. When I woke up, I was on the platform. That's all I remember," she finished, her patience waning.

"What did this passenger look like?" Detective Landon inquired, his gaze still fixed on his notepad.

"I have no idea."

"Could you determine their gender at least?"

"Male."

"Could you describe their ethnicity?"

"I don't know."

Maxine's responses grew curt, as she aimed to deflect suspicion away from Kam.

"Tall or short?"

"I already told you, I don't know," she snapped.

Finally conceding that he wouldn't get much more detail, Detective Landon jotted down the scant information he had gathered. Looking up from his notes, he regarded Maxine with an attempt at reassurance. "I didn't mean to intrude, but seven lives were lost, and the fire's origin remains a mystery. No signs of oil or gas leakage, electrical mal-functions, or anything of the sort. Furthermore, there are reports of a person flying into the sky." Maxine's surprise was palpable, though she tried to mask it. She leaned back, feigning a casual expression. "What?" she asked, trying to sound genuinely puzzled.

"Yes, some witnesses claim that. I believe it might have been some object or misinterpretation, but it's quite perplexing that multiple witnesses describe a similar event. Any thoughts on that?" Detective Landon's gaze was probing.

Maxine knew she couldn't share the truth, as it would likely be dismissed as nonsense. She shrugged nonchalantly and replied, "I didn't see anything."

Detective Landon looked intrigued yet baffled by her response. Tapping his pen against his pad, he nodded slowly. "Alright, this investigation is ongoing. I'll have to look more into this.…. 'hocus pocus phenomenon,'. In the meantime, here's my card." He retrieved a card from his blazer pocket and handed it to Maxine. She took it begrudgingly, clutching it tightly without even glancing at it.

"Feel free to reach out if you remember anything or if you have any questions. I'll stay in touch," Detective Landon said with a friendly smile, rising from the stool. Maxine offered a brief nod, her mind still tangled in a web of confusion and disbelief.

Maxine nodded slowly, her smirk tinged with pain. "Take it easy, kid," he said, getting up from the stool and walking out the door. Maxine twirled the card in her hands as she gazed at it. She knew she wouldn't contact him even if her life depended on it. She ripped the card to shreds and carelessly tossed the debris onto the floor. The door flew open again. "Sis!" She heard. It was Kincade. His face held a mix of relief and shock. She lit up the moment she saw him and wrapped her arms tightly around him, feeling as if she could stay in his embrace forever. "Thank god," she murmured into his shoulder. She stayed, clinging to him, her eyes welling with tears but not spilling.

He released her and placed his hands on her shoulders. "What's up with the George Stacy in the fancy suit? What did he want?" He asked, nodding his head towards the door. "Don't worry, just casual detective interrogation tactics. I'm not in any trouble," she said as she sniffled. "You good?" He asked with a look of concern. Maxine nodded, smiling through her sadness. "Looks like I have another demon to fight," Maxine said, her chuckle masking her sorrow, taking a deep breath to steady herself. Kincade smiled. "Nothing you can't handle," he reassured.

Maxine nodded, her tears held back. She unconsciously turned around, as if to wipe away a tear, but found her face still dry. "I manage," she said, her voice quivering as she fought back tears. "The Harley is outside. Let's get the hell out of here," he said with a grin. Maxine beamed, feeling a surge of excitement to ride it. He put his arm around her shoulder, kissing her on the cheek as they left and headed for the front desk to check out.

**.

"I knew my bestie was indestructible," Ava said cheerfully as she released Maxine from a hug.

"I wouldn't set the bar that high," Maxine replied.

"Aw, don't kill us with your modesty. I mean it!" Ava exclaimed.

Kincade was perched at the round wooden dining table, which looked slick and pristine as if it were just bought. He had a smirk on his face as he observed Ava and Maxine on the opposite side of the kitchen, standing in front of the counter near the refrigerator.

"Even steel has nothing on you," Ava added as Maxine timidly tucked her face away, her hand clasped to her mouth.

"I like that description, it's fitting," Kincade said.

Ava raised an eyebrow. "Are you agreeing with me?" Ava asked, her tone filled with amusement.

"I find your disbelief hilarious," Kincade said with a sarcastic grin.

"I'm looking for my alarm clock to bring me out of this twilight zone," Ava replied as she sarcastically darted her head in every direction.

"Twilight zone, huh?" He asked, then continued, "I was just admiring the fact that you actually said something valid." Maxine chuckled at this.

"I felt the backhand of that," Ava said with a laugh.

Maxine let out a small laugh, amused by their banter full of sarcasm. "Dad working late again?" Maxine asked. She had the feeling he was, but couldn't help but ask.

"Yeah, he's playing hide and seek again. Everyone seems to be it except for him. Go figure," Kam said as he shrugged casually.

"Can't lie and say I'm surprised," Maxine sighed, feeling dejected.

"Ship me to the moon the day he can withstand adversity and not fold," Kincade added.

"Isn't that your dad?" Ava asked, partly serious.

"He might as well be your dad, too. As often as you're here," Kincade said as Maxine held back a laugh.

Ava pierced her eyes at him, annoyed. "You live here now, so you might want to switch that little Mister title you gave him," Kincade chuckled, finding Ava's displeasure entertaining.

"He makes a valid point," Maxine said with a laugh.

"Hey, you're supposed to be on my side!" Ava said humorously.

"Blood before... whatever you are," Kincade said as Maxine laughed more loudly than she anticipated.

Ava grinned wide as she gave Kincade the finger. "I eat those," He said with a cocky grin.

"You look like you eat nothing but air, looking like a badly drawn stick figure," Ava retorted.

"Aww, suddenly I'm flustered! I think my self-esteem boosted by a few points!" Kincade replied in a mocking tone. But she wasn't far off. Kincade was really slender and slightly below his optimal weight.

"Y'all are priceless as hell," Maxine said as she finished her laugh attack.

Kincade and Ava's second-nature ability to conflict with each other brought back her sense of normalcy. So much so that she temporarily forgot about the horror she experienced earlier that night.

They all glanced up in surprise as a key slid into the lock of the front door. Tobias stepped through the doorway, clad in a large brown coat and a matching fedora. His Kodak camera was attached to his waist as he hung his coat on the rack. His short, dark hair was neatly cut and combed, and he now sported a plain gray shirt, black slacks, and a pair of polished boots without laces.

He made his way to the kitchen, spotting Kincade sitting at the table, wearing a shirt with alternating light and dark blue stripes. "Oh look, it's the man of the hour!" Kincade quipped as Tobias walked in.

"Hey, son," He answered casually. He scoured the room, spotting Maxine standing next to the stainless steel fridge. His face formed a wide smile as his eyes remained still. "Hey, baby girl!" he exclaimed, his voice animated as he embraced her, and she hesitantly returned the embrace. "If he knew what happened, why didn't he visit?" She thought. The words wouldn't dare find her lips.

He released his grasp, his eyes wide, finally matching his smile. "Smile baby, you made it!" He exclaimed, ignoring the awkwardness in the room. "I'm in one piece, dad," Maxine said, forcing a smile.

"My baby survived. Something in me knew you'd be okay." His lips slightly twitched, his eyes barely holding on to Maxine's. Maxine kept up with her smile, despite the tension in the room. "She truly is unbreakable, isn't she?" Ava said proudly, attempting to break the tension. Tobias smiled and nodded, analyzing Maxine again.

"Everything is okay, dad. Pinky swear," Maxine said reassuringly. "I'm sorry work ran so late. Things got a bit hectic today. The press is running rampant right now with everything going on," He said.

"Don't apologize, dad. I understand." Maxine said, not meaning it.

He embraced her one more time and held his gaze, his smile starting to fall apart. "I'll be upstairs okay?" He said as Maxine slowly nodded. He smiled as the others waved back, although the atmosphere remained tense. He walked upstairs as if he wanted to flee, feeling a surge of guilt ping at his chest. The others watched on until they heard his door shut.

"That was sufficiently cringe," Kincade said. Maxine said nothing, although she agreed with him. "Didn't even ask if you were okay, just assumed it," Ava added. "Valid," Kincade agreed. "I'm on a little valid roll tonight aren't I?" Ava quipped. "Your luck is close to the edge, don't push it," Kincade replied as Maxine chuckled lightly and Ava half smirked. "He acts like visiting you would have broken him in half," Kincade said to Maxine as he rose from the table.

"I hope you feel better in the morning," He said as he patted Maxine on the shoulder. "Why hope? Why not know?" Ava asked.

"Because it's up to her to feel better, not us," Kincade said as he planted a kiss on her forehead.

She felt a wave of relief as Kincade gave a final smirk and ascended the stairs. Ava offered a small, comforting smile as she passed her. But her thoughts soon drifted back to her father - how he had chosen to work late rather than face her in the hospital. That knowledge stung her deeply.

It wasn't just him avoiding Georgette that triggered her. Tobias had a long-standing habit of fleeing when times got tough. He also had a long standing history of playing off their feelings and not taking their vulnerability seriously. His history of hiding was long, hiding when things became strained between him and Georgette a few years back, when Maxine had been hospitalized over two years ago, and when Kincade almost died from an asthma attack.

Rather than visit Kincade in the hospital, he had relied on her and Georgette for updates, citing work as an excuse for his absence. He would always talk up bravery, but when it was time to act, he would always flee.

| 12 |

Kam

Kam had finally arrived home, the moonlight casting a gentle radiance upon the worn appearance of the earth house. Shadows of tears still clung to his cheeks, remnants of his brief cry just moments before. His head wound, miraculously healed in an incredibly short amount of time, now bore only a faint scar. Climbing the weathered wooden steps, he noticed the door slightly ajar. At first, terror flickered in his eyes, but then realization settled in – this was his request to Bliss before he left.

He wedged his hands into the small opening, pushing the door aside. Upon entering, the living room and kitchen were bathed in a soft blue hue emanating from the kitchen. He treaded lightly down the hallway, reaching his room on the left. He slipped inside, carefully removing his laceless black shoes before settling onto the bed, his head bowed. A soft knock on the door suddenly disrupted his thoughts. Kam raised his head, unease settling in. Could it be Meeka or Ala coming to chastise him?

Relief washed over him as Bliss's face appeared in the doorway, as if on a top-secret mission. Her perfectly sculpted cheekbones were slightly dulled by the faint moonlight filtering through the window. In her hands, she held a steaming black mug. "I brought tea," she announced, strolling in and placing the cup on the bedside table before sinking into the beanbag chair across the room, allowing her body to relax.

A sense of secrecy hung in the air as Bliss noticed the dread etched on Kam's face. "Nothing... Nothing makes sense," he muttered, his gaze fixed on his trembling hands. "What happened?" Bliss's curiosity took over. Kam looked up, fighting back the urge to cry, and began recounting the events: the train derailment, seeing Maxine, the city bombings, and the rumors of a death camp. After he finished, Bliss was visibly astonished. "You were more right than you know," he admitted, still trying to process the staggering information. "But from what I heard, the city bombings happened all at once, in one night. And they weren't fireballs. More like planted," Kam shuddered at the implications. Bombs? Planted? How could he uncover the truth? He was certain it wasn't just bombs that attacked him; there was something far more sinister at play.

Then, a sudden realization struck him. His breath quivered as he said, "I think we were targeted." Bliss raised an eyebrow. "You?" she asked incredulously. Kam shook his head, clarifying, "I don't know, but someone knew we were there." Bliss appeared lost in thought. "It's possible you were caught in a crossfire," she suggested. Kam disagreed, explaining, "The fireballs followed us as we moved through the train. It was like someone was aiming." Bliss sat there, her hands clenched and resting on her chin as she leaned forward, deep in contemplation.

"It's possible someone knew I was Axpherian. I doubt it was random," Kam mused. "She might have died because of me," he added solemnly. "But she didn't. You saved her," Bliss reassured him. Kam couldn't help but smirk. "I feel like I've finally redeemed myself. I listened to my gut this time. I had a feeling something was going to happen, and I was able to intervene." His gaze shifted away, the weight of the passenger he couldn't save heavy on his mind. Returning to the train attack, he looked up at Bliss, his expression resembling that of a scolded puppy. "You have such a complicated hero complex. It bothers me sometimes," Bliss said, a mix of seriousness in her tone. "I hate to say this, and you might argue," she continued, "but you're going to have to tell the folks. As gut-wrenching as it sounds."

An ache of anxiety settled in Kam's chest. "But why? All they're going to do is scold me to death, like they always do," he retorted, a hint of defiance in his voice. Bliss glanced over her shoulder, hoping to keep their conversation from waking their parents. "They might be able to help. You nearly died tonight. Are you not aware of that?" she asked, a touch of frustration creeping into her voice. "I was there, Bliss. Of course, I'm aware," he replied. "Then why not seek help when we literally have two scientists working with the Axpherian army? It's not the time to be so prideful, especially after I almost lost you tonight," Bliss reasoned. "I'm here! I'm here, and I survived without them," Kam responded, his voice carrying more determination.

Exhaustion hung heavily on Kam as he placed his hands on his head, wearied by the heated exchange. "This is silly. I'm sorry," he admitted, a pang of guilt washing over him. Bliss rose from her seat and settled beside him on the bed, her fingers intertwining in her lap. "This isn't silly. It's too important to be dismissed as such," she assured him. She apologized for the heated discussion, her gaze meeting his, the violet of her eyes seeming darker in the dimly lit room.

"We should hurry our discussion of this intricate plan," he said, his voice drained. "Let's put a bookmark in it until morning. We'll have plenty of time then," she suggested with a yawn. Kam nodded slowly, his gaze on his folded hands. "You saved a life tonight. Someone almost kissed and waved her goodbye for the last time. But you intervened. You're a hero. And every hero needs support. That's what I'm here for," Bliss reassured him, her words prompting a slow grin from Kam. "Thank you," he sincerely said. "Shut up. And you're welcome," she playfully retorted, a snicker escaping her.

A familiar scent wafted from the mug, and Kam wrinkled his nose in recognition. "Smells like Blue Fralik leaves." These leaves, grown in the Pata forest in Axpherial, were alluring with their light blue color. The forest was a breathtaking sight with its blue leaves and light brown bark. The leaves acted as a sedative and relaxant, though their bitterness was quite pronounced. Bliss smiled knowingly. "Indeed, it'll help you sleep and take some weight off," she said. Kam's frown turned into a smirk. "I thought you wanted me to feel better." Bliss responded with a playful, "I knew you'd say that," and they shared a laugh.

Seeing Bliss's knowing smirk, Kam realized she was serious. "I have all night. I'm not leaving until you've consumed every cringe-worthy drop," she declared, eliciting a nervous laugh from Kam. He reluctantly took sips from the lukewarm blue liquid, cringing with each gulp. Finally, the mug was emptied, and Kam declared it "torturous." Bliss collected the mug, assuring Kam that he would thank her later as she headed toward the door. As she spun around, her gaze met his as he sat upright, staring at the desk. "When does the part where I thank you come?" he said in a sarcastic tone. "When you're deep in dreamland." Kam chuckled nervously. "Hopefully, no Ferris wheel this time." He hesitated, surprised at his own attempt at humor. Especially about that.

Bliss smiled warmly, "Get some rest, rebel," she said as she finally left the room. It didn't take long for the effects of the tea to kick in. Soon, his body felt heavy with sleep, and he lay down without bothering to tuck himself in. Bliss's words echoed in his mind as his eyelids grew too heavy to resist.

****
****

Kam jolted awake to the sound of intense conversation. He detected a tinge of unease in the voices, indicating that something was amiss. It was now early morning, and sun rays beamed on him from the window. He recognized his parents' voices, but there was another voice he did not know. Trying to shake off the grogginess of sleep, he quickly got up. He decided to investigate the source of the noise. It appeared to be coming from outside of his room. He leaned in closer to the door to hear.

An unfamiliar voice, deep with baritone, said, "We all have to tread lighter from here on if we want to safeguard our citizens as much as we can." Then, Ala's voice, not in its usual passive tone, asked, "Do you think it really was one of our own?" She spoke in a quavering voice, her fear palpable. Kam continued to listen in.

"Multiple civilians have attested to having seen a figure hovering in the air during the train assault, with the recordings being widely circulated in both major and minor media outlets, and on something they call social media. This could very well be sufficient grounds for initiating another attack," The unknown man said urgently. Anxiety stabbed at Kam's gut as he realized how many people could now be aware of the situation. Kam looked down, feeling overwhelmed.

Ala and Meeka paused for a moment, pondering a quick response. Meeka posed the question to the unknown man, "Any idea on who it could've been?" The man sighed deeply before showing them a glass screen that contained the footage. The image was blurry and taken from far away, yet they were still able to recognize Kam taking off into the sky. Their eyes widened in astonishment as they viewed the scene before them, unable to believe what they were seeing.

He switched it off as he observed Ala and Meeka seemingly per-plexed. They were unsure of how to process the information. The man standing before them was a lieutenant in the DAA. He was tall with a trim beard and had a similar muscular build to Meeka. He was wearing an all-black suit with red stripes on both sleeves that glowed like dim LED lights. Ala inquired, "Do you suggest we leave?"

"Certain measures, though drastic, must be met to protect their citizens and ours," the Lieutenant replied. Meeka then asked, "What about the Aphlama? Do you think that'll be safe? We're still perfecting the prototype. The math still needs modifications."

The Aphlama was a significant machine that could save lives, and its loss could be devastating. The Axpherians were working closely with the US government to come up with a cure, though they kept their true identities under wraps. "Continue your work. But get your children to safety before any more potential casualties. I'll talk to the council at The Great Strength about deprogramming the delfonas from earthly travel. Only DAA personnel will have access to this realm. No civilian access until we can resolve these ongoing onslaughts. There are only

7 immunity cities left in the United States. That number can dwindle easily with continued missteps," The lieutenant said.

Meeka stood with his arms folded as the man delivered the news, while Ala just looked at the floor, still recovering from the shock. Kam muttered, "No access" while continuing to listen. "It's quite drastic, but it's necessary," Ala commented. "It's a necessity to save lives. I'll touch base on what the council decision will be at The Great Strength. As outlined in the Axpherian's Bylaws for tranquility, we can bypass a democratic vote to protect the planet from war, genocide, and societal collapse if the members can come to a 70 majority vote." Both Meeka and Ala nodded, seeing a glimmer of hope.

Kam listened with apprehension as the man gave a reassuring smirk and declared, "We'll be in close contact," as he marched out the door. Ala and Meeka stood side by side, processing the situation. The implications of no earth access and bypassing the vote raced through Kam's mind, making the need for plans more urgent than he had anticipated. He slowly backed away from the door, his thoughts still spinning.

"Bliss, Kam! In the sitting room now!" Meeka said, his voice hot with frustration. Kam jolted back and slowly dragged his feet out of the room as if they were weighed down by two tons. He lurked into the hallway, witnessing the weariness on Bliss' face. Both of them showed signs of dread as they looked upon one another.

Bliss and Kam slowly marched to the living room. They both took a seat on the longest couch cautiously, as if they were sitting on hot coals. Meeka had an expression of anger that could turn away a lion. Ala, on the other hand, had a worried look, as she failed to appear stern. Bliss and Kam looked up in anticipation, aware of what was to come.

"Didn't I make myself clear when I told both of you no antics?" Meeka asked. Neither of them responded. "You both have mouths, so speak," Meeka hissed. They looked at each other, hoping the other would speak first. Then they searched the room, avoiding the fire in Meeka's eyes.

"Your father and I....." Ala said, trailing off. They turned to Ala, dreading what she would say. "Your father and I work diligently to provide protection for both of you. We trusted that you would at least do what was told, given the circumstances." Suddenly words bubbled up in Kam, but he decided to wait for Ala to finish.

"So when we tell you to do something, we expect you to follow through." Kam couldn't take the pressure anymore. "Why didn't you tell us what was really going on then?" Kam asked. Ala tilted her head and raised an eyebrow. Meeka's intimidating stare became more intense. Bliss's mouth was open, like she couldn't believe he said that.

"Excuse me?" Meeka hissed. "Why keep the details of the pandemic from us? Why not tell us about the bombings? Why isolate us?" Meeka angrily spat out, "Our missions are none of your concern. I had to keep a tight leash on you both. Every time I leave you two or particularly you Kam, alone; I can't help but receive insubordination and an inability to display well-rounded enough discipline to follow simple instructions."

"Instructions? If I followed your instructions someone would be dead right now!" Kam said, almost yelling. Meeka squinted with confusion. "Dead?" He asked intensely. "Yes, dead. I saved someone on that train. The girl who was in the car that day. I saved her."

"Are you aware of the magnitude of the harm you have caused?" "No. But I saved her. And that's what matters most. Do lives here not hold weight unless they're Axpherian?" "Kam, you're missing my point." "Point? But dad...." "Enough you two! Now!" Ala said, raising her voice.

Kam and Meeka stopped, caught off guard by the rare fire in Ala's tone. Ala continued, "I commend your act of bravery, Kam. But it doesn't negate the fact that you still disobeyed us and caused our plans to become even more top-heavy. You could've very well put millions of people in a compromising position from your actions." Ala then glared at Bliss. "And you. I know he required your assistance. And for that, it's just as much your fault we are in this predicament." Bliss attempted to defend herself, "Mom, please see it from our perspective. We..." "Save it Bliss." Ala hissed. Bliss fixed her mouth to say something else, but the words never left.

"You both are going back to Axpherial effective immediately. Your delfonas will be deactivated until we conclude our mission. No leaving Axpherial, no leaving the island, understand?" Meeka said, arms folded. Kam and Bliss put their heads down, not having anything else to say. "Good. Go pack. We'll have an official come get you soon. Make it quick." Meeka said. "This is for your safety. We love you." Ala said, her voice soothing again.

The two of them trudged to the basement, and Bliss and Kam silently pondered their situation. "That was...." Kam struggled to finish. "Selfish." Bliss said, finishing for him. "They treated her like she was disposable. They didn't so much as..." Kam swelled with anger as he trailed off. He balled his fists and clenched his jaw, not helping himself. Bliss was a bit shocked seeing him so tense with anger.

"Brother, you have to relax." Kam nodded, trying hard to pull back. "I feel like they know more than they're leading on," Kam said, eyes gazed on the floor. Bliss raised an eyebrow. "I feel like they might know why I was attacked, but they think if I actually knew who that..." "That you would put yourself in harm's way to save everyone." Bliss finished as her lips curved upwards and her eyes lit up with a knowing expression. "And they feel like me sneaking out provoked the attack. And maybe it did.." Kam muttered, his tone defeated. Bliss planted her hand on Kam's shoulder as he fought the lump in his throat threatening to turn into a thunderstorm of emotions. "I think they were trying to protect me and I just put us in danger." "No. Not this again, big bro." Bliss laughed out of frustration. "Wow, you're such a frustrating pain in the..." Kam chuckled as Bliss trailed off.

"You're not gonna villainize yourself again. You're too great of a person, well great is a stretch but you're definitely no one with I'll intent." Kam chuckled again as he nodded, trying his best to fully believe her, despite the ping of guilt still settling in his stomach. "We have to find a way to come back, before they or the council turn off the delfonas." Kam said. "Looks like the first draft of this master plan is coming to pass. I'm all ears." Bliss said, leaning forward.

"I'm gonna find a way to come back and go through the basement. I can then see all the info they're tucking away. Go to my cabin and we'll communicate through my computer in the basement. I'll send back pictures, documents, the complicated math equations, everything that looks even partially important. I'll dig a fine-tooth comb through it." Bliss smirked, beaming at the idea of snooping through the top-secret files.

"Intriguing. When do we execute?" "Three days, no sooner." "But the trackers on our delfonas won't turn off even with portal deactivation." "Bliss, you should know your brother's brain better than that." Bliss grinned. "I forgot there was a genius underneath that abnormally large skull. I keep forgetting it's not all air in there." Kam chuckled.

"Air-headed or not, I have a couple of backup delfonas in the cabin. Safe and parent-proof." Bliss grinned at this. "Remember that emergency council votes usually take around 9 days to take effect. So we may have just enough time." "But in case we don't?" Bliss asked. "We have to find one of our parents' government spares or clone their originals. As you know, the government delfonas won't be affected by the deactivation. And the folks are only gonna deactivate our current delfonas, not the two spares I kept at the forest house." Bliss smiled.

"Then what?" "We'll talk about phase two of this plan after we execute this one. Remember that we only have 9 days if we can't get a hold of a government delfona. We don't have much time to try to save everyone." Bliss and Kam gazed at each other, realizing they needed to pack. They quickly rose as Bliss said with a grin, "You were right. Antics are fun." Kam replied, "These antics will save lives." Bliss beamed with excitement as they thought about their plans. As they were packing their bags, there was a knock on the door. It was the official.

| 13 |

Maxine

Maxine woke to the beams of the early morning horizon on her face. She yawned as she rose from her bed. It had been three days since the train wreck, yet the shock it caused was still fresh in her memory. She recollected the terrified eyes of the middle-aged woman who was unaware as the fireball engulfed her. She thought of Kam, the young man with the single, beautiful violet eye that soared into the sky. As strange as he seemed, she was more than appreciative that he had saved her.

She heard a gentle knock at the door and lightly jolted. "It's open," she said sleepily. "Hey, still in bed sleeping off this peaceful afternoon?" he said. Her expression betrayed her mixed feelings. She was glad to see him, but wished Kincade or Ava had come in instead. She still found his inability to visit her or Georgette in the hospital cowardly. He sat at the end of her bed, folding his hands in his lap. "You've been catching a lot more zzz's than usual," Tobias quipped. Maxine faced him, seeing the twitch on the corner of his mouth, knowing he was faking his banter. A part of her felt empathy, the other was half full of resentment.

"I have been hibernating, haven't I?" Maxine said, realizing how often she'd been in her room, avoiding having to look at him for too long. Tobias grinned as he looked at his hands again. "I'm sorry for not visiting Georgette. I know you probably feel a way about that. But work has been unusually needy lately. I hope you understand." Maxine nodded, hiding her distaste. "I know Georgette is fighting an uphill battle right now. It's like yesterday...." He huffed into a laugh, then continued, "She was posing for the camera. Long hair, dimples, looking like the Picasso of an angel. But I know she'll be okay. I have all the faith in the world." He said, sounding unsure.

Maxine listened intently, desperately wanting to embrace him, yet also wanting him to take accountability and actually listen to her for once. It was a constant battle within her. "I still remember seeing her eyes light up when I told her how beautiful she was. I remember she gave me her email instead of her number. Told me I had to earn it," Tobias said into a laugh. Maxine couldn't help her lips that curved into a light grin. "But I can't front. I miss her," Tobias said as his voice began to quiver. "Then be a man and go see her," Maxine thought. She just nodded, listening to him reminisce. "I miss her too, Dad. I want her home so bad, but...." Maxine trailed off, exhaling hard and gazing downward as she thought about her.

Tobias gently put his hand on her leg that was still under her blanket. "You, your mom, and Kincade are all I've got. And I....." His smile faded and he quickly turned away as he quietly sniffled and wiped his tears, careful not to show Maxine his face. "Dad, you okay?" He nodded, quickly blinking away tears and fixing his face. "I know you're sick of me talking about her so much. Like that'll help change anything." Tobias said. "I am sick of it," Maxine thought. She had a hard time wanting to hurt his feelings. She really loved him but knew her love for him didn't blind her from facts.

He smirked at her, as she attempted to plaster a smile on her face, pretending to be okay. "I love you, baby girl," He said. "I love you too, Dad," She replied. His light brown eyes took on an even lighter hue in the rays of the early morning sun. His thick black beard sparkled in the light. His skin was supple and smooth, making him look much younger than his actual age of early forties. Although he was always a handsome man, he never sought to exalt himself. In fact, he was often oblivious to the compliments he received for his looks over the years. His earlier memories of being bullied as a child put a damper on his self-esteem even as an adult.

"I promise I'm not going anywhere," Maxine smiled. She meant it, even though she didn't fully want to. Tobias nodded, though he still felt the quiet tension between them. Maxine could tell he didn't fully believe her. "I mean it," Maxine reassured him. Tobias smiled as he rubbed her cheek. "I know," He said quietly. Maxine looked down, disappointed he couldn't bring himself to fully believe her. He took a gentle hold of the back of her head and planted a kiss atop her head before striding out of the room. She stayed rooted to her bed, examining her fingernails anxiously as she struggled to find the words to express her true emotions. She knew that it wouldn't be too much longer before she would.

****
*****

Maxine creaked open the door to the garage, her heart in her throat as she stared at the car that filled her with immense dread. She took a deep breath, trembling fingers hovering on the door handle. She inched into the garage and began counting to five, her breaths shallow and uneven. One, two, three... Her chest tightened with each number. Five breaths passed, but her racing heart didn't seem to notice. She squeezed her eyes shut, as if shutting out the fear.

She forced herself to continue. She began to Inhale for five seconds. She held her breath for five seconds more, then exhaled slowly, as if releasing the tension that coiled within her. She repeated this four more times. By the end, her chest felt a little lighter, and she tentatively inched towards the driver's side. Her heart pounded so hard she could feel it in her ribs as her hand brushed against the door handle, as if it were a hot stove.

She shut her eyes once more, attempting the five-second breathing technique yet again. Unfortunately, it failed to produce the desired effect. Rather, her heart rate escalated and heat surged through her body. Every inhalation felt like a struggle. She grasped the handle and opened the door with her eyes still closed. "You can do this," she murmured to herself, her voice trembling. Her hands were shaking as the distinct smell of a new car filled her senses.

She peered inside, taking in the muted charcoal-hued seats and the faint beeping from the open door. Her gaze shifted to the glimmering black steering wheel and the small navigation screen and push-start button. The last time she was in this seat was when she had her panic attack; she closed her eyes and attempted to banish the recollection from her mind. Taking a deep, steadying breath, she carefully lowered herself into the driver's seat. Still feeling the ache in her chest and her heart pounding, she sat there, her fingers trembling as she ran them along the leather-clad steering wheel. She closed the door, but the storm going on within her did not subside.

She kept her eyes shut and took long, deep breaths, counting each one. After several attempts, her pulse started to slow, and the fire in her veins cooled down. She opened her eyes and repeated the technique, feeling like each breath was a small victory. Kam's voice echoed in her mind, "Focus on your breath. Mindfulness." Taking a deep breath, she honed in on the sensation of her lungs expanding and contracting. After a few moments, she felt the tightness in her chest dissipate, and the rapid thumping of her heart slow. She had done it.

A sense of accomplishment filled her, and she opened her eyes with a self-satisfied smile. As she opened the car door, she repeated her breathing technique one last time, mastering her fear. She stepped out of the vehicle, closing the door behind her. She was proud of herself for managing to get in a car without succumbing to a panic attack, something she hadn't been able to do in two years. With a sense of pride, she walked away with her head held high, proud of her progress.

| 14 |

Kam

"So what did you need to show us again?" Talo asked. Kam stood before his lake house, beaming. The sun shone brightly in a clear, light blue sky. Beside him, Bliss, Talo, and Orna eagerly awaited what he had to show them. He was anxious about revealing his secret basement, yet he knew he had to do it eventually. After all, if he ever needed help, they would need to be familiar with his arsenal. But that wasn't the only thing he wanted to show them.

"It's almost perfected; I'm taking it to Earth in two days," Kam smiled. Orna peered at him, puzzled, then asked, "Earth? You're crossing over to the forbidden?" Talo smirked and rolled her eyes. "The council hasn't banned it yet. Do you even listen to the announcements when they come on or..." "I got distracted like always." "Of course you did." Talo grinned.

"Anyway, we also have something important to tell you guys," Bliss said. "Oh?" Talo said, face beaming with curiosity. "We have four days before the council votes. And even then we...Bliss did you get the delfonas from our parents?" Bliss smiled, taking one out of her pocket.

Kam beamed as he saw her reach for it. "Rebel skills. I learned from the best," She said, tossing it to Kam. "Now all we have to do is clone it and bam! Earth is a revolving door," Kam said as he dangled the watch in his fingers. "Anoba!" Talo said excitedly. Anoba was a term used in

Axpherial to describe someone or something as cool. "Okay so what is this magnificent thing you wanted to show us?" Orna asked. "Follow me." Kam said with a hard grin.

He took the lead as they entered the cabin. He arrived at the end of the shallow hallway behind the living room and pressed his hand against the wooden wall. A red light shone, and the wall opened up to reveal a staircase. "Secret chamber," Kam said, taking in everyone's wide-eyed expressions except for Bliss, who was already aware of his armory. "What else are you hiding from us?" Orna asked, his shock evident. "Is it like a house within a house or something?" Talo asked. "Come with me, and you will find out," Kam replied, leading them down the stairs.

As they trailed after Kam, they exchanged glances. The stairway was initially long and dark, but each step they took triggered bright lights that illuminated the space in a brilliant white glow. They stepped into the chamber, and he flicked the light switch, illuminating the room. In front of them stood the three rows of steel tables, with various weapon designs strewn across them. In the middle of the room sat a motorcycle, its rims encircled by a blue light, appearing as if it had already been assembled. The motorcycle was perched on the center table.

Talo and Orna were dumbfounded. "Impressed is a harsh understatement," Talo said. "You, impressed? I could cry a river of joy right now," Orna said with a broad grin. Talo casted a disgruntled glance at him, while Bliss struggled to contain her amusement. "Over here!" Kam exclaimed, gesturing to the motorcycle at the table. "What's with the wheels? It reeks prehistoric and It's very..... earthy." Talo frowned. "That's the point. It's for travel there," Kam said proudly. "Wait? You want to ride this thing just for that? Who hit the insanity button on your brain?" Talo asked, half kidding.

"Hey!" Bliss exclaimed, partly serious. "That's my brother!" Bliss maintained a humorous stance, although she was very protective of Kam and would sometimes cringe when it seemed like Talo and Orna's insults seemingly went too far. She couldn't help but come to his defense, something programmed within her since childhood. "Building something that's completely useless on Axpherial doesn't exactly ring logic," Talo said. "Not everything requires logic. Some things just require thrill. You know, just for fun," Orna said. "Yeah cause Prehistoric transportation is just full of thrill," Talo said, rolling her eyes. "Don't worry, it has a flight feature too," Kam replied. Talo felt a sense of ease wash over her as she breathed a sigh of relief. "It's amazing brother," Bliss said as she analyzed it.

"Thank you! The radiator and swingarm needs a little work, but by the time I need it, it'll be ready for at least a test run. I'll do that in a minute." Bliss beamed excitedly then asked, "Ohh can I volunteer as the testee?" Kam chuckled, then replied, "Well, I don't quite qualify testee as a word, but yes, of course." Orna's face contorted with concern. "What about helmets?" He asked. "Don't worry, our skulls will break the fall," Bliss quipped with a smile, eliciting a chorus of chuckles. Orna shrank back, feeling as if they were laughing at him.

"Don't be embarrassed man, no question is a bad one," Kam reassured. "Says you," Talo said into another laugh. Bliss gave Talo a light "Stop it" tap on the arm, her mouth twitching as she tried to stop herself from bursting into laughter. Orna straightened, hoping to conceal his lingering embarrassment. He didn't want to show that he was still affected.

"But anyway, we need to tell you guys the plan," Kam said, diverting the attention. Bliss positioned herself beside him, and they both faced Talo and Orna, "All ears," Talo said. Bliss quickly went over the pandemic, the bombed cities, the train attack, their parents concealing their work in the basement, and the council emergency voting. "So in other words, time is of the essence," Talo said. "Precisely. But luckily, we have that on our side for now," Kam said before continuing, "And as for the motorcycle, flying around in plain sight in a dimension where flying contraptions like this are foreign is asking for death. That's why I built it. And motorcycles are just solid. I've been fascinated since I first saw them on Earth as a kid."

Talo nodded, glad to have a clearer explanation from him. "As soon as we get to the basement and get what we need, we'll need the strength in numbers, so we will call you guys up in about eight days. That's how long it'll take to fully clone the government delfona. Until then, you guys can look around to see which weapon suits you most," Kam said. Talo and Orna were beyond intrigued. "Weapon?" Orna asked, dumbfounded. "Yep. Learn how to be deadly soon, man. You very well might have to be," Kam said. Talo and Orna both felt a mixture of excitement and trepidation. "Wait. So if we fail, Earth is obliterated?" Orna asked. "And potentially here, too. But I don't fully understand how yet, but they mentioned something about putting Earth and here in danger," Bliss said. "I'd like to participate in the later prep of these plans, I have my own inputs," Talo said.

"No," Kam said plainly. Talo appeared perplexed, as though she was having difficulty accepting what he said. "Testing your fire again. Pick your jaw off the floor," Kam grinned. Talo attempted to force a chuckle, trying to indicate that Kam hadn't succeeded in affecting her, though he had. "We don't know all that we are going up against. But whatever it is, I hope this is enough manpower for now," Kam said. "Soooo, what about that test run?" Bliss asked. Kam beamed as he glanced at her. "You wanted a test run of what again?" Kam said with obvious humor in his voice. Bliss let out a chuckle and gave a semi-amused expression. "Give me just a minute," Kam smiled. "What about us?" Orna asked. "What about y'all?" Bliss replied with a grin.

Orna just half smirked while Talo rolled her eyes. "You guys can pick a weapon out of the armory room and have your way. Bliss is already good with guns and is... intermediate with swords." He said. Bliss cut her eyes with her smile still intact. "Intermediate meaning exceptional," She rebutled. "That's a hard oxymoron," Talo said. "Oh, you know what I meant," Bliss said, partly serious. "There's a small training room in the corner. You can utilize the simulations. Try not to die while we test this thing out," Kam said with a hard grin. "Die. Funny." Talo said, unamused.

Kam gave a smirk as they headed to the arsenal. Bliss watched Kam, in awe, as he manipulated the parts of the bike with his mind, waving his hands around the cycle softly as the parts assembled together. When

Kam was done, he levitated the bike and set it down, pleased with the final outcome.

****

Kam rode his motorcycle through the stillness of the night. Arriving at the Earth house, he was clad in all-black attire with a full-face helmet. The cycle's glowing blue lights encircled its wheels, creating a mini lightshow. The cycle's radiance illuminated the barren fields dotted with bristly yellow grasses, swaying softly in the breezy night.

"BB to K-man, what's the status?" Bliss's voice crackled through what sounded like a walkie-talkie, coming from Kam's delfona, which glowed a light blue.

"K-man to BB, I'm at home base, about to infiltrate the premises," Kam replied, a hint of humor in his voice.

He turned off the engine and dismounted from the cycle, standing before the ancient-looking home. "Fancy words there, K-man. When did you expand your vocabulary?" Bliss retorted playfully.

"Do you really think I'm incapable of above-average literacy?" Kam teased back. "Yep," Bliss jestured.

"Aren't you the sweetest?" Kam replied with a grin.

Kam began pacing toward the house, not noticing anything unusual, but his hands buzzed with a sense that something was amiss. He stopped, cautiously surveying his surroundings.

"Something feels... I'm getting a tingle," he remarked.

"Tingle? You gotta pee or something?" Bliss joked.

Kam laughed. "I should've used a better word."

"You think?" Bliss replied with a playful tone as Kam smirked. He inched toward the home, feeling his stomach drop. His hands continued buzzing as he stepped onto the creaky balcony. He noticed the wooden board door creaked open, just as it did when he had snuck out the night of the train derailment. His eyes widened in surprise, realizing his parents were already home in Axpherial, and no one else should know their location.

"Status?" Bliss asked, growing concerned.

Kam stared, astonishment etched onto his face as he tried to comprehend how the door had been opened. "I might have company," he said with shaky breaths.

"What?" Bliss exclaimed, her worry evident.

"Shhhhhhh!" Kam urged her to silence. He ventured into the house, and all appeared as it had been left, including the faint blue light illuminated from the Chef Variety monitor in the kitchen. He took out his delfona and shone a bright light across the living room, then moved on to the back of the couches, the kitchen, underneath the tables, down the corridor, and finally into his bedroom. He looked around carefully, moving as gently as possible.

He visited every other room in the house, examining them thoroughly, yet he found no one. Returning to his room, he stuck his hand behind the headboard, let out a grunt as he stretched his arm, and withdrew a lengthy, black sword tucked inside a glossy black scabbard with a shoulder strap. As soon as he pulled it out, the tip of the sword lit up in a bright, crimson red.

He brandished the sword as he turned around, strapping the scabbard to his chest. His gaze swept the hallway, illuminated by the red glow. His steps were measured as he made his way through the living room and towards the kitchen. Taking a deep breath, he returned the sword back into the scabbard, and the red glow vanished instantly.

He slowly creaked open the door by the fireplace and glanced down into the darkness of the basement. He couldn't make out the bottom of the stairs, but it seemed like a deep, bottomless abyss.

"K-Man, you okay?" Bliss's voice came through again, making Kam jump slightly.

"Main areas clear, now heading for the main course," Kam whispered, trying to maintain his humor. He slowly descended the steps, illuminating the stairwell with his delfona light to guide him.

"I love main courses. Not mom's main courses, but this one should be good. Don't tell her I said that," Bliss quipped, and Kam stifled a chuckle.

"Keep it down, not in the clear yet," Kam cautioned, still whispering.

"Sorry, bro," Bliss replied, lowering her tone significantly.

When he arrived at the bottom, the bright laboratory lights switched on automatically, causing Kam to squint his eyes in surprise at the sudden brightness. As his vision adjusted, he found himself before a long black counter that occupied half of the wall. There was a black microscope with a purple marking at the base of its eyepiece and a square glass tablet standing upright nearby. Beside the microscope was a black device similar to a small touchscreen phone.

Above them, black doorless cabinets loomed. Near the counter was a mini sitting area with a huge whiteboard on the wall, containing various math equations and numerous crossed-out formulas. Kam quickly pointed his delfona at everything, taking pictures. The delfona emitted a small white light every time a photo was taken. He sent the photos to his computer, while Bliss watched in awe as they captured everything their parents had tried to conceal.

"My curiosity has never been so satisfied," Bliss commented.

Kam smiled and said, "After so long, we finally get to..." He froze in his tracks as he observed deep gouges on a black knob-less filing cabinet, situated next to the sitting area. The scratches seemed to be quite deep, as if someone had attempted to open the cabinet with great force but to no avail. His eyes widened as he snapped more pictures.

"Someone got so desperate they became careless." Bliss remarked.

Kam then realized the significance as he carefully examined the cabinet. "Wait. This is pure Polakiem. That mineral is nearly indestructible," Kam marveled at the deep dents. Polakiem was a crystal discovered in multiple caves within the Axpherian mountains, known for its near-indestructible properties.

"It takes not just desperation, but hours of effort to even leave a crack. Even with the best tools," Kam said, his voice shaking.

"And they left a lot of cracks. They did a whole arts and crafts project on it," Bliss added.

"That's impressively scary," Kam replied.

He then noticed a black file folder on the counter that he hadn't seen before. He raised an eyebrow and slowly crept over.

"What's going on now?" Bliss asked.

"Folder," Kam replied with brevity.

"What does it say?" Bliss inquired.

"Don't know yet," Kam said as he gingerly opened the folder. It contained various documents printed in black ink, with a few highlighted in a more urgent-looking red. Kam's gaze moved to the red-inked letters, reading the following:

"The investigation into the Viola virus yielded a baffling conclusion; laboratory results identified the virus as Hephoma 818 aka the Viola poison, a fatal toxin. The toxin's behavior mimics that of viruses found on Earth. It was created during a rebellion, approximately 150 Loza's ago, in the somber realm on the planet of Zemo. This toxin was used by the government to wipe out its citizens, however, this caused an inability to reproduce, thus spelling doom for the Herloid civilization that once inhabited the planet. Although the toxin was believed to have been eliminated after the rebellion, it somehow managed to find its way to Earth, leading to a deadly pandemic. Fortunately, the Aphlama prototype is close to completion, and when the antidote is released into the atmosphere in approximately six weeks, it should eradicate the toxin."

Kam finally realized everything. The virus was a poison. The pandemic was man-made. His parents were trying to develop and cure it, and someone knew exactly what they were doing.

"Bro? Any word?" Bliss asked anxiously.

Kam was at a loss for words and unable to respond. He stared at the file, still trembling, when something on the floor caught his eye. It was a broad silver bracelet with an unknown language imprinted in small letters surrounding it.

He tentatively stretched out his arm and retrieved the object. It was a zemano, the shape-shifting device utilized by the Herloids - and with that realization, a chill of fear ran through him, making him shudder at the thought of the danger they were in.

"BB to K-man. Say something. A breath even. You're scaring me," Bliss said with trembling in her voice.

Kam grasped the polished silver bracelet, twisting it in his hands and examining it. "A zemano. Found it next to the file cabinet," He said, his voice quivering.

Bliss was beyond dismayed. "What? Are you... What?"

"This is bad, Bliss. Really bad."

| 15 |

Maxine

"The doctor said I'm almost ready to go home," Georgette said. Maxine gazed at her, smiling to keep her composure. She'd been with her for over an hour, and Ava and Kincade had been there until shortly before midnight. They had both grown weary and gone home, but Maxine was too filled with apprehension to leave her mom's side. Maxine nodded as she continued gripping her hand. "Did you like the poem? It was an oldie, I still have severe writers block." Georgette peered her eyes with worry. "You didn't have a lot of blocks until..." She decided not to finish, knowing it could trigger Maxine.

Georgette's hands were long and smooth, radiating a youthful golden hue. Maxine's hands were just as velvety, although slightly darker. "The fact you finally wrote something says a lot. I think that's the first sign that you're healing," Georgette said. Maxine nodded, concealing her skepticism. "I um..." Maxine's eyes dotted the room like she was about to reveal a deep secret. "I finally got in my birthday car," She said as if she didn't take pride in it. Maxine often questioned her capabilities, a consequence of her pursuit of excellence. She felt her self-esteem wavering. Georgette smirked and exclaimed, "I'm so proud of you!" Maxine's lips curved up in a smile as she turned her head to brush away a tear. "Not again," she thought to herself. "Tears are like rain. Without rain, everything would be in flames," Georgette assured.

Maxine gave a nod to Georgette as a tear rolled down her cheek. Georgette moved closer, gently wiping it away. "You and Kincade are the biggest gifts I have. I love you. Me and Tobias love you. I know he's not here but I'm okay, baby." Maxine nodded quietly as she suppressed her grief. She couldn't help but not believe that she was truly okay with Tobias not by her side. "Thank you," she said in a trembling voice, holding back tears. "Don't ever take your vulnerability as weakness again. It's the ones with the most pride who wear the biggest mask," Maxine nodded as she took heed to her words. "Thank you, mom. I'm getting tired. I have to get some rest," Maxine said as she began to straighten up. "Sleep well, sweetie. Tell Tobias I said hey," Georgette paused and said, " And go easy on him." Maxine rose to her feet, readying herself to depart. Maxine remarked as she made her way towards the exit, "I'll try to keep my words and hands to myself."

"Remember what I said when you were little?" Georgette asked. Maxine grinned. "Leave kisses, not bruises," Maxine said with her grin intact. Maxine desired for Tobias to feel the emotions that seethed inside her. Her mother's meekness meant nothing to her, yet she still cherished her. This was something that had long irritated Maxine- her mother's docility and her willingness to forgive and forget. Maxine returned and kissed Georgette on the forehead, gifting her one last enigmatic smile before departing.

As she walked through the hospital's front doors, she noticed a sleek motorcycle with glimmering blue wheels and a man astride it, dressed in dark clothing with a full face helmet. She smiled and said, "Kincade! I thought LED's were criminally trendy and unappealing. What made you change......" Kam took his helmet off before she could finish. Her jaw dropped in astonishment and her gaze went blank. She felt like the air had been sucked from her lungs. Meanwhile, Kam sported a grin as if he was unaware of her surprise.

Maxine's throat constricted as she struggled to find words. "How the hell did you find me?" she uttered with a low voice. "We dropped you off here, remember? I've been out here the last fifteen minutes. I had a feeling I'd find you here," Kam said, beaming. Maxine was still uneasy. "Okay dude, either you're psychic or a damn good stalker," She said, sounding both miffed and anxious. Kam frowned, now feeling remorseful for causing her distress. "I'm sorry, but... There is something... well some things I got to tell you," He said urgently. "Things?" "You saw me fly that night. I'm pretty sure everyone else in your world saw me, too. But you actually *saw* me. Get it?" Maxine's expression initially seemed perplexed, yet quickly shifted to comprehension.

She was now certain that what she had seen was real. "From the looks of it, it looks like it was written off as something called a conspiracy theory. Your world doesn't seem impressed by anything deemed supernatural here," Kam said. "Movies, TV, Netflix, it definitely desensitized our imaginations for sure. An alien can casually beam us into a warship and we'd still be looking for a camera crew," Maxine said, now seemingly relaxed. "Interesting," Kam said, tapping his chin. Maxine's eyes lit up as she exclaimed, "Wait? Did you just say *our* world?" Kam smiled nervously. "I'll explain that later," He said. "I'm no less confused from when we first met," Maxine said into a frustrating laugh. Kam waited a beat then asked, "You believe what you saw don't you?" "At first no. Well I guess I just didn't want to believe it," Maxine admitted.

"Well to relieve any other doubts, I want to take you somewhere," Kam said. Maxine grinned and asked, "Trying to kidnap me for a date?" Kam returned a grin and said, "No, but I feel obligated to share some things with you." "Oh? So you're finally the one spilling the tea?" Maxine quipped as she and Kam shared a chuckle. "Whatever that means, I guess I'm spilling away!" Maxine giggled at his awkward charm. In fact, she was beginning to find it alluring. "You mind ensuring my protection on the way and taking me home safe and sound?" Maxine asked.

Kam half grinned as he stepped off the bike and opened the seat, offering her a helmet. "I wouldn't do anything less." His smile broadened as she returned a grin and accepted it. It was polished and jet black, just like his. "Dark and fancy," She beamed. "Glad you like it." He said as he got back on the cycle. He donned his helmet and started the engine. She followed suit and hopped on the back as he set off to the Earth House.

****

Kam and Maxine kicked up a dusty trail on their way to the Earth House, a cloud of dust swirling in their wake. After dismounting, they stowed their helmets in the seat compartment. Maxine surveyed the peculiar building and quirked an eyebrow. "Is this really your humble abode?" she asked, puzzled.

"Yeah, but not quite home, though," Kam replied with a proud grin. Maxine raised an amused eyebrow. "Dude, you're a walking, talking question mark," she remarked. Kam blinked in confusion. "What?"

"A cute walking, talking question mark. But a question mark nevertheless," Maxine clarified with a smile. "Well, like I said, I hope I become less of a... question mark in due time," Kam replied, grinning shyly.

Maxine smiled, feeling a mixture of confusion, charm, and nervousness. She was strangely comfortable around him, although she couldn't explain why she had such strong feelings for someone she barely knew. Kam led her to the door, and her confusion persisted. She glanced around as if expecting to be observed. When a wolf's howl echoed, she jumped, the wooden porch creaking beneath them. "Was this house built in the 1850s or something? It's giving serious creep vibes," Maxine commented.

Kam turned to face her, grinning. "It's supposed to look dead on the outside. It un-arouses suspicion," he explained. Maxine scrunched her nose in response. "Suspicion of?" Kam continued to grin as he touched the wooden door, which glowed red before opening. Maxine's eyes widened in amazement. "Well, you sure showed me," she quipped as Kam led her inside.

The darkness within the house felt unusually heavy. Kam sensed something wrong and stopped in his tracks. The living room lay in ruins, the blue glow extinguished. Kam's face contorted as he grabbed his delfona flashlight. The couches lay torn apart, glass tables shattered, and the Chef variety screen in the kitchen split in half. Kam was left speechless by the destruction.

"What happened?" Maxine asked, her voice filled with concern. Kam took quick, shallow breaths as adrenaline coursed through him. His heart pounded like a drum in his chest. "I don't know," he admitted, aware of who might be responsible. He hurried to his room, Maxine following closely. He frantically searched but couldn't find his sword. "Who made this mess?" Maxine inquired.

"Someone came back again. Someone watched me leave," Kam replied urgently. Maxine looked puzzled. "Who watched you?" she asked. "Someone is targeting us, someone who wants me to know they're watching. Whoever they are, they damaged these things but knew what they were really after is in the basement. They wanted me to know that it... or they can see everything."

Kam scrutinized the room and located his sword in the closet. He retrieved it, its red glow filling the room. "It glows, like something from Star Wars," Maxine commented. Kam, puzzled, asked, "Star Wars?" Maxine rolled her eyes. "I keep forgetting you're a Martian," she said, shaking her head. "The glow keeps the sword sharp," he explained as he guided her out of the room and into the basement.

In the basement, Kam continued to hold the sword tightly as he ventured forward, scanning the area carefully. When he switched on the lights, everything appeared as he'd left it, adding to his confusion. Despite this, he tucked his sword back into its scabbard and wrapped the strap around his chest. Maxine observed the room, her eyes settling on the equations on the whiteboard. "Math. Me and math have a tumultuous relationship. Imani used to save the day every t...." Maxine stopped herself, huffing and shifting her gaze toward the wall, fighting the urge to cry.

Kam noticed and sympathized. "We grieve the same," he pointed out. Maxine attempted to conceal her emotions, but her expression gave her away. "I'm sorry?" she said, trying to sound composed. "I said we grieve the same. I turn my head too when I get emotional," Kam shared.

Maxine, relieved by the connection, gave a small smile and admitted, "I try not to cry so much." Kam nodded in understanding. "Yeah, sometimes it feels like there's a lake filled with emotions inside of me that may drown a city one day." "Same," Maxine said, stuffing down her tears.

Maxine's gaze landed on the test kit they used upon entering the city. "What's that doing here?" she asked, surprised. Kam, too, was puzzled and hadn't noticed it before. He picked up the device, labeled: ANOMALY TEST KIT VERSION 17.5, in bold red letters on a black background. Kam raised an eyebrow. "Anomaly test kit," he murmured.

"Yeah, they used it on us when we enter and exit an immunity city," Maxine explained. Kam's eyes widened as he held the device to Maxine's forehead. "What the actual hell?" she exclaimed, jerking back. "I just want to see how this thing works," Kam reassured her, laughing a little. Maxine, albeit skeptical, agreed, "Fine, but no surprises."

The device beeped twice, and the screen displayed Maxine's DNA in vivid hues, then showed the words, "No anomaly detected." Kam scanned himself with the same result. "Dude, is everything good?" Maxine asked. Kam looked up, his expression tense. "I'm not sure," he replied.

Maxine raised an eyebrow. "What do you mean?" she inquired. Kam anxiously scanned the room, his attention drawn to the file. He seemed lost in thought. "Hey, did you forget that you had something important to tell me?" Bliss reminded him.

Kam, snapped back to the present, said, "It's about the virus." Maxine groaned, rolling her eyes. "Oh, brother." Kam, feeling remorseful for causing her distress, continued, "No, it's not a virus. It's..."

"It's?" Maxine pressed impatiently. Kam finally confessed, "It's a toxin." Maxine contorted her face in disbelief. "Come again?" she asked, astounded. "This so-called virus was made in a lab. It was created by a thought-to-be extinct species from the somber realm. But obviously, a few had to have survived because I found this," he explained, showing her the zemano. Maxine's eyes widened at the sight. "I guess they put necessity over fashion because that thing is hideous," Bliss commented, lightening the mood.

Kam handed the bracelet to Maxine, and she examined it with curiosity. "All of this is new to me. And realms? You sound like my brother when he rants about his sci-fi-packed conspiracy theories. He'd have a blunt and a field day hearing this."

Kam chuckled, and Maxine joined in. "But, dude, I have like a billion questions, and I feel like I only scratched the surface," Maxine said. Kam looked intrigued yet slightly puzzled. "Me?" Kam asked. Maxine clarified, "You said I'd be less confused. But I think you also doubt how complex my mind actually is. I'm more open-minded than the average skeptic. Pinky swear," she said with a reassuring smile.

Kam beamed. "What do you want to know?" Maxine smiled and replied, "Tell me as much as you think I can handle." Kam paused, then took a deep breath, feeling certain that this was the right moment. There was something about her that instilled trust in him. The words flowed as he began to share more about his family, his real name, and his home planet. He also explained the items he had found in the basement. "Dude, saying that's a lot is an understatement," Maxine remarked, bewildered.

Although overwhelmed by the new information, Maxine felt reassured that she had answers, however bizarre they might seem. "Was that enough tea for you?" Kam asked with a flirtatious grin. She chuckled and replied, "Kam fits you better. You don't quite look like a Joey."

Kam laughed and said, "I second the distaste for that name." The tension between them shifted from awkward to subtly romantic. They gazed at each other, feeling the attraction grow.

As they talked, Kam suddenly halted, realizing something crucial. "Those people at the gate, you said they scanned you, right?" he asked. Maxine looked confused and then narrowed her gaze. "Yeah, so?" she said casually. Kam's expression became tense. "That device doesn't just tell you if you're infected," he revealed, panic edging into his voice.

Maxine stopped in her tracks, her face displaying growing concern. "What?" she asked. Kam concluded, "It also tells you about where you're from, your name, and... realm of origin." Maxine's expression shifted to one of unease. "I'm a bit spooked," she admitted. Kam's words hung in the air as the implications settled in. "You're not from Earth, Maxine."

| 16 |

Maxine

Maxine contemplated her thoughts about Kincade, Tobias, her mother, Imani, and Ava. She remembered how she had been told from a young age that she resembled Tobias. This created feelings of betrayal and sorrow within her. Taking a deep breath, she hesitantly asked, "What are you talking about?"

"The people at the gate," he began, "may not have been ordinary soldiers. They knew exactly who you and everyone else are. They were not only looking for those who were infected, but also those who were not from the planet."

Maxine's gaze lowered to the ground as she processed his words. "I think you're being watched. And I think you're in danger." The gravity of his words hit Maxine.

"Watched? What?"

Kam gazed downward, feeling a twinge of remorse as he watched sorrow wash over her face. He observed her deep dimples, the dark circles around her eyes, and her hazel-brown eyes shining in the brilliant basement illumination. His attraction to her seemed to grow more intense. He shook his head to clear his thoughts.

"Herloids," He said it like the words were daggers on his tongue.

"Her what?" She questioned, her voice trembling as if she was on the verge of crying.

"They created a lot of intriguing technology. Some dangerous and destructive technology. It doesn't surprise me that they knew how to bomb an entire city. And be so calculated with their execution," Kam said.

Maxine was disoriented, but slowly it dawned on her what he was saying. Memories of her family's escape from the doomed city flooded her mind, and she recalled the barrage of explosives that rendered one section of the city to rubble after another. She could still feel the smoke burning her lungs as she had awoken that fateful night, just barely making it out of her hotel alive.

Kam continued to explain, "As advanced as they were, they had their share of wars and societal collapses. And their laws made the harshest dictatorships on your planet look euphoric."

Maxine struggled to keep her emotions in check, unable to accept the news she was hearing. She vehemently shook her head in disbelief. "I have a hard time believing all of this is any less than a bad dream," She said as she tried to suppress her tears.

Kam sauntered up to her and gently placed his hand on her left shoulder. Maxine felt a wave of warmth wash over her at his touch. Though her eyes kept searching the white marble floor, her heart was filled with a flurry of emotions.

Kam tried to assure her by saying, "I know this is a lot to take in, but if you stick with me, I promise we'll figure out a way to save everyone," Kam felt a pang of guilt as his attraction for Maxine seemed so wrong in the midst of so much fear. His mind filled with visions of the Ferris wheel, and the terror in Zina's face. He stepped back, taking a deep breath.

Maxine smiled tenderly, her eyes conveying her appreciation for Kam's concern. "Thank you," she murmured.

"You weren't lying when you said we were carrying a lake," Maxine said as she forced a wry grin and chuckled wistfully.

Maxine's face contorted, and she dropped to her knees, tears streaming down her face. Kam bent down and embraced her as she sobbed, the sound reverberating throughout the basement.

He tenderly held her head close, letting her unleash her emotions. Her cries echoed through the air for several minutes, until her sobs finally softened, and her breathing steadied. Kam's arm was drenched, yet he didn't care; all that mattered was her.

"My family... they..." She pushed out the words through her sorrow, "I can't believe they aren't my family." She continued, "And mom, just seeing the scars on her body. I drag myself to the hospital to see her every night..." Her words were nearly inaudible through her tears. "And Dad he...he's a coward!" She said angrily through her raspy voice.

She continued sitting up as Kam retrieved a few paper towels from the electric dispenser by the sink. He passed her a handful as she delicately dabbed her face and blew her nose. "I'm a wreck, dude," she said, her voice still heavy with emotion.

Kam looked curious, but he forced his eagerness to know more down. He gently lifted her up from the ground and realized how much taller he was - standing at a towering six feet. She barely reached his shoulder when they embraced. He held her just a little too tightly, but she appreciated his embrace even if it was a bit clumsy. In this moment, she could care less.

"Sorry. I didn't expect to projectile vomit my grief all over your basement floor," She said with a nervous laugh.

Kam smiled as he released her and planted his hands on her shoulders. "Don't worry, I did the same on the top of my roof a week ago," He smiled reassuringly.

"We do grieve the same after all," She said with a stiff smile.

"Yeah, we do," He said. Kam and Maxine paused, their eyes locked in a gaze. Kam felt a strong desire to kiss her, imagining her lips pressed against his. He could tell Maxine was feeling the same way, yet her feelings ran deeper. There was a special romantic attraction between the two of them, but it wasn't just romance Maxine craved.

Instead of a kiss, Kam tenderly enveloped her in his arms. He was still healing from the wounds of his first love that he lost a year prior, and wasn't sure if he was ready to open up his heart again. Taking her hand, he guided her up the stairs and to the door. Despite the mess, he paid no mind to it, focusing only on her.

Kam stopped in his tracks as he thought about the house. He paused, then uttered, "Wait, I....need to do something." Releasing his grasp on Maxine's hand, he stepped away from the entrance. He scoured the walls and spotted the security system, a square, blue-glowing monitor on the wall beside his parents' room. He tapped the screen a few times and activated the home's security, this time disabling fingerprint entry and switching to keycards.

The keycards were small and square, about half the size of a credit card. He made sure to secure one from the basement. The cards were impossible to duplicate. As he and Maxine exited the house, the security system began counting down from sixty. If anyone were to break in or occupy the house, the house would detect them and release a lethal gas that would kill them in mere seconds.

"Had to rearm the house," Kam said, striding alongside Maxine towards the cycle. He still wore his sword across his back, ready to act in an instant if necessary.

Maxine gave a slight smirk, though it was obvious she was still greatly disturbed by the events. "You're gonna make it?" He asked.

"You're taking me home, remember?" Maxine said sarcastically. "I don't mean that, I meant you. Are you gonna be alright?"

Maxine shook her head. "Not now, but I will be," She admitted, smiling more convincingly. Kam gave a concerned glance as he passed her the helmet. "Please stop staring at me like I'm glass. Pinky swear, I'll be fine," she said, her lips curling into a smile.

Kam felt his worries lifting as he smiled back and fastened his helmet. He revved up the engine, and they sped away into the darkness, the events of the evening still lingering in their minds.

****

Kam and Maxine halted at the entrance of Maxine's driveway. Kam silenced the motorcycle, and both of them dismounted. He placed his helmet in the seat as Maxine handed him hers. A heavy mask of disappointment clouded her face, though she soon swapped it for a feeble grin. "Does it look like I wasn't crying my life away yet?" She said as she attempted to smile more convincingly.

Kam felt unsure of her wellbeing but found solace in her inner strength. He beamed and said, "I don't see anything other than strength." Maxine's painted smile became more genuine. "Thanks." Maxine said as she gazed at the motorcycle, hesitant to go into the house. She was worried that her true emotions would be written all over her face for everyone else to see. "Let's just keep this whole meltdown thing between us friends, okay?" She said as she grinned.

Kam sauntered up to Maxine, his smirk radiating a mysterious charm. She could feel her stomach quivering with anticipation as he drew near, and when he stood inches away, Maxine felt her heart skip a beat as his indigo eyes ensnared her in their powerful gaze. Despite these feelings, she was able to keep them well hidden. "Oh? We're friends now?" He asked. "I don't plan on retracting that title anytime soon, so wear it proudly, weirdo."

Kam raised an eyebrow and took a couple of steps back. "Weirdo?" He said, half serious. Maxine was amused. She chuckled at Kam not catching on to her sarcasm. "Let me run some game on you real quick," She narrowed her eyes and continued, "If I insult you, it's a good thing. In fact, insults are my love language." Kam squinted, then broke into a chuckle. "Oh no, I get it! My dialogue around my friends is just as lethal as yours."

Maxine laughed, relieved he caught on. "Have to say, you scared me for a second, but I'm officially impressed," She said. She felt a sense of relief wash over her. Suddenly, it was as though the events of the past few hours had been nothing but a distant dream. "And by the way, I'll wear this little friendship title like a snug bulletproof vest." Maxine laughed again, finding his awkwardness cute. "I'm going to try to sleep off this unusually interesting night. You rest easy, too," Maxine smiled. "Goodnight," he said with a smile, as she made her way to her door. Maxine watched as he donned his helmet and rode off into the night.

She lingered for a moment, then reluctantly made her way through the front door.

She stepped into her room, flicking on the light switch connected to the ceiling fan. Her space was quite large, her walls adorned with posters of R&B musicians, LED lights around the corners, astronomy images including a poster of the earth from the moon, and a dream catcher given to her by Ava above her queen-sized bed. She perched on the bed, removed her tennis shoes, and glanced at the full-length mirror in front of her. She was wearing light blue jeans and an over-sized black hoodie.

She sat there, observing someone whose mask was disintegrating. She wasn't sure if she was prepared for that moment to arrive. Recollections of her mother's words about people wearing masks crossed her mind, and she couldn't help but ponder if she was included. Then something hard was detected beneath her pillow, prompting her to draw out a bottle of brown liquor in a sizeable glass container. She slowly swirled the bottle in her hands before taking a gentle sip. Despite this, she wasn't in the mood to consume any of it, and hence shoved the bottle back beneath her pillow.

She startled at a sudden knock on her door. "It's open," She said, expecting it to be Kincade or Ava, as Tobias was likely at work. The door opened gently. Tobias. Maxine struggled to smother her annoyance as she took in his presence. Her fury towards him was resurfacing, and she really wasn't prepared to face him. "Is this a bad time?" He inquired as he partly entered her room. He bore dark circles beneath his eyes, like he hadn't slept in days. Maxine's fingers began trembling, trying to stuff down the hurricane of emotions she had inside of her.

"You look drained, baby. But I bet it's nothing. I know you're strong enough, whatever it is," Tobias smiled. She seethed with rage, her body radiating heat. She also felt the uncontrollable need to spare his feelings dissipate. He witnessed the shadow of tears under her eyes and contorted. "Baby girl, you been crying?" Maxine shook her head as she felt her anger consume her. "Don't let a bit of rain stop your shine!" He quipped, reaching for her cheek. She drew back quickly, and gave him a grave look of disgust. He was taken aback, looking so flustered he could cry. Maxine let out a short, furious chuckle and asked, "Dad, am I adopted?"

Tobias's jaw slightly dropped. He was so flabbergasted that he wondered if he was dreaming. "What?" He asked, sounding lost. "I need to reiterate, so you can catch it again. Now, am I adopted? Yes or no?" She hissed. Tobias stiffened as tears welled up in his eyes. "No. Of course not," He answered like it was the only answer he knew. A single tear trickled down Maxine's cheek as she absent-mindedly wiped it away and turned her head.

She spun around in a flash, her eyes aching with the hurt he had inflicted. She wanted him to witness the anguish he had caused. She wanted her emotions to break him. "You can't even so much as to look me in the face and tell the truth. Always running away," She said as her voice cracked. "Running?" "Like Kincade said, always running from diversity. Never taking the time to listen to me. Or any of us." She stood, disregarding the grief that was plainly written in his expression, despite her empathy for him still crying out. "Always waving the white flag and making me think it was okay to run away, too."

The sorrow radiating from Tobias's expression could even make a hardened sociopath feel sympathy for him. "Mom in the hospital keeps asking for you. Her eyes keep wandering behind me to see if you finally....." Maxine's tone rose as she struggled to finish, "Finally had the strength to be her husband and my father again." Maxine's face twisted in agony as she let out her emotions in tears. Tobias too began to weep, filled with deep remorse and regret.

"I make excuses like you'll come around but she isn't fooled. I mean, not anymore at least." Tobias's cries became subtle as silent tears came down his cheeks, knowing she was right. "Baby, I'm so..." "Shut up!" She screamed. Tobias gazed downward, speechless as he wiped away his endless tears. "You taught me and Kincade strength, but your actions proved how much of a coward, and walking contradiction you are! And as bad as I want to hate you, my heart won't let me. And I'm done making excuses for you. You need to man up for once, and take accountability for the pain you cause me! Look what you've done to me! Look what you've done to all of us!"

Tobias, consumed by his guilt, embraced her tightly as she sobbed. "Let me go! Get off me!" She yelled as he cradled her. She was too feeble to shove him off, so she shifted around in his embrace, wishing he'd release her. Promptly, he obliged, taking a step back and still sobbing. Tobias stood by the dresser near the entrance, furtively wiping his eyes.

"Baby girl, I'm so sorry," Tobias said through sobs. Maxine stood with her arms crossed, feeling a pang of guilt but not regretting her words.

Her sobs began to cease, a sign that her emotions were finally released. "My promises were never kept, and I'm so sorry for that. I'm so sorry for hurting you," He said, his voice low and raspy. He sniffled, attempting to compose himself. "But I know one thing I'm not lying about," He said. Maxine gazed up, her anger bubbling to the surface once more.

"You are not adopted," He said, sounding sure of his statement. "Stop lying," Maxine hissed.

"I swear on my life, baby. I'm not lying."

"Stop! Stop lying to me!" Maxine screamed.

"I'd never lie to you about that, baby. I swear," His voice was loud but pleading.

"Bullshit!" Maxine exclaimed as she wiped another tear.

"From the moment I cut the cord and held you in my arms, I knew I created something beautiful. I swear I fought with my life to protect you, your mother, your brother, and your sister. You all gave me a reason to live."

Maxine's jaw gently dropped in disbelief as she realized he was speaking honestly.

"I had cancer. Stage three cancer when I was only a child. I was twelve. I couldn't even pull out my own chair or pick up a remote. I was suicidal after I went into remission, but you guys gave me a reason not to give up. And maybe, yeah, I let my own trauma prevent me from hospital visits, and to be honest, that's still not a valid excuse. But it's like that experience broke me. Now I can't help but just run to find peace when things get hard. And to see Georgette like that, I just can't..." He began sobbing once again.

Maxine had stopped sobbing, yet she was still in a state of confusion. She could not shake the feeling that something felt off. Why was her DNA saying those things? Why did Tobias sound so sincere when he said she wasn't adopted? These questions spun through her mind.

"So baby, I'll work on not running again when things happen," Tobias said. His voice was barely audible, overwhelmed by the aftermath of his emotional breakdown.

"It's not just about knowing better, Dad. It's about doing better," Maxine said, sounding a bit cold.

Tobias placed his hand tenderly on Maxine's shoulder and kissed her on the forehead. His voice was quiet yet sincere as he said, "I love you. I promise I'll do better." His apology was met with silence. She was proud of herself for finally standing up for what she believed in. As he closed the door, Maxine crossed her arms and leaned against the wall. She was overwhelmed by everything that had happened, and she knew she still had a long way to go to get the answers she was looking for.

| 17 |

Kam

"Wait? Herloids?" Talo said. Kam had just shared the events of his mission with them. They were all gathered at their usual spot at the top of the waterfall. They were wearing the same swimsuits they had on during their prior visit. Kam was sitting with his knees drawn up to his chest, while Orna sat beside him with one leg stretched out in front of him. Talo stood above them, the thundering waterfall flowing behind her.

Amidst the lush, green grass, there were daisy-shaped blooms with blue and red petals. They were known as Pokaz, and they only came out during Zay, the Axpherian spring. Axpherians had four seasons, just like Earth, but they lasted almost twice as long. Naka, Lula, and Maz were the names of their respective winter, summer, and autumn. Elmana's winters were particularly brutal; temperatures could drop below 30 degrees Fahrenheit. Summers were humid but bearable. Spring and fall offered more pleasant temperatures - not too hot and not too cold - making them the best of the four.

Kam nodded. "I thought their species was as dead as a boulder," Orna said. "I agree. They had a civil war that turned their cities into literal dust towns. I bet you could hear an atom sneeze on their planet now," Talo said as Kam and Orna laughed at this. "Yeah, pretty much a skeleton floating in space," Orna added. Kam chuckled, but suddenly a question brewed in his mind. He thought, "Why kill the people of Earth? There has to be a serious motive behind it." The Herloids were quite brilliant and always planned their assaults with careful precision. This was a fact that made Kam question their motives even more. "But why Earth?" Kam asked, perplexed. "Yeah. Why use the very poison that killed off your old civilization? I definitely second your suspicion," Talo said. "And Herloids were detailed. They were scary, calculated, and vicious." Orna added.

Kam gazed downward, deep in thought. It didn't seem like a typical assault - there must've been something more at play. "I get the feeling that the agenda is a lot bigger," Kam said, as his worried expression scanned the grass. Talo and Orna exchanged a shocked glance. Their eyebrows shot up in surprise. "Bigger?" Orna asked. Kam nodded, not quite sure about what exactly the agenda could be. "I'm sensing a promising theory coming on," Talo beamed.

He contemplated something. The Herloid race fell apart due to their incapability to comply with such a strict dictatorship. Most of their technology was eradicated. The planet was ravaged beyond recognition. However, there must have been survivors for him to locate the shape-shifting device. Then it hit him. "Maybe….." He swallowed hard before finishing. "Maybe the poison isn't just poison," Kam said. He didn't know exactly what, but he just knew it had to be something more sinister.

Talo peered downward, as if the answer were on the tip of her tongue. "Hold on," she said, and Kam and Orna shifted their focus to her, feeling certain she had an intriguing theory to offer. "I did some research about different dimensional civilizations. I found a lot more out than what the palace ever taught us," Talo said, sounding like she couldn't wait to deliver the news. "Think you're smarter than the training masters at the palace?" Orna said with a sarcastic smirk. "Listen, don't envy my anomalous quest for knowledge, okay?" "Anomalous eh? What qualifies your research as more unique than the average genius?" Orna asked, sounding amused. "Well, if you listen I will gladly explain," Talo said, thrilled to share her research.

"The Herloids didn't quite see eye to eye. Their species were, as you know, tech geniuses. They evolved very quickly. They even became masters of disguise hint, the shape-shifting device. They had a mandatory test that determined their jobs in society. High-scoring individuals were scientists, teachers, doctors, any job that required much more than a sliver of intelligence. Those that scored average had the boring jobs like construction, mining, things like that. Those that scored low, they were um, dumped from society for lack of more vicious words."

Orna and Kam seemed unimpressed. "Okay, can we get to the good part?" Orna asked. "Yeah, most of this info is available at the palace library. I'm waiting for this anomalous part that you made sound so intriguing," Kam said. "I never said I was finished," Talo said nervously. Orna and Kam rose up as Orna said, "Hey Kam, wanna go swim while she figures out how to regurgitate info with fancy four-syllable words and ego-driven dialogue?" "Hey! I'm almost done. Patience and participation. Please." Talo pleaded. "Fine. Proceed," Kam said, as he grinned reassuringly with his hands up in surrender. He and Orna returned to their positions and leaned in, eager to hear the rest of Talo's story.

"Anyway, this process went on for generations. But it's people, and this is where the not-seeing-eye-to-eye part comes in; its people eventually rebelled, and around their world, people gathered and attempted to dismantle the government. Riots, bombings, destroying government buildings. But the government was one step ahead. They released world-shattering bombs, killing everyone. Then they gave birth to another generation and attempted to teach them unquestionable obedience."

Kam and Orna's mouths lightly dropped as Talo continued, "A few generations later, they rebelled again. Then they erased them again by manipulating the weather. Hurricanes as big as entire territories. Thunderstorms that drowned cities. Hail the size of mini hovercrafts. Then the last time, they got through only one or two generations without rebellion. But it was like they couldn't help but, you guessed it, rebel. Then they developed the Hephoma poison, and they took their people out again. But the fourth time, something was well... different.

Instead of waiting generations for them to multiply, the same number of Herloids killed in the third rebellion were mysteriously reanimated."

Kam and Orna stared at Talo in awe, impressed. Talo beamed, delighted that they had taken in the new information and smirked as she finished, "But they seemed much more obedient. And their memories were wiped. But after a couple more generations... you know how this cycle goes. So they ended up destroying them for good this time. But many government officials and their king were also killed in the process, and the planet was already near inhabitable with all the man-made, or in this case, Herloid-made exterminations of their people. The last remaining of their kind were seemingly dead, and there was thought to be no one left. The planet then became a dead red globe floating in space."

Talo finished up, wearing a satisfied grin. Kam and Orna were astonished. This was exactly the reaction Talo had anticipated, and she gave them a smug look. Kam soon realized the most important part of Talo's story, and his eyes lit up. "Wait. You mentioned something about them reanimating their civilization," Talo and Orna looked at him, feeling he was onto something. "Maybe the survivors that we thought were dead are using the people of Earth to resurrect their people." Talo and Orna were astounded by the revelation. Their eyes grew wide in shock. "And maybe they aren't just regular survivors. Maybe they're former government officials trying to create a more subservient generation," Orna said as he shuddered at this. They all grasped how treacherous the situation on Earth had become. "But why did your folks say you might have put our planet in danger, too?" Talo asked. Kam didn't think about this, nor did he have an explanation. "I do know that I was targeted. And I do know that Axpherians are immune thanks to the shots." He tapped his chin. "At first I thought they would simply try to bomb us like earth but..."

Kam thought deeply about this. An ominous thought came to him, yet it was too unsettling to voice. His heart raced, and his stomach churned with anxiety. He averted his gaze, not wanting to face the truth. "Maybe they don't just want a new generation of people," Kam swallowed hard as he pondered his theory. "I'm sensing the thickening of a plot," Talo said. "Maybe they also want soldiers." Kam paused, hesitant to continue. Yet, he gathered the strength to finish. "Soldiers to destroy Axpherial," Kam said, feeling the weight of the words as they slipped from his tongue.

| 18 |

Maxine

A lush meadow stretched out endlessly, adorned with gorgeous blooms that swayed gracefully in the gentle breeze. Hills and valleys were carpeted with these colorful flowers. In the heart of this meadow, Kam and Maxine stood side by side, gazing at the breathtaking sunset. Their fingers intertwined, Kam dressed in a crisp white shirt and black pants, while Maxine donned a stunning white dress embellished with delicate pink roses. "You're more beautiful than the sunset itself," Kam whispered.

Maxine turned toward him, her cheeks flushing. "I'm not really one for mushy stuff, but that was cute," she admitted, a warm smile playing on her lips. Kam's grin radiated happiness, causing Maxine to feel a weightless sensation deep within her. Kam's eyes drifted to the field of flowers around them, and he plucked one with care. Gently, he wove it into her thick braids near her left eyebrow, completing her look with a romantic touch. "I might not be the mushiest stuffed animal you've met, but," he stammered, his cheeks reddening, "I can't help what I say when I'm around you."

Maxine's gaze lowered as she smiled bashfully. "I appreciate that you can be yourself and be so unapologetic about it," she replied, her voice soft and filled with warmth. Kam reached up, tenderly lifting her chin. Their eyes locked, expressions bursting with joy. Their smiles widened uncontrollably. Kam leaned in, so close they could share a single breath. His head tilted as he moved closer to her face. She closed her eyes, anticipation tingling through her as she awaited the warmth of his lips.

Suddenly, she jerked awake, sunlight streaming onto her face. Her heart continued to flutter from the remnants of her dream. Maxine glanced at her hands, still feeling the sensation. Checking her phone, she saw it was 2:12 in the afternoon. She rubbed her eyes, rose from her bed, and retrieved the bottle of liquor hidden beneath her pillow. After changing into loose blue jeans and a red plaid shirt, she left her room and made her way to the garage.

****
****

Maxine reclined on the hood of her birthday car, lost in reflection over the past two days since she had bravely shared her inner turmoil with Tobias. Thoughts of Kam danced through her mind, and a growing realization dawned upon her - she was falling for him, deeper than she'd ever anticipated.

She pondered the last encounter with Kam and the anomaly test kit. The notion that she might not be from Earth seemed impossible to reconcile with her already chaotic state of mind. The events of the past few months had added another layer of complexity to the trauma and PTSD she'd been grappling with for the past two years. Now, Kam's words and a series of eerie, supernatural experiences from her past swirled in her thoughts, prompting her to question: "What if he was right? What if those mysterious occurrences weren't mere dreams or coincidences?"

When she was a teen, she dreamt of entering a room filled with shattered bones. In her dream, she witnessed Kincade, one leg missing, desperately searching for it. The sensation of her hands buzzing accompanied her awakening, and strangely enough, just a week later, Kincade broke his leg. These peculiar dreams occurred periodically, but she had always kept them to herself, fearful that no one would believe her. However, they seemed to take on a new significance now.

Lying there, she clutched a half-empty bottle of liquor. Ava had already consumed most of it. Her desire to drown her worries in alcohol dwindled. She yearned for relief that didn't involve drinking or smoking. Those vices only masked her trauma without providing healing.

As the door opened behind her, she kept her eyes fixed on the bottle, feeling somewhat detached from reality, as if existing in another world. "Infiltrating headquarters without me, I see," came Kincade's voice from beside her. She turned to find Kincade, his face glowing, sporting a new, shorter hairstyle that accentuated his precise hairline. A well-groomed beard lent him an air of maturity, making him resemble Tobias more closely than ever, especially with the facial hair, an unusual sight for him, given his preference for a clean shave.

"I see you're entering your scruffy era," Maxine quipped with a smile. Kincade chuckled, replying, "Finally embracing my post-puberty look."

Concerned about her father, Maxine asked, "How's Dad?" She had been avoiding him, much like a frightened stray cat, ever since that confrontation. Part of her felt remorse, while another part wished him to face the consequences of his cowardice.

"Well, he's home more often now," Kincade remarked. "I can't give him too many bravery points for that. He spends most of his time in his room, much like you." Maxine acknowledged the similarity between her behavior and his, both retreating into isolation.

"I've noticed that I hide a lot too," Maxine admitted, a note of defeat in her voice.

Kincade shook his head. "Max, you're not like him," He said.

"I don't know," Maxine replied. "When things get tough, I find myself hiding as well."

Kincade looked at her, recognizing her inner strength but sometimes struggling with her moments of defeat, especially in times like this. "You mean that girl who checks on Mom almost every day? The one who casually walked through torrential rain to get to her? The same girl who sat by my side in the hospital for over a day when I had an asthma attack?" Maxine contemplated these examples but replied, "For others, yes, I'm there. Not so much for myself. I'm also the girl who can't get into a car without feeling like I'm drowning. The one with too much pride to let others see her break down. The one who can't even look Dad in the eye after telling him off."

Maxine glanced down at the bottle in her hands, struggling to contain her tears. She shook her head, determined not to cry again, fearing she wouldn't be able to stop if she started. "But you're also the girl who, despite everything, keeps fighting," Kincade reassured, lightly squeezing her shoulder.

Maxine nodded, wanting desperately to believe his words. Yet, she couldn't help but feel her fragility was akin to Tobias'. "And I do want to be that girl who keeps on fighting," Maxine admitted. As she finished speaking, she pulled a keyless car key from her pocket. Kincade raised an eyebrow, asking, "Are you sure?" He studied her expression, searching for any hint of hesitation.

Maxine nodded, her confidence unwavering. Kincade paused briefly to ensure she was resolute. "Alright, let's conquer these demons," he said, grinning.

****

Maxine sat in the passenger seat, her hands trembling. She tried to keep her shallow breaths quiet. Her heart felt like it was hammering against her chest, with occasional palpitations. A tightness gripped her throat. Her grip on Kincade's hand was so strong that his palm was turning red. He ignored the throbbing in his hand as they sat in the driveway, the engine rumbling.

Kincade peered at her, seeing the tension in her expression. She was gazing downward, her eyes slowly scanning the floor. It was the same look she got when she attempted to bury her anxiety in the back of her thoughts. He always noticed it. "You sure you're ready, sis?" he inquired, his gaze fixed on the fear that clouded her eyes. Maxine merely nodded, her body language illustrating her desire to be done with this as soon as possible. However, she refused to let herself completely unravel.

Ava dashed to the car and scurried into the backseat before Kincade had the opportunity to lock it. He rolled his eyes in exasperation. "So you didn't bother telling me my superhero bestie was demon slaying today?" Ava asked, shutting the door. "No. On purpose I didn't. And this was Diana Prince's idea, not mine," Kincade said, gesturing his head toward Maxine. "It's okay, Kincade. She can stay," Maxine reassured him. Kincade paused, then said, "Fine. As long as she doesn't become a grade-A pain in the ass, I'll let her stay." Ava stuck her tongue out, feeling like she had won.

"Max?" Kincade asked. Maxine uttered a terse, "Yes?" as she fought to contain her panic. "I need my circulation to switch gears," He said, masking his pain with a seemingly composed smirk. Maxine jolted back to reality and let go of his hand. "I said you can hold my hand, not kill it." Kincade grinned. "Sorry, bro." "Don't apologize, let's just focus on the task at hand," Kincade said as he put the car in reverse.

After they drove for a few miles, Maxine employed the breathing technique Kam had taught her. Ava and Kincade did their best to make Maxine comfortable, with Ava lightening the mood by poking fun at Kincade's driving abilities, while Kincade drove cautiously to soothe Maxine. Fifteen minutes in, Kincade and Ava got into an argument over which route to take and what music to listen to. Maxine, however, was mostly lost in thought, replaying the last time she saw Imani alive in her mind—the color draining from her face, the blood smothering her body, the bruises and deep cuts on her smooth honey-colored skin. Despite a series of panic attacks, she somehow managed to make it through the ride. She wanted to eradicate her fear with every ounce of strength she could muster. She was determined not to give up.

****
****

That evening, Maxine lay in bed, reflecting on the day's activities. After about two hours of driving, she'd had enough. She stepped out of the car, feeling dizzy and seeing spots in her vision. Her heart pounded in her throat. Thankfully, she reached the house before she vomited in the guest bathroom by the garage. She tried her utmost to conceal her fear from Ava and Kincade, but they sensed it, though they chose to overlook it as she wished. They cared enough to let her preserve her pride. She felt weak. She felt strong. She felt conflicted.

Suddenly, a knock came at her window. She froze, taken aback by the strangeness of the situation. She was on the second floor, and there wasn't a single ladder in sight that could help someone reach her window. With trembling fingers, she pulled open the thin white curtain to see a pair of dark violet eyes staring back at her in the darkness. It was Kam. She opened her window immediately. She was elated, yet very caught off guard. "Dude, this is the most cliché thing I've ever seen," Maxine said, beaming. "If this is what your world calls cliché, it's pretty thrilling," Kam said with a wide smile.

Maxine swiftly spun her head behind her at the door. "Your room smells great," Kam said with his head partially in. "Gee, thanks. Just come in before you fall and break something." "Oh, you don't have to worry about me falling." Maxine felt the familiar fluttering of butterflies in her stomach, and paused briefly, distracted from her task of locking the door. She shook her head and caught herself. "Hold fast, let me make sure the door is locked," she said, just as Kam was already halfway in.

She hastily locked the door and gestured for him to enter. Kam tottered slightly as he clambered through her window. His tall frame made it so he just barely fit through. "How did you even get up there?" Maxine asked. "I flew over with my mystical alien powers." Maxine gave a smirk, recollecting the time she witnessed him soaring through the sky. "So what do I owe the pleasure, Martian boy?" She asked, grinning. "You ask a lot of questions, earth girl." Maxine's smile broadened in response. "Insults are my love language, too," he winked. Suddenly, they both heard someone in the hallway, and they both glanced at the door. "You sure it's locked?" Kam asked nervously. "It's airtight, dude. Trust me," she said, reassuring him.

Kam sat on the bed, and she approached, settling down beside him. They were almost shoulder to shoulder. Kam rose to break the tension, now standing close to the window. "Look, I have a few things to tell you. That's why I'm here," Kam said. Maxine's eyes lit up. "There's more to tell?" Kam gave a light chuckle in response. "Yes. And unfortunately, it's not all good news," he said. Kam's eyes widened with glee as he remembered something. "But before that, I got you a surprise," he said, rummaging behind his back.

He slowly presented her with a flower, the exact same one from her dream. Maxine was taken aback by the sight, her expression a mix of surprise and delight. "They're Pokaz. They bloom during Zay, Axpherian's version of spring," he said as he planted it gently in her hair, the exact spot he did in her dream. Maxine looked down, comprehending the situation. "Funny thing. I had a dream the other night that I was in a field of these, and we were holding hands. And I know you branded us friends and all, but in the dream, I planted this in your hair, and in the moment of it all...." "We almost kissed," they said in unison.

They both looked up, their faces brightening with surprise. "Wait, how'd you know?" Kam asked, genuinely puzzled. Maxine's eyes paced the floor, mouth partly open as she came to a realization. "I haven't been able to do that since Imani died," Maxine said under her breath. "What?" Kam asked. "I don't know how to explain it without sounding like a freak, but I can sort of... dream walk. And sometimes visions, too." Kam still looked puzzled. "Look, maybe this was a bad idea." "No. I'm genuinely fascinated. Continue," Maxine smiled, feeling secure enough to proceed.

"I used to be able to... sort of go into other people's dreams. Or dream of things happening before they do. Like my dad. He often dreamt about mom. Kincade's dreams were always just weird. Just comic geek type of dreams where he'd fight crime or battle some evil villain from one of his twelve hundred dozen comics. When I was a kid, I used to even join him sometimes. That's when it was the most fun. My sister used to paint a lot. In her dreams, her paintings were alive. They were just so immaculate. Full of color. Full of exotic animals and beautiful landscapes. She'd get freaked out when I used to tell her about it the next day. But when she died, it's like I lost the ability," Maxine examined the curl of her palms in her lap as she reflected. "But you did it with ease last night," Kam reminded her. "I'm not sure how. Maybe..." She trailed off as she pondered this and said, "Maybe mom was right. Maybe I'm beginning to finally heal." Kam settled next to her once more, disregarding the intensifying romantic atmosphere between them. He softly caressed her cheek, while she kept looking down at her hands. His warm hand filled her body with electricity. It was like every part of her lit up.

Kam's eyes widened as he suddenly recalled his message for her, and he jumped to his feet, pacing the room nervously. "What's up?" Maxine asked, watching him pace back and forth. "We might be in more danger than I previously anticipated." Maxine contorted. "What are you talking about?" she asked. Kam told her about the Herloids, went into brief detail of their history, and told her about the possibility of soldiers invading Axpherial. "Damn, that isn't good news," she said, processing this. "It's not exactly a walk in the park to process, but the cloning soldier theory isn't concrete. I still need to find more proof." Maxine peered her eyes at him. "How?" "I'll meet you in front of the hospital in a few days. We can find out together," he said. Maxine nodded. "Hey Kam?" Maxine asked suddenly. "Yeah?" "Why do you trust me with such valuable info like this?" She asked. Kam gave a little smirk, not daring to reveal to her the reasoning behind it, fearful of being embarrassed.

"My gut doesn't lie; if I couldn't, I would've abandoned this whole friendship thing after the train." Maxine beamed, as this made her feel warm inside. "You can continue to talk to me on here," Kam said, pulling a delfona out of his pocket. Maxine looked puzzled. "It's a delfona," he said. "Like an Apple Watch?" Kam laughed. "Its capabilities are beyond the current evolution of your planet's technology." Maxine cradled the device in her hand. She was perplexed by the circular glass screen and black straps. "Does Axpherial accept long-distance calling?" Kam chuckled again. "Interdimensional communication is one of its basic functions." Maxine smirked. "You're calling our technology dated?" "Yes, very much," Kam said as they shared a laugh. "I'll use it wisely," she said. "I'll discuss my plans further with you. But we'll keep in touch." Kam smiled. He opened the window as he prepared to exit. "Kam?" she queried, with him already halfway out the window. He stopped and turned to face her. "Be safe, okay," she said, sounding genuinely concerned. "Of course," he said with a reassuring smirk. He clumsily crawled out of the window, then he briefly hung on to the window sill until his fingers disappeared. Maxine sat, looking at the delfona. She held it in her palm as she lay down, still processing everything.

| 19 |

Kam

"They made the announcement today," Bliss shrugged, as if it were just another tidbit of information. She stood before Kam in the basement of his cabin. After a few days, the council had declared that no delfonas in Axpherial would be allowed access to Earth until further notice, effective immediately.

Kam's voice held a weary undertone. "I must've slept through them this morning," he admitted. Bliss asked with a tone of concern, "Nightmares again?" Kam gave a solemn nod in confirmation. "Except... Instead of seeing Zina on the Ferris wheel..." Kam nervously cleared his throat before finishing, "it was Maxine."

Bliss looked perplexed. "Why do you think you saw her?" She asked. Kam inhaled deeply, his gaze wandering across the room. "I think something inside of me feels like I can't save her. I don't know, maybe I can't," He said.

"I bet your little lover boy cape fits so snug it's suffocating," Bliss said, and they shared a chuckle. "But seriously, I need to get back to Earth and find out what other information is in that basement," Kam said.

"Wait. Their filing cabinet requires the golden key cards. How are we even supposed to access that? Our folks never gave us one, remember?" Kam stealthily extracted the glimmering golden card from his pocket. "Of course," Bliss said as she rolled her eyes, smiling. "I stole a spare from the top basement drawer."

Bliss couldn't help but feel thoroughly impressed. "You often forget that my resourcefulness is top tier," He said with a smug grin. "Meh. It's like a notch above modest. But I'll give you this one," She said, smirking.

"Did you finish the clone?" Kam asked. Bliss's eyes suddenly gleamed with excitement. "Almost forgot! And yes, let's check it out," she said, gesturing for him to follow her to the steel desk in the far left corner.

Bliss was undoubtedly a prodigy, inheriting her mathematical prowess primarily from her father. When it came to crafting technology, she effortlessly outshone her peers. Her contributions to Kam's intricate designs were invaluable, often taking the lead in complex calculations. She played a pivotal role in programming and constructing his computer. Like Kam, she was also an Ocria. Her unwavering reliability made her an indispensable ally.

She went to the large glass computer screen with a small glass container containing a delfona hovering inside of it. Bliss tapped the screen a few times, and the glass container disappeared beneath the desk, with the delfona still hovering. Bliss carefully picked it up and gave it to him. "Revolving door it is," Bliss grinned.

Kam beamed as he donned the device. He lightly tapped the screen a few times, the Axpherian logo clearly displayed: A person silhouetted in darkness with dozens of wings spreading out, with dozens of dark wings that stretched from each side. Even smaller wings stretched out from the bottom with the final two wings connected to the figure's feet, encircled by a thick black ring. It was just like all government delfonas. "Wow," he murmured in admiration, proud of her work.

"You know, my resourceful skills put just a slim dint in yours," Bliss beamed like she couldn't help it. "That remains to further be seen," Kam smiled as he continued to examine the delfona. "Well if you count me coming up with elaborate excuses for you, I say I have you very much beat," She uttered, eliciting a giggle from Kam. "You do alright," Kam quipped.

"That's excellent in your language, so I'll take it," Bliss smiled. Kam gazed at her and then embraced her in an unexpected, tight hug. It took Bliss a few seconds to reciprocate the hug. "You're welcome," Bliss said, sounding like he was squeezing too hard. "Sorry!" He exclaimed as he drew back. "Don't sweat it. Now go on, loverboy. I'll be here waiting," Bliss said. Kam grinned as he lightly tapped her chin and straddled his motorcycle to return to Earth and reunite with Maxine.

****

Maxine stood outside of the hospital, glancing at her phone. The clock read 8 o'clock, exactly as Kam had told her to meet him. The two had been speaking almost every day since he had gifted her the delfona a week prior. Chit-chatting late into the night, it was casual and safe conversations, with them often falling asleep with each other. A couple of minutes passed, and Kam pulled up in front of her. A smile spread across her face as she saw him wearing a black motorcycle jumpsuit with slim blue stripes running down the shoulder, back, and leg.

Maxine's face lit up as he removed his helmet, prompting him to return her smile. "You're a little late," she said, her voice tinged with excitement. "Well, I humbly ask for you to excuse my tardiness," Kam smiled. Kam's eyes narrowed as he analyzed her. Her voluminous, oversized white sweater, slim black jeans, and pristine white sneakers. She wore a minimal amount of makeup, yet her beauty was effortless. "What?" Maxine asked, snapping him back to reality. "You have a thing for oversized clothing. It looks very natural on you," He said, beaming.

Maxine was slightly taken aback. She didn't really think much about how she dressed that day. But she highly appreciated the compliment nevertheless. "It's my cool, unorthodox sense of fashion," Maxine said into a smile. "Well, unorthodox looks exceptional on you," Kam grinned.

"Trying to charm me?" her voice laced with playful curiosity. "Is it working?" He jested playfully. "Not at all." She smiled. Maxine glanced away, her cheeks flushed with embarrassment at the ease he brought out in her. "There is something I wanted to tell you tonight," Maxine said. Kam quirked an eyebrow. "What's that?" He inquired. "Something I was... that I was too afraid to let you in on before," Maxine said as her voice trembled. "I have something I want to show you, too," He said. "I like this little game of show and tell," Maxine said, curving her lips into a slender smile. "Do you hear that?" Kam asked, frantically looking around. "Huh?" Maxine said, checking her surroundings as well. "Those walls finally crumbling down?" Kam said, beaming wide. Maxine caught on immediately and laughed out of relief. "Making fun of me?" She asked jokingly. "Making fun of us, actually." Kam said, suddenly serious. Maxine's gaze was met with urgency as she peered into his eyes. Her demeanor suddenly shifted to a more serious tone. He hopped off his motorcycle and offered her a helmet and a matching motorcycle jumpsuit. "Come with me. I'll spare no details for this," He said. She grabbed the jumpsuit, and tension grew as they both realized she had to change. "I'm about to be semi-naked, can you play as my shield for just a second?" Maxine asked. "Of course," He said. "Keep your eyes on the outside, not on my temple, Martian boy." Maxine jested as Kam's lips curved upward as he chuckled. Kam awkwardly turned his head as Maxine quickly switched clothes. The jumpsuit fit perfectly, and she stuffed her clothes inside his seat as she strapped on the helmet Kam gave to her. Kam quickly revved his engine and they took off quickly into the night.

****
****

As they rode, they raced swiftly through the city streets. Without warning, they weaved across the lanes, narrowly avoiding a few cars. It was clear that even though Kam had some skill with the motorcycle, he was oblivious to the rules of the road. "Hey! If you want to keep the blood in both of our bodies I suggest you slow down!" Maxine yelled over the engine. "Sorry! I think I just got caught in the rush!" "Less rushing, more safety! Please, dude. I'm begging you!" Maxine yelled.

"So the dashing white lines separate the lanes?"

"Yes!"

"And the white solid lines?"

"Just dont cross! Unless you're turning and you see the big white arrows!" Maxine rolled her eyes in exasperation as she tightly grasped Kam, her fingernails digging into his side. "Your nails are stabbing me!" Kam yelled. "Sorry!" Maxine yelled as she slightly released.

****

As they approached Kam's Earth home, an eerie orange glow replaced the usual moonlight and the faint streetlamp illumination. They came to a halt a few yards away from the house. Kam swiftly dismounted his motorcycle, tossing his helmet aside in one fluid motion. Maxine followed suit, discarding her helmet and hastening to catch up with him. Just as she reached him, Kam froze in his tracks, his chest heaving as he gazed upon his home consumed by furious flames.

Maxine attempted to inquire about what was happening, but her words were drowned out by the crackling fire. Inside that inferno were the files, the test kit, the memories, all devoured by the merciless blaze. Kam's terror-stricken eyes darted around, noticing crimson lettering etched onto the ground. Maxine, too, glanced down and spotted the letters: G, O, O, D. Slowly, the pieces of the cryptic message fell into place.

A chill crept down their spines as they deciphered the letters A and S beneath, forming the word: AS. Their hearts pounded in unison as they continued to decode the ominous message, revealing the final, dread-inducing revelation. In bold, red capital letters that dominated half the ground, the ominous message spelled out: AS GOOD AS DEAD.

| 20 |

Kam & Maxine

Kam sped through the city streets on his motorcycle, Maxine perched on the back. His driving had improved, staying in the lanes despite his speed surpassing the limit. His mind was preoccupied with the potential peril facing not only him and his family but also Maxine and her family. He suddenly pulled into a gas station, needing a moment to catch his breath as he experienced a panic attack.

Kam slowly removed his helmet, revealing a mortified expression on his face. He was able to stabilize his breathing, but his culpability remained. Even the blindest man in the world could see the weary in his face. Resting his arms on the helmet that was placed on the handlebars, he felt a wave of guilt wash over him. Maxine followed suit, removing her helmet and showing a more composed face, yet the shock of the situation was still evident.

Kam spoke in a low voice, "It's my fault." Maxine put her hand on his shoulder and gave it a reassuring squeeze. He fought back tears, his mind plagued with memories of his rebellious actions, despite the fact that his actions saved Maxine's life.

"Everyone's gonna die because of me, Max. Because I can't stay still enough to consider how serious everything was until people got hurt; Including you." He wiped his nose and blinked away tears, wanting to remain sturdy though he felt so small. Maxine attempted to be encouraging as she uttered, "I'm not hurt," She smiled and added, "I'm in mint condition." Kam still felt at fault.

"But whoever attacked us on the train, maybe I was their target and you just happened to be there." "You gotta give yourself more credit than that. You saved me." Kam shook his head. "But maybe if it wasn't for me you would've…" "No. I'm not gonna let you do that. I'm not gonna let you blame yourself for something me nor you had any sort of.….." Maxine swallowed hard before finishing, "There's nothing you can do to take back the way I felt after that night. You reminded me that I have more than enough to live for. Yeah it traumatized me but you know what I did the next day?" Kam suddenly gazed at her with eyes swallowed by grief. "I finally began the journey to finally healing myself. And every day I'm slowly progressing. I have nobody but you to thank for that," Maxine smiled as she thought of this. Instead of feeling the urge to shed tears once more, she felt empowered. This astonished her a bit, but she welcomed this newfound power.

Kam felt this wave of relief flush through him hearing her words. His throat felt less heavy, and he no longer felt himself on the verge of tears. "You make me sound like I'm a god or something," Kam said, his smile tinged with sorrow. "I make you sound like you. A hero. Definitely on the strange side of the tracks, but I'd put your signal in the sky any day," Maxine smiled warmly as Kam gazed intently into her eyes, recognizing the honesty in her expression. "That means the world," Kam replied, smiling hard.

"Dude, it better," Maxine said, grinning. "Come on, let's get you home," Kam said. "Yeah, just ease up on the speed, dude. You keep flirting with death, she just might flirt back," Maxine said as she put her helmet back on. "I'll ease up," Kam replied as he also strapped his helmet on. "Ease up by like a mile, man," Maxine said, half serious as they began riding away.

Kam tried to follow her advice, but soon his adrenaline got the better of him. He resumed driving recklessly, darting past cars at a speed exceeding the limit by at least thirty miles per hour. "Isn't this thrilling?" Kam yelled.

"Terrified yet exhilarated!" Maxine shouted back, her voice barely audible over the wind.

"Good!" Kam replied.

However, his thrill was short-lived as he spotted red and blue flashing lights in his rearview mirror. "What's that?!" he exclaimed in alarm.

Maxine's response was drowned out by the roar of the wind, but she gestured frantically. Kam finally understood when he saw the flashing lights. "Who are they?!" he exclaimed.

"Cops!" Maxine yelled.

"Cops?" Kam replied.

"Pull over if you value your life!" Maxine yelled.

"My life?" Kam asked, bewildered.

"Two people driving like they're in a pole position race on city streets? Two black people driving like that? Just... pull over and do what the officer says!" Maxine urged.

"Why does my skin tone matter?" Kam asked, perplexed.

"Unfortunately, it does here," Maxine replied.

Kam quickly decreased his speed and pulled over to the curb. A police officer parked behind him, and the officer soon approached Kam's vehicle. The officer was around 50 years old, tall, with fair skin and a receding hairline. He eyed Kam suspiciously.

"Do you have any idea how fast you were going?" the cop asked, already annoyed.

Kam shook his head, his heart racing and his hands trembling. Maxine tightened her grip on his hips, causing a quiet moan to escape him.

"You ran several stop signs and were speeding at 45 miles over the limit. License and registration, please," the officer demanded.

Kam's mind raced as he realized he hadn't considered credentials when constructing the cycle. "So, we were going too fast, officer?" Kam stammered nervously.

"Yes, and you don't have plates, son. Where are your tags?" the officer inquired.

Kam fumbled for an answer. "I was in a hurry, and I, uh..."

"I get the feeling you're stalling. It won't work. License and registration," the officer insisted.

Kam felt paralyzed, his lips refusing to cooperate. Maxine held onto him, her fingernails digging into his flesh.

"What's your name, son?" the officer pressed.

Kam struggled to come up with an answer, and Maxine's mental encouragement was palpable. Finally, he blurted out, "Joey."

The officer eyed him skeptically, unconvinced. "Joey what?"

Kam glanced at Maxine, his desperation evident, before saying, "Joey Wilson."

The officer grunted and headed back to his patrol car, leaving Kam and Maxine in anxious silence. Kam's heart raced as he feared the worst. The phrase "If you value your life" echoed in his mind, and his trembling hands revealed his fear.

As they waited, Kam felt an overwhelming sense of dread. The officer's voice came through the walkie-talkie, and Kam's stomach churned as he realized they were in trouble.

"Sounds like two adrenaline junkie kids thinking they can drive lawlessly through the streets. He gave a fake name. Kid has no identification. I suspect the cycle is stolen. I'll bring him in for a sobriety check. I might bring the young lady in, too," the officer said.

Kam's fear escalated as he heard this, and he knew he couldn't face the consequences. He quickly made a decision and sped away. The police officer yelled into his walkie-talkie as he chased after them.

Maxine's scream filled the air. "What the hell are you doing?!"

Kam didn't answer; he just kept driving. The police car pursued them, and Kam's evasive maneuvers included running a red light and narrowly avoiding a white SUV. He knew that staying would lead to a lose-lose situation – possible arrest or even death.

"In my left pocket, there's a square device! Press the button!" Kam shouted.

"Why?" Maxine yelled.

"Just trust me!" Kam replied.

Maxine hesitated but found the small device in Kam's pocket. She pressed the button, and a surge of energy coursed through her, causing her to nearly lose her grip on Kam.

"What was that?!" Maxine exclaimed.

"You'll see in a moment!" Kam replied, sounding both excited and nervous.

Just as two more police cars joined the chase, the motorcycle's wheels vanished in a flash of blue light. The patrol cars screeched to a halt as the motorcycle levitated and soared into the sky, leaving the police officers bewildered.

Maxine was speechless as Kam closed his eyes, concentrating. He conjured a white sphere of light, and they stepped inside the portal, which disappeared once they were safely inside.

The sphere materialized again, this time in the vast darkness of space. Kam and Maxine slowly descended on their motorcycle as the wheels reappeared beneath them. Kam removed his helmet, taking a deep breath, and Maxine stepped off to survey their surroundings. All she could see was a grey, rocky terrain with circular craters in every direction. She turned around and saw a bright blue ball partially silhouetted against the darkness, with broken white clouds floating in the distance.

Then it hit her – they were on the moon.

Maxine held her chest, trying to keep from fainting from disbelief. She tightly shut her eyes, then opened them again with a hint of desperation. Her chest heaved, and her pulse pounded. She wondered if this was just another dream.

"Kam, can I see the time?" Maxine asked.

Kam was puzzled. "Of all things, you want to see that?" Kam asked.

"Yes, please."

Kam walked over and pointed to his delfona; the clock read 11:45 pm Mountain time - the same time zone that they came from.

She hurriedly rushed to the left side of the motorcycle's rearview mirror, scrutinizing it carefully. Her gaze ran over her brown skin, her even cheeks, and the faint circles under her eyes from fatigue and stress. She inspected herself solemnly. Kam was utterly perplexed.

"What are you doing?" He finally asked.

Maxine continued checking the mirror, going as far as to check her teeth, analyze her braids, and even inspect between her eyelids. Kam just folded his arms, still looking lost.

Maxine abruptly glanced up, almost having forgotten about him. "Time and a clear reflection. Both are impossible to see in your dreams," Maxine said.

"Wait? You thought we were dreaming?"

"People don't go on high-speed chases, fly to the moon, or fly through clouds every day, Kam." Maxine and Kam exchanged a nervous chuckle.

"Well, unless you're high," Maxine added, and they shared another laugh.

"That's valid," Kam grinned.

"How'd you do all that?" Maxine asked.

"Adrenaline, I guess. I didn't want either of us getting hurt by that red and blue guy back there."

"It's called a cop, martian boy," Maxine smiled.

"Yeah, he was scary," Kam said.

Maxine gazed around in disbelief, still unable to fully comprehend that they were there. "My mind tends to be a ticking time bomb around you," Maxine said.

Kam raised an eyebrow. "How?"

Maxine chuckled in amusement at the realization that he had no clue. "It's always blown," Maxine said as Kam hardly chuckled. "Okay, bad joke. But you get the point," Maxine beamed.

"Don't be so hard on yourself. I'm not that funny, either," Kam said, grinning.

"Oh, shut up!" Maxine said as she and Kam laughed.

There was a brief pause, with both of them seeing Earth from afar, enjoying the view.

Maxine asked, "How'd you do it?"

Kam appeared bewildered. "What do you mean?" He questioned.

Maxine gave him a piercing look, implying that the question was too obvious for him not to catch on. Kam suddenly understood as his eyes lit up. "Oh, you mean this! Let me show you," he exclaimed, brandishing a blue square device with a small black button in its center.

"It's a Zakkra. It allows you to withstand pressures underwater and in space, and it's pretty much a space suit without, of course, the spacesuit."

"Thats..." Maxine trailed off, lost for words.

"Still feels like I'm front row on a mushroom trip or having one hell of a lucid dream," Maxine said.

Maxine paused, her eyes darting to the ground as she had a realization. The fact that he had that device of all things had to mean something. She suddenly gazed at him with a smug smile. Once again, Kam looked clueless.

"You planned this, didn't you?" Maxine asked.

Kam smiled knowingly, his face radiating warmth as Maxine let out a sweet, timid chuckle. She felt a sudden rush of fascination as their eyes met.

"Except the high speed chase part but yeah, I did," Kam admitted.

Maxine chuckled lightly as she kept her gaze fixed on him.

"I saw the poster in your room like this from Earth's moon. I've learned that a person's choice in decorations says a lot about a person's personality. I figured that..."

"You figured that you would blow my mind with a space odyssey-themed first date, am I right?" Kam beamed.

"Surprise?" He said shyly as Maxine laughed. "I still feel like I'm dreaming," Maxine said.

Kam chuckled, as he inched closer to her. "I can assure you that you're not in a dream," he said kindly, as he approached.

"Oh?" Maxine asked nervously. She felt the weightlessness of butterflies once again. Her pulse raced as Kam stood mere inches away from her. She felt her heart flutter with anticipation.

"Remember that dream we had in the field the other night?"

"Yeah?" Maxine asked, her voice shaking.

"And remember when you woke up, right when we were getting to the good part?"

"Yeah?" Maxine said, her voice more shaky.

Kam's face was just inches away from hers when he uttered, "You owe me one." He tenderly cupped her chin and pressed his lips to hers in a soft, gentle kiss. A surge of electricity shot through them. They felt complete and in perfect harmony with one another. When Kam pulled away, their eyes met and her lips parted in awe. She couldn't help but to capture his face once more and embrace him in a passionate kiss. She wanted him, completely and entirely.

Kam felt satisfied, like he finally scratched a burning itch. Suddenly, he felt this heavy feeling of terror and anxiety. Anxiety so over-whelming that he quickly pulled back like he regretted the entire thing. Maxine looked shocked, like he was rejecting her. Kam glanced down-ward, feeling a pang of guilt for his actions. Maxine peered her eyes and asked, "Did I come on too strong?"

Kam just shook his head.

"I guess I'm just a little afraid," He admitted.

Maxine gave a small smile, quickly banishing his worries as if they were nothing more than mere shyness. "You can't be scared of how you feel. Cause I feel it too."

Maxine gazed into his eyes, seeing the fear take over his expression. "I didn't think I would... you know, find you this attractive. I always thought you were cute, but I didn't know I wanted you this much," Maxine admitted.

Kam smiled, feeling a pleasant sensation in his heart. He was aware that he shouldn't be feeling this way, but his genuine feelings for her were hard to resist.

"No Max, I feel very much the same. It's just I...." Kam trailed off, not wanting to say it.

"I'm afraid to lose you," He admitted.

Maxine arched one eyebrow in surprise. "Why?" Maxine asked.

"Because the last time I fell for someone like this, she was gone before I could say goodbye," Kam said as his eyes scanned the ground.

"You think we're moving too fast?" Maxine asked.

"No, I'm actually fond of the pace. It's just…" Kam suddenly remembered exactly what he needed to tell her.

Kam stopped for a moment, uncertain of how to tell her about Zina, but he realized he had to. He inhaled deeply, then spoke, recounting the night of Zina's accident at the Ferris wheel. He spoke of the emotions he experienced, the nightmares he endured, and the guilt he felt for not being able to prevent the tragedy. When he finished, his face held a look of defeat as he cast his gaze downward.

Maxine felt nothing but sheer empathy for his story. She felt even closer to him now than ever before. "I'm so, so sorry, Kam. I…" Maxine gently placed her hand on his left shoulder, providing him with a sense of solace. "I can definitely relate. And I know people like to say things like that when in reality, they're just projecting fake empathy and making their scripted compassion sound sweet. But I say this with sincerity and honesty. I know exactly how you feel." Maxine swallowed hard before finishing. "And it's time I let you know why."

| 21 |

Kam & Maxine

"I guess I trust you enough to finally let you know why I keep having these... triggers. Or why every time I say her name, it feels like it's burning on its way out," Maxine admitted, her gaze fixed on Kam, who stood before his motorcycle.

"I like this game of show and tell," Kam responded, a grin forming on his face.

"More like post-traumatic show and tell," Maxine replied, and they shared a laugh. "But anyway, there's a lot to tell, unfortunately." Kam offered a reassuring smirk as he perched on the edge of his motorcycle seat, ready to listen.

"Okay, so..." Maxine grappled with her inner thoughts, contemplating whether revealing something so sacred, so distressing, was worth it. She smiled softly, reflecting on the security Kam provided, his consistency, and the fact that he saw her beyond her physical self. Finally, she decided to continue.

"It was about two years ago. I was 17, before the world took a complete nosedive into hell," Maxine began with a nervous laugh. Kam's grin widened in response.

"That's neither here nor there. But anyway, I had an older sister, Imani. She was the oldest among Kincade, me, and herself. She was a sophomore in college, on her way to becoming a teacher. Dad treated her differently after finding out she was a lesbian. I thought the obvious was... well, obvious. She and Kincade wore the same clothes, she couldn't name three makeup brands to save her life, and they competed in video games, sports, anything labeled 'for boys' by society. Maybe Dad saw it, but knowing him, he'd run from the truth as usual. My dad would demolish a marathon the way he likes to run," Maxine shared as Kam lightly chuckled.

"It was almost like having two big brothers, but she tried to be more of a typical girly girl around me. She even let me paint her nails, which took some convincing, but she agreed, though I ended up painting them jet black. That was one of the last nights we spent together," Maxine said, her gaze averting as she reluctantly pushed forward.

"She was the only one who knew I was..." Maxine swallowed hard, never having shared this with anyone else. "I was three and a half months pregnant. The guy who was the father was killed in a school shooting two weeks after I found out. He was my first, but he was a narcissistic dick whose maturity peaked in middle school. He had a charm that briefly made you forget about his repressed self-loathing, masked by his pretty looks and insufferable god complex," Maxine laughed, though it was laced with bitterness.

Kam tenderly clasped her left hand, his thumb running soothingly across the back of it. "I was leaving a party. I wasn't quite drunk, but I was a shot or two away. I no longer cared about my pregnancy. I don't know if I was trying to drink teen pregnancy away or..." Maxine's voice trailed off, and she felt like she was transported back to that night, engulfed in guilt.

"I was too inebriated to drive, so Imani picked me up. We were driving down the highway. I don't remember the conversation verbatim, so I can't give you a play-by-play, but I remember my sister being pissed that I was drinking in the first place with an entire human being inside me. I actually took into account what she was saying and felt like glorified crap for doing something so reckless. Then, Ava texted me a meme, and I showed Imani, who laughed. Ava always sent me memes, always trying to give me a good laugh. But as soon as Imani and I looked back up, we saw the back of a black Honda with brake lights that came to a sudden stop. She had no time to stop, and we flipped over at least a few times. I woke up feeling dizzy, bleeding from my head and stomach. I was bleeding a lot between my legs, and I knew my baby was in trouble. Imani was covered in blood and not moving. I tried to wake her, and she did. The first thing she said was that she couldn't feel her legs. I remember the ambulance and police getting us out of the car. I remember being on the stretcher and hearing my heart rate monitor flatline in the hospital..."

Maxine began hyperventilating, feeling as if she was back in the accident all over again. "I was dead. I was watching them trying to revive me from above the room. I didn't believe much in ghosts until that day when I thought I might have become one," Maxine said, smiling painfully.

"When I woke up, Kincade was by my side and told me I had a near-fatal miscarriage. I was in a coma for three days. However, the doctors were surprised at how fast I was healing. My scars were nearly gone, and I was able to walk out of the hospital without the physical therapy they thought I'd need. Kincade told me that Imani died an hour after she arrived at the hospital. They said a shard of glass punctured an artery, and she bled to death."

Maxine's tears streamed down her face as she finally allowed herself to feel. She nestled into Kam's embrace and wept into his chest. "I felt like I killed her and my baby. I still haven't forgiven myself for what happened that night. I still feel..." Maxine wiped her tears as she backed away a couple of inches from Kam. "I still feel responsible," she admitted as Kam gently wiped her tears.

Kam's face lit up with a grin as he gazed into her eyes and lightly brushed his fingers against her cheeks. The sensation filled him with warmth and longing for more of the softness of her skin, making the world around him vanish. He felt a bit of fear, but he chose to push forward instead of retreating. Kam tenderly held her face in his hands, and their lips met in a passionate embrace. She clung to him as his kiss sent a wave of emotion through them both, more intense than they had ever experienced. They had the urge to lock up and stay intertwined. Kam pulled back again, his heart racing with a mixture of anxiety and a tension he hadn't felt since Zina.

On Axpherial, their hormones worked differently. First came romantic attraction, then sexual attraction. Kam was now starting to feel the latter, which only made him more nervous. "The Earth looks beautiful from here," he said, quickly changing the subject. Maxine's face lit up with a smile, understanding what he felt. She was pleased that he was feeling the same. Kam took Maxine's hand and wrapped his arms around her waist. They gazed at earth, their eyes swallowing the breathtaking view. Despite their brief relationship, they felt like they knew each other forever. Kam rested his chin on her shoulder, and Maxine gripped his arms, feeling at home in his embrace.

✳✳

Maxine and Kam arrived at Maxine's house, the motorcycle purring to a halt in the driveway. They both removed their helmets, Maxine handing hers to Kam with a smirk. Kam grinned back at her as he removed his.

"So the elephant in the room wants to know something," Maxine said.

"Intrigue me," Kam said with a tired grin.

"What are we?" Maxine asked. Kam stopped, unsure of how to respond. Maxine's grin diminished slightly, though she was well aware of what they were. She was just waiting for Kam to say it.

"I guess we are one beautiful trauma bond, huh?" Maxine smiled. Kam chuckled softly, still feeling a bit uneasy at the prospect of engaging in intimacy again.

"Yeah. I think we are," Kam smiled. His smirk vanished as he swept his gaze across the ground.

"I sense a but is coming," Maxine said, sounding a little disappointed.

"But you have to bear with me, as I'm still kinda scared," Kam admitted as his voice shook. Maxine's smirk widened again as she gazed into Kam's deep violet eyes, illuminated by the dim white light of her driveway. Mesmerizing as always. Maxine smiled and said, "Let's make a deal. I'll kiss your scars, you kiss mine," Kam's face softened into a bashful smile as he gazed into her eyes. "It's a deal," He said.

Maxine glided over to Kam, who was beginning to feel a wave of panic wash over him. She tenderly planted a kiss on his cheek and slowly stroked the spot where she had kissed him.

"You're so adorable, even when you're anxious," Maxine smiled as Kam returned a nervous grin. He knew that he couldn't help how he felt, but he felt guilty all the same. His mind raced with a jumble of feelings. "Goodnight," he said, his smile tinged with anxiety. Maxine's smile remained as she waved softly and stepped inside her house. Kam was jolted by a gentle beep, like an alarm. He was astonished when he realized the source of the signal - it was coming from the earth house.

| 22 |

Kam & Maxine

"Max! Max, wake up!" The cloudiness of Ava's voice was all Maxine heard as she shook herself out of a deep sleep.

"What's up?" Maxine inquired drowsily as she rubbed her eyes.

"Insanity is what's up! Come on, let's get downstairs!" Ava said excitedly, pulling on Maxine's arm.

Maxine yawned, remarking, "I'd rather be fully rested first."

"Just come downstairs, pleeeease?" Ava sang, still tugging her arm.

"Down those stairs?" Ava rolled her eyes as she tugged a little harder. "Alright, alright!" Maxine groaned as she finally caved and allowed Ava to rouse her from the bed.

She walked downstairs half-walking, half-dragged by Ava. Maxine entered the living room, where Kincade and Tobias were absorbed in the TV. Tobias was pinching his bottom lip with his fingers, deep in thought. Kincade had his arms crossed, his face displaying suspicion. Maxine stood beside him as he glanced at her and grinned before turning back to the screen. Tobias nervously nodded in her direction, and she responded with an awkward nod. The atmosphere between them was as heavy as a storm cloud. Maxine felt pain in her heart, but she didn't know how to spark up a conversation with him.

Maxine spun to the screen, her heart racing as her eyes alighted on the image. An indistinct shot of a motorcycle with two riders dressed in black hovering in the sky was enough to cause her to gasp in disbelief. She could barely comprehend the words of the reporter, as her mind was eclipsed with shock.

"Total mysterious phenomenon, Clearance. Is it fact or fiction? That is the ultimate question as the debate on social media rages on. Right out of a Stephen Spielberg script into reality, two mystery people were captured flying into the sky late last night as people are questioning the authenticity of this footage…." Maxine kept her gaze fixed on the television screen, her expression seemingly solemn as the reporter went on and on about the possibility of the footage being a hoax. She then remembered something she told Kam only a little bit ago, "An alien can casually beam us into a warship and we'd still be looking for a camera crew." Her statement making even more sense now.

"Well, of course, they want us to question something like this, so they can continue distracting us with their corporations, their MK ultra programming, and subscription services with our happily ever after television shows. God, I also bet they…"

"Shut up!" Maxine and Ava uttered in unison.

"Hey, just your friendly, neighborhood critical thinker here," Kincade said with his hands up in surrender.

"You are one of the main reasons I use alcohol to cope," Ava said as she rolled her eyes.

"I'm not your source of your alcoholism, sweeetheart. Your inability to cope with your own demons are."

"Do humanity and me a favor and shut up forever, please," Ava said, annoyed.

"Pay me first," Kincade replied, smirking hard. Ava just shook her head and rolled her eyes as she glanced back at the television.

"Good reason to wake up, huh?" Ava asked Maxine, who was lost in her own world.

Her heartbeat was in her throat, and she squeezed her hands into a fist to conceal her trembling. She felt caught, though there was no evidence that she was the one responsible.

"Max?" Ava asked as she snapped her back to reality. Maxine jolted as she glanced at Ava nervously.

"You look like you saw a monster under your bed, hun. You okay?" Ava asked.

Maxine nervously nodded. "Not fully awake yet," she lied. Ava tilted her head and studied her intently. Her eyes then brightened with understanding. "Aww, you probably just need some caffeine. I'll be back," Ava said as she skipped to the kitchen. Maxine wordlessly nodded, gazing at the TV screen. A beautiful middle-aged woman with olive skin appeared on the news station, and Maxine watched her intently. She went on about gas prices and talked about the pandemic, like an alien wasn't literally flying casually on the screen moments earlier. Maxine turned to walk away when a voice stopped her in her tracks.

"I got a surprise for you tomorrow night. I hope you don't mind," Tobias said.

Maxine was overcome with a sense of relief and elation, yet a spark of resentment smoldered within her. Despite this, she was unable to prevent herself from loving him, though she still thought he lacked courage. Maxine turned and gave a soft smirk that looked painful and said, "Okay, dad."

Maxine quickly ascended the stairs without hesitation. Tobias remained where he was, his face displaying sorrow as he observed her. Kincade's lips curved with delight as he noticed Tobias's shame after Maxine told him off. Despite his love for his father, he was certain the guilt would eventually lead him to take responsibility and halt his second nature ability to scurry at adversity.

****
******

Kam zoomed through the streets, doing his best to obey traffic regulations until his impatience pushed him to accelerate beyond the speed limit. He drove recklessly in his bid to get home quickly. When he arrived, he stopped to analyze the charred remains of his earthly home. The once-sturdy wooden structure had been reduced to a mound of charcoal-colored debris. The red warning he had received still glared boldly on the ground.

Removing his helmet, he gazed sadly at his home, realizing that the vast memories, designs, and perhaps even the answers he sought in the basement had all turned to ashes. Glancing at his delfona, which still flashed bright red with the distress signal, he quickly hopped off his vehicle and advanced towards the house. He moved cautiously, surveying his surroundings, ready for anything.

He noticed that the porch leading to his house was mostly intact, except for one section which had been severely charred. Climbing up the creaky stairs, he passed through the remains of the entrance. He began to rummage through the debris, his palms turning black from the soot.

Then he spotted the edge of his black scabbard, with his sword still tucked inside. With a sense of relief, he grabbed it and secured the scabbard around his chest, the sword now securely on his back. His attention was then drawn to the partially covered door that had once led to the basement.

His eyes lit up with recognition as he remembered the Polakiem filing cabinet. Without wasting a moment, he bolted down the stairs and activated the flashlight on his delfona. Panting, he shone the light around the basement, only to find the dark, dilapidated remains. His brow furrowed as he spotted the desk and realized that the file had been charred beyond recognition. However, when he directed the light towards the filing cabinet, he noticed that, aside from some ash scattered on top of it, it remained unscathed.

A sigh of relief escaped him as he sheathed his sword and tapped his delfona. The cloned-government device contained the access code to his parents' cabinet. When he opened the top drawer, he saw several black filing folders, each labeled in white: Formulas, ADA Forums, Photos, Dimensional notes, Pandemic. His gaze immediately fell on the last one, and he removed it from the cabinet and placed it on top.

Opening the folder, he began skimming through the documents, searching for any clues. His eyes landed on the plans for the Aphlama, the weapon Kam's parents had mentioned as the means to disperse the cure into the atmosphere. Noting two valves filled with a dark blue liquid and a syringe encased in a plastic bag, he quickly looked over the papers behind the valves, discovering they contained samples of the antitoxin. Without hesitation, Kam stowed them away in his pocket, sensing they might come in handy later. He then examined the prototype of the structure.

The structure was colossal, boasting eight gargantuan silver barrels with a black neck linked to a black cube-shaped stand housing the fuel for the antidote. The machine measured 35 feet by 20 feet tall, and Kam noted that, once the prototype was perfected, it would be duplicated and stationed at multiple other base camps.

Kam couldn't help but ponder the mysterious dents he had noticed in the filing cabinets on his last visit. It became clear that the herloids were desperate for the maps contained within; possessing such advanced and destructive technology would make the camps completely vulnerable. He set the folder aside and resumed rummaging, determined to find the maps. Eventually, he located the folder tucked away in the back of the cabinet. Inside, all he found was a thin, rectangular glass device that fit snugly in his hand.

Tapping the screen, a shimmering blue hologram materialized, displaying a spinning globe in the air. Kam's gaze swept across it for a moment before he tapped North America, causing several red points of light to illuminate. He read the names of the base camps, listed alphabetically, and chose the one closest to him: Basecamp K, which lay about 82 miles beneath the surface of the Chihuahuan desert. With a simple tap, the map dissipated, and Kam tucked the device into his back pocket.

His attention then turned to the mysterious pandemic file, and he recalled his theory of the poison potentially reanimating the deceased. He hastily seized the file and began scanning it, primarily finding accounts of potion advancements. To his surprise, he discovered that only a scant amount of antidote was available. Kam understood that the immunity cities were populated by those who had either been vaccinated or were innately resistant due to their inter-dimensional DNA.

The realization hit him: the immunity cities were a ruse, designed to gather all those who had managed to elude the poison in one spot. Recalling Maxine's words about the scanners, Kam realized that the soldiers were not human; but were herloids. Dread washed over him as he continued to sift through the file, reading about the Helphoma 818 poison's ability to resurrect and even reproduce, allowing the herloids to multiply.

It became clear to Kam that the herloids needed to build up their numbers to create an army, just as he and his friends had predicted. He then predicted that they had destroyed his home in an attempt to hinder Axpherian plans to refine the prototype his parents had been working on. The herloids sought to buy more time to demolish the immunity cities, clone enough soldiers, and send them to destroy Axpherial. These revelations terrified Kam as he took the blueprints from the file and tucked them away in his back pocket, along with the glass device containing the maps. He knew that with their technology, it was only a matter of time before they found a way to crack open the filing cabinets.

As Kam slammed the cabinet shut, his delfona's distress signal blared once again. He hastily made his way up to the surface, unsheathing his sword and surveying the area. A loud beeping beside him startled him, and he spun around to find Bliss, her face mirroring the concern etched across Kam's.

"Did you activate the distress signal?" he asked, puzzled. Bliss looked equally confused. "What? I assumed you had done it," she uttered. Kam cocked his head and arched an eyebrow. "Who did it then?" he inquired. Bliss's eyes gleamed as she scanned the debris.

Kam motioned for Bliss to get behind him, and she complied. The two of them carefully stepped through the rubble, their flashlights illuminating the ruins. All around them was an eerie silence. "What happened?" Bliss asked in a hushed tone, her eyes wide with worry. Kam shook his head and replied, "I think I've found the motive."

Bliss glanced at him curiously. "Oh really?" she said, her interest piqued. Kam halted and spun around, just as he was about to say something, he heard the sound of footsteps. Both he and Bliss turned warily, Kam holding his sword and Bliss brandishing a jet black laser gun, which was slimmer than a typical pistol. Meeka then stepped out of the darkness, a sword that was identical to Kam's in his hands. "Dad?" He asked. "Which one of you activated the distress signal?" He demanded.

Ala trailed close behind him, both dressed in black ADA army jumpsuits. "Clearly none of us," Bliss said. "Why are you guys here? How did you have access to this realm?" Ala demanded. "I mean, he is Kam," Bliss said with a slight chuckle. Kam let out a laugh before quickly regaining his composure. "Dad, you gotta listen. Someone is..." "Someone is clearly trying to talk their way out of an explanation. Now again, how did you two get here?" Bliss and Kam exchanged a glance, uncertain of what to say. All of a sudden, Kam had a feeling that something was off. His hands started to tingle, confirming his hunch. "I'm waiting." Meeka said with his arms folded.

Kam stopped in his tracks, a strong feeling of danger washing over him. He heard a voice call from behind him, "Kam!" He recognized the voice immediately and spun around to see....Bliss! She was panting, her attire far different from the other Bliss. She had on a snug black sleeveless shirt and snug black pants, while the other wore a white sleeveless shirt that exposed her midriff and baggy black pants.

They stood there, weapons drawn, each one pointing their firearm at the other. The tension was palpable as they faced each other. "It's a trap! They called the distress signal. I saw them on the cameras above the house!" The Bliss in black exclaimed. He turned and faced the Bliss in white, who had her gun trained on the Bliss who just arrived. "Kam don't believe her. She's the one who set the signal. We all were lured here by her. She's the imposter!" The Bliss in white said. Kam backed up, confused. "Kam please, it's me!" The Bliss in black said. "Kam, don't believe her! Look at me!" The Bliss in white exclaimed.

Kam stared at them both, not sure which one was being honest. His lips slightly parted as he studied them both; both with thick, dark, curly hair with violet tips. Fear was visible in their eyes. But Kam's gaze fell on the Bliss in white as her hands shook, her gun trained at the other Bliss's head. Kam's eyes widened with shock as he beheld the Bliss before him: with a single blink, one of her eyes had turned a dark, dirty yellow shade, before it shifted back. He had barely lifted his sword to strike when he was suddenly plucked from the ground and thrown aside, just as the sound of a gunshot echoed through the air.

| 23 |

Kam

Kam winced as a wave of pain shot through his back, a searing sensation, like a thick, sharp object prodding him, intensifying. He clenched his teeth and took a deep breath, summoning the strength to drag himself away from the mound of ash he lay on, his glowing sword still in his grasp.

He rose to his feet, eyes widening in shock at the scene before him. Real Bliss and herloid Bliss both laid motionless; it was uncertain if they were alive. A presence lurked behind him, and he swiftly spun around to see "Meeka" hurtling toward him, wielding a sword similar to his own. Kam leaped aside just in time, narrowly avoiding the strike aimed at the very pile of ashes he had been lying on.

Meeka's complexion suddenly went ashen, and his black military shirt transformed into a bare chest covered in yellow, serpentine scales. His head became bald, his face devoid of color, yet still human-like, except for the yellow scales from the neck down, dark yellow eyes, and razor-sharp teeth. Kam stepped back in awe, his imagination failing to grasp the menacing sight before him, far different from the pictures and illustrations he had seen in some of the Training Palace books.

The herloid charged at Kam, swords clashing as their fight began. The clinking of blades echoed in the night air. Suddenly, the herloid delivered a kick to Kam's groin, sending him tumbling to the ground, a cry of agony filling the night. His back throbbed with searing pain. The herloid exerted immense strength, pushing Kam's sword against his. Kam strained every muscle to resist. In a matter of seconds, the herloid had both blades poised at Kam's neck like a pair of scissors.

The sharp blades neared Kam's skin, and he teetered on the brink of defeat. With a surge of energy, he used his telekinetic power to send the herloid crashing into a charred wall, which collapsed into a heap. Gasping for air, Kam stood up, clutching his sword tightly. His eyes darted around, searching for his adversaries, but they were nowhere in sight. "You can't beat us, just let it happen," came the dark menacing voice from ahead. Kam felt his sword vibrate in his trembling hands.

Suddenly a fireball sped towards his head and, thinking quickly, he ducked at the last moment, tumbling into a blackened heap of wood. The heat of the blaze missed him by a hair's breadth and he scrambled upright, ready for the next attack. His gaze darted around, and when he spotted another fireball speeding towards him, he sprinted away, then dropped, rolled, and sprung up again.

"If you surrender the maps, I promise we'll spare you," a dark, menacing voice called out. Kam's initial fear turned to rage. He knew surrendering was not an option. "Sorry, but I'd prefer these to be in less lethal hands," Kam replied with determination.

"How about I play the screams of your loved ones as they take their last breaths? You can listen to it while you're dying of an agonizing and slow death," the voice threatened. Kam's throat tightened, but he maintained his composure. "We can do this the easy way..." Kam let out a frustrated shout and wildly swung his sword around, but he struck nothing but empty air. "Or the deadly way."

The final words sent chills down his spine. "That's sweet of you, but you underestimate how far I'll go to protect the ones I love," Kam retorted as he spun on his heel. The herloids chuckled, genuinely entertained by his defiance.

"Hand over the maps, or I'll bring your severed head to your girl-friend's doorstep," the voice taunted. Kam trembled at the thought, realizing Maxine was also in danger. He tried to control his quivering breath and asked, "How do you know about her?"

"Because she's expendable, just like your family. How would you like to lose another loved one because of your bad timing? Again." Kam's throat tightened further as he remembered the tragic incident from his past. He let out a scream of frustration and desperately swung his sword to his left, reliving the traumatic memory. He trembled, tears threatening to spill.

"If you want these maps, you'll have to take them from my dead hands!" Kam declared.

Suddenly, he felt a tight constriction around his throat. His sword clattered to the ground as his lungs burned from the lack of air. Desperate to free himself, he used his telekinetic power to push both himself and the herloid against a charred wall. They crashed to the ground with a thud, but the herloid held firm. "Your dead hands will certainly do!" The herloid exclaimed through gritted teeth. Kam's efforts were futile as darkness closed in around him. His muscles grew limp, and he slipped into unconsciousness.

The herloid that had been holding him let go with a satisfied smirk. The one in the guise of Ala approached Kam's unconscious form, joining her companion in a triumphant grin. "You look better when you're not breathing," the male herloid remarked, still wearing a menacing grin.

"His determination was admirable, but his strength was his downfall," the female herloid added. "Pathetic Axpherians. Our revenge against them is sure to come to pass," the male herloid said. They gazed at each other as the male herloid extended his arm to retrieve the maps and blueprints.

Kam's eyes widened in astonishment as he quickly raised his arm and tossed both herloids into the air. They crashed to the ground, their motionless forms painting an eerie picture on the debris-laden battlefield. Kam stood up breathlessly, clutching his neck, still feeling the ghost of the herloid's grip. He scanned the ground for his sword and, with a wave of his right hand, it levitated into his left palm.

A familiar presence behind him made him spin around. It was Bliss, panting but alive. She lifted her shirt to reveal a steel bulletproof vest beneath, a life-saving choice. Kam glanced back and saw the herloid that had been disguised as Bliss still lying on the ground, a dark pool of liquid surrounding it.

"Shot her point-blank in the head," Bliss said, her voice tinged with a mix of triumph and relief. Kam smirked. "I knew you were a good shot," Kam said. "Shut up. Of course I am," Bliss quipped as Kam shakingly chuckled. They both gazed ahead, searching for any signs of the other two herloids. Kam couldn't help but remark, "They had us fooled."

"They had you fooled," Bliss countered, a playful glint in her eyes as she eyed Kam.

He smiled back, his eyes darting across the debris-strewn battlefield. Suddenly, something in the corner of his eye caught his attention. He nodded to Bliss, a silent signal. Then, with a swift motion, he swung his sword with all his might.

The next sound he heard was a blood-curdling scream, and he felt a spray of black liquid next to him. The herloid materialized on the ground, writhing in agony, clutching the spot where its left forearm used to be. Kam and Bliss gaped at the sight, completely taken aback.

"While we're at it..." Bliss said as she aimed her weapon and fired behind her without looking.

Suddenly, the female herloid materialized, her head jerking back as a spray of black blood shot into the air. She dropped to the ground, her body going still as a puddle of dark liquid pooled beneath her. Her lifeless eyes stared blankly ahead, a few final twitches passing through her body before she drew her last breath.

"Now who has the dead hands?" Bliss said with a cocky grin.

Kam smirked at her, a mix of admiration and astonishment. "No one messes with our family," Bliss said, her voice filled with determination.

Kam then glanced over his shoulder at the male herloid. His cries had softened to a low moan, muffled by gritted teeth. Kam directed the sword at his face. "Tell me," he demanded, "who sent you?"

The herloid lifted his head, his face drained of color. "You and your pathetic family...," he groaned in pain. "Your pathetic army...they destroyed us all! Their story of what happened to us is a lie! And you haven't even destroyed a tenth of us! We will be everywhere. On every planet. Our species will reign over all the dimensions with an iron fist! And every world, including yours...will be ours! You, your families, Earth, and Axpherial...they're on the top of the kill list! You're too late!" The herloid groaned again as he pushed himself to finish, "We will have our revenge!"

He let out another yell as he eventually succumbed to his injuries, his body going limp. Kam and Bliss stared at each other, not knowing how to process this new information.

"Revenge?" Bliss asked, her gaze fixed on the ground. Kam scrutinized the herloid's corpse, a jumble of emotions coursing through him.

"That's the word I'm at a loss for, too," he responded. They both examined each other's faces, searching for answers in their shared gaze.

"Alright," Kam declared, determination in his voice. Bliss contorted her face in confusion. "What?" she asked.

Kam swallowed hard, his expression becoming more serious. "Let's tell our parents, get the army involved," Kam declared, his smirk broadening.

Bliss gave a faint grin, her eyes shining with agreement. "I guess even your pride has its limits," She said coyly.

"Don't push it," Kam replied, half serious as his smirk grew wider. "Two down, many to go," Bliss said. "I like those odds," Kam replied, his grin stretching from ear to ear.

He was still mulling over what the Herloid had said about revenge and the Axpherial government's possible deception. He was itching for answers, but now he knew for sure that their lives were truly at stake. Their parents had to believe them, or they might perish in much less time than they all believed they had.

| 24 |

Maxine

Maxine had just returned from a day of driving. The panic attacks that had plagued her throughout the day still lingered, though this time, she had managed to meditate with Ava for ten minutes before setting off. While the intensity of the panic attacks had been lessened, they were still very much alive. Perched on the edge of the bed, her face exuded a sense of defeat as she held a pink flower that Tobias had left on her pillow earlier.

The sweet, aromatic smell of the rose was comforting, and she appreciated the thought, however the disappointment was still there. He had yet to visit Georgette and seemed to actively avoid her. Was his apology and gift-giving, a mere facade, a way to avoid facing his trauma?

At that moment, a light knock sounded at the door. "Come in," she beckoned. The door swung open, and there stood Kincade. "How you feeling?" He asked. "Like I have the world on my shoulders," Maxine confessed, her face beaming with embarrassment as she gazed at the floor.

Kincade smiled as he sat in the corner of her bed, beside her. His gaze fell on the rose in her hands, and he couldn't help but smile knowingly. "Roses are red, well in this case, pink.." Maxine laughed as he continued, "violets are blue. Maning up is a bitch, so roses will do…"

Kincade and Maxine burst into laughter. "There, you see? Already feeling better!" he exclaimed as Maxine's laughter died down.

"But on a serious note, don't beat yourself up about today. You're progressing, and you've earned a few good pats on the back for that." Maxine grinned, though she was still berating herself for how she handled the car ride. However, she also knew her brother was right.

"You can't microwave your way out of grief, sis. Be patient with yourself, just like I'm patient with you. Even what's her face ummmm... Ava! Yeah, even her with her severe, undiagnosed Attention deficit disorder is patient with you." Maxine lightly chuckled, but took in his words.

Kincade was often quite the joker, but he had a knack for being wise beyond his years even when they were kids. Maxine was often impressed by how mature and perceptive he was underneath his more carefree, comical demeanor. "I'm glad you're finally facing your shadow self. We often demonize the shadow self as trauma, anger, and depression, but these things are really teachers and manifestations of the side of ourselves that we need to work on the most." Maxine nodded as he continued, "Society, the media, and even our loved ones program us from birth to run from it, but Only a true, strong person can face it and learn from it."

Maxine took in what her brother said. She nodded slowly, deep in thought. "Thank you," she said softly. She smiled at him, feeling an immense surge of gratitude. This exchange made her even more appreciative of him. "I still think I sucked royally today," Maxine said into a nervous laugh as Kincade chuckled himself. "Yeah, my hand is still trying to come alive from you cutting off my circulation, but hey, like I said, you're getting stronger," He said as he wrapped his arm around her shoulder.

Suddenly, Ava arrived at the door and gave it a light tap. "Max! And Peter Parker!" Ava exclaimed in a sarcastic tone. "Funny. What's up, Ava?" Kincade asked, unamused. "Your dad has a surprise for both of you," Ava said. In an instant, Maxine's emotions transitioned to unease and mild frustration. "What surprise?" she questioned.

"That's the point of a surprise, superwoman. You're not supposed to know until it's revealed." Maxine gazed downwards with no enthusiasm. Ava's expression immediately altered to one of worry. "Max, you okay, babe?" she inquired in a concerned tone. Maxine was unable to respond, her throat constricting and preventing any words from escaping. "Just give us a minute, okay?" Kincade asked. Ava smirked painfully as she left the room, defeated.

Maxine felt his offerings and presents were just a way of masking the fact that he was still running. "Is this really what I get instead of a hospital visit? Instead of an ear for once?" Maxine snapped, her voice laced with anger. Kincade looked down as he searched for words. "Max..."

"No! He thinks he can just buy his way out of visiting her?"

"Sis, I definitely agree, but...."

"Don't you dare make any excuses for him, Kincade!"

Maxine paced the room, eventually stopping and slumping against her dresser. Kincade remained on the bed, guilt weighing heavily on him. "It wasn't my intention to excuse the inexcusable. Because the way he keeps letting us down all these years made me resentful, too," Kincade said. Maxine gazed downward, her temper seemingly subsiding. "But for the sake of me gaining strength for myself, I couldn't keep holding a grudge. I know dad's emotional maturity is buried deep somewhere in that mess of a head he has," Kincade said as Maxine let out a soft laugh. He continued, "But at least give him a chance to try to make things right with you. No matter how corny or even pathetic his form of apology may be."

Maxine considered what he said and gave a nod in agreement. There was a newfound optimism that maybe, with his efforts to put things right, he could find the courage to take action, and confront his fears, just like she had done. Just maybe he'd be emotionally available for once and stop shutting them out. "Okay. You're right. I love him...." Maxine paused for a second before she finished, "But he's definitely pathetic. Pathetic until proven otherwise." Kincade grinned, a mischievous expression on his face. "I definitely second that," Kincade said as he and Maxine shared a laugh. "Alright, sis, see you downstairs, okay?" Kincade said as he stood up and approached the doorway. His gaze held hers for a moment, and she gave a timid smile. He returned the smile before he descended the stairs.

Maxine felt a peculiar, heavy feeling in her hands, a sensation she hadn't felt in years. As the feeling disappeared a loud crash startled her. She turned and saw a shattered mug on the floor. She examined her hands, then took in the broken glass. The sense of heaviness seemed to linger in her left hand this time, and she chose to go with it. When she swirled her index finger, the glass shards levitated and circled her head. First slowly, then as she sped up the swirling of her finger, the shards swarmed faster and faster until the heaviness in her hands was gone. The shards crashed back to the ground. Maxine scanned the room, ensuring nobody else had witnessed what had just occurred. She collected herself and went downstairs, bewildered at being able to do that. Again.

These occurrences appeared sporadically, and she never had full control. But when it did happen, it definitely amazed her. For instance, when she was only sixteen, she woke up to find herself sleeping on the ceiling. She screamed and dropped onto her bed. When her parents rushed in, she, of course, covered it up and put on a false, convincing smile to fool them. Typically, she could lift smaller things, but once in a while, she'd have an incident like the one on the ceiling. However, shortly after Imani died, her supernatural occurrences seemed to die down too.

****

Maxine descended the stairs and strolled into the kitchen, where the glass patio doors opened to the dining table. Her eyes widened as she took in the sight of yellow tents dotting the expansive backyard. The patio featured a stainless steel BBQ grill, a white sofa nestled before a fireplace, and two ceiling fans lazily spinning above. Nearby, two cozy armchairs encircled a small table, complete with a glass ashtray for smoking. The backyard, a vast 5500-square-foot square, cradled a grand oak tree in the far left corner, a jacuzzi in the opposite corner, and a trampoline positioned in between.

Two tents stood about five feet apart, and in their midst, four folding chairs awaited, two blue and two black. Seated in the blue chairs, Ava and Kincade roasted marshmallows on lengthy plastic sticks over a mini, crackling BBQ pit. Trap-style hip-hop music provided a rhythmic backdrop. A blue and white cooler rested near Kincade's chair, accompanied by a sizable blue plastic lunch bag.

Maxine's face lit up, although a lingering ember of anger toward Tobias simmered beneath her joy. Nonetheless, the camp setup delighted her; it had become an annual tradition to camp on this day, but amidst the chaos, she'd completely forgotten. It marked the first time they'd technically go camping without Georgette. She swung open the patio door and was greeted by the tantalizing aroma of sizzling hot dogs and hamburgers, causing her mouth to water.

"There she goes!" Kincade exclaimed as he spotted her. Maxine beamed, genuinely thrilled to see them. "Come indulge in adult activities with us!" Ava called out. Kincade playfully contorted his face, as if she'd said something vulgar. "Pause!" He exclaimed jokingly.

Ava extended her left hand, pinching her right fingers together as though holding something as tiny as an ant. "This is your mind," she said, alluding to her tightly clasped fingers. "This is the gutter," she added, gesturing with her palm. "Get your mind out of the gutter," she concluded, releasing her pinched fingers. "But it just sounded so wrong," Kincade said with a laugh.

Ava dramatically mimicked him, her lips moving to replicate his response. "It did sound a little wrong," Maxine said, her smile widening. "See? Case closed, Madame Hydra." Ava's face twisted in confusion. "Madame Hydra. Viper. Enemy of Captain America, X-Men, big villain in the Marvel universe? Not ringing any bells up there? Oh, I forgot, you have the attention span of a squirrel, no way you could get through a comic." "Ugh, stop, you're getting geek everywhere," Ava said, feigning the removal of something from her shoulders. Maxine let out a hearty chuckle, louder than expected. "You're not laughing at me, right?" Kincade asked, beaming. "Yes, she is!" Ava said with a laugh. "Yeah, if you and your ego say so," Kincade quipped.

"Hey, baby," Maxine heard from the side. It was Tobias, wearing a black apron, coming away from the grill. Maxine's grin immediately vanished. Tobias inched closer, offering her a painted smile that barely concealed his grief. Maxine despised that look, yet she didn't step away when he embraced her. She unconsciously hugged him back, disregarding the tension.

Although her feelings toward him remained unchanged, her unconditional love for him was undeniable. "Hey, dad," she said into his shoulder. He gently let go and put her forehead to his. She inhaled a blend of BBQ and fresh citrus cologne, a fragrance steeped in cherished memories. That cologne had accompanied so many moments of happiness, from her high school graduation to her first ninth-grade prom and, especially, her sophomore-year high school talent show. During that performance, she'd forgotten the last two lines, watching as Tobias mouthed the words from the audience. It led to an awkward pause, and she lost the first-place trophy she'd longed for.

Instead, it went to a stern-looking girl whose singing barely surpassed mediocrity, with several missed notes. Maxine sobbed backstage, feeling that the countless late nights spent perfecting her performance had been in vain. Her perfectionist tendencies haunted her. When she left the stage, she concealed her true emotions, knowing Tobias would simply wipe away her tears and just tell her she'd be okay and to toughen up, instead of listening to her. To lift her spirits, he'd taken her, Kincade, and Imani to Liby's soul food kitchen, her favorite restaurant. However, she still chastised herself, repeatedly memorizing her poem until it became second nature. She held herself to high standards and was unforgiving when she fell short.

Those memories highlighted how Tobias had always expressed his support through gift-giving. She wished that, instead of urging her to be tough, he'd offered a more empathetic ear, not teaching her to resent her vulnerability. She always appreciated the gifts, but they felt less sincerely heartfelt, causing a deep ache.

"I'm sorry, okay," Tobias whispered in a low tone. "I'll make it up to you, no matter how long it takes," he added as she stepped back. He gently caressed her cheek and brushed a few braids away from her face, tucking them neatly behind her ear. Maxine felt a familiar warmth, even as conflicting emotions waged war within her. She smiled shyly as Tobias placed a hand on her left shoulder.

"I know it's tough with Georgette not being here. Due to the quarantine, we can't venture to the great outdoors this time, but I hope this will suffice," Tobias said, his voice quivering. "This is great, dad," Maxine said, attempting to conceal any bitterness with a gracious display of appreciation. "It's the least I can do for you. All I hope is that we can work through this together," Tobias said. "Me too," Maxine replied. A moment of awkwardness hung in the air between them, while Ava and Kincade engaged in an amusing conversation in the background. Their words were mostly inaudible to Tobias and Maxine, who continued to gaze at each other, yearning to break the silence but unsure how to do so.

They both burst into laughter at a joke Kincade made, diffusing the tension. "I'm gonna finish cooking. You should rejoin them, I'll be over shortly," Tobias suggested. Maxine gave a silent nod as Tobias tapped her cheek before returning to the grill. She glanced up at Kincade and Ava, her smile returning as Ava motioned to the spot beside her. Maxine grabbed a marshmallow-laden stick, took a seat, and joined them in toasting marshmallows by the campfire.

"Hey, remember when we went camping last year, and Kincade fell out of the boat while we were rafting?" Ava said as she and Maxine chuckled. "Yeah, because drowning is such an exhilarating festivity," Kincade said, half seriously. "He was like, oh my god! Oh my god!" Ava mockingly imitated, prompting Maxine to crack up.

Kincade rolled his eyes, clearly unamused. As a child, he'd never held much enthusiasm for water. Whenever there was a pool party, for instance, he'd find an excuse to avoid it, citing concerns about his hair, homework, or simply being too cool to swim. He'd managed to overcome his fear about a few months ago, but some reservations still lingered when it came to bodies of water.

Ava glanced at him, noting his lack of amusement, which only fueled her laughter. "Come on, that water was as shallow as a rain puddle," Ava said. Kincade silently mimicked her, continuing to roast his marshmallow. "Rafting isn't exactly my cup of half-sweetened green tea, but I digress," Kincade said. "Aww, do I see some tears?" Ava taunted in a mocking tone, provoking another bout of laughter. Maxine chuckled lightly, though she was starting to feel sympathy for him.

Kincade took a deep breath, gripping the arms of his chair as he prepared to leave. "Well, if you'll excuse me," he said, rising to his feet, "I'm gonna go get high." With that, he headed off to the far corner of the yard, in the direction of the oak tree. "He's so gonna cry in the tent," Ava predicted. Maxine gently nudged Ava, barely suppressing her amusement. "What?" Ava asked. "He's man enough to take my insults with pride," she replied with a shrug, as she picked up a s'more from the stick, her marshmallow now slightly charred. "I can't with you," Maxine said with a laugh. "But you love me anyway," Ava quipped as she took a bite of her s'more.

****
******

Maxine awoke the following morning with a sensation of weightlessness. A sharp, wooden point dug into her back, and with a sense of curiosity mixed with disbelief, she slowly unzipped her tent and peered outside. Her eyes widened as she realized she was perched high up in a tree.

The ground lay several feet below her, and the vivid memory of her dream from the previous night rushed back. In that dream, she had crawled out of her tent and soared into the sky. Now, as she gazed down from her unusual vantage point, she couldn't deny that it wasn't just a dream. Her extraordinary abilities had finally surfaced.

Kam's words about her unique DNA echoed in her mind as she gingerly stepped out of her tent. Her movements were uncertain, and she partially stumbled, her hands reaching out to grasp a stout tree limb. She found herself dangling in the air, teetering on the edge of a precipitous fall. Panic surged, and her grip slowly weakened.

Desperation set in, but Maxine remembered the breath control techniques Kam had taught her and the meditation methods Ava had imparted. She closed her eyes, attempting to regain control. Over and over, she repeated the process, her breathing slowing, and her body descending gradually. Mindful of her thoughts, she continued to breathe, feeling a strange sensation of lightness as her feet touched the ground. She opened her eyes, exhaling a sigh of relief, grateful to have landed safely.

Suddenly, her gaze was drawn upward, and a shiver ran down her spine. Something among the branches caught her attention. As she squinted to get a better look, she made out two eerie, yellow eyes staring back at her. The figure's massive shape remained shrouded in darkness, intensifying her fear. Instinctively, she began to back away, only to collide with Kincade, causing her to scream in terror.

"Max, it's just me! What's going on?" Kincade asked, gripping her shoulders tightly. Maxine's wide-eyed gaze shifted upward to the tree, but the mysterious figure had vanished. Kincade noticed the dark circles under her eyes and voiced his concern. "Did you sleep?"

"I think it was more like sleepwalk," Maxine replied, trying to assure him with a nervous smile.

Kincade embraced Maxine, and she returned the hug, thankful that he didn't press the issue further. After releasing her, Kincade gave a faint smirk, and Maxine responded with a mixture of relief and amusement. "Dad cooked swine and stale eggs on the campfire. Want some?" he offered.

Maxine chuckled, her mood lightening. "Sounds appetizing," she replied, and Kincade slung his arm around her shoulders as they walked together. "Let's go and clog our arteries together then," he quipped, prompting another laugh from Maxine. Her gaze briefly returned to the tree, her thoughts still lingering on the mysterious figure. "Could it have been my imagination? Or was it an animal?" she wondered silently before turning her attention back to the campsite, her mind filled with questions and a sense of unease.

| 25 |

Kam

"Is it still possible to change my mind?" Kam asked, his frustration evident. He lay on his bed, his gaze fixed on the ceiling, filled with anxiety. In the room, Bliss perched on a wooden chair, facing him.

"We have to tell them, big bro. Especially after what happened." Bliss paused, her conviction unwavering.

"I know," Kam admitted with a deep sigh of exasperation, his thoughts lingering on the events of the past week.

"I just wish this whole confession thing wasn't as dreadful as it is," Kam muttered. "Confessing to another so-called antic just to be scolded, it's the story of my life."

Bliss sensed Kam's reluctance and redirected the conversation. "Look, if you don't tell them anything... this isn't just about you or us anymore. It's about two planets potentially being vaporized into extinction if we keep this between us," Bliss asserted, her voice tinged with concern.

"My stomach is doing backflips right now," Kam confessed, his nervousness growing with the weight of their secret.

"Mine too. But we're in this too deep to seek other options. We've exhausted the whole 'do it ourselves' thing, at least for now," Bliss said reassuringly.

Kam let out a nervous huff and asked, "Are you sure there isn't another option?"

Bliss tried to ease Kam's anxiety with a smile. "I mean... we could die," she said with a shared laugh, trying to lighten the mood.

"That sounds like heaven compared to this," Kam replied, sitting up on the bed. He clasped his hands together and examined them nervously. "I feel like I'm walking into my execution, sis."

Bliss offered a comforting embrace, reminding him, "Add 'we' to that, and that'll be accurate." Kam managed a tiny smirk, finding solace in the fact that he wasn't facing this ordeal alone.

"Hey, we both had everything to do with this. But if we tell them that our antics this time were for the greater good, maybe, just maybe, we'll live," Bliss reassured him.

As they prepared to leave the room and reveal their secrets to their parents, Kam and Bliss exchanged glances, a mixture of fear and determination in their eyes. "Ready?" Bliss asked.

"Nope," Kam admitted with a nervous laugh. Bliss gave him a comforting smile, taking his hand, and together they ventured out the door. They moved slowly down the hallway, their footsteps echoing their trepidation.

When they arrived at their parents' room, they stood outside, both too nervous to knock. An awkward silence hung in the air as they waited for the other to make the first move. "Psst. What are you waiting for?" Bliss whispered.

"I would ask the same of you!" Kam retorted, his nerves palpable.

Facing the door once more, they both took deep breaths, trying to summon the courage to proceed. "Suddenly I feel like I'm gonna pass out," Kam confessed, his anxiety reaching a crescendo.

Bliss rolled her eyes but raised her fist towards the door. Kam hesitated, feeling paralyzed. "Kam, if you don't do this... remember what's at stake."

"I know what's at stake. I'm just..." Kam searched for words but came up empty.

Taking a deep breath, Kam raised his fist hesitantly to knock. Just as he was about to make contact, Meeka flung the door open, his appearance suggesting he had not slept all night. Both Kam and Bliss were startled and jolted backward in unison.

"Why are you guys whispering so loudly by the door?" Meeka asked with an intense stare, adding to their unease.

Bliss and Kam exchanged nervous glances, then shifted their gaze to Meeka. "We, umm... we..."

"What's going on out there?" Ala's voice came from behind Meeka, interrupting Bliss's faltering explanation.

The siblings stood in silence, feeling the tension in the air. Kam nervously tried to stifle his pounding heart. "We've got a few things we need to tell you," Kam finally managed to say.

"Need?" Meeka asked, raising an eyebrow.

"And you may not like how I got this information," Kam admitted, his anxiety mounting.

Meeka scrutinized him, his expression betraying his skepticism. Ala, on the other hand, wore a worried expression, eager to have her confusion resolved.

Meeka gestured for them to enter the room. "Get in," he ordered, his tone unwavering. Bliss and Kam hesitantly complied, stepping into their parents' room.

Bliss trailed Kam as they walked further into the room. Both moved as if their legs weighed a ton each. The room was vast, with polished wooden floors and walls adorned with ADA accolades and family photos displayed on holographic screens. In one corner, a large bed suitable for three people stood against a headboard. On one wall, a massive holographic screen displayed equations and a blueprint of a weapon resembling a double-barreled shotgun.

Kam and Bliss stood by the door, their parents a few feet away. Meeka had his arms crossed, waiting for an explanation. Ala appeared concerned, her hands clasped tightly behind her back.

As Bliss and Kam scanned the room, they couldn't help but feel like they were searching for an escape route. "You obviously wanted something, so I'll give you both the floor," Meeka finally said, his deep, intimidating tone filling the room.

Kam took a deep breath, gathering his courage. "We're being targeted." Meeka's and Ala's faces immediately contorted, the gravity of the statement sinking in.

"No, Dad, hear us out. We were attacked by..." Bliss glanced at Kam, seeking reassurance. Kam gave a slight nod, urging her to continue. "We were attacked by..." Bliss struggled to finish.

"Herloids," Kam interjected, completing her sentence. Meeka's anger flared. "By what?" he demanded, his voice rising.

"They torched the Earth house. I received a distress signal. They showed up looking exactly like you," Kam explained, his voice quivering as he recounted the chilling details. He bit his cheek so hard he tasted blood.

"And they left a very... sweet message, written in bold red letters," Bliss added.

"Sweet?" Ala questioned.

"Come on, Mom, you and I both know what 'sweet' really means," Bliss replied. Meeka continued to gaze at them suspiciously, not entirely convinced.

"How did you two get access to Earth through the Delfona block?" Ala asked, her tone stern.

Kam looked down, apprehension surging through his veins. He then confessed about the cloned government Delfona, the cure he found in the files, the maps, and other details, including his battle with the Herloids and the message written on the ground.

"So, you two not only stole government property but also dug an even deeper hole for yourselves. You broke into the Earth house, accessed classified documents, and now you want to fabricate an attack? The Herloids are long extinct. Some of their technology, however, was stolen. And..." Meeka's voice trailed off.

Kam grew suspicious. "I get the feeling that I'm not the one fabricating something here."

Meeka's face contorted, his anger escalating. "What has gotten into you? You went out of your way once again to defy me and your mother, and you have the audacity to talk to me in such a condescending manner?"

"Dad, I saw the notes. I think you know a lot more than you and Mom let on. I know what the Herloids are trying to do. And I know that you and Mom know too. When they attacked, they mentioned maps. Maps to the bases."

"And that information should have been none of your business to explore," Ala interjected.

"Mom, I was attacked twice, and neither of you seemed to take it seriously. I just want you to trust me this time. Just let me show you what they did and why you should act fast before Earth and Axpherial are destroyed!" Kam exclaimed, his voice filled with desperation and anger. Meeka remained unconvinced, even as Kam held back tears, visibly distraught.

"Show me," Meeka finally said.

****

A shimmering blue and white portal materialized beneath the single streetlight outside the earth house. The atmosphere was dreary, the sky overcast, and the rain threatened to pour down in bundles. Kam, Meeka, Bliss, and Ala emerged from the portal one by one. In an instant, the portal shrank and vanished behind them. Kam and Bliss exchanged dismayed glances as they took in the sight. The earth house stood in pristine condition, as if untouched. The ground beneath their feet was plain dirt and gravel, devoid of any trace of the message that had previously marred it.

"No," Kam muttered under his breath. Meeka seethed with anger as he gazed at the house. Ala wore a similarly distressed expression, noticing that everything appeared exactly as they had left it. "No, No! They burned it down! I was there!" Kam cried out with desperation in his voice. Meeka's eyes narrowed as he regarded Kam with suspicion. "Do you take pleasure in deceiving us?" he hissed. Kam shook his head in dismay, his face etched with despair. "No! I swear I wouldn't lie about something like that!"

"He wouldn't. I have the footage to prove it," Bliss interjected, her fingers deftly working her delfona. A holographic projection emerged, replaying footage from the camera above the streetlight. As she fast-forwarded to the night of the attack, the footage showed the house untouched and serene. She anxiously scanned the recording but found nothing to substantiate their claims.

"So, both of you thought that by making it seem like you had a valid excuse to return to Earth, you could indulge your curiosity, steal government files, and assume that by acting convincingly, we would be fooled into accepting anecdotal information without evidence?" Meeka questioned, his tone heavy with skepticism.

Kam and Bliss opened their mouths to defend themselves, but Bliss spoke first. "Dad, you know better than anyone how intelligent the herloids are. You understand their ability to manipulate technology. You have to trust us. I witnessed it with my own eyes, and they even shot me." Bliss pointed to a brown, circular bruise on her left shoulder, revealed after she pulled down her shirt.

Meeka examined her scar closely, his eyes betraying his inner turmoil. He ran his thumb gently over her scar, but still doubt lingered. He surveyed both of them, noticing the earnest expressions of concern on their faces. It perplexed him, as their looks seemed to suggest they were telling the truth. However, lacking any solid evidence, he chose to reject the information they provided.

"Both of you will return to Axpherial immediately. Surrender the cloned delfona, and do not set foot here until we complete our mission. Is that clear?" Meeka's voice dripped with stern authority.

Kam inhaled deeply and reluctantly handed the cloned delfona to Meeka. "Understood. You've already caused enough chaos. Stay put, or you'll regret it," Meeka warned with an undertone of menace.

Bliss and Kam felt their thoughts constrict as they heeded his warning. They fully grasped the gravity of the situation. Meeka opened a shimmering, multicolored portal resembling Axpherial. Without a word, they all stepped through. Kam realized that Meeka now held the sole means of reaching Earth, and he had no idea how he would return. But he knew that time was running out. Just as the portal closed, the earth house rippled like a giant holographic screen. In an instant, it vanished, revealing only charred remains in its place. The herloids' plan had been executed flawlessly.

| 26 |

Maxine

Maxine, Kincade, and Ava embarked on their journey to the hospital to visit Georgette. Kincade assumed the driver's seat, Maxine occupied the passenger's seat, and Ava perched herself carelessly in the middle of the backseat, forgoing the seatbelt.

Maxine and Ava had engaged in a thirty-minute meditation session that morning, part of their daily routine for the past two weeks. It had gradually lessened Maxine's anxiety during car rides, although she still experienced occasional panic attacks. Maxine leaned back in her seat, her eyes closed, basking in the warmth of the mid-afternoon breeze. The sky was clear, not a single cloud in sight. But her thoughts weren't on the car; they were consumed by those eyes—the pair of dark, yellow eyes with their distinct squared pupils that had fixated on her so intently that day in the tree.

Lately, she'd been plagued by terrible nightmares. In one, enormous black birds with hawk-like features and those ominous yellow eyes pecked relentlessly at her flesh, inflicting deep, gaping wounds that bled profusely. Another featured an anaconda, also with those same haunting eyes, coiling around her and squeezing the air from her lungs until she was on the brink of suffocation. Every time she awoke, it was with a sharp gasp and a sense of lingering dread. The nightmares had become so unbearable that she had resorted to over-the-counter caffeine pills and energy drinks. However, they only succeeded in keeping her up partly, only for her to drift off into another nightmare. Even when she did sleep, the nightmares seemed to stretch on endlessly. Eventually, she decided to flush the remaining pills down the toilet.

But the night before, she had a different dream—a vision of Imani. Imani was painting a mural on the walls of Maxine's room, transforming the previously bare walls into a vibrant depiction of her and Kam, hand in hand, clothed in white, standing in the same field from Kam's dream. Yet, the joyful hazel and violet eyes gradually morphed into the same lifeless yellow of the herloids. Maxine watched helplessly as the faces in the painting began to bleed, cracks splitting open in the walls at an unsettling speed. Imani grabbed her hand, and together they passed through the wall just before it exploded, drenching the room in a terrifying flood of blood. As they soared into the night sky, the fear that initially gripped Maxine gave way to an inexplicable serenity.

When she awoke, it wasn't with a scream but with a smile. She interpreted the dream as a sign of moving beyond her trauma, a symbol of moving forward. Still, those piercing eyes from the painting haunted her thoughts as she tried to relax in the car.

Meanwhile, Kincade and Ava carried on with their casual conversation. Maxine, however, remained so deeply immersed in her thoughts that she was oblivious to their chatter.

"Max, hello!?" Ava's voice cut through Maxine's reverie.

Maxine startled, snapping back to reality. "I said, do you want some Darla's?"

Maxine's mouth instantly watered at the thought. She hadn't realized how hungry she was. "Darla's sounds amazing," Maxine replied.

Ava couldn't contain her triumph. "Ha! Two to one, I win!" she declared, sticking her tongue out victoriously.

Kincade chuckled, adopting a smug expression. "Well, it's my hands on the steering wheel, and this isn't a democracy."

Ava retorted with a grin, "According to geography, we're in the United States, bozo."

Kincade laughed heartily at her witty response. "You call the mountain-sized walls and death camps free? More like land of the misled, and home of the enslaved."

"Hilarious. Anyway, you know the rules, majority wins," Ava insisted.

Kincade, playfully sulking, remarked, "This is North Korea. And as supreme leader, I officially devalue your input on said eating establishment."

Maxine couldn't help but smile as she stifled a giggle with her fist. Ava slumped back into her seat, crossing her arms, and adopted a feigned look of sadness, as if conceding defeat. "I was kidding, pouty face," Kincade said, and Ava quickly resumed her triumphant smirk.

"Spoiled ass," Kincade teased.

"Drug addict," Ava shot back.

"Oooh, I got chills! Did you get chills, Max?" Kincade asked with a sly grin.

Maxine nodded, bursting into laughter. "I'm with Ava this time; how dare you sleep on Darla's?"

"Their burgers are mid, their fries taste like they added a few cups of high blood pressure and a pinch of heart disease, and they have limited drink options. The ones they do have are filled with high fructose, and fructose makes sugar look like alkaline water."

"Shut up!" Maxine and Ava exclaimed in unison.

Kincade smirked mischievously. "Sure, shut me up when I'm spitting facts."

"Yes, we are definitely shutting you up," Maxine said with a grin as she and Ava shared another bout of laughter.

Kincade, grinning, couldn't help but join in. For that moment, Maxine pushed her nightmares and trauma to the back of her mind and savored the warmth of the camaraderie around her. She had unwavering faith that they would never abandon her—a sentiment she deeply cherished.

****
*****

Maxine walked into Georgette's room, clutching a crumpled white bag. On it, in an orange graffiti-style font with a red outline, was written with the name: Darla's. "I got you something, Ma. Your favorite!" Maxine exclaimed as she handed her the bag. "Twelve piece nugget and a small fry," Maxine said as Georgette beamed and sifted through the bag. "Thank you, baby! That hospital food is wearing me out," Georgette said, sounding more than relieved for the meal. Maxine smiled warmly as she watched Georgette slowly take a bite out of a nugget.

Georgette's eyes rolled back as she savored the tender nugget in her mouth. "It's like a long-lost friend," She said with a mouthful as she quickly took another bite. Kincade and Ava entered, Kincade clutching a bouquet of red roses. Ava sipped from a white cup with the Darla's logo on it, and they both beamed at Georgette, who returned the smile. "I got the most clichè gift I could give, but I know your uncanny obsession with red, so I said, why not," Kincade said as he handed Georgette the flowers.

Georgette smiled as she inhaled the scent of the flowers deeply, and then carefully placed them on the tray next to her bed. "I love them, Kincade," She said as she smiled. "You look great, Mrs. Hewitt," Ava said. "Thank you, sweetheart. How's your parents?" Ava made a casual side nod. "They hate me. But I figured." Georgette made a sad face like this troubled her. "Don't sweat it, I'm not quite head over heels for them, either." Georgette still looked concerned.

Ava grew up with a not-so-easy mom to deal with, and her dad was an abusive alcoholic. Her mom was on almost every drug under the sun, and would tell Ava often that she was the reason she never went back to nursing school. Truth was, she got arrested for drug possession and lost grant funding, forcing her to drop out. She discovered she was pregnant with Ava just a few weeks later. As Ava grew up, she received lots of unnecessary beatings for the simplest of things. Lots of strict rules, like being in before the streetlights turned on. Even on weekends and even when she was in her late teens. She'd be beaten, verbally abused, and called everything but her name. It made matters even worse when her parents found out she was bisexual. They found out by going through her text messages one day when she was in the shower. They then beat her with a slipper so bad that a bloodied Ava took the bus to Maxine's house, where she never left.

Georgette could relate, as she had a similar past. Her mom was abusive towards her and her siblings. She ran away and lived with her grandmother, who fully supported her modeling dreams. She was a pageant princess, winning many of them with her naturally long hair and smooth brown complexion. She then began print modeling, and met Tobias at a shoot when she was 20. Her mom died from a stroke that year, and she still attended the funeral. She still found it in her heart to forgive her, despite the trauma she inflicted still lingering.

"Anyway, Maxine has been riding in the car every day for the past week," Kincade said as he attempted to shift the conversation away from Ava. Georgette arched an eyebrow, impressed. "Yeah, we finally took the birthday car for a spin. Well, a few spins, as you heard. I think I'm starting to genuinely heal, ma," Maxine said excitedly. Georgette gave a proud smile. "Okay, girl! Look at you flying past your fears like I knew she would!" Georgette exclaimed as Maxine shyly chuckled. "I always had an undying faith in you. No matter what, I was always your cheerleader."

"So am I!" Maxine heard from behind her. The voice was too familiar. Like it was…. "Dad!?" Maxine called out. There he was, standing tall against the doorframe. The top of the frame just a few inches above his head. Everyone's eyes planted on him. Everyone's jaw to the floor. "Dad? Oh my god!" Maxine exclaimed as she wrapped her arms around him. Maxine held him tightly as a tear rolled down his cheek. Kincade followed suit, and soon Ava too. The three of them stayed embraced, their tears mingling. Maxine wanted reassurance from him that he was truly remorseful and making an effort to turn things around, and he finally did in the most meaningful way.

She felt she finally had the best version of Tobias thus far. It took all of them a minute to let go, and when they did, he wiped the tears from each of their faces, then his own. He went over to Georgette and they shared a similar embrace as Tobias apologized over and over again in her ear. Maxine, Kincade, and Ava continued wiping their tears of joy as they watched them reunite. Maxine in particular, was so happy that he was finally showing the progress she and Kincade longed for.

After releasing Georgette and exchanging a few words, Tobias rose and beckoned Maxine to accompany him outside. Standing in the hall, they looked at each other for a few moments, until Tobias mustered up the courage to speak. "I know you heard me apologize so many times, but I can't help myself. I abandoned you on more than one occasion. I abandoned my wife, my kids, and myself for so long. And nothing kills me more than for my own daughter to resent me," He said as he slouched against the wall in front of Maxine and gazed downward. His hands tucked stiffly in his pockets. "Dad, what counts is your effort. It killed me, too. Every time we'd be in the same room, the elephant was obvious. And the tension was most definitely suffocating," Maxine admitted.

"But I knew you loved me. And I knew I loved you. But I also wanted you to stop with the baseless apologies and trying to use gifts to excuse yourself from putting in real effort to make things right." Tobias nodded, not disagreeing with anything she said. "Your attempts at apologizing were appreciated, but felt disingenuous, with the whole backyard camp thing or the random pink rose on my bed the other day. I want you to be more emotionally present in my life, and stop expecting us to be so tough all the time and shutting down when you can't handle things." Tobias gazed at his shoes, feeling his grief take hold of him as he took in what she said.

"But this is worth so much more than all of those gifts you gave me. I mean like, so much more, dad," Maxine smiled as Tobias returned a painful grin. "I'm glad you at least acknowledge my efforts," Tobias said. "Just know that I'll be more of an ear, I promise to be more vulnerable with you guys, and I promise that there was nothing disingenuous about those gifts I gave you. I never want to make you feel like that again," Tobias assured. "As long as things like this stay consistent, our relationship can continue to repair itself," Maxine said.

Tobias agreed with her as he sniffed away tears welling in his eyes. "It's a vow I'm willing to commit to wholeheartedly," He said as he looked up at her, observing her grin, no longer seeing tears in her eyes. He added, "Seeing you, driving around in the car did something to me. I see you tremble and I see you trying to fight off all the anxiety that had harbored inside you for so long. And I saw myself, except you were putting in effort, and I wasn't." Maxine kept grinning as she listened, doing her utmost to prevent her tears from returning.

"You inspired me to get rid of my own demons. Right now, my heart is pounding so hard, and my hands are in my pockets because they won't stop shaking, and I'm most definitely a mess everywhere else," He said into a nervous chuckle as he continued, "But I'm still here, and I have you to thank for that, baby girl." He wiped away another tear and tried to force a smile. Maxine smiled, genuinely proud of him. "No, dad. You have you to thank for that," Maxine beamed. "I might have given the push, but you were the one who decided to man up and be here. You decided that you wanted to be there for me again. And you gotta give yourself cred, dad," Maxine said as she wiped a tear that fell automatically from her left eye.

Tobias nodded, his tears still wet on his cheeks. He and Maxine hugged tightly, Maxine pressing her head to his chest. For a moment they stayed like that, neither wanting to let go. Finally, they stepped back. "I love you so much," He said as he wiped his tears and gently held on to her shoulders. "I love you, too," Maxine said as she smiled at him.

They both composed themselves before entering the room again to rejoin the others. They enjoyed the time spent together, filled with laughter, unity, and prayer. The atmosphere in the room was so vibrant that it could be sensed from hundreds of miles away. They encircled one another, conversing and making plans for when Georgette would be released from the hospital. Maxine, however, would periodically drift off into her own thoughts, pondering the unanswered questions that had been plaguing her lately - the Anomaly test, Kam, and the mysterious yellow eyes. Answers were about to be revealed, though they would come much sooner than she anticipated.

| 27 |

Kam

"Okay, let's see if operation revolving door is a hit again," Bliss announced. Kam, Bliss, Talo, and Orna were in Kam's cabin basement. They had been experimenting with different formulas on the computer to craft a delfona that would bypass the Axpherian government's block. Additionally, they were honing their fighting skills in the basement. Talo had become exceptional with guns, whereas Orna initially struggled with the weapons but eventually found his strength with the small axes, whose blades emitted a faint blue light and were sharp enough to cut through even the toughest of concrete.

Their attempts at hacking through the government block had so far proved futile. Every time they thought they were at the finish line, something was always just a little off. Last time, Bliss accidentally opened a portal to a planet in the Somber realm. The world exhibited exotic creatures that were twice the size of dinosaurs. Thankfully, that portal closed quickly.

Bliss began to pass the delfona to Talo, who tested it the most. Her pride couldn't help itself. "Wait! I think I can do it this time!" Orna exclaimed right before Bliss could place it in Talo's hand. Everyone gazed at him like they wished he was joking. "You're not serious, are you?" Talo asked. Orna nodded his head. He was serious. "I promise,

I've been practicing." "You need about another eternity's worth of practice," Talo replied. Orna stopped in his tracks, defeated.

"Let me try it," Kam said calmly. Talo grinned, pleased, and remarked, "That's more like it." Orna mimicked with a smirk, "That's more like it, mehhh." Talo rolled her eyes in her usual expression of annoyance, but Orna just grinned in satisfaction. "Here, Kam. And you two!" Bliss said as she pointed her eyes at Talo and Orna, "Stop flirting! It's giving me a headache." Talo stuck out her tongue like she was disgusted. Orna just laughed, he nor Talo had any type of romantic chemistry towards each other. In fact, they were both repulsed at the thought of it.

"Okay, hopefully this is the climax. Hopefully," Kam declared, stepping forward and training his delfona on the wall between the wooden tables. Kam shut his eyes and focused intently. A brilliant light shot from his delfona, and a portal materialized before him, casting a violet radiance over the basement. Kam opened his eyes to see the light violet portal before him, disappointed. "That's Arome, an anarchy dimensional planet in the Orecka galaxy. The planet is a lifeless gas giant floating around a red dwarf. Epic fail," Kam said as the portal dissolved.

Kam hung his head, anxious that they wouldn't succeed. It wasn't something he often pondered, as he was known to have an exceptional fighting spirit. "I'll keep working at it. Don't sweat it, big bro," Bliss said as she gently took the delfona from his hand. "Hey! This is just a little setback. We haven't tried every formula yet. We're just one more try away," Bliss assured as Kam gazed at her and gave a disappointing nod.

"I promise the second we get access, we'll let you guys know," Bliss said to Talo and Orna. "I don't know, Bliss. It's looking kinda bleak if you ask me," Orna said. "It may seem bleak, but I have enough faith in my sister that we'll get it right," Kam said. "You don't seem very confident in your statement," Talo said, examining the lack of faith painted on his face. "Yeah, it's like your words say one thing, but your eyes say defeat," Orna said. Kam had all but lost hope, their words proving to be true. The look of despair was evident on his face, and he did a terrible job at hiding it.

"Say it like you're actually convinced. And you'll convince us," Talo added. "Well, I'm convinced. And I'm convinced that one of these formulas on my unusually long list will breeze through this little hurdle," she quipped, her tone dripping with sarcasm. "Also, I need to tell you guys about something the herloid said to me when we were attacked," Kam said, changing the subject. Talo and Orna's eyes lit up with curiosity. "They said something about how the Axpherial government killed them. About them lying to us about their history. It rang a few alarms, to say the least."

Bliss cast a glance at Kam, unsure if she desired for him to share this information with them at the moment. "Sounds like glorified manipulation tactics at hand," Talo said. "Manipulation?" Bliss inquired, seeking clarification. "What makes you think they weren't?" Talo replied. "It was one of the last words one of them said before they bled out," Kam said. "Bled out?" Orna asked as he raised an eyebrow. "I decapitated his arm." "Ouch!" Orna cringed. "Their camouflage disguise had a solid flaw. I could still see their body movements, although I did have to look very carefully," Kam said. "Hmm, not really buying the whole dying confession thing. My own alarms are going off, to be honest," Talo said as she rolled her eyes. She added, "They thought by including that in their last breaths that you'd have no choice but to soak it up."

"You bring up a good argument, but I didn't quite read deception from them. I think we need to investigate their claim further before we just write it off too hastily," Kam said. Everyone nodded in agreement, but Talo remained fixated on her suspicion.

✳✳
✳✳✳✳✳✳✳✳✳✳✳✳✳✳

The following day, Kam was back at his usual spot. His gaze was fixed on the flow of the waterfall. He perched atop the violet grass that stretched before the glossy black rocks that sloped into the glimmering river below. He was wearing his swimming trunks and was thoroughly drenched, having already plunged into the water and swam a few times. His thoughts were like the river, rapidly coursing and chaotic in their flow.

Maxine and he were able to connect earlier, but she didn't tell him about the strange yellow eyes - something she was still questioning the reality of. Keeping things from the people she trusted the most was a bad habit of hers. She did, however, let him know how her progression in the car was going, how she and Tobias were slowly mending their relationship, and of course told Kam how much she missed him.

In turn, he updated her on his progress in getting back to Earth, and they discussed potential dates, things that happened during their days, and more. Hours went by in the blink of an eye, as usual, but certain topics - the ones concerning the dangers that laid ahead of them - were left unspoken, as they would rather discuss them in person.

They craved for each other so much, although there were times Kam would ignore her calls or avoid calling her altogether. He was still imprisoned in his intimacy anxiety. He was however, opening up more, although the Ferris wheel dreams still reoccurred. Thankfully not every night, but around two times a week on average. It switched between Zina and Maxine, but Kam found himself being able to go back to sleep easier without waking Bliss.

But last night, he had a nightmare that he saw Maxine trapped in the Ferris wheel with a herloid who had her by the throat. When he tried to rescue her, the car burst into flames. He awoke with a loud grunt, his body drenched in sweat. He still feared that his relationship with her would end in her demise. Despite this, he still made a strong effort to try to keep building an intimate relationship with her. He found himself helplessly captivated, unable to deny the strong feelings stirring inside him. He was scared to accept it, but he was truly falling in love.

"A lot on your mind?" He heard from behind. He jolted and looked up to see Talo with a lime green shirt that covered just her chest and loose black pants. Her warm brown skin glimmered in the early after-noon sun, her hair in two long braided pigtails. Kam just nodded as he looked down. "A lot on mine, too," She said as she sat down next to him. They paused and sat in silence for a few seconds, until Kam finally spoke up, "Is there something wrong with a hero complex?"

Talo squinted, perplexed by the suddenness of the question. "Depends on how said person handles such a complex," She replied. "I just want peace. Not just for me or for those close to me. But peace and safety for everyone, even if that means my own demise." Talo processed this, she shivered a bit at the word demise. "I want peace, too. But logically, not everyone is peaceful or has great intentions. Not by a long shot." Kam nodded as he listened. "But you," Talo said into a small laugh before she continued, "You want to be thee hero sometimes. And you have the tendency to volunteer the load of the world, and you always want to try to clear a war by yourself. But sometimes the enemy has the winning hand without your own army behind you." Kam smirked at this, her advice hit him deep. "Yeah, it's definitely a curse and gift. But I still wouldn't trade it for the world," Kam admitted.

Kam suddenly fixed his gaze upon Talo, as if he were trying to read her mind through her eyes. Talo raised an eyebrow in apprehension, feeling invaded. "What?" "You have a complex, too." Kam smirked. Talo rolled her eyes in exasperation. She was well aware of what he was referring to. "My need to compete is just a manifestation of my perfectionism," Talo said. "Why aim for perfection? I haven't met a perfect person yet. Except you," Kam said as he and Talo shared a laugh. "I just expect the best from myself. My parents are always quick to bring up my older brother. They make it seem like he's the epitome of godhood. I grew up competing with someone who I could never beat. So I guess part of it stems from that. But I think it's both a nature and nurture thing," Talo said as her eyes wandered through the soft, shallow grass.

She was right. Her brother was quite the overachiever. Always excelling in training, sports, and even mastered his abilities at twice the rate as Talo's. They both competed in Maka: A sport where a colorful beam was shot into the sky, and whoever brought back their beam first won. Her brother always won, which irked Talo. She was then determined to dedicate her time to acquiring as much knowledge as her brain could hold. She was constantly striving to appear as the most intelligent in the room. Though she was definitely competitive, what she truly desired was companionship. She felt isolated at home, and being around Kam, Orna, and Bliss made her feel seen.

"You don't have to compete with me or anyone else," Kam said. "I know, but I can't deny that it's still fun," Talo said with a grin. "We accept you for who you are, unfortunately," Kam said into a laugh. "Stop!" Talo exclaimed as she and Kam chuckled. "But seriously, Kam. Once we crack this code, we knock these weirdos back into extinction," Talo said with a mischievous smile. Kam smiled upon hearing this. He realized then that he couldn't face this challenge alone. Recalling the night of the attack on the house, he thought of how he would have surely perished were it not for Bliss.

"Thanks for reminding me," Kam said. "As much as I hate you, I'd be beyond crushed if something really bad happened to you," Talo grinned as Kam beamed back at her. "Don't worry, I'll be around to get on your nerves the rest of your life," Kam said. "You better be," Talo replied as they exchanged a smile. Talo scooted closer to Kam as they watched the waterfall. Their eyes followed the flow in unison, feeling at ease in each other's company. They had little time for peace, though. Because time was quickly running out.

| 28 |

Maxine

Kincade and Maxine had been driving for the entire day, and Maxine's driving PTSD was gradually waning. Maxine's yellow-eyed dreams dissipated, and her dreams began to feel normal again. She often dreamt of Imani or Kam, and she pushed the limits of her dream-leaping abilities. The night before, she appeared in Kam's dream, and together they soared through the cosmos, gliding past various planets and admiring the stars. She also drifted into Tobias's dream, seeing him taking snaps of Georgette, a lovely, healthy Georgette at the summit of a snow-capped mountain. This made Maxine wake up in tears, yet she was still able to drift back off into sleep.

Maxine was able to drive for a second time, which provided her with a greater sense of ease than when she was simply riding along. She realized that her Post-traumatic Stress was more associated with riding than driving, yet it still had a strong presence in both. She focused on her breathing during the trip, which made a huge difference. Without her calming techniques, she most likely would've had at least one minor panic attack.

It was nearing midnight as they returned from visiting Georgette, who was only two days away from coming home. They had already begun to plan the celebration - balloons, cake, gifts, and various other decorations. Tobias hadn't visited this time, but he had come by a few times a week, and this marked a big milestone for him. Maxine and Kincade were immensely proud of him. Ava and Maxine even taught him the same breathing exercises that had worked for them. It seemed to be helping him even more.

Maxine beamed as she stopped the car. She felt a surge of gratitude that things were seemingly going smoothly for her. In the depths of her subconscious, something still seemed amiss, but she chose to dismiss that sensation for the present. She was tired of feeling stressed.

"You're glowing, sis," Kincade said as Maxine put the car in park. They sat in the car at an isolated gas station, their vehicle parked beside a fuel tank. A few other buildings lay nearby, but each appeared abandoned.

"Thanks, dude," Maxine replied. "No, like you're glowing, glowing. This is the happiest I've literally seen you in years." Maxine's grin broadened at his words. He was correct; she hadn't realized the amount of time she'd been pretending until this point. "I never paid attention to how long I've been faking this whole happy-to-be-here thing, but I'm glad to actually be content for once," she admitted.

"I'm glad you ain't gotta keep faking the funk anymore, either. I know depression when I see it."

Maxine appeared perplexed. She had never considered herself to be suffering from depression. Recalling the time after Imani had passed away, she could hardly eat or leave her room. On one occasion, she went to the rooftop of a parking garage and perched at the edge, believing that it was her fault and that the only way to deal was to end her own life. She barely graduated high school, failing nearly every class, despite being an honor student before.

She started drinking and smoking heavily, to the point that even Ava and Kincade had to caution her to take it easy. But, around a year after Imani's passing, she began to cut back, although she still relied on alcohol and marijuana as a way of dealing with her pain, especially when Imani's birthday or death anniversary came up. In the most recent weeks, however, she only resorted to these substances on small occasions.

"Yea sis, you were pretty isolated up until now. I'm really proud of you."

"Thank you," Maxine said shyly. "Instead of continuing to dwell, You're choosing instead to save yourself. And you even pushed dad out of his paralyzing, manic cowardish, I meant, cowardward umm... Did I mention that I'm smarter than my grade point average?" Kincade said with a flustered smirk.

Maxine chuckled and said, "I'll take the grade point average thing with a grain of salt, dude."

Kincade gave a broad smile, not taking himself too seriously. "It's cowardice, big bro, and yes, I agree. Dad was definitely the poster child for not practicing what he preached," Maxine said.

"I wish I had a joint and a good nap right now," Kincade said into a yawn. "I second that, man," Maxine replied.

"Thought meditation sessions with your alcoholic, hipster friend were helping you cope."

"I also like options."

"Oh god, you're even talking like her!" Kincade let out a chuckle, and Maxine followed suit. "I'm gonna be a gentleman and pay for the gas," Maxine said. "Wait! Let's get some pregame snacks." Maxine glanced at him with a sly smile. "You know most of those snacks have unfavorable ingredients like the ones you preach about."

"Meh, I don't mind being a high little hypocrite tonight. Let's go," Kincade said as Maxine chuckled. Maxine and Kincade then exited the car, and Maxine double-checked that the door was locked.

Maxine and Kincade began walking towards the store when Maxine sensed a presence behind her. She spun around but there was nothing there, only their vehicle at the fuel pump labeled 1. Maxine cautiously rotated to face forward again, trailing Kincade into the store. Just as they entered, a black bird as big as a flamingo descended upon the hood of their car. The bird had ghastly yellow eyes and wings that were nearly a foot long each. It bore an eerie resemblance to the bird from Maxine's nightmare. The bird perched on the car as three others joined it. One of them perched on the hood. They stared at the store ominously.

Kincade and Maxine began getting snacks as they ranted on about comic book characters, conspiracies, and other casual things. Kincade started replacing items with a hint of annoyance, as he was used to reading the ingredients list on everything. Outside, the number of birds had grown to an alarming degree. At least twenty of them had encircled the store, their piercing yellow eyes staring menacingly. The car and gas tanks had been surrounded, forming a frightful army of feathered, yellow-eyed creatures.

Maxine and Kincade finally stopped talking as they approached the empty counter. "Cashier, cashier, come out with your hands up!" Kincade said jokingly. "Hands up? Really?" Maxine asked, beaming. "You know we can make a run for it," Kincade said. "No, you can make a run for it," Maxine said, laughing. An elderly gentleman with tattered overalls and a stained red checkered shirt emerged from the door behind the counter. "I agree with the young lady; that would be downright deadly. I keep a loaded shotgun at all times." His voice was raspy, as if years of cigarette smoke had taken a toll on his vocal cords.

"That's cool and all, but just this, please," Kincade said unamused as he pointed at a bag of hot chips, some organic popcorn, two green teas, gummy bears, and some peppermint gum.

The cashier remained silent as he scanned their items and started to bag them. None of them noticed the increasing flock of birds that had taken over the parking lot and the gas pumps. "The total is $17.28. Cash or card?"

"That, my friend, will be paid by my buddy, Andrew Jackson, the seventh supreme ruler of the United States," Kincade said as he handed the twenty-dollar bill to the cashier, who rolled his eyes. Maxine rolled hers too. "Does everything have to be so damn extra with you?" She asked, half serious. "Yes, sis. At any and all times."

Maxine smiled and shook her head, but her expression suddenly changed to one of horror as she glanced out at the glass doors. It was exactly like her nightmares. She then questioned if she was dreaming as she quickly looked at her phone for the time and saw it was 10:55 pm. She looked up in the circular mirror in the corner of the store and saw their reflections as clear as day. She then realized that it was definitely real. "Kincade," Maxine said with terror in her voice. "I got the change already; we will use the card options on the pumps."

"Kincade!" Maxine said louder. "Maxine!" Kincade mocked. "Kincade, look outside!" Maxine exclaimed as she backed up a few steps.

Kincade's smile disappeared rapidly as his eyes fell upon the terrifying sight. At least one hundred birds now filled the area. "You got a secret demonic bird meeting going on tonight, man?" Kincade asked, spooked. "A what?" "What I meant to ask was, how many bullets are in that shotgun?" The cashier looked at Kincade like he was crazy, until he saw the obvious outside like they finally did. The cashier swallowed hard, his mouth opened as he watched in horror. Kincade and Maxine both backed away slowly, not quite sure of an escape route.

"Go to the back room where I keep my supplies; I'll hold them off if I can," The cashier said as he dug in his overalls for his keys. He pulled them out and flung the keys to Kincade, who raced off with Maxine towards the back, just as the lights went dark. They rushed to the back, the piercing squeaks of the birds following behind them. They huddled behind the coolers, surrounded by stacks of boxes of various soft drinks lining the back wall.

They frantically scanned the area with the light from their cell phones. A periodic flash of light, followed by the sound of a shotgun, echoed through the store alongside the sounds of feathers flocking and the squeaks of the birds. The cashier let out a blood-curling scream as he fired again and again. Then, just as the final gunshot rang out, the birds moved closer.

They heard the relentless tapping of beaks against the metal door, leaving deep indentations. Kincade made a break for the back door, the EXIT sign still glowing. The door had a long swing handle that would not budge. "Come on, not today of all days, please," Kincade said through grunts. Maxine looked above her and noticed the entrance to the vents.

Kincade looked back at her and followed her eyes and immediately caught on. The entrance was above a stack of beer in gold and white boxes. "There! Let's go!" Kincade said as he and Maxine began to climb the half pyramid of boxes. The birds were starting to slowly pry open the door.

Kincade was in the lead as he frantically tugged at the gate that was barring the entrance to the vent. It didn't move. "It's not budging!" Kincade yelled. "No, shit!" "What do you suggest, then?" "Just pull like our lives depend on it!" "You had to be literal!" Kincade said as he pulled much harder. This time the gate ripped off and fell on Maxine's shoulder, delivering a sharp pain and causing her to groan. "My bad, sis," Kincade said. "Let's just go before we're a hashtag!" Maxine exclaimed, ignoring the pain. Kincade peeked his head in and realized how snug the vents were. He looked back at Maxine, looking lost. "You go first!" He exclaimed. "What? Bro no..." "Max, no time for that. Take my hand!"

Maxine pondered this, not wanting to leave him behind. She then hesitantly took his hand as he led her inside. Maxine struggled to crawl through the shallow vents. She managed to pull herself inside but the vents were snug against her body. Too snug. She didn't know if Kincade could even fit.

Kincade was climbing up when the birds suddenly came bursting through the glass coolers, shattering them into pieces. He was more than halfway in when the birds swarmed the room. His screams filled the air when the birds began to viciously peck at his legs, chunks of flesh flying off as he thrashed around in agony. Maxine screamed in terror as Kincade oozed blood from his wounds. Kincade finally lifted himself inside as he let out another scream.

Maxine quickly crawled ahead as Kincade trailed behind, leaving a path of blood as he struggled to navigate the vents. The birds began to make their way inside and began to peck at the back of his legs as Maxine screamed for his name. He began to viciously kick them away as he continued moving. Kincade felt a sudden rush of terror as a bird squeezed its way past him. Its beak viciously attacked Maxine's left calf, causing her to scream out in pain. Maxine reacted quickly, kicking the bird in the beak and sending it squealing all over the vent. In a fit of adrenaline, Kincade grabbed the bird by its throat and with a swift movement, snapped its neck. Maxine, though in agony, kept pushing forward, ignoring the throbbing in her calf.

As the birds started to swarm in, it seemed as if their doom was certain. Kincade desperately tried to shield Maxine, while kicking away the birds. The birds began to struggle, as they struggled to fit into the vents all at once.

Kincade felt a chill run down his spine as another bird squeezed past him and began pecking at Maxine, just below her first wound. She screamed, kicking at the creature, and then felt the vent start to collapse beneath them. With a loud crash, the vents broke away, and the two of them fell back into the store. They landed hard on the floor a few feet away from the dead cashier. His body was riddled with tiny, penny-sized holes, and there were a few dead birds lying in pools of dark blood.

Maxine jumped and covered Kincade, willing to sacrifice herself to the demonic birds. Maxine felt the birds encircle her, yet there were no pecks. She looked up and noticed a transparent, bluish force field over her head, which the birds were swirling and jabbing at, yet unable to breach. An innumerable number of birds blanketed every bit of the store. This went on for several minutes until the birds slowly began to fly out of the store in unison. As the last bird flew out, Maxine suddenly awoke from her trance and brushed herself off, as if ridding herself of imaginary birds.

She inspected her calf where the bird had pecked. There was a small pool of blood surrounding the wound, and the throbbing increased as the adrenaline started to fade. The pain was becoming more and more unbearable. She peered down at Kincade, whose eyes were barely open. She noticed the same penny-sized holes in his legs that she had seen in the cashier. His tan pants were drenched in blood. She knew that, without urgent medical attention, he could easily bleed out.

Maxine cried into his chest, but relieved he was alive. "We were really attacked by angry birds," he said weakly. Maxine laughed nervously as she squeezed her brother's hand. "Thank you for saving me," he said as he swallowed and struggled to keep from losing consciousness. Maxine was certain it was the end; she was unable to comprehend how she created the force field. Despite the confusion, she was elated. It saved their lives. "I knew your healing would come around," Kincade struggled to say. Maxine nodded her head as she wiped more tears streaming down her face. There was something about what he said that struck a chord with her, yet she decided to put it aside for the moment and continued to watch over him. She attempted to avert her gaze from the pool of blood he was lying in, but nevertheless, she kept her grasp firmly on his hand.

They both glanced up to hear the sound of police sirens outside. The red and blue flashing lights illuminated the previously neat store, now destroyed with toppled shelves, broken coolers, a smashed front door, and countless dents in the walls. "The man is actually here to save us," Maxine said as she sniffed more tears away. They lay together as ambulances, fire trucks, and cops flooded the store. The paramedics and police officers quickly removed them from the scene and took them to the hospital. Just as Kincade began to lose consciousness from blood loss, they drove away.

****
**

"No wound." The doctor gave Maxine a puzzled expression. Maxine mirrored the expression right away. "A lot of blood but no wound. Are you sure your calf was punctured?" Maxine's face remained one of confusion. "Ma'am, I am going to accompany you to the sitting room, where you can wait for your brother and take a moment to clear your thoughts. Please sign these discharge documents and we'll send you on your way," The doctor said.

It was a middle-aged woman with toffee-colored skin and dark green eyes. Beautiful, to say the least. The doctor grinned as she passed the tablet to Maxine for her to sign. Maxine quickly scribbled her signature, and the doctor beamed in response. "I'll be right back to walk you out, okay? Just stay put for me please," The doctor said as she headed out the door.

Maxine perched at the edge of the cot, stuck in her thoughts. She gazed at the folded hands in her lap, not catching on to what healed her so quickly. She ran through dozens of scenarios in her head to theorize why she got spared, and Kincade didn't. Kincade was luckily saved when he arrived at the doctor's office and was staying in the ICU.

The doctor returned after around ten minutes, guiding Maxine to the waiting area. The room was almost filled to capacity, with only a few open chairs remaining. Maxine took a seat near the wall, with two empty chairs between her and a thirty-something woman who was struggling to keep her child still. She slouched against the seat as the doctor gave one final reassuring smile before she walked through the double doors behind her.

Maxine's mind continued to spin, as she once again thought about the night Kam told her about her DNA. "You're not from Earth, Maxine." The words tormented her. The force field, the unexplained healing, the dream walking, the visions, and the flying was all making sense, but at the same time not.

She also recalled what Kincade said about her healing. She still felt there was something more to what he said. She was just stuck on the ulterior motive why. She shut her eyes and allowed herself to relax, breathing in and out slowly, letting her breathing technique begin to rock her to sleep.

"Maxine!" She heard through shut eyes. She gazed into Tobias' sorrowful expression. Maxine leapt up and embraced him tightly, as if it were the last time. Maxine savored the citrus smell of his cologne. He kissed the top of her head, and they let go while Tobias held onto her shoulders. "They said Kincade is in room 209. What happened?" Maxine had no idea how to tell him. She had no idea how to tell anyone. Maxine cast her gaze across the floor, pondering how to explain everything to him. Her brow was creased in thought, her expression grim. "I don't know," was the only answer she could manage.

Tobias just nodded, not pushing it any further. "I'm just glad you're both okay. Were you hurt?" Maxine shook her head. She felt tears well up as she thought about Kincade. The last thing she remembered was watching him fade into unconsciousness before they reached the emergency entrance.

She blinked her tears away as she tried to remain calm. Tobias gazed at her and whispered, "I'm here for you, no matter what. Let's talk outside about it, okay?" Maxine glanced at him, pleased that he was staying true to his promise of putting in more effort. Just as they were about to leave, four men in military attire stormed into the room. "It is mandatory that all individuals remain seated. We have been informed that a Viola virus patient was admitted approximately two hours and forty-five minutes ago. In order to ensure the safety of everyone present, we must conduct tests to check for infection. We will do our best to expedite this process," The lead soldier said.

Maxine's anxiety surged as they pulled out their Anomaly test kits. Kam's words about the soldiers not being soldiers echoed in her mind, and she struggled to keep her composure. However, Tobias gently guided her to a seat, and they sat down. Maxine's heart raced, thumping against her chest. The soldiers paced around, running their kits over each person in turn. Her breaths quickened as her fingers dug into the seat of her chair. Tobias noticed it and peered his eyes at her, worried. "Maxine, you okay?" Maxine slowly nodded. She suddenly felt lightheaded as her breaths became more shallow.

She slowly began to practice breathing again, just as the soldiers were two people away from them. She closed her eyes, hoping she could just vanish. She felt the coldness of the monitor on her forehead as it beeped twice. "She's clear," The soldier said. She began to calm a bit until she heard three beeps beside her. "Infection detected," The soldier said.

| 29 |

Maxine

"What?" was all Tobias managed to say. Maxine's eyes widened with terror. She thought, "How could he be infected? How did he become infected? Was Kam right about the poison?" All questions Maxine could not answer herself.

"Come with us, Mr. Hewitt," the soldier directly above him said. Tobias's face was a picture of sheer astonishment. Maxine shook her head. "Not him," she thought.

Without a second thought, she stepped in front of Tobias as he reached for the soldier's hand. "You're not taking my father anywhere!" she exclaimed through gritted teeth. "Miss, this is your first and only chance to move out of the way."

"No! I said you're not taking him!" She held her ground, standing in front of Tobias, her arms outstretched. "This is for your own good, ma'am," the soldier said as two other soldiers began to pull a kicking and screaming Maxine away from Tobias.

They grabbed an arm each as they struggled to control her constant flailing. She continued to scream to the top of her lungs as she felt her body slam hard onto the marble floor. One soldier put a knee on her back, and another tried to fold her arms behind her as two other soldiers picked up Tobias, who complied without protest.

"Baby, I'll find you okay! I love you! Find Kincade!" He yelled as Maxine huffed against the polished floor as her eyes followed Tobias out of the automatic exit doors. She continued to struggle as she heard the sound of handcuffs. She continued to flail and jerk away, as one officer called for backup.

They then overpowered her and held her arms firmly behind her back. The soldiers began to place the handcuffs on her wrists when, all of a sudden, she vanished. They looked around, mystified. The people in the waiting room's faces dropped. Maxine looked around, now camouflaged with her environment. She rose with a deep breath, panic-stricken as she attempted to locate her arms and legs. Incredibly perplexed, she observed the soldiers who had drawn their weapons, carefully surveying around them.

The soldiers peered through the air, seemingly unaware of the Invisible Maxine who stood right before them. She then looked into one of the soldiers' eyes and dimly saw a flash of yellow. She backed up as she panicked, then quickly raced to Kincade's room. The soldiers could hear her steps but still not see her. They had their guns aimed, yet unsure of where to fire. As she got further down the hall, she heard the thunder of gunshots ring off. This caused her to sprint faster as she breathlessly ran to her left.

The booming echoes of gunfire followed her as she entered the stairwell and sprinted up the stairs. The thunderous shots then softened to a series of faint pops as she ascended to the second floor. She crumpled to the ground, gasping for breath as her lungs felt like they were on fire. It took her a moment to steady her racing heart and get her breathing back to normal. She rose slowly and glanced at her arm. Her arms were visible once more. She looked down and found that her whole body had now come into view. She exited the stairwell and hastened down the hall, her face filled with panic.

She observed that the second story was much more deserted than she anticipated. Her suspicions began to stir as she saw a young nurse with an olive complexion in pale lavender scrubs tapping away at the desk in the center. Then she caught sight of a male and female doctor conversing in a relaxed manner as they walked by. The man gave her a faint smile as they veered left down the hall behind her.

As she ventured further, she searched for room 209, taking five rooms to find it. To her dismay, the room was vacant. Her expression contorted in confusion, yet she attempted to remain calm. Could Tobias have been wrong? She hoped so, yet her gut was saying otherwise.

She strode up to the reception desk. "Excuse me, ma'am. Was a man named Kincade Hewitt in room 209?" The woman seemed perplexed. "Kincade Hewitt?" she inquired. "Yes! My brother! We came in last night." The nurse tapped the name into the computer. "Aha! Kincade. It looks like he was admitted to room 109." Maxine exhaled with relief. "But it also says here that he has already been discharged." Maxine's hopefulness instantly evaporated into panic.

"What? He was bleeding a lot! They said he would be in the hospital for at least a few days!" "He was discharged by Zeus City soldiers. He tested positive for Viola."

Maxine's whole world crumbled. Her pulse quickened, her muscles tensed, and her breath came in shallow gasps. Her breathing technique was out the window. Maxine's heart was heavy as she considered her family's fate. All she could do was shake her head in despair and angrily pound her fist into the desk, causing the nurse to startle. The thought of her family in the hands of soldiers, possibly en route to death camps, was too much to bear.

"Please find him! Can you find him!?" Maxine yelled. "Mam, you need to relax, okay? It's not in our jurisdiction to..." "Please! Get him back!" She then detected a door opening in a hallway which was out of her view. It was the same hallway the nurses were headed towards when they left. Maxine heard the same soldier bellowing the same command as before: mandatory testing. Frantic, she searched for a route of escape without being noticed. With no hesitation, she bolted in the opposite direction of the soldiers.

She veered into another passageway and saw an elevator open, disgorging a middle-aged doctor with a bald crown. She raced over, her cries for the doctor to wait ringing out. Georgette was the sole focus of her thoughts. She had to reach her before the soldiers. She dashed into the elevator as the doors were about to close. "Floor eleven please!" She said breathlessly.

The concerned doctor pressed the button for the 11th floor, as Maxine positioned herself in the corner as she struggled to regain her breath. As the elevator stopped at the ninth floor to let the doctor out, she trembled as she neared Georgette's floor. The old metal doors opened slowly, and she slid out before they were fully open, her fear intensifying at the sight that greeted her.

Maxine's heart began to race as she took in the gruesome scene. Before her lay two doctors, motionless in a sea of their own blood. She stepped closer and saw the bullet wound in one of the doctor's temple. Maxine stifled a gasp as she noticed the other doctor had been shot four times in her chest and stomach. The horror of the situation was almost too much for her to bear.

Maxine's gaze fell upon the reception desk, her eyes widening in horror at the sight of a young Asian doctor slumped there, a multitude of bullets piercing his chest, his body drenched in a sea of blood. His eyes were closed, looking as if he were asleep. The faint pop of shots echoing through the hallway alerted her to the truth - they were getting rid of the infected, then mercilessly slaughtering the rest. It was evident that no one was meant to leave this place alive. Maxine's heart sunk as she thought about the first floor, realizing that any innocent individual she had seen there was either kidnapped or dead.

As soon as the grim truth set in, she hastily ran to her mother's room. Room 1117. When she barged in, her bed was not occupied as she had expected. Instead, the bed was saturated in blood and there was a thick line of it leading into the bathroom. In a panic, she rushed to the restroom and spotted her mother lying seemingly lifeless next to the toilet bowl. "Mom!" she yelped, bending down and lifting her mother's head. The sight that met her was of her mom's blood-smeared face and her mouth oozing with blood.

Georgette slowly cracked open her eyes and drew a deep, shuddering breath, as if she had been resurrected from the dead. "Mom!

Mom, what did they do!?" Maxine screamed. Georgette coughed as she struggled to talk. "They tested everybody for in...." She began to cough before she could finish. Maxine began to cry hysterically as she cradled Georgette's head in her lap. She felt her heart sink as she saw the bullet wounds in her abdomen, torso, and arm. She knew there was no hope for her.

"Mom! Don't die, please, mom! Please stay with me! Please!" Maxine cried out. She let her tears stream down her face as she held on to Georgette's dying breaths. "You have to let me go, baby. I can't be saved. And that's okay," Georgette said into several more coughs. Maxine nodded as she continued to cry. "Imani was never your fault. None of this is your fault. Continue to heal and..." Georgette coughed more as she struggled to get her last lines out. "I love you so much. You are a light. Continue to be a light. No matter how...." She coughed again, this time non-stop. Maxine's grasp was firm as Georgette shut her eyes. Gradually, the coughing ceased and her breathing steadied. Her lips formed a smile then she inhaled deep. No more breaths followed. Maxine continued to rock back and forth, with her shirt stained in blood.

Maxine closed her eyes and envisioned a vibrant Georgette, cheerfully preparing breakfast in the morning, taking her to school, and attending her graduation. Recollections of her, youthful and joyous, flooded her mind. When Maxine opened her eyes, Georgette was lying there, her beauty still evident even in death. Maxine quickly turned her head, her tears streaming down her face. She pulled Georgette's limp hand away as she cried into her hands. She laid there for several minutes, no longer caring if the soldiers came for her.

She kissed her temple and rose from the floor. She backed away hesitantly, averting her gaze from Georgette. Wiping her tears, she remembered that she still had to locate Ava. She walked out the bathroom into Georgette's hospital room. She gathered herself as she wiped her tears and thought about what Georgette said. She knew she was right. But something in her still felt fully responsible. A habit she couldn't shake overnight.

****
****

Maxine frantically ran into her driveway. Miraculously, she had managed to make it past the soldiers and carefully descended the stairway before sneaking out through the back door. However, the sight she encountered before leaving was truly horrific. The hospital was set on fire , and the massacre of so many innocent lives - men, women, children, and even her mother - by herloid soldiers that executed every one of them, made her shudder. But she already figured that they weren't real soldiers.

She understood that without her mysterious abilities, she would have met the same fate. She was baffled as to how she had so little control over them. Nevertheless, she was aware that the less trauma she carried, the more potent they became. She just couldn't make them activate at her command. That was what bothered her. She yearned for nothing other than the security of Tobias and Kincade. To her, it was imperative that she reach them. She was determined to locate them, even if it cost her her life.

She raced to the front door, throwing it open and shouting Ava's name. She searched the area in a frenzy, her heart pounding. The television in the living room was set to the news channel, the same blonde news reporter speaking as before. "A freak hospital accident took the lives of at least 77 people although authorities are still frantically searching through the wreckage for more casualties and more importantly survivors." The lady continued speaking as images of the hospital appeared on the screen. The building had been reduced to rubble, the charred remains shrouded in billowing black smoke. Firefighters rushed to the scene, desperately trying to contain the blaze.

Maxine felt the house tremble, and then suddenly the television switched off. Clutching the stair railing, she felt weightless as the shaking persisted for a few moments before it abruptly ceased, sending her crashing to the floor. She felt waves of pain reverberate through her spine as she laid there, groaning.

She jumped to her feet and peered out the window, utterly dumb-founded. Instead of the usual view of the streets and similar-looking vintage homes, she could now see a great expanse of the city, including the towering gray walls that encircled it. An empty square now sat in the place the house stood. She stumbled back, unable to fully comprehend what she was seeing. Was this her powers manifesting again? Was this someone else? She was beyond lost for words.

She then heard a sudden call for her name that sounded like Ava. Quickly, she ran to the kitchen and was horrified to find Ava bound to the kitchen table, lying across it with thick ropes entwining her body. "Ava!" Maxine screamed. "They were here, Max! They came and asked for you!" Ava yelled as Maxine frantically looked through the drawers and cabinets for knives. The knives were all cleared out. Every sharp object was removed. Someone clearly planned this out well ahead. She hurried to the table and surveyed the area, searching for the source of the ropes.

She searched high and low, but all she found was a length of rope without any knots. "What did they look like? Did they have yellow eyes?" Maxine asked. "Eyes were dark brown. The basic, regular-looking ones. They were soldiers. Scary as hell looking." For the life of her, she couldn't find the rope's origin. Maxine started to become increasingly anxious; she sensed something was off.

If the soldiers were likely not real, then she knew they could really be anybody. She decided to test her out. "Ava, what's my favorite color?" Ava contorted. "What does that have to do with saving my ass, superwoman?" Maxine chuckled a bit. "And it's blue. Midnight blue, to be specific. Happy?" Maxine was impressed but still unsure. "And you have a half-moon-shaped birthmark on your left shoulder." Maxine's suspicion began to wane.

"Just for extra points, you're the most stubborn Gemini I've ever met."

"Okay, you're you. but how the hell do I get you out of these?"

"I wasn't exactly conscious when they put me here." Ava replied.

Maxine chuckled as she continued to survey the rope. Suddenly her eyes lit up. "Hold on, I'm going to check upstairs for my hair-cutting scissors." Ava contorted and raised an eyebrow. "Those scissors? Those might snap in half trying to cut through this."

"Well, dude, if you have an idea that's more genius, I'm not opposed to suggestions."

Ava looked up for a second, but couldn't think of anything. "I'll play the unfortunate hand I've been dealt for now," Ava said. Maxine grinned.

"Thanks. I'll be back."

"Obviously," Ava said as she smiled back.

Maxine gave a final smirk as she began to climb the stairs. Suddenly, she felt a force tackle her, and she screamed as she was lifted into the air. She heard a few loud beeps as the person who tackled her carried her away from the house.

Maxine closed her eyes and felt cool air as she heard a deafening explosion that created a faint ringing in her ears. The house burst into flames, and she was still soaring in the sky.

She opened her eyes, and to her surprise, there was somebody lying on her waist. She recognized the dark hair and golden skin. As her eyes traveled down, she noticed the bloodstains on the back of their white T-shirt. This made her even more anxious than before. She was unsure if she should feel safe or if she was still in danger. She then relaxed as she recognized who it was. It was Ava. Bloodied and still alive.

| 30 |

Kam & Maxine

"It'll work for an hour. Then you'll have to come back," Bliss said, her eyes locked onto the computer screen, deciphering lines of intricate code. On Axpherial, time flowed differently from Earth. Axpherians operated on a twelve-hour cycle, where 1.2 Earth minutes equated to a single Axpherian minute. For instance, an Axpherian hour translated to two Earth hours. Their time notation was different too. Instead of the familiar 0-60 minute structure on Earth, Axpherians used 0-99 minutes without a two-dot time separator. For example, instead of writing 9:80, they would write it as 980.

"And it'll really bypass the block?" Kam asked cautiously.

"You still sound doubtful," Bliss remarked, her gaze shifting from the screen to him.

"No, no, just cautious," Kam assured her. Bliss couldn't help but notice a hint of skepticism in his tone.

"You gotta stick to telling the truth, because you literally can't lie to save your life."

"I embrace that."

"Boy, don't you?" Bliss rolled her eyes and smiled.

Kam returned her smile as Bliss handed the new device, the delfona, to Kam. However, she hesitated for a moment before relinquishing it.

"What?" Kam asked, puzzled by her sudden pause.

"Ignore your instincts. Just get the pretty Earth girl back here, and that's it. One hour, bro," Bliss said urgently as she finally placed the delfona in Kam's hand.

"I'll try my best," Kam promised.

"Kam, I mean it." Bliss's tone was laced with genuine concern, and her eyes glistened with tears. Kam noticed her worry, and his smile faded. He simply nodded in response.

"I need you. I won't know what to do with myself if you go now." Bliss's voice quivered as her eyes welled up with tears. She welcomed the warmth of his embrace, knowing it might be their last.

"Hug too tight?" Kam asked, trying to inject a touch of humor.

"When isn't it?" Bliss replied with a gentle smile, brushing away the remnants of tears from her eyes.

"Sorry."

"Don't apologize. You just have a clumsy, bone-crushing way of showing affection," Bliss teased as Kam chuckled.

"I'll take the compliment," Kam said.

"Eh, not that you have a choice," Bliss said with a playful smirk.

Kam strapped the delfona to his wrist and headed toward his motorcycle parked nearby. He swung a leg over the bike and aimed the delfona at the wall in front of him.

"Mission revolving door is on in three..." Bliss shouted as Kam revved his engine.

"Just get Maxine. Nothing else," Kam muttered to himself.

"Two..."

"Don't do anything too heroic," Bliss thought as Kam donned his helmet.

"One!" Bliss exclaimed as Kam released a blue and white portal from the delfona. She watched with satisfaction as Kam revved his engine one last time and drove into the portal, which promptly vanished. Anxiety gripped Bliss as she contemplated her parting words to him. All she could do now was hope.

Kam pulled up to the spot where he and Maxine usually met, except he was directly across the street from the hospital. His heart sank as he took in the horrific scene: the hospital engulfed in flames, surrounded by fire trucks, police, and a small crowd of onlookers. The firefighters battled the blaze tirelessly. Despite the growing dread, Kam had a gut feeling that Maxine was still alive, and all he could think about was finding her. He quickly revved the engine and sped toward her house.

His pulse raced as he recklessly weaved through the streets, narrowly avoiding a collision with a fire truck and a pristine white Camry. A few people recognized his motorcycle and dark gear from viral videos, snapping pictures and videos with their phones. Kam paid no attention, his singular focus on rescuing Maxine.

Kam arrived at Maxine's house, only to find it missing. He came to an abrupt halt, staring at the open patch of dirt where the house had stood. Suddenly, an explosion jolted him out of his daze. Looking up, he witnessed the house consumed by flames, with two figures soaring away from the wreckage. Without a moment's hesitation, Kam mounted his motorcycle once more and gave chase, his gaze locked onto the distant shapes.

Maxine was in a daze as Ava descended with her to the ground. When they reached the pavement, Maxine found herself in an empty alley within the heart of the city. Regaining her composure despite the dizziness, Maxine noticed that Ava stood before her, a trickle of blood flowing down her head, although there was no visible wound.

"No wound," Maxine observed as she caught her breath.

"I know," Ava responded casually. Maxine's confusion deepened as she tried to make sense of the situation.

"Well, this is definitely the part where I ask what the hell is going on," Maxine exclaimed.

Ava chuckled nervously, aware that she needed to explain everything. "Well, this is an awkward plot development," Ava began, searching for a way to convey the new information.

Maxine's confusion intensified as she fixed her gaze on Ava, her eyes heavy with anticipation for answers. "I... well, we are not exactly Earthlings, as you may have already figured out."

"I know that part," Maxine confessed.

Ava's eyes lit up. "Wait? So you know where we're from?" Ava asked excitedly.

"No, but I was already told I wasn't from Earth," Maxine said, taking a deep breath. Ava raised an eyebrow. "Who told you?" Maxine's gaze shifted as she struggled to say Kam's name. "Okay, the point is, I don't know where I'm from, and you do," Maxine continued, "Where the hell am I from?"

Ava laughed nervously again as she finally confessed, "We're from Utok. From the Tranquility realm. Fourth dimension. I've only known for a little over two years. When she told me everything."

Maxine's face contorted in confusion. "She?"

Ava sighed heavily as she prepared to tell her the next part. "She. She meaning our mother."

"Our mother?" Maxine's heart raced, and she clenched her shirt tightly in her fists as she continued to absorb this new information.

"We're sisters, Maxine. And Kincade is not just your earthly brother. We're triplets." Maxine was absolutely stunned, her jaw unhinged in shock. It all made sense now. She and Kincade were of course twins, and she and Ava were always the same age, although Ava pretended to be four months older.

"Our planet was destroyed in a war. Our mother was pregnant with us. She extracted our embryos and implanted them into two separate Earth parents. Georgette's womb could only handle two, so I was given separate parents, of course. Parents who were hateful, abusive, and unaccepting of my quote-unquote unruly sexuality."

Ava cleared her throat, continuing. "My mother found me one day. I was like you. My powers would spontaneously show up, and she taught me how to control them. Through meditation, of course. The better control I had over my thoughts, the more control I had over my abilities."

Maxine peered at her suspiciously. "How did you know I...." Maxine paused as she realized. "Of course you did." Ava chuckled, then finished, "Mom died shortly after I met her. Apparently, she was in a hovercraft explosion. But she told me to find you, and it just happened I enrolled in Montgomery High during junior year."

Maxine vividly remembered the first time she met Ava. It was just two months before the accident. During their second-period algebra class, she had watched Ava stroll in fifteen minutes late, casually sipping iced coffee and clumsily clutching her books. Maxine couldn't forget her white hairband, tie-dye shirt, and the clear crystal necklace she wore. She also remembered how some classmates whispered derogatory remarks, labeling her a "hippy" and suggesting she was merely following a trend.

"Look who rolled in from Woodstock," a male student had quipped from behind her, inciting laughter from a few others. Maxine, however, paid them no mind and instead looked at Ava as she took the seat next to her.

There was an instant connection, an inexplicable sense of comfort, especially when Maxine noticed the quartz crystal around Ava's neck. She couldn't help but compliment her on it, to which Ava replied with a smile, "Aww thanks! Got it from Sarah's psychic shop across the street. I'm kind of a crystal addict." Maxine smiled back and introduced herself, shaking Ava's hand. "I'm Maxine. But everyone calls me Max, as if saying two syllables would break their jaws." Ava laughed immediately, endearing herself further to Maxine. "I'm already intrigued," Ava said with a wink. Maxine laughed too. "Same here."

Ava's playful banter made Maxine like her even more. "I felt the spotlight on me when I entered; I can tell I'm going to be loved here," Ava sarcastically remarked. Maxine chuckled, admitting, "Girl, they love me, too." They continued talking throughout the class, passing notes and exchanging sarcastic jokes. Before the period ended, they swapped phone numbers.

It was only later that Ava realized they were sisters when she noticed the half-moon birthmark on Maxine's chest, identical to her own and their mother's—a mark unique to citizens of Utak. From that day on, Ava vowed to protect Maxine and planned to reveal the truth when the time was right.

As Ava continued to recount their shared history, she explained, "I taught Kincade first because you were still traumatized by the car accident. It's much tougher to teach your abilities when you're grieving. Too much grief, anger, or guilt can hinder your powers. So, Kincade and I made it our mission to heal you. It was pretty easy for him to accept his true background when I told him. As a top notch conspiracist, It definitely made the unusual, sounding usual."

Maxine's mind raced back to the time when she had those dreams of yellow eyes. She realized they weren't just anxiety but premonitions. "I had visions of this pandemic thing," Ava continued, describing purple clouds suffocating everyone, causing them to pass out and awaken as zombies with yellow eyes. "Kincade saw it too."

Maxine, now intrigued, asked, "So, you know what the virus actually is?" Ava responded, "Not exactly, but I have an idea. It's the same virus they tried to use on our planet and failed."

Maxine was puzzled. "I've been confused so many times these past weeks," she said with a frustrated laugh. Ava reassured her, saying, "I guarantee my word is as good as a bond." Maxine's mouth curved slightly upward. "As good as a what?" Maxine laughed. "Sis, you know what I meant," Ava grinned.

They shared a moment of sisterly laughter before Maxine's emotions got the better of her. Tears welled up as she realized that her only known mother was gone. Ava comforted her, holding her as they heard a motorcycle engine nearby.

Maxine's eyes lit up when she saw Kam. "Kam!" she shouted. Ava, bewildered, asked, "Come again?" Maxine didn't hesitate and ran to him, embracing him without a second thought. Kam, although awkward and strong in his embrace, provided the support Maxine needed. When she released her grip, tears continued to flow as Maxine confided, "They took my brother, they took my father... and they got Mom. She's dead."

Kam, empathetic to her grief, could only say, "I'm so sorry." Feeling overwhelmed, Maxine urged, "We have to find them and get them back."

Ava, walking over, declared her intention to help. "I'll find them and get back to you on their whereabouts," she assured Maxine.

Before Maxine and Kam left, Maxine's eyes lit up. "I'm sorry, Ava, this is Kam; Kam, this is Ava," Maxine said as they awkwardly shook hands. Ava, playfully inquisitive, asked, "Oh? He's handsome. When did you swipe right for this one?" Kam replied with humor, "Alien lovebirds dot com, found only on the dark web." Ava chuckled, seemingly impressed.

Ava issued a protective warning to Kam, saying, "Take good care of her. I may look pretty, but I'm both protective and irrational if you push me." Kam accepted the responsibility with a promise, saying, "Solemnly swear."

Maxine handed her delfona to Ava. Surprised, Maxine asked if she knew how to use it. Ava replied that her mother had taught her. With final words and reassurances, Maxine and Kam roared off on the motorcycle, heading towards Axpherial, their mission looming ahead.

| 31 |

Kam & Maxine

A portal materialized inside Kam's basement. Kam and Maxine arrived immediately and came to a stop. Kam and Maxine got off the motorcycle and put away their helmets. Maxine's face was shrouded in heavy grief. Kam saw the tears shimmering in Maxine's eyes and went to her. He wrapped his arms around her, and she let herself cry, her body shaking with each sob. After a few moments, Maxine pulled away, her eyes still shimmering with tears. Kam tenderly wiped them away with his thumb, and she smiled, grateful for his compassion.

Kam gazed at her intently, not with pity but with admiration. Through her, he realized that letting yourself break down was actually the strongest thing a person could ever do. "You didn't turn your head this time," Kam said with a shy grin. Maxine smiled as she sniffed away at her tears. "I'm just done hiding from myself. Done hiding from this trauma that I thought would shatter me," Maxine said as she grinned through her grief.

"I always looked down on my dad for always running from himself, but he was just a reflection of my own flaws. I thought always having a tough exterior made you strong, but it just makes you hide from yourself." Maxine sniffled, her tears having dried up. Yet her grief still lingered. "Kincade mentioned the whole shadow self thing. But he was definitely right. I think I'm finally embracing it," Maxine grinned, sniffling once more.

Kam gazed at her, awestruck by her strength and self-esteem. He knew he didn't have to offer too many encouraging words. She already knew how to encourage herself. But he also knew offering his encouragement wouldn't do any harm. "I have to say, your strength is definitely one of your greatest assets," Kam said as he gently held her cheek. This made Maxine feel warm all over. "Being around you is also helping to strengthen me. When you have that quality, you can't help but emit that energy onto others," Kam said. He and Maxine were now sharing a breath, both of them feeling shy and nervous yet entirely content in each other's presence. They weren't two halves becoming whole, but two completed beings becoming one.

"You gotta give credit to yourself, too," Maxine said. "You were afraid to be too close to me once upon a time. Now look at us, sharing air like it's the only oxygen in the room." They both shyly laughed as Kam admitted, "I am still afraid. But just like you, I've become one with my shadow side, too. I don't let my trauma dictate my actions. I try my best to control my actions despite the voices in my head," Kam said. As he said this, he gently put his lips to hers. Maxine embraced him tightly, her arms wrapped around his neck. He responded by caressing her waist and drawing her close. Their lips met in a gentle, tender kiss that swiftly grew passionate and intense.

They could feel themselves becoming magnets. They were as close as close could possibly be. Kam swept her off her feet and gently placed her on the table before him. Their passionate kisses continued as they embraced one another. They were ready to cross the intimate threshold and take off everything weighing them down. Their traumas, worries, and futures. Just before they were about to succumb to their desires, Kam suddenly pulled back.

Maxine felt a longing for more, yet she was careful not to rush things. Kam could feel her breath on his face as he stepped back, his heart pounding. He didn't feel the time was right. Maxine straightened up, worried. "What's going on?" Maxine asked. "It just doesn't feel right," He said. "Why? I feel ready," Maxine admitted. Kam smiled nervously. "I feel the same, too. But I just feel like I want to know much more about you before we..." Kam was too shy to say it. Maxine had to ask, although Kam came off as strong and experienced. "Have you ever... you know."

Kam grinned and nodded his head. Maxine felt slight relief, as she would rather he be experienced, too. "I think you're beautiful Max, every part of you is beautiful to me. But I want to help you. I want to heal you. I want us to heal each other, I mean." Maxine's lips curved into a gentle smile as she listened to his words, nodding in agreement. "I think I want to know how to control these supernatural occurrences I keep having." Kam's eyes lit up at this. "What other abilities did you discover?"

Maxine relayed to him all that Ava had shared with her, including how her powers manifested when she was in danger, and began to manifest more and more as she proceeded on her healing journey. "So you're from Utak? They're about four galaxies from us. In the Narmoa galaxy. Their planet went through one of the worst wars in the entire universe. The war lasted several Loza's. I knew Axpherial and Utak had an allegiance, but I don't know too much else."

Kam sensed a mysterious connection between them. His recollection of the herloid's dying words was particularly persistent, especially when it came to what he had mentioned about Axpherial lying about their past. He felt that he was missing some vital details, yet he couldn't seem to figure out what it was. And thought it would be dangerous to make a baseless assumption.

"You good?" Maxine asked, noticing the calculated look on Kam's face. Kam snapped out of his thoughts and looked up. "Yeah, I'm fine. It's just something about the war and what the herloid said." Maxine tilted her head and peered with curiosity. "What do these herloids look like?" She asked. Kam suspected she was onto something. "Do they have dark yellow eyes?" Maxine asked. Kam's face dropped as he realized she must've seen them too. "When did you encounter them?" Kam asked.

Maxine let out a heavy sigh and finally opened up to him about the figure in the tree, the troubling dreams, the ominous birds, and the military personnel at the hospital. As she brought up Tobias and Kincade, her voice trembled, still coming to terms with it. Kam looked flustered, his eyes suddenly filled with agitation. "Why did you keep that from me?" Kam asked. Maxine looked surprised, feeling the fire coming from him.

"I didn't know how to tell you."

"I see you still have your vulnerability wall sitting between us."

"What? Kam, I've updated you about my progress in healing from my sister. I've told you everything about my family, my past, and you really have the audacity to talk about walls?"

"So you couldn't tell me about you being stalked and nearly killed? Was telling me about you being in danger... grave danger really too much to ask?"

Maxine was absolutely dumbfounded at his lack of understanding.

"Dude, you trippin. I told you about my accident. I haven't shared that with anyone in two years. And what the hell were you gonna do about the crows or the soldiers murdering my mom and taking the two people I'd take a bullet for? You were stuck here, remember?"

"It's the fact that you've kept away some of the most significant things that happened to you. I would've definitely found a way to get to you if I knew how dire the situation was. Just like I found a way this time."

"You didn't rescue me! Ava did. And I rescued myself from the hospital. You think I really need you like that?"

Maxine's last words cut Kam deep. Maxine immediately felt bad but was too prideful to immediately take it back. Kam huffed and puffed, feeling anger swell inside of him. Unable to contain his rage, he swung around and slammed his fist into the metal table, leaving a deep dent. Maxine jolted, surprised by his strength. Kam's face drained of color as he realized his mistake and he slumped against the table, his hands covering his face in regret. "I don't want you seeing me like this," He murmured, his face buried in his hands. Maxine got up and glided to his side. She gently laid her hand on his shoulder. "Hey, it's okay. You accept my vulnerability, and I accept yours, too." Kam stood up and gazed at her. "I'm sorry for keeping those things from you. I just didn't want you to worry too much." Kam smiled and massaged her cheek. "I'm sorry, too. I'm sorry for not understanding you," Kam said.

His anger cooled down as fast as it came up. "I guess I can't help how I am when I'm around you," He said as he curved his lips into a grin. "Besides, I think your feisty side is kinda sexy." Kam chuckled shyly at this. "So you enjoy my highs and lows as is?" Maxine gazed into his eyes, smiling. "I accept yours, just like I'm learning to accept mine." Maxine said. "Looks like we're on the same path with that," Kam said.

They gazed into each other's eyes, entranced. They savored the feeling of getting lost in one another. They could remain in that blissful state forever. Kam's voice grew soft and low as he spoke, "I want to show you something." Maxine grinned, genuinely curious. "I'm open." Maxine said in a similar tone. Kam grinned as he took her hand and led her out of the basement and into the main area of the cabin.

****
****

Kam and Maxine now stood in the living room, looking up at the sky illuminated by one and a half full moons glimmering with a pale blue hue. Maxine was in awe of the scene before her. "How many moons do you guys have?" She asked. Kam smiled warmly, understanding that this was an entirely unfamiliar experience for her. "We have three. Kahlofa, Moto, and Talpo."

"I bet your shores are like mini tsunamis," Maxine said. Kam looked confused. "The moon affects the tides. At least on earth they do."

"Our tides are actually pretty weak. But here the more moons a planet has, the weaker the tides. The moons are actually saving us from having daily tsunamis." Maxine seemed genuinely fascinated by this. "I'm a bit of a cosmos geek," Maxine said. Kam beamed, genuinely interested in more details from her.

"It's a secret exploration of mine. I used to read books about space and planets just for fun as a kid. I got called a space cadet for like a year. The kids used to be like, 'Earth to Max, space geek, over.'"

Kam let out a booming laugh, genuinely amused. "Hey, don't laugh at my pain and suffering!" Maxine said into a chuckle. "Sorry, you made it kind of easy," Kam laughed, as Maxine delivered a soft tap to his shoulder. "Don't feel bad, I'm a space cadet, too," Kam said. Maxine squinted her eyes, slightly surprised, then realized that he might be, as he did take her to the moon. "I guess that little moon date might've given part of that away," She said. Kam grinned. "We went on a what?" He asked jokingly. Maxine folded her arms and gave a smug grin. "If you thought that was a date, let me really show you how much of a space cadet I really am." Maxine appeared eager.

Kam smiled slyly and stepped away. "Axpherial orbit!" He called out into the ceiling. Maxine glanced around, uncertain of what awaited her. "We're about to lift off," He said to Maxine. "Lift what?" Maxine asked, her face fully contorted. Kam smiled and grabbed her hand and sat her on the coal-colored couch leaning against the wall. "We're wearing seatbelts right?" Maxine asked, partly petrified. Kam laughed and said, "The interior has its own gravitational pull to keep us in place. Plus seatbelts suck! They're restrictive." "They're the perfect death condom." Kam laughed hard at this. "Oh god, you're killing me." "Don't be killing me with your lack of secure restraints in this unusually homely spaceship."

Kam chuckled and drew Maxine close as they felt themselves become weightless as the house lifted off into the sky. They soared through the air until they reached the stars, where they beheld a breathtaking view: the colorful lands, the bright oceans, and luminous white ring around Axpherial with the three uniquely placed moons. Maxine was spellbound as she quickly got to her feet and made her way to the window next to the door. Kam followed suit, and when they both arrived, they beheld the radiant sight of Axpherial, its hues of colors radiating out into the star-filled sky. She was entranced by the beauty of it all, and

Kam came up from behind, encircling her waist with his arms and resting his chin on her shoulder.

Maxine sighed blissfully, "This is the most romantic shit anyone has ever done. Or ever will." She nestled into Kam's embrace, feeling his arms wrap around her. "I know you're not big on romance, but I hope to continue to expand your horizons," Kam said. Maxine beamed. "Tell me more," She said. "How about I show you more." Maxine looked up at him with a puzzled smirk. Kam looked up and yelled, "Outer dimensional viewing!" Bliss nervously smirked as Kam released her from his grasp. "What's going on?" She asked, her voice shaking. "Don't be afraid, trust me." He said.

| 32 |

Kam & Maxine

Maxine stiffly nodded as she grasped his hand, and they gazed out of the window. A brilliant white beam surged from the base of the house, opening a dazzling white portal. Without hesitation, the house passed through and emerged to an enticing view. They were well above a pure white sphere half shrouded in darkness. A circular black hole was in the center of the illuminated side, and a circular white one in the center of the dark side. Attached to this mysterious orb were seven beams of light, each connected by a delicate, silver cord.

Each beam of light represented a different dimension. Kam went on to tell her about what each color was. The red was the Pits Realm, the orange was the Somber Realm, yellow was the Anarchy Realm, green was the Tranquility Realm, blue was the Eutopia Realm, indigo was the Guardians Realm, and violet was the Bliss Realm.

Maxine was absolutely astonished. She couldn't believe her eyes, her mouth agape in shock. "Need a mirror or the time?" Kam asked jokingly. Maxine just shook her head, her mouth now buried in her hands. She eventually lowered her hands and kept gazing at the wondrous view, her mouth still agape. "The half-dark sphere in the middle, we call it the Eye of All. Your planet calls it god. As you can see, it looks just like…" "Like the Yin/Yang." Maxine finished.

"Yeah, the dimensions are separated from darkest to lightest to maintain balance and order. The gods created the dimensions eons ago when the realm of Guardians was the only one that existed. The dark influences of the Eye of All started to corrupt the realm, so they created the other realms to prevent the self-extermination of their universe. The Death Realms are not just places souls are trapped forever but serve as either paradise or punishment. Then your soul is placed back into the living to evolve and eventually graduate reincarnation to become immortal gods."

Maxine was completely dumbfounded. "Wow. I'm lost for logical words," she admitted. Her eyes darted to the floor as she said, "And you were right about earlier. I definitely find an overabundance of mushy behavior cringe. But you have a distinctive charm that's just too damn good to pass up on. It's like you're challenging everything I used to believe in. My pride usually wins in those situations. But I'm still wondering where the hell my pride goes when I'm around you." Kam tenderly brushed his lips against her cheek as she cradled his head in her hands. "I feel free," Maxine said. "This is why I built this place. To feel free," Kam said.

Maxine's eyes lit up all of a sudden. "Speaking of freedom, I wrote a poem a few days ago. I was looking up into the sky, and I thought of the dream I had with me and Imani. She saved me from a room that turned into a river of blood. That's the moment I ended my writer's block." Kam looked intrigued. He released his grasp, and they stood facing each other. Kam gazed at Maxine as she became bashful in an instant. "Let me hear it," he said. "It's a rough draft. It needs a few more nips and tucks and maybe a line lift or two." Kam chuckled hard, sensing her shyness. "Rough or not, I'm sure it came from the heart." Maxine blushed as she prepared herself to read. She took a deep breath and said, "Alright, here goes nothing," as she extracted her phone. She scrolled through her notes until she discovered it in her poems folder. She cleared her throat nervously before beginning to read the first line.

"I envied the vacant wings in the sky. The eyes of the stratosphere gazed at me with its lies. I crashed and burned from fantasies of flight.

I lost my path, forfeited my sight. I was serenaded by the kiss of the ground. I found the poke of flames, I found death all around. Just when my fate was too bleak for saving grace, I found redemption, with its smiling face. Now together, we're soaring high. I gained my wings, and I'm beyond the sky."

Kam grinned, feeling beyond elated. "That was exceptional. Your play on words and metaphors seemed to flow with ease." "Thank you," Maxine replied, still feeling shy. "Hey, you have a gift. You should keep at it," he said. "I can't help but be modest. I haven't been able to write for so long. I guess I was inconvenienced by my sinking ship of a life the last couple of years." Kam smiled softly as he gently held her chin in his hands. "Look at you. You're gifted, too. You built this space house, built weapons, built vehicles. How'd you do it?" Maxine asked.

Kam gestured to his head with his index finger. "Mindfulness. If I focus on what I want to build for long enough, all I have to do is imagine every fine detail, and then I materialize it. First, I draw it, then it all goes from there."

"Wait, from thin air?"

"Yeah, we don't need solid materials to build everything. Just a clear mind." Maxine was speechless. It seemed almost too good to be real. But she had heard of so many other strange things lately that she had an easier time accepting this. "I want to learn to control my abilities, too," Maxine said. Kam smirked at this. "I meditated with Ava, but I still don't feel I've mastered the control aspect yet." Kam grinned and said, "I'll be glad to assist." Maxine beamed immediately at the offer. "Thank you." Kam shouted "Home," and in an instant, a beam of light shot out, and the house was instantaneously set back in its original location. The moons illuminated the night sky with a deep blue hue, the sun still yet to rise.

Kam led Maxine up the stairs and into the room. To the right of the bed lay a red mat. Kam dug under the bed and pulled out a second one, placing it next to the first. Sitting down, he crossed his legs on one mat as Maxine followed suit. Closing his eyes, he folded his hands and went through the breathing technique he had taught her. They sat in stillness for a few moments. "Now, I want you to focus on being unseen. Concentrate on that and only that," he said.

Maxine did as she was told. "If a thought comes, observe it, don't react," he said. Maxine fought against her instinct to break down as memories of her family came flooding back. She took deep breaths and concentrated on her body being transparent. She imagined that she'd open her eyes and see nothing. After a few moments, Kam spoke up, telling her to open her eyes.

When she did, she looked down and immediately tried to study her hands. She saw nothing. She was elated as she scanned the rest of herself and saw the same thing. She did it. So did Kam. Invisibility was another ability Kam kept to himself. He liked it that way, he felt some things were better kept private. However, around Maxine, he couldn't help but let this slip. He'd do anything to help her, including revealing parts of himself he never told anyone else.

Maxine smiled. "Oh my god!" Maxine exclaimed. Kam beamed with pride as he saw her progress. "Now close your eyes and focus solely on being seen again," he said. Maxine obeyed the instructions and soon emerged, although it took more focus this time than she anticipated.

Kam took just mere seconds. Maxine was ecstatic. She was over-joyed to finally have some mastery over her abilities. "Thank you so much," Maxine said. Kam gently planted a hand on her shoulder. "Thank yourself, too. You were able to do it, despite the reality of everything. That's how you control your abilities, by focusing on your inner world, and putting the outer world aside, just for the moment," he said. "I just hate how spontaneous my abilities seemed before," She muttered. "If your abilities were dormant for so long, they may be harder to turn on and off. And they usually show themselves when you're in imminent danger."

Maxine understood why her powers had manifested during the crow attack and in the hospital. She wondered, however, why they hadn't surfaced during the train ride and the car accident with Imani. She posed this question to Kam, who put his finger to his chin in concentration. "Think about it a little more. Are you sure it didn't?" He asked. Maxine began to go through those events.

She reflected on the speed of her recovery. Even after her fatal car crash, her healing was remarkably swift. She recalled her wounds from the accident had disappeared in only a few days after she awoke from her coma. Furthermore, she remembered having no visible marks from the train incident. Even when she fractured her arm as a child, the cast was off within a week. Realization dawned on her that they were always there, protecting her.

"I guess they did," Maxine realized. "And now, as you progress, you'll learn more on how to do it at will," Kam said. Maxine smiled. "I'm new to this whole supernatural thing. So forgive how clumsy I may be at taking all this in," Maxine admitted. "You gotta learn to be vulnerable more often, and not be so quick to apologize." Maxine chuckled and took heed. This was something she definitely struggled with. "Being vulnerable meaning detoxing my addiction to rocking a painted smile. Right?" "Sounds like you got the self-awareness down. Let's just focus on turning awareness into practice," Kam said.

Maxine glanced downwards and let out a soft chuckle. "Cute, wise, exceedingly romantic, adorably awkward, superhuman. You're a walking mythology, especially when it comes down to most men in general." Kam blushed as he tried to stifle a grin. "My point is, you're this amazing person, and I'm still picking pieces of myself off the ground. What is your fascination with me?" Kam let out a chuckle. He was fully aware of why he was so smitten. "You remind me so much of myself. Someone striving to be perfect, masking their trauma and flaws. Someone who's still recognizing how beautiful they are. Someone learning to become one with the darkness and not letting it dictate. You're like my reflection, and I'm like yours. We point out every single aspect that we love, and ones we try to avoid within ourselves. So all the things you love about me, you have within yourself," Kam said.

Maxine and Kam rose to their feet. Maxine understood this and knew that Kam was absolutely correct. They existed in each other's lives for a single purpose: to heal one another. They reclined in the bed and felt completely exhausted. They nestled together, picturing their worries and the world fading away. "Is it a shame that I might be falling for you?" Maxine asked. "I feel the same. But I often fear losing you." Kam admitted. "Losing me is the last thing that should be on your mind," Maxine replied.

They lay in each other's embrace, and within a few minutes, they felt themselves get sleepier by the second. They had been so busy lately that they had forgotten how good it felt to just rest. "Do you want me? In every way?" Maxine asked. Kam knew exactly what she meant. "I'd rather cherish you first. There's a soul in there I want to get to know. We'll know when it's time. We won't have to question it," Kam said sleepily. Maxine clung to his words, allowing herself to drift into a peaceful slumber. Wrapped in each other's embrace, they were able to take the rest they both desperately needed.

| 33 |

Kam & Maxine

Kam couldn't tell if it was the sun rays or the beeping sound on his arm that woke him up. Maxine slept peacefully on his chest. He groggily gazed at his blaring delfona, its red light flashing aggressively. Maxine simply shifted, clinging on to sleep. Kam tapped his delfona, and a holographic image of Ava materialized before him.

"Rise and shine, violet eyes," she said. Kam chuckled drowsily as he massaged his eyes. "Hey, can you do me a favor and wake up, superwoman? This concerns her too."

"Nope," Kam said with a playful smirk as he spun around and nudged Maxine awake. Maxine groaned loudly, dreading having to open her eyes.

"Max, it's Ava," Kam said, with sleep in his voice. "Tell her to go away," Maxine said into a yawn.

"Hey! I'm like five feet away!" Ava exclaimed. "Good. I don't like you anyway," Maxine said. "I love you, too. Anyway, major update on the yellow-eyed freaks. They plan on demolishing the city tonight. 11 pm to be exact. It's 6 am here, so we have to crash this party soon before it blows up in our face. Literally."

Kam and Maxine paid close attention, grinning broadly at Ava's lively banter. "I did some snooping. I stole a zemano and keycard from one of the herloids so I was able to see this narley shit in person."

Kam and Maxine gave a light chuckle as Ava continued, "There are underground bombs controlled with electricity. They're using the city's power supply to control them. The plant is fifteen minutes away from the city. We'll need to get to that or it's permanent lights out for everyone."

"What about Kincade and Tobias?" Maxine asked. "They were seen at the death camp outside the city. Turns out it's actually a training facility for the zombified herloids. They're imprisoning the infected and using them as experiments for soldiers. They've already turned some of them. But thankfully, Kincade and Mr. Hewitt are still alive."

Kam tapped his chin, taking it all in. Maxine looked understandably worried. "The power plant is heavily guarded, so I suggest we split up, and one group is team rescue, while the other is team warrior."

"What if there's too many of them? Why can't we all go rescue first, get Kincade and Tobias, then we all go to the power supply together? You know, strength in numbers," Maxine suggested.

"I recommended the split up because if we can kill two birds with one, well... two stones, we can find a way to throw them off and because I think it's the most logical plan so far."

Kam thought about this but thought Maxine had a point. "What if there really were too many guards to handle? I'm not too keen on fighting the guards head on. I think we need to be more inconspicuous. Find our way around them. Maybe..." Kam trailed off, not sure how to continue. Maxine looked up, hoping he'd come up with something. "Maybe?" Ava asked.

Kam raised an eyebrow and asked, "What if we deactivate the bombs one at a time?"

"The bombs are planted in completely different areas around the city. The only sure way to stop them is to temporarily disable the power supply. But the herloids will know something is up." Ava tapped her chin. Her face then lit up with a bright grin. "But if you have a tonch, then we have something more concrete."

A Tonch was an electrical gadget that could permanently disable bombs and other explosives. To make the deactivation work, they needed to ensure each Tonch was placed accordingly, since it was controlled by a computer signal programmed into a delfona. Kam had possession of the device's blueprints.

"Me and Bliss can work on creating those. How many bombs?"

"Ten. Keep in mind that just like the power plant, the bombs are guarded, too. But how many guards I can't say. I'll have to get back to you on that."

There was a brief pause before Ava wrapped up, "Okay, so any other plans to discuss in case these fall through?"

Kam ran through numerous potential outcomes in his mind, all of which resulted in calamity. Maxine did the same, both of them anxiously scanning one another in the hopes of finding an alternate solution. Unfortunately, no such answer presented itself.

"None yet, but I'll bring this back to Talo, Bliss, and Orna. Maybe five heads are better than two in this case," Kam said as Ava chuckled.

"Okay, get back to me when you do. Remember, tik tok, you guys are on a clock." Maxine and Kam shared a laugh. "You're such a cornball! We'll talk to you later," Maxine said as she stretched. Ava giggled and bid farewell as her image faded away.

Maxine finished her stretch and nestled into Kam's chest. She yearned to drift off into a seemingly endless sleep to forget the last 48 hours of her life. She still clung to the hope that everything that took place was all just a dream.

"Max. We have to get up," Kam said, still drowsy. "Can I see the time?" She asked. Kam grinned as he showed her the delfona. It read: 469. Maxine's face twisted in confusion as she stared at the clock, bewildered at what time it read.

"What in the alien is that?" She asked. Kam was initially perplexed, yet he started to chuckle once he realized she hadn't understood.

He broke down axpherian time to her. He told her how different their clocks were. For example: 469 would be 7:22 am on earth. He also broke down an Axpherian year and talked about their version of months. The Axpherian months were: Topa, Mozz, Arki, and Lim respectively. Each month was 375 days. It took exactly 1500 days for their planet to rotate their sun. Below the time it said: Arki, 288. Which meant month three in the 288th day of 375.

When he was done explaining, she looked like she could bash her head against the wall. "You look like I did when our parents taught us about earth dates and times," Kam laughed. Maxine exclaimed, shaking her head in disbelief, "My brain hurts like hell just thinking about it!" Kam let out a hearty chuckle, and Maxine couldn't help but respond with a soft giggle.

"I think I need something that guarantees a blackout and hangover for this," Maxine said as she planted her palms to her face. Kam chuckled softly as he playfully swept her hands away. "I love your morning face," He smiled. Maxine gave him a flirtatious grin and then playfully puffed her breath in his direction. He was taken aback and shut his eyes tight. She just laughed and said, "My morning breath is another story." They both chuckled joyfully as they rose up. "Ready to save the world, superwoman?" He asked. Maxine cringed slightly. It was a little awkward as the only one that called her that was Ava. "Let's leave that to Ava," Maxine said. "What should I call you then? Cause earth girl isn't exactly valid anymore." Maxine smiled as she thought about this. "Let's start with just Maxine. I think it's more fitting." He smiled blissfully as they both rose from the bed, "Maxine, got it."

****

It was still early morning, and the sun glinted off the lime-green water, casting a bright purple tint over the sky. The sun always started as violet before transitioning to a brilliant yellow and then light blue, giving their sunrises and sunsets a purple hue instead of the orange ones on Earth. Maxine got lost in the breathtaking scenery, observing the lime-green waters and the distant metropolis as people commuted on hovercrafts. She and Kam were now perched on the beach side by side.

She was startled by the sound of laughter above her, and when she looked up, she beheld three children soaring high in the sky. She was captivated by the floating landscapes and the joyous smiles of the people around her. The atmosphere was absolutely exhilarating; it seemed like everyone was in a state of bliss. "What are you thinking about?" Kam asked with a grin.

Maxine didn't notice until now that she was frowning. "It's so freeing here," She said as she continued to gaze at the scenery. Kam frowned a little, as he knew the significant differences between there and Earth. "I mean, the unwavering smiles. The overall feeling of safety, love, and I don't know...It just reminds me of how dark my planet is. I love my home, but I see why you always came off with such careless, beautiful energy. You came from a place like this. I can't help but slightly envy, but it's just the flaw of human nature I guess. Instead of being happy for others, we instead want what they have for ourselves."

Maxine gazed downward as the emotions of her words hit her. She continued, "Instead of realizing that we can have unconditional happiness now. From within. Something I'm far from having right now." Kam's grin broadened as he scooted closer to her. Maxine felt like she could melt into him. Their eyes locked, and the world around them seemed to disappear. They were transfixed in each other's gaze, neither of them wanting to break the spell. They simply soaked in the moment, allowing themselves to get lost. Kam yearned to give her that unconditional happiness she craved. But he knew realistically that he couldn't. She had to get it herself.

The air around them felt alive with tension, as if a current of electricity was passing between them. He tenderly cupped her chin and looked into her eyes with a look of understanding. A small smile tugged at his lips and her heart soared as the fluttering in her stomach made her feel weightless.

He sweetly pressed his lips against hers and savored the moment as he kissed her slowly and passionately. She let her eyes drift shut and allowed herself to be swept away. They stayed locked into each other for a few moments, briefly unable to let go. Kam released his grip, and their gaze intensified. An indestructible feeling of bliss swept through them. Their faces stayed inches apart, closely sharing a breath. Kam felt the urge to kiss her more, but knew that he would kiss her forever if he could. His heart thumped heavily in his chest, as he was still consumed with terror that his worst nightmare might still come true. He was haunted by the thought that her demise could still manifest, and that it would be his fault.

"Did I come to the right meeting?" Kam heard from behind him. Kam and Maxine spun around to see Bliss. She was beaming down at them with a broad grin. "Hey, I'm Bliss. His sister," She said as she held her hand out to Maxine. Maxine beamed and shook her hand. "Nice we can finally meet," Maxine said. "Under less awkward circumstances," Bliss smirked. "Definitely agreeable," Maxine replied.

A blood-curdling cry came from the skies. They turned up to see Orna almost free fall to his feet, fumbling and gathering his breath. A few seconds later, Talo came and landed considerably more smoothly. She was taking a breath as well. "I gave you that head start!" Talo exclaimed. "Just take the loss! You're always full of excuses!" Orna retorted. Maxine watched as the two conversed, trading insults back and forth. Eventually, they turned to her and introduced themselves, then exchanged a few final jabs at one another.

"Um, hey! This is about Kam. He has something important to tell us," Bliss said as she interrupted their passive confrontation. Talo and Orna fixed their eyes on him, eagerly wondering what the purpose of their gathering was. "Y'all are so precious," Bliss said as she rolled her eyes. Kam rose to his feet, taking in everyone around him. He rehashed Ava's instructions from earlier that day; the bombs, the plan to separate, and the rescue mission. "And you believe we are capable of doing all of this?" Orna asked with skepticism. "We tried to get the folks to agree to get the Axpherian army involved, but of course they didn't believe us. So yeah, we got to be our own army," Kam said.

Talo also looked doubtful. "I'm on Orna's side, this plan definitely has a lot of wrinkles in it." "I know it doesn't look pretty, but if we want to save everyone, we're the best shot as of right now," Bliss said. "Kind of a crooked shot, but I'm following," Talo said. Orna's eyes paced the ground as he pondered their situation. "I wish I could say that if anyone felt unsafe to back down now, but I also feel like I need all of you," Kam said. "I know you do. We're definitely gonna have to fix the holes in this plan but we're also not gonna let you be an idiot by yourself," Talo grinned. "Yeah, we are all in this glorified suicide mission together," Orna quipped.

Kam and Maxine found their sarcasm amusing and chuckled, but Bliss didn't seem as entertained. "I think my brother and I can guarantee that the last thing you need to worry about is going on a death mission," Bliss said. "I agree with her. If we come up with a solid enough plan I'm sure we can ensure our safety. And the safety of my family," Maxine said. Talo and Orna reluctantly nodded their heads, as they all headed back to Kam's cabin to finish out their plans.

****
******

For the next few hours, they went over various drafts of their plans while Bliss worked on the Tonch prototypes. She finished cloning a substantial number of deactivators, then placed them in a small black bag. Earlier that day, Ava had informed them that the explosives themselves were guarded by at least three invisible herloid soldiers who were keeping a close watch on them. They decided that Kam, Bliss, and Orna would handle deactivation, while Ava, Maxine, and Talo would be responsible for the rescue mission.

Bliss also replicated the zemano device that the herloids had used and provided one to each of them. They planned to disguise themselves as Herloid soldiers to create a smooth diversion. In addition, they equipped mini cameras on their collars to live-stream footage directly to the Axpherian army database. Bliss had spent a couple of years honing her hacking skills, and this was the perfect opportunity to leverage her expertise. She was confident that once the Axpherian Defence Allegiance (ADA) saw the live footage of the death camps, they would be compelled to take swift action and offer the necessary assistance. With the plan firmly in place, everyone was on board.

"Wait. Kincade and Tobias are infected. How do we deal with that?" Maxine asked. Bliss reached inside the silver computer desk drawer and retrieved the blue valves and syringe that Kam had acquired from the basement during the home herloid assault.

"The rescue team will carry these with them. Administer the antidote right after the rescue. It should take effect within a few minutes," Bliss explained. Talo swiftly took the syringe and valves, leading Maxine to raise an eyebrow in question.

"I've used needles and equipment like this before, just being cautious," Talo explained.

"You pronounnced controlling wrong," Orna chimed in, half-joking.

"I think I'd feel more comfortable if I did it. After all, they are my family," Maxine asserted.

"Have you ever used a syringe before?" Talo inquired, with a hint of skepticism.

"My mom was a nurse, dude. I know enough not to be reckless," Maxine replied. As she spoke about her mother, a wave of emotion washed over her, but she managed to keep her composure.

Talo remained hesitant to hand over the syringe. "Just let her hold one valve," Orna suggested, almost pleadingly. Talo looked at Maxine, shaking her head. In response, Maxine reached out and deftly snatched it from her. Talo made a desperate attempt to retrieve it, but Orna positioned himself between them.

"Hey! I'm just trying to save you from doing something potentially destructive!" Talo protested.

"Sorry, not sorry. Truth be told, I don't know you, and you don't really strike me as medically coordinated," Maxine said as she tucked the valves and syringe into her back pocket.

"Earth medical practice and Axpherian medical practice are significantly different! That is Axpherian medical equipment, and I was trained at the palace to use such equipment!" Talo argued.

"Looks earthy enough to me," Maxine retorted, standing her ground.

"Just let her do it, Talo. She's not the enemy. We're all a team, and we can't complete this mission if we're not united," Orna reasoned.

Talo straightened up, took a deep breath, and conceded, "Fine."

"Like Orna said, we're a team. We only have a few hours left. We have to set everything in motion now. We managed to extend the portal for two hours, equivalent to four hours on Earth. Time is of the essence, to say the least. We've reviewed the plans multiple times. If any of you have last-minute changes, speak up now," Kam said. Everyone turned their expectant gaze toward him, eager to proceed. No one interjected.

Kam nodded with satisfaction. Maxine, Bliss, and Talo readied their laser guns, which gleamed white with elongated barrels. Kam secured his sword in its scabbard, ensuring it lay securely across his back. Orna, on the other hand, carried two axes strapped to his back, with two bands crossing his chest.

"Ava will meet team rescue outside the camp entrance, near the electric fence guarding it. The deactivation team will rendezvous at the first bomb location, which is situated beneath a willow tree in James Polk Forest Park in the southwest. I'll display the maps with the exact locations for planting the Tonch devices. Our aim is to draw the herloids away by creating diversions, as we've previously discussed. We just need to select one diversion at each location," Kam explained with urgency.

They all tapped the shapeshifting devices on their wrists, transforming into Herloid soldiers with smooth scaly skin from the neck down, dark yellow eyes, sharp teeth, and sharp nails, all of which repulsed them.

"Let's promise to never do something this gross ever again," Talo suggested, prompting a chorus of chuckles.

"Agreed. Let's get this over with," Orna added, sharing the feeling of disgust.

As Bliss was about to activate the delfona, Orna interrupted. "May I have a go this time?" Bliss reluctantly handed it over, her expression tinged with trepidation. Talo appeared on the verge of vomiting. Orna squinted one eye and took aim carefully. He mumbled something inaudible as he unleashed the portal, its white and blue hues mirroring those of Earth. He staggered back but managed to remain upright.

He, Kam, and Bliss walked into the portal leading to the park. Talo activated the second portal just east of the death camp's entrance. As they cautiously advanced, their hearts raced within their chests. In an instant, the portal vanished, and they found themselves inside. It was now too late to turn back.

| 34 |

Kam

The portal closed behind Kam, Orna, and Bliss. They found themselves standing in a park, illuminated by a starlit sky. To their left, a concrete path meandered around an empty playground, dotted with a swing set, all resting on a bed of white, crumbly sand. Beyond the playground, the path disappeared into the shadows of the trees. They carefully made their way into a cluster of trees to discuss the route of the first bomb.

Kam tapped his delfona, and a hologram of the park appeared. He pinpointed the location of the isolated willow tree, a quarter of a mile past the playground down the dimly-lit path. "Okay, so we need one to act as a diversion, one to aim, and one to plant the device under the tree," Kam said.

"I'll aim," Bliss said quickly. Orna's face was filled with dismay. "Look Orna, you're great with the Ax, but I don't think you're quite ready to fire a gun," Kam said. Orna narrowed his eyes in disapproval. "Why does everyone think I'm so incompetent?" Bliss and Kam gazed at him with puzzlement. "Nobody would have brought you here on such a life-threatening mission if we thought you wouldn't be useful," Kam said. "I have a feeling that those words, just like my presence, are sympathy-based." Kam slightly contorted as he scrutinized his expression. "Maybe I'll just go home. Maybe your repressed ability to frown upon my worthiness is starting to bring me to the realization that I'm a glorified tag-along."

Kam was astonished by what he heard. He was becoming increasingly frustrated by Orna's lack of assurance. "Orna, stop. We have never thought of you like that. And as hard as it is to believe sometimes, neither does Talo. I brought you here because I know your potential. I've seen you progress. I've never seen someone learn to aim so accurately before with those AX's. Ever. You're a fast learner. That's why I brought you here," Kam said. Orna gave a smirk as he listened to Kam's words. He felt his spirit lift as he knew Kam was right.

"I will distract, and you can plant the first deactivator," Kam said to Orna. Bliss unzipped her backpack and presented Orna the Tonch. The Tonch was long and slim, with a blue luminescent encircling its tip. "Plant the Tonch about two feet from the front of the tree. It will sink into the ground, and you'll see it blink blue twice from the gravel. That will let you know that it's planted." Kam said as Orna accepted the device. He delicately turned the lustrous gray device in his palm. "Why'd you guys have blueprints for this thing anyway?" He asked. "Kam's unusual fascination with military weaponry and my willingness to support it. And because, well, he needed my expertise," Bliss said with a hint of self-satisfaction in her tone. "See how she's always reminding me that she's my right hand?" Kam grinned. "It's second nature to humble you," Bliss remarked, a smile tugging at the corners of her lips as she and Kam shared an amused glance.

Kam groaned from the weight on his knees, unaware of how long they had been crouching. "You didn't break a bone, did you?" Bliss jested. Kam chuckled softly as he gathered himself. Orna gazed up and grinned at them both. "Thanks for reminding me that I'm not a disappointment," Orna said. Kam gave a smirk as he placed his hand on Orna's shoulder. He recalled all the times Orna had been teased for not mastering certain skills. Orna often had a tendency to quit prematurely to avoid being mocked. But when he finally stuck with it, he would usually surpass his peers. He was aware that their words hurt him, and it still caused him distress at times. Sometimes, Talo and Kam's jesting remarks affected him more than he let on. He knew they were just having a bit of fun, but it still managed to hurt him a bit.

"Don't ever refer to yourself as a disappointment, man," Kam assured. "Mmm, I think you're a notch above insufferable sometimes, but that's my opinion," Bliss said, eliciting a chuckle from the group. Kam glanced at his delfona, which was switched to earth time. It was 7:39 pm. "We gotta move out, let's go," Kam declared as they all tapped their shapeshifting devices and became invisible. Keeping their footsteps as soft as they could muster, they stealthily moved onto the concrete path and into the forest shrouded in darkness.

They stopped short of an opening to the willow tree and Kam tapped on his shapeshifting device and materialized. He glanced to his left and saw Bliss, her form still recognizable despite her camouflage. He gestured towards the tree and Bliss nodded, gliding into the dense foliage. Kam cringed as the tree shuddered with her movement. She perched atop the highest branch and trained her gun on the solitary willow. Kam emerged from his hiding place and cautiously approached the tree, which seemed to be abandoned.

Orna knelt low, despite still being invisible, as he kept a close eye on Kam approaching the tree that still appeared seemingly unguarded. Kam stepped forward and uttered a strange, unfamiliar language. It was Modonii, the language of the Herloids. It sounded like fancy gibberish to the average ear. In their language, he told them, "You guys are needed in midtown. The leader wants you guys to search for an escaped prisoner from the camps. Just come down in your disguises. Me and my partner will guard the tree." Three Herloids suddenly appeared, fitted in all-black military attire with long laser guns strapped to their backs. There was a male Herloid with dark brown skin, and two others, one male and one female, with pale skin. "We have not obtained those directives. Generally, the chief communicates with us through our earpiece," the brown-skinned Herloid said in Modonii. "The earpiece is experiencing communication errors. He notified me to convey this message to you."

Kam continued to communicate with them in Modonii as it took several minutes to fully convince them to move into action. "Where's your partner?" The female Herloid inquired with a hint of suspicion. "Soldier 228, let's go!" Kam called out in Modonii. Orna remained motionless, for he was unfamiliar with the language. Kam repeated himself, fighting to keep his composure. Eventually, Orna understood and tapped the shape-shifting device, becoming visible. He stepped forward as the Herloids' expressions became increasingly dubious. "He's stiff for a soldier," One male Herloid murmured in Modonii. "Fresh trainee. I'm his mentor," Kam assured.

Orna silently shook their hands, attempting to mask the fact that he did not comprehend their words. Kam thanked them in Modonii, and they reluctantly walked away. Kam and Orna waited patiently for five minutes before Orna spun and carefully placed the Tonch two feet away from the tree. Kam withdrew his sword vigilantly and scanned the area around him. A blue light briefly flashed twice from the gravel beneath them. Orna rose up with a satisfied grin.

"See what happens when you believe in yourself?" Kam said, elated. "Thanks! But man, you've got to teach me Modonii. I had no clue what that gibberish meant!" Orna said. "You should consider taking it at the palace. It's an optional curricular, but in this case, it was..." POW! A loud gunshot reverberated, drawing the attention of Kam and Orna. Drawing his sword, Kam whirled around, while Orna snatched up his ax. Just as they began to retreat, two more shots rang out. Suddenly, a Herloid man came barreling towards them, clutching his shoulder as though he had already been wounded. Orna hurled his ax, but the Herloid managed to catch it with perplexing accuracy.

Kam and Orna were struck with dread as Kam raised his sword. But before he had a chance to strike, the herloid was shot right between the eyes, just as he was only a few feet away. At the sound of the gunshot, both of them reflexively ducked. Then, they looked up and saw Bliss swooping down from the trees, no longer in disguise.

"They all started running back when they realized what was going on. I saw them quickly and killed the other two before they even made it close. He's lucky my first shot was in the shoulder," Bliss said as she stood beside them.

Kam and Orna's pulses raced with the adrenaline that flooded their bodies. They felt their hearts hammering in their chests.

"This is the part where you thank me for saving you, right?" Bliss gestured. Kam and Orna released a gust of laughter, a sense of relief washing over them. "You annoy me greatly," Kam grinned. "You're welcome," Bliss beamed.

They glanced at the delfona; it was now 8:02 pm. "We got under three hours to keep up this little winning streak," Kam said. "Score!" Bliss exclaimed, as if she relished the challenge. "Let's try to pick up the pace this time," Kam said. Bliss and Orna nodded in agreement as they pored over the maps for the next bomb locations.

Orna then spied something in one of the herloids' pockets. It appeared to be a pair of small fishing goggles. He delved into his pocket and produced the goggles. When he put them on, the night became almost as bright as day. The goggles had no straps and fit snugly over his eyes. Instantly, he realized what they were used for.

"Kam! Bliss!" He called out. Kam and Bliss gazed at him, captivated. "What are those?" Bliss asked. "They were on the herloid. It allows you to see in the dark. And maybe it..." He trailed off. "One of you disappear really quickly," He said.

Kam and Bliss both appeared perplexed initially but shortly obliged. Kam vanished from sight, yet the goggles revealed him as plainly as the sun in the sky. "Wow! Looks like the herloids can say goodbye to their little camouflage hiding spot. Well, in this case, spots," Orna said excitedly. Suddenly, they were visible again and exchanged glances. Kam could sometimes see them with his own eyes, but not always. This convinced him enough to accompany Bliss to the two other bodies.

The two of them located a pair of goggles on the corpses of the herloids. Hastily sliding them on, they tested their power by disappearing from one another's sight. The goggles operated efficiently, and the duo understood that their task would be considerably easier now.

The second bomb was buried beside an aged brick building, close to an active gas station. Bliss activated her goggles and spotted three herloids nearby. She took aim and shot two of them above their eyebrows and one in the throat. The herloid shot in the throat was mortally wounded, bleeding out within seconds, and the tonch was planted within minutes. They hastened as they pinpointed each bomb. Most of them had only three herloid soldiers safeguarding them, whereas a few had as many as seven.

With each planted tonch, they became more skilled at diverting the herloids and executing with sharp precision. Bliss took care of most of the casualties with her gun, while Kam had to fend off a couple with his sword. Orna even employed his shape-shifting powers, becoming a snake to strangle a guard to death. Kam was deeply ashamed to admit it, but he experienced a thrill from killing the soldiers. He later felt much remorse and hoped each kill would be their last, yet he couldn't deny that part of him was enjoying it. Fortunately, his heroic, compassionate side was much more powerful than the darker side of him.

Kam checked his watch and saw that it was 10 pm. They had made it to the ninth location just in time. Ahead of them, looming ominously, were the towering gray walls. These walls stood at an intimidating 25 meters and were topped with three lines of humming electric barbed wire. Turning away from the walls, they walked back to the bomb location that was tucked away inside an ancient brick building.

A sign with faded red lettering on a white background remained at the top of the building, its bold cursive still legible enough to make out the words, "Lee's meat market." The building had been deserted for decades.

Kam and Bliss crept up to the entrance of the factory, donning their goggles. The bomb was dead in the middle of the room, guarded heavily by twelve soldiers stationed around the perimeter. As they peered through a faded window, they carefully surveyed the scene.

"This bomb must be sacred as hell. They're everywhere and then some," Orna pointed out. Kam nodded his head as he continued to observe.

"This diversion is gonna be challenging, to say the least," Kam said. Kam and Bliss's original plan was now pushed aside as the three of them came up with various ways to enter the premises, only to discard each plan quickly. They began to argue in hushed tones until they came to an unfortunate stalemate. Kam glanced at his delfona; the clock read 10:11 pm.

"We aren't getting anywhere. Time isn't gonna wait for us to finish arguing. Millions will be dead in less than an hour, so can we please, put logic over feelings? Just this time," Kam said. You could hear the shakiness in his tone as he had fully taken in what was at stake. Bliss and Orna perceived the gravity of the situation and nodded in agreement.

"Okay, me and Bliss will march in disguised as soldiers. Orna, I want you to go out undisguised and bait them into the forest. Bliss will plant the Tonch this time, then we go to the final location. We have to act fast. Very fast," Kam urged. Orna let out a smirk as he turned off the disguise. Slowly, he stepped back with a boastful grin spread across his face. Kam and Bliss were a bit puzzled, seeing the excitement in his expression.

"Herloid soldiers! We know exactly what you're doing! Now come out slowly and surrender yourselves!" Kam and Bliss quickly camouflaged as the soldiers erupted in chaos. "I'll set this place on fire in 3...2..." Orna screamed as he shifted into a colossal gray wolf. He then quickly ran into the shadows of the woods ahead of him. The soldiers gave chase to him as Kam and Bliss looked on. When the last soldier had vanished from sight, the two of them sprung into action, hurrying inside.

Kam's delfona pointed to the exact spot where the bomb was. The factory was empty and dilapidated, with a second-story balcony crumbling away and a thick layer of dust coating everything in sight. Kam and Bliss had to stifle coughs as they got down on their hands and knees to plant the Tonch. Kam swiftly planted it, and Bliss and him beamed as they saw the ground take on a flashing blue hue. They both removed their goggles and faced each other, beaming. "One more before we save the world," Kam said with a grin. "The worlds, you mean," Bliss replied. "Exactly," Kam said with a wink. "Let's hurry and get Orna before he's..."

Kam's eyes widened in astonishment as a herloid soldier abruptly appeared and clamped his hand over Bliss's mouth. Kam was then flung across the room with such force that he landed in a pile of empty barrels with a loud groan. Bliss's screams were muffled by the herloid's hand. "Imposters, General. Just as I suspected," The herloid said as he deactivated Bliss's disguise.

| 35 |

Kam

The soldier yanked the zemano from her arm as the General herloid loomed before her. He was a colossus - seven feet of toned muscle and black scales from neck to toe. His human-like face was dark brown, and his eyes were a piercing yellow. He grinned devilishly as he faced Kam. Kam attempted to lunge at him when two more herloids seized him by the arms, turning his disguise off. The General plucked Bliss's bag and yanked out the last tonch. He gazed at her and sneered as he crashed the tonch onto the floor and destroyed it with his pistol-shaped laser gun. "That was foolish," He said with a dark laugh.

Kam let out a desperate cry as he attempted to reach Bliss. He attempted to use his telekinesis to escape, yet realized that his powers were useless, leaving him perplexed. The General laughed mockingly. "How does it feel to be the helpless one?" He asked. "What are you talking about!?" Kam angrily exclaimed. "I knew you'd be here. That's why there's a force field blocking your worthless sixth sense," The General said with a smug grin. He spoke with a voice that was deep and menacing. It sent shivers down Kam's spine and filled him with an intense feeling of dread.

Kam strained with all his might, desperately attempting to wrench himself from the guards' grip, yet they were simply too powerful for him. "I said helpless, because I saw what you did to one of my other guards. I'll admit, your perceptiveness is impressive. But that's not the only thing I'm referring to," The General said. This confused Kam. "What else could he be referring to?" He thought. Kam recalled the words of the herloid he had slain, about how the Axpherians had lied about their past. He was slightly mollified by this insight. The General smirked, as he caught on to Kam's revelation.

"Your government and army have damned our species to near extinction. They snatched away our only hope of restoring our world. They helped the rebels annihilate our people. Millions perished at the hands of your soldiers. We tracked down the planet Utak where the Viola poison could be used against its inhabitants. We were more than willing to sacrifice another species to keep our own alive. But instead of killing them, the poison merely stripped them of their powers, but still had the ability to turn them upon death. We had the advantage until the Axpherians arrived with their anti-poison drones. We none-theless managed to take over Earth, a planet too primitive to put up a fight against us. Now our army continues to grow and soon billions will be reanimated. Your planet is doomed, your military are no match for our forces. Our retribution will be absolute. We will have two new worlds to call our own."

Kam's rage only intensified as he heard the herloid speak. Bliss froze, realizing she was powerless against the soldier. "Why earth? Why did your attempts to reanimate your own failed?" Kam asked. "You're very inquisitive for someone with so little time on their hands," The General said, sounding like he already won. "But since this will be…." "And why was I a target?" Kam snapped.

The General was initially perplexed, but then his features contorted into a devilishly mischievous grin. "Because you and your family were a hindrance to our plans, and we knew we had to eliminate you first. But my assassins failed me, and they paid a fatal price for it," He said. "What about my other question?" Kam asked as he boiled with rage. The General's lips curled upwards in a sinister smirk, relishing in Kam's inquisitiveness. "For some reason, it was in several herloids' DNA to transgress past totalitarian leadership. The most logical leadership when keeping order and balance of one's world. We figured another species' DNA just might be more amenable and less questionable to our rulers. And also, our planet became inhabitable. Thanks to your species. So I'm not the villain here. Thank your planet for inciting this war that caused two different worlds to collapse. Now Earth and Axpherial will be next, we plan on making sure our species never face extinction again. We will invade more worlds, and none of you will be alive to witness it."

Kam fixed his gaze on the General, not dumbfounded by the news, but appalled by the General's apparent lack of remorse for what he had done. "So..." Kam swallowed hard before he continued, "So you figured that getting rid of the existence of other worlds was the best choice because your own had been destroyed. It was you who made the resolution to massacre your own species. Eradicating them, then reviving them. Your people were no more than just lab experiments to you. And now you want to play this anti-hero role like your crimes are justified? I find way too many holes in your logic. So excuse me for reading past your excuses. The truth is, you're an evil dictator who masks their fear with power. People like you deserve death." Kam's face was bright red with fire as he spat the words at him.

The General's sinister grin quickly vanished from his visage. "I may deserve death, Kam. But it's you who will face it," A wicked grin resurfaced across his face, though not as bold or assured as before. "Kill them," He said, sounding bored. The guards forced Kam and Bliss to kneel, guns trained on the backs of their heads. Fear gripping them both, they could feel the cold metal of the barrels against their skin. "Rest easy, kid," The General said as the soldiers cocked their guns.

Kam looked at Bliss, knowing they failed. Kam saw a tear fall from her eye as they looked at each other and knew this was the end. "I love you, sis," Kam said as the tears in his throat made it difficult to talk. Bliss nodded tearfully as they looked at each other and braced for the gunshot to put them to rest. Kam, though, immediately felt a powerful desire to live. He believed that it wasn't the end and shouldn't be. Not this close. Not this far. Not like this. The herloids then pulled their triggers.

Kam shut his eyes tightly, expecting the end. But, no gunshots fired. This left Kam puzzled, as he watched the soldiers pull the triggers a second time, yet still nothing. The General stared at them, clearly baffled. Kam then took the opportunity to try with all his might to levitate his sword from his scabbard. Closing his eyes tightly, he focused on his sword leaving its sheath and piercing the guard who held Bliss. He was determined to protect her, even if it meant forfeiting his own life. When he opened his eyes, he saw his sword had done the job, as it was now firmly embedded in the guard's head.

The soldier let out a blood-curdling shriek as the blade slowly tore through his flesh. His eyes rolled back in his head, and a sickening gush of black blood cascaded from the top of his skull. The sword had penetrated through his entire body and was now being pulled out, leaving a trail of death in its wake. The sword spun like a helicopter propeller, slicing the General's gun in two. Then, with a swiftness of a wraith, it beheaded the two guards that had Kam in their grasp. The General emitted an inhuman-like scream as the sword plunged into his chest. He collapsed to the ground as the sword returned to its place on Kam's back.

Bliss stirred, feeling a wave of surprise and relief wash over her at the realization that she was still alive. She gazed at Kam, with the need for an explanation written on her face. Just when Kam fixed his mouth to say something, Orna burst through the door, breathless. "I led the soldiers into a portal to a planet in the somber realm. The planet was made of fire. Can you say, ashes to ashes?" Orna joked breathlessly as Bliss and Kam nervously chuckled. "Using earthly terms for dark humor?" Kam laughed. Orna's grin broadened. "Well, I could have also said that they were burned from that joke." The group emitted a brief chuckle. "Well tell me, did you turn off the force field?" Bliss asked. Orna looked confused. Kam and Bliss were shocked. "Wait, so how did you…" "Nah I'm kidding, I killed the force field, and their guns." Orna cast his gaze around, aghast at the circle of corpses encircling him, a shy smirk playing on his lips. "Wow, looks like a black river of corpses," He said. "Courtesy of Kam, and his rotating blade of death," Bliss said as she grinned at Kam, who shyly smiled back.

Just as they began to leave, the General suddenly awoke and thrust his hand onto the ground. Sparks flew, and Orna and Bliss were jolted with electricity. Kam let out a shrill scream as he witnessed their bodies twitching with the power of the shock before collapsing in a heap. The General grinned smugly as he rose up. Kam let out an exasperated scream as he charged the General, and the two of them soared into the heavens. They climbed ever higher, nearly brushing against the thin white clouds. Kam and the General traded blows as they flew, until finally Kam cast the General towards a tall building in the center of town.

Terrified spectators either fled or began filming the interaction. The General hurtled through the structure and collided forcefully with a Taxi cab. Kam hovered in the air, observing him. Then the General grinned as he rose, seemingly unscathed as he ascended and hoisted half the construction he had penetrated and threw it at Kam. Kam gasped hard as the building was hurled at him. He dashed through the structure, brandishing his blade. His fury escalating, he sprinted to the end of the building and rose up, soaring into the air. The building ascended beyond the gray barricades, plummeting downwards. Thankfully, the building was mostly vacant, and no casualties ensued.

Kam was astonished at his strength, and then he flew after the General, who was running away. It was like he was a bird of prey, with a blazing fury coursing through him. He pursued the General up a towering skyscraper, sword drawn. As they neared the summit, the General unsheathed his blade. They clashed blades a few times, their swords crossing to form an X as they each attempted to overpower the other. The General was taken aback by his strength. "This Viola might seem like mere poison with reanimation properties, but it's much more than that!" The General said through gritted teeth. "What?" Kam asked.

"The Viola, it contains traces of DNA from the Gods! It has more powers than you could ever imagine! I tested a non-lethal version on myself, and now I'm unstoppable!" The blades drew nearer to Kam, their sharp edges glinting in the moonlight, as he desperately fought against the General's immense power. "This one will create an army of God's!" Kam used his telekinesis to hurl the General away. The General crashed into the concrete structure beside a window, and Kam towered over him, sword aimed at his temple.

"How did you obtain Godly DNA?" Kam demanded. The General merely chuckled, understanding he wouldn't provide him with a response. "You won't break me that easily," He declared, heaving Kam into the sky. Kam executed a graceful flip before facing him again. With a furious yell, he lunged at the General, and their swords collided, creating a metallic ringing that echoed through the night as they fought on the side of the building. Kam and the General clashed swords once more, Kam feeling the weariness creep up on him as the blades formed another X and neared his face.

"Just know that everyone you love will soon be nothing but dust!" The General said through gritted teeth. Kam felt the cold steel of the swords nearly brush his face as he struggled fiercely against their razor-sharp edges. "And your species will be my loyal subjects!" The General said as he was seemingly close to finishing Kam. Kam let out a shriek of anguish as he exerted all his strength to force the General back. The General descended onto a window, his weight causing a loud groan and a deep crack in the glass. Kam towered him and was about to deliver the finishing strike when the General suddenly thrust his sword into Kam's abdomen.

Kam let out a gasp of shock, then a faint cry as the General's lips curled into a sinister smile. The General hoisted Kam up, and the sword began to lift them both into the air. Kam let out a terrified screech as the General's smile broadened into a wicked grin.

"You thought you could be the hero in this story, didn't you? You thought this would play out like every other fairy tale but guess what?" The General clamped his hand around Kam's throat, his grip tightening as a trickle of blood escaped from Kam's lips. "This time the hero is the casualty," He said as he got close to Kam's dying face.

Kam clenched his eyes shut, his body shaking as he desperately attempted to fight off the inescapable feeling of death looming over him. "You are a worthless Axpherian who sacrificed his best friend and sister only for you to watch them die with just a snap of my fingers. And now, you and your friends will dwell in the afterlife, and my reign will begin." He clenched Kam's neck tightly as he rose ever higher into the air, and Kam's strength drained away from his injury.

"Your ambition. Your skill. Though exceptional, still wasn't enough," The General's lips curled into a grin as he observed Kam slowly drift off into unconsciousness. "This is the end of you, and the dawn of my kingdom," He declared as he rifled through Kam's back pocket and seized the maps of the Axpherian army's base camps. He spoke with a sinister tone, "And this... I'm afraid, is mine to keep." Kam slipped from his blade and his unconscious body began to descend. In what felt like an eternity, Kam plummeted from the top of the highest skyscraper and into a fragile, empty pedestrian bridge, shattering it into pieces before finally plunging into the murky depths of the water below.

The General sneered viciously as he wiped Kam's blood off his blade. He seemed pleased as he watched the destroyed bridge spew debris into the river below. He then soared to the power plant outside the city to use the energy supply to trigger the bombs. Once the lights of the city flickered on then off, the city would be turned into a sinkhole.

| 36 |

Maxine

Talo and Maxine stood in awe as the portal shut behind them, revealing a colossal building with an imposing barbed-wire fence. Maxine gasped as she gazed upon the building. "So all the rumors were true," she muttered. She looked up at the large, ancient-looking white structure, which was split into multiple sections. From the exterior, it resembled a deserted prison, and it was. It had been closed for two decades.

"Rumors?" Talo asked. "Death camp. I told dad it existed. He thought they all got taken to the isolation shelter at the stadium," She said. "Wow, Earth is truly hell," Talo said. "Thanks," Maxine replied casually. "I wasn't being nice, you know," Talo said. "I know, but facts are facts," Maxine shrugged.

Ava materialized abruptly in front of them, undisguised. Maxine and Ava both recoiled in shock, screaming. "Even under disguise, the scared little girl instinct never fails does it?" Ava laughed. Maxine and Talo deactivated their disguises as they stood before her. Although their terror had abated, their astoundment was still visible.

"Dude, did you enjoy almost obliterating my heart?" Maxine asked. "Only a lot," Ava smiled. She swiveled her head and glanced at Talo, giving her a warm smile. "Hi, I'm Ava. Her sister slash bestie," She said as she held out her hand.

Talo grinned and accepted her hand. "Wow, you're really pretty!" Ava smiled. "Thank you," Talo beamed as she and Ava concluded their handshake. "So you think you're really pretty?" Ava said with jest in her voice. "Huh?" Talo asked, confused. "It's a movie reference. You should watch it sometime on earth. It's a pretty wicked chick flick." Talo remained slightly bewildered, while Maxine chuckled at her cluelessness. "I sometimes prey on people's ignorance. It's kind of funny to see people crumble," Ava said. Talo seemed slightly flustered by Ava's wit, while Maxine appeared amused. "You'll get used to her, I promise," Maxine assured. Talo just nodded, hardly amused. "Anyway dude, what's the plan?" Maxine asked.

Ava gave a smirk as she tapped her delfona, and a 3D map of the camp's interior appeared before her. The image zoomed in to reveal seven floors packed with cells.

"They keep the prisoner cells underground. They keep the men, women, and children separated into three different sections. Kincade and Tobias are in a cell together on the top floor in cell room B605. We march in as herloid soldiers with our livestream cams activated. We rescue Tobias and Kincade, give them the antipoison, then place them in Kam's cabin in Axpherial for safety. The army should respond and take over from there."

"Sounds solid enough," Maxine said. Talo peered, her face laced with skepticism. "What if the army doesn't reply? What if there is a communication error? Why can't we send everyone back to Axpherial for safety?" Talo asked. "Because for one, there isn't enough room for stray refugees in the tens of thousands to come to Axpherial. And for two, this is sleeping hours in the camps. Only a select few are chosen for experiments. It's the least guarded time, and they will be caught completely off guard by the Axpherian army. And three, you should know how fast the army is in dangerous situations like this. And four, they're infected. Do you have enough antidote for all of them? I didn't think so," Ava said.

Talo crossed her arms, her expression stern. "Girl, lose the pouty face and put on a brave one. You're gonna need it," Ava said as they all turned on their herloid disguises. "Okay ladies, feminist power on three?" Ava cheered. "Feminist?" Talo asked. "You grew up with equal privilege. Earth is as divided as.. I don't know, but they're the definition of divided and conquered," Ava said. "You sound like Kincade, dude." Maxine said, slightly weirded out. "Wow, that is something he'd say. I think he's rubbing off on me. Gross," Ava said as Maxine giggled. Talo stifled a giggle and tried to disguise it with her fist. "Glad my humor finally caught up to you,I knew you'd adapt," Ava said as she led the way. Talo removed her fist from her face, and her expression quickly shifted to one of seriousness. The trio approached the front gate, which appeared to be deserted. As they arrived at the gate, two herloid soldiers suddenly materialized at the entrance.

Ava presented the guards with her stolen badge. The soldier nodded, prompting the guard at the upper left guard post to permit their entry. With a buzzing sound, the gates opened on either side. "Glad to see you, soldier," Ava said in Modonii. "Same here, soldier," The soldier replied in Modonii as they both saluted each other. As they entered the entryway, Maxine's gaze swept across the area. There were several other guards, yet they were hidden from view, pacing stealthily about. Suddenly, Maxine thought she could make out a guard that seemed to be blending in with the surroundings. She dismissed it from her mind, however, and continued to trail Ava and Talo.

As they walked through, Maxine whispered, "What in the tongues were you speaking?"

Ava laughed and said, "Modonii. Mom taught me some before she died, but I became fluent on my own."

"Dude, it sounded like two toddlers going back and forth."

"Get used to it in here. Most speak English, too, but some of them are hardly fluent," Ava said.

"I understand Modonii, too," Talo said. "You like letting people know that you're a search engine, don't you?" Ava said, rolling her eyes. Talo raised an eyebrow. "You're a know-it-all. Did I read that right?" Ava asked.

"I don't know everything. But when I'm right, I'm usually spot on," Talo replied.

"So I read it right," Ava said as she scanned her badge to the large metal door in front of her. The door beeped as it let them inside.

The hallways gleamed, illuminated by a bright white light. The beige marble floor shone, its glossy surface reflecting their every move. Each step they took revealed a startling clarity in the floor's mirror-like surface. Maxine and Talo shivered, feeling the immediate coldness of the halls that smelled like fresh paint. Ava sped through the compound, as if she were one of the soldiers. In contrast, Maxine and Talo were making their way with cautious, calculated strides, as if they were sneaking around. Suddenly, Ava halted, no longer feeling their presence.

She glanced back and noticed them, her face scrunching up in annoyance. "Can you guys try to blend in better? Significantly better?" Ava asked anxiously. "Sorry, dude. Forgot about this scaly costume for a minute," Maxine exclaimed, now aware of how peculiar she appeared. "They have a lot of eyes in the sky here. If you look even a little out of place..." Ava paused for a second before continuing, "Try to look more severe. Like you secretly hate life but at the same time like a subservient, brain-dead soldier."

Ava tried to sound as quiet as she could. "In other words, upright, straight, just pretend we're not here to blow their plans up in their faces," Ava said. Maxine quickly straightened as did Talo. Talo was dubious of Ava's leadership, but since she was unfamiliar with the area, she reasoned that the most reasonable choice was to follow her guidance. But she found it a bit perplexing that Ava knew so much, which aroused her suspicion.

Ava spun left at the end of the corridor, Maxine and Talo hurrying to keep up. The hallway was identical to the rest, Maxine lifting her gaze to spot a myriad of cameras in the ceiling - seven in this single passageway. They arrived at the end of the corridor and encountered a glass elevator. Ava pressed a pair of wiggly lines on the panel, and the glass lit up with an ethereal orange glow. The numerals displayed were Mondonii, looking like strange shapes that didn't belong to-gether. "Mondonii numbers," Ava declared, observing the bewildered expression on Maxine's face. "I know," Talo said.

Ava couldn't help but roll her eyes at her for what felt like the millionth time as they entered the elevator and the glass doors shut in front of them. "Wait? So many people went missing from the govern-ment's hands. How did all of this slip past them?" Maxine asked as the elevators descended. "The city is taken over by these herloids. They killed the government officials here, and they misled the real military out of the city. The infected were supposed to be transported out of the immunity cities into safe camps to await the antidote, not the so-called immunity stadium. The infected were instead led to this prison slash training ground for new soldiers that they plan on sending to Axpherial and a couple of other planets. This is one of several training grounds." Maxine swallowed hard and Talo gazed intensely as they took this in.

Ava then continued, "Most of the infected were left for dead, to transform them into regular herloid citizens. Also, they had to make this whole thing look like a real viral pandemic. Too many missing with no explanation would've roused suspicion. The world govern-ments and Axpherians were working on the Aphlama prototype, Kam's parents played a huge role in that. But after their house was torched, some of the final blueprints were destroyed, and the Axpherians now have to give the limited supply they do have through injections until it's finalized. They keep some of the cure at the base camps, but it will be at least a couple more weeks until another full batch is fully ready. They do however, have just enough for the people in this prison camp. The herloids already feel like they have enough soldiers here, and they plan on invading the next city soon. They figured already that the other citizens in Zeus city are disposable. They're either immune to the poison or had the antidote already. So they know they can't turn them into anything. That's why they're turning Zeus city into a tomb. The citizens left are useless to them."

Talo and Maxine took this in solemnly. Maxine's mind raced to the hospital, picturing the carnage of those who had not been infected.

Maxine shuddered at this. "I'm sorry, but all of this info doesn't surprise me. The herloid government was one of the most vile. The herloids depended on power like air," Talo said.

Talo fixed Ava with a suspicious glare and abruptly pressed the button that halted the elevator. Ava and Maxine stared at her, bewildered, as if she had gone off the deep end. "I find your intelligence a little too suspicious," Talo hissed. Ava looked surprised yet slightly amused by her suspicion. "Does my knowledge offend you?" Ava asked, puzzled. "Your arrogance reminds me of..." Talo trailed off as she took her gun from her back and trained it at Ava's head. "It sounds like a herloid trying to lead us to our execution!" She growled viciously. Maxine then trained her own gun on Talo's temple. "I wouldn't do that if I were you," Maxine hissed.

Ava stood motionless with her hands raised, her lips curved in a smug grin. "Someone's cognitive dissonance can't take that her genius can be outmatched. So I have to be one of them to be this intelligent? Am I right or am I right?" Ava asked.

"Maxine, you don't find her unusual knowledge about this place and this pandemic a bit odd?"

"No, I don't."

"What if she's one of them and she pulls the reverse card on us and takes us out?"

"I'll take my chances. And you will take yours, too. Now do the smartest thing you've done since I've met you and put the gun away."

"You're not the boss."

"But right now, I'm deciding your fate. And we can have a two-for-one special or we can follow through with the plans. Make a choice. The smartest one should be easy," Maxine said, not taking her gun off Talo.

Talo paused, the gun still pointed at Ava's head. Ava's smirk remained fixed on her face. Finally, Talo slowly lowered her weapon. Maxine followed suit, holstering her gun at her hip. "Glad we're on the same page," Maxine said. "More like different pages, same book," Ava replied. "Okay but if she's wrong..." "Then I'll take her out." She glanced at Talo like she could cut her in half with her stare. Maxine snarled, her voice a menacing growl, "Whether she is Ava or not, you don't touch her." Talo attempted to keep her composure, though inside she was trembling - she had never seen Maxine so enraged.

Talo hit the button for the elevator to resume its descent, her body retreating into the corner as she kept her distance. "She's a grade A bitch," Ava whispered to Maxine. Maxine smirked and gave a agreeable nod to Ava. Talo glanced over at them, her arms crossed defensively. She seemed on the verge of tears, but her stubbornness wouldn't allow it. As the elevator came to a stop, they all stepped out and were greeted by a seven-story housing unit.

The prison was an imposing structure, bathed in a harsh light. The concrete walls were gray, and the metal tables in the center gleamed coldly. The cell walls were made of thick, unbreakable glass, with the number of each cell painted in bold yellow with a black outline. The only way to reach the seven floors was a long, winding staircase. Forty cells occupied each floor, with seventy cells on either side of the two walls, each cell containing fifteen inmates. But the prison contained many more cells, many more housing units. Maxine gasped in disbelief, "How long have they had this place?" She surveyed the room of young and elderly faces. "It's been a few years," Ava replied solemnly. "The herloids marked their territory a long time ago."

Maxine desperately wanted to let out a piercing scream. Her compassion begged her to do something to help this abominable place. "Let's walk around for a bit and get footage," Ava said as she fixed the mini camera on her collar and led the way. They trudged by the prison cells, witnessing a multitude of men who appeared to be malnourished, famished, and exhausted.

"Okay, I'm gonna go to one of the experiment labs. I have to show that to the army. Just please go to Kincade and Tobias's cell. Here," Ava said as she handed a badge to Maxine. "If a guard questions you guys, then I need you, Talo, to tell them in Mondonii that you're taking them to experiment room A. Meet me there, I know the way out." Talo uttered in a caustic tone, "Ah, so you finally need me, huh?" "You are so pretty, yet all that beauty doesn't cover up your repressed insecurity," Ava said, with a wicked smile. Talo stood there, arms crossed in a dramatic gesture, seething with rage. Despite her fury, however, she could feel the guilt lurking beneath her emotions. "Anyway, just stick to the plan, ladies," Ava urged as she headed towards the exit doors to the left and saluted a herloid guard on her way out.

"I'm not insecure," Talo said, sounding insecure. "Look, you don't have to try to be so harsh, arrogant, and right all the time. You gotta loosen up, dude. And she's right, and my mom used to say, 'arrogance is just insecurity with makeup on,' and I think you're definitely a top-tier case and point for that statement. I see someone that's a potential sweetheart underneath all that bs. I hope you work on that," Maxine said. Talo suddenly felt like she could hide. Maxine read her insecurities very accurately. Talo also felt like she definitely let her parents' seeming neglect and over-attentiveness to her brother play a bigger role in her life than she imagined.

Maxine and Talo trudged up the steps, attempting to mirror the stern and emotionless expression of the other soldiers. Maxine was panting heavily by the time they'd reached the third floor. Talo secretly longed to simply soar to the sixth story. They both attempted to keep their breathing steady as they labored up the last few steps. They both straightened their posture and tried to fit in with the other soldiers, who marched resolutely and stood perfectly upright. It's like the herloid soldiers were machines. Trained down to a science. They reached the cell, and Maxine peered in, her gaze lingering on the prisoners slumbering in the bunks that ran along each wall of the cramped cell. At the end of the room was a toilet and a sink—the only amenities offered in the dismal space.

Maxine found Kincade asleep in the farthest corner of the cell, curled up on the lowest bunk. There was no sign of Tobias, which she found peculiar. She then examined the glass door, seeking where to present her badge. It was a plain door, with the cell number B605 written on its upper side. Talo suddenly had a vivid vision of a scaly hand pressing a badge against the left side of the door, so real it felt like reality. She shook off the trance and decided to offer her assistance.

"Just place the badge against the left of the door," Talo said. Maxine gazed at her doubtfully. "Just trust me. I know I haven't been so nice to you, but I wouldn't mislead you either. Trust me," Talo said. Maxine paused, then gave a solemn nod as she firmly pressed the badge on the left side of the door.

The door gilded open, allowing Maxine and Talo into the cell. Maxine surveyed her surroundings with a heavy heart, feeling sorrow for the inmates. She wished she could do more to help them, yet was aware of the Axpherian forces keeping an eye on every move. All she could do was to pray for the swift arrival of their troops. She found Kincade sleeping in a fetal position. Maxine knew every time he slept like this, he was having a nightmare. Maxine shook him gently, and his eyes flickered open. He gazed up at her, not recognizing her in her disguise, thinking it was just another guard. The light in his eyes dulled, and the usual smile that usually graced his lips was nowhere to be seen. Maxine's heart ached to see him like this, more despondent than she had ever seen him before.

"Kincade, Kincade, it's me," Maxine whispered. Kincade's eyes suddenly sprung to life as he recognized her voice. "Max? Why do you look like...." "Kincade, where is dad?" Maxine whispered. Kincade's face suddenly fell, his expression one of grief. "They took him last night." "Where!?" She exclaimed. "They might've taken him to the experiment room. I'm not sure," He said. Maxine felt a sudden surge of anxiety, her heart thumping rapidly in her chest. "Come on, we're gonna get you out of here," Maxine said. Kincade gazed around at his cellmates. "What about the others?" He asked. Maxine yanked Kincade from the bed, her voice low and resolute. "They're gonna get help. Let's go."

"Pst!" Talo said, gesturing her finger to Maxine's back pocket. Maxine's mind raced as she recalled the antidote. Talo kept a watchful eye to ensure no one would spot them, and Maxine retrieved the syringe and valve from her back pocket. Maxine examined the syringe, somewhat confused. The needle's plunger resembled scissors and demanded two fingers, but aside from that, the equipment was not much different than what she was used to on Earth. Marked in black characters, there were five lines running up the side of the syringe, numbered from one to five. "Fill it to two," Talo whispered. Maxine obliged and did as she was told. She accidentally filled it slightly past that, but it proved to be no harm. Talo watched closely as Maxine pulled off the plastic cap from the syringe. Taking a deep breath, she injected the serum into Kincade's arm, who slightly cringed. Quickly, Talo handed her a sanitizer pad, which she used to clean the injection site.

"Thank you," Maxine said. "No problem," Talo replied. "Did she tell you?" Kincade asked. Maxine squinted, confused. "Ava? Did she tell you how you're the real-life Diana Prince yet?" Maxine let out a soft chuckle and gave a slight nod. Through her laughter, however, the sadness she was trying to conceal was still visible. "Good," Kincade said as he rose up, and they began to slowly walk out of the cell. "She better have."

"Stop right there! Where are you taking 771?" A herloid soldier demanded just as they reached the door. Maxine, Talo, and Kincade stood motionless, a chill of fear sweeping over them. "We need to take him to Experiment room A," Talo said in Mondonii. The soldier scrutinized them suspiciously. "We're not doing any more experiments tonight. Not until the town is demolished. We'll start again by morning," The soldier replied in Mondonii. "Please! It's ordered by the sergeant. We need just this one for tonight," Talo assured. The soldier fixed his gaze on them, his gun raised menacingly. They were all frozen in fear, their hearts pounding with dread. It seemed their mission had been doomed to failure. It very well may have been.

"Just joshing you! Follow me," the soldier said with Ava's voice. They all looked relieved when they realized it was her. "I think I just died a little," Kincade said as they began to walk out of the cell. "Did you see a light at the end?" Ava asked. "I saw fire and brimstone," Kincade grinned. "Save a spot for me," Ava said as Kincade and the others emitted a quiet chorus of laughter.

They made their way downward towards a few corridors and headed to the elevator. Ava pressed the button with the circular shape, and the doors opened. They quickly piled inside as Ava selected three slim lines with a squiggly shape at the end. The elevator began to ascend. Maxine still wondered what happened to Tobias. She thought, "Why was he taken? What happened to him?" "Where is my father?" Maxine asked. Ava looked puzzled. "He wasn't with Kincade?" She asked. "They took him last night," Kincade said. Ava looked even more perplexed. "Weird," She said as they reached their floor.

They stepped off the elevator and were guided down a shadowy hallway. The walls were a deep black, the metal doors blending seamlessly into them. They all couldn't help but smell something rotting as they marched along. Maxine and Kincade scrunched their faces and exchanged a glance, sensing something off with the unusual smell.

They turned down two corridors before reaching a glass door displaying the words 'Experiment Room A'. Ava swiped her badge, and they stepped inside. The room was crescent-shaped. The cells were like the glass prisons in the cell houses, but these cells were only large enough for one person. The rooms were lit by bright white bulbs and a large, red lamp hung from the ceiling. The rotting smell was stronger than ever, causing Maxine, Kincade, and Talo to briefly cough. They felt the source of the smell had to be extremely close, as they all felt a thick presence behind them.

As they glanced back, they saw a grim sight of lifeless prisoners sprawled across the floor; men, women, and children alike. Maxine gasped in horror at the gruesome scene. Then at the end of the line of bodies, she saw him. Tobias. His eyes closed and his clothes stained with blood. "Dad!" She wailed in terror as Kincade restrained her. Her cries of despair echoed through the room as the others attempted to calm her down.

Talo was paused by a vision of a scaly mouth clamped around Ava's mouth as she tried to calm Maxine. She paused, coming face to face with one of the cells. Inside was Ava, sleeping on the cot, her body positioned as if someone had placed her there. A chill ran down her spine as she took in the scene. She realized with dread that they had been deceived. The real Ava ushered them into the building, but when she ventured into the Experiment room, they detected her presence and locked her in a cage before dispatching one of their own to find the others. Too late, Talo realized what had happened and felt a sharp blow to the back of her head before succumbing to darkness.

| 37 |

Maxine

Talo awoke to the harsh light of the cell beaming on her face. She slowly rose to her feet, her eyes widening as she took in her surroundings. She recognized the same green jumpsuit she wore as the one from the other prisoners. Despair washed over her as she glanced out of her cell and saw Maxine lying on the floor, restrained by black cuffs. She let out a loud cry, pounding on the glass in desperation.

Ava jolted awake in her cell, hearing Talo's cries emanating from the adjacent cell. She rushed to the door, pounding on the glass and screaming Maxine's name, desperately trying to use her telekinesis to break free. However, the cells had a control mechanism that prevented the use of their powers. Realizing this, Ava's screams intensified, echoing through the room. Kincade remained unconscious in his cell, oblivious to their cries.

Maxine jolted awake to the terrified screams of Ava and Talo. Peeling her eyes open, her vision blurred by the alternating red and white hues of the room. Her wrists were pinned down by tight handcuffs, and she immediately began thrashing her body, trying to break free. She screamed for her father, desperate for help. She then glanced at the row of lifeless bodies, noticing he was now gone.

The metallic doors of the room opened with a loud creak, and Maxine's eyes widened in terror. In walked a soldier, dragging a figure behind him. It was Tobias, but he was no longer the father Maxine recognized. His skin had mutated, taking on a scaly appearance from the neck down. His eyes had turned a deep shade of yellow, like those of the other herloids. He was expressionless, his hands bound behind his back.

Maxine gasped, her chest heaving in terror as the soldier walked over. She could hardly believe what was happening. "What have you done?!" Maxine shrieked, her voice edged with horror. "What have you done to my father?!"

"Young lady," the soldier intoned, a hint of dread in his voice, "you and your companions have illegally entered a restricted, confidential training ground." Maxine contorted her face in disbelief. "Training ground!?" She screamed, "You call this hell a training ground!?"

"Yes, training ground. We are training future soldiers for invasion and for the fight of proliferation of our species." Maxine listened incredulously as he detailed their intentions to conquer the planets and exact revenge on Axpherial for the wars he believed they ignited.

"So, to repopulate, you create genocide. That's revolting," Maxine hissed. "Revolting to you, revolution to us. Your idea of who's the villain in this situation is full of diluted fallacies. Earth is a wasteland full of people who are insubordinate, immoral, and careless. Which is why it was already on the edge of imminent annihilation even before our invasion. And now, our new and improved species will clean up this planet, and thrive in harmony. With the resurrection of our people, they will be much more susceptible to obedience and order!" The herloid soldier smirked at his explanation, as if it was godlike.

Maxine looked like she could vomit. "It sounds like a bunch of glorified bullshit. You really think that someone like you can thrive in harmony? You call the death of innocent people harmony? You call susceptible obedience harmony?" Maxine hissed. The herloid smiled wickedly, seemingly amused. "You may have been fortunate enough to flee from your planet before, but I will relish in watching you all mutilate each other."

Maxine looked confused at how he knew about her home planet. "How the hell do you...." "Your birthmark on your chest. All Utak possess it," Maxine gulped from this realization. He grinned smugly and said, "It's a shame I know more about your dead planet than you." Maxine's eyes averted his, thinking about the train, the hospital attack, the crows, and her house being blown to bits. Her eyes widened as she asked, "Was I a target?" The soldier formed a sinister grin, on the edge of laughter. "You are associated with the Axpherians. Fraternizing with the son of renowned scientists. Scientists with the cure. We had to make sure you and anyone you came into contact with were eliminated promptly, as you now became a threat to our plans." The soldier's grin broadened as he added, "Until today." Maxine quivered, her mouth slightly ajar as a dawn of realization hit her.

Maxine was still confused at what he meant by relishing in watching them mutilate each other. The herloid soldier continued to grin as he read the confusion on her face. "Your father, former father I mean, will enjoy drowning you in a pool of your own blood," He smiled wickedly. "Then after your agonizing last breaths, you will spill their blood."

Maxine took this in, shuddering in sheer terror at the very thought. She screamed as she tried to yank free once more, prompting the herloid to laugh. "You and all your friends were injected with the viola poison. When you die, we will reanimate you as one of our own. Axpherians and your kind may be immune to death from the poison, but the infection will quickly disable your sixth sense, and once you die, you will live again as a great, noble soldier who will fight alongside us. You guys will all be brought back greater than you've ever been before. You will spend your days on beautiful, renovated worlds with our species. But before that will transpire, your previous form will need to be demolished. And you will cleanse your allies and all will be balanced."

Maxine continued to yell and thrash on the floor after she heard his speech. The herloid untied Tobias, who brandished a razor-sharp dagger in his right hand as he glared at Maxine menacingly. Maxine's gaze shifted upward to the corners of the room, where she noticed numerous cameras. She knew they would record every moment of the atrocity that was about to unfold.

"You have front row seats to this entire thing," Maxine said with realization. The herloid grinned malevolently. "Make her suffer," he sniggered wickedly to Tobias as he left the room. As Maxine beheld the remains of Tobias, she was aware that he was gone, yet her eyes still begged for mercy while her tears trickled down her cheeks.

"Dad!" She cried out as Tobias towered over her, gazing at her with pure apathy. Maxine's heart raced as she gazed into Tobias' dark, yellow eyes. He raised the knife, ready to strike, as she felt her body tremble in terror. She screamed as he lunged forward, the dagger glinting in the light. Maxine rolled away just in time, hearing Tobias' deep, guttural grunt as the blade sailed past her. He began to stalk towards her as Maxine desperately sought a way out. She could hear Ava's distant cries, and she felt herself coming closer to her cell door.

Tobias let out an eerie scream as he lunged at Maxine, just barely missing her head and striking the glass of Ava's cell. Fortunately, Ava remained unharmed, as the glass door was exceptionally thick. Maxine began to pant as she started to lose self-control. She rose to her feet as Tobias started to bolt in her direction once more. He pursued her around the room, slashing the blade wildly with each step he took toward her. Terror filled her veins as she desperately tried to evade him.

Maxine felt her lungs burning as she struggled to draw in air. With every breath, it seemed more and more impossible to take it in. Finally, her strength gave out, and she collapsed in front of Kincade's cell, who was still unconscious, lying across his cot. Her lungs were in agony, and her head was spinning as she fought to catch her breath. "Dad, please! Dad, I know somewhere in there you can still hear me!" She cried out breathlessly.

Tobias was panting, unable to lunge at Maxine at that moment. She shut her eyes, focusing on Kam's words. She struggled to calm her breathing so she could take deep, steady breaths. She slowly closed her lids and felt her breaths gradually slow. She imagined herself transparent, blending in with her surroundings. Her strategy began to work as she was becoming less visible with each inhale. Then, Tobias grasped her neck with his left hand.

Maxine began to feel the flames back in her lungs. His hand crushed her throat so tight that she immediately saw black spots dancing in the corners of her vision. Even as she suffocated, she closed her eyes and concentrated again. This time she was able to become fully invisible, right before she would have passed out from the lack of oxygen. Tobias let her go and rose to his feet, bewildered and enraged.

Maxine felt relieved it worked, as she still felt the shadow of his grip lingering on her throat. She attempted to muffle her breathing as Tobias surveyed the area for her. She cautiously leaned her back against the wall and rose, moving along it bit by bit. As her breath evened out, she gradually backed away from him.

Ava and Talo were no longer screaming, their eyes darting around in search of Maxine. Both of them had their hands and faces pressed hard against the cold glass doors of their cells, their heartbeats pounding in their throats. Maxine began to inch even further away as Tobias savagely swiped the dagger around the room, hoping a stray stab would penetrate her. He began to scream loud as he swiped more and more, his eyes viciously scanning the room. Maxine then concentrated on breaking the cuffs. She felt the heaviness in her hands as she concentrated hard as her telekinetic ability forced the cuffs to give way. She was proud of herself, this was the first time she was able to do that willingly.

Tobias heard the clatter of the cuffs, and he bolted in that direction, shrieking as he brandished his dagger. Maxine was able to locate the needle and valve containing the antipoison and fled out of the way. She cautiously filled the needle with the antidote, keeping her distance. Tobias, now seething with anger, frantically scanned the room for her. Maxine began to circle the room, her grip on the needle unwavering.

She crept closer to him as he menacingly brandished the dagger. He gasped for breath as he desperately searched for her. She noticed that part of her hand was becoming visible again, a sign that the poison was taking effect. She gazed downward, noticing her legs beginning to materialize. She stayed behind him, feeling her control slipping away. She strained to maintain her abilities, but to no avail. She was becoming visible again, and quickly.

She tried not to panic as she looked down and saw her upper half appear. Only her left hand and right arm were still unseen. She continued to circle behind him as he continued to angrily look for her. She finally got close enough to his back and with the thrust of her left arm, she jabbed the needle into his shoulder.

She pressed on the plunger as Tobias turned around and she felt a sharp sting penetrate her back. Maxine gasped in agony as the sharp pain seared her spine. He had plunged the dagger deep into her just seconds before he fell to the floor and lost consciousness, taking the dagger with him. Her cries of anguish pierced the air as she crumpled to the ground. Ava and Talo screamed in horror as Maxine hit the floor with a thud. Kincade slowly rose from his cell, his eyes wide with terror as he saw Maxine lying on the ground, blood pooling around her. He pounded on his cell door, shrieking her name.

Maxine found herself unable to utter a word, her throat still raw from Tobias' grip. She attempted to concentrate on healing her wound, but it seemed impossible. As she lay there bleeding on the ground, she felt her energy slipping away. Kincade pounded and kicked at his cell door, desperate to get to her. She could hear, "No Maxine, please!" and "Stay with us, Max! Stay with us!" coming from the cells, but was too weak to make out who said what.

Her breaths became shallow as she started to succumb to her injury. She was bleeding out fast, as the pool of blood that surrounded her became significantly larger than before. She closed her eyes as she accepted that this was it. This was how she felt she would die. Bleeding out, but a hero. Maxine's heart raced as she turned her head to the right, seeing a vision of Imani, smiling in a pristine white gown. She managed a crooked smile, relieved to be reunited with her. Just as she closed her eyes and accepted death, the entire facility plunged into darkness and the sound of explosions filled the air.

****

Meanwhile, the general, who had just defeated Kam, Bliss, and Orna, was now descending toward the Zeus City power supply. He landed between two buzzing power boxes, right in front of towering metal structures that buzzed with electricity. He gripped the novuk tightly, a circular device that held the power to detonate the planted explosives.

The area was encircled by a metal gate, with its top adorned with menacing barbed wire. The general, whose real name was Ko'mas, was the one-time ruler of the Herloid world, now serving as the army's powerful general. He had taken the life of the former general and concealed the truth of his death as a case of accidental poisoning. In actuality, it was the deadly viola poison that had taken its toll on him.

Now the soldiers followed him with unquestioned servitude. He spun around, bellowing for the soldiers who were safeguarding the city's energy supply. Twelve soldiers materialized as they encircled Ko'mas. Ko'mas' face lit up with triumph as he gazed upon the guards.

"Our primary threat has been neutralized. Tonight, we witness a further step in our insurrection. Another stride towards reconstruction. We still have a battle before us, but after this, we will obliterate another lingering peril. The Axpherial regiments occupying the base camps. I now have the maps, and we will initiate an ambush within 48 hours. Our other soldiers will be apprised, and that's when they will take part in the onslaught. All I have to do is dispatch these maps to the other databases and the Axpherians will be just as dead as Utak and the rest of Earth will be," he declared in Mondonii.

General Ko'mas had a charm that easily drew people in, particularly the herloid soldiers who already viewed him as a god. Striding over to one of the colossal metal structures shaped like a dome, he planted the nuvak. It emanated a dim blue light from its center and began emitting short, soft beeps. Ko'mas and the soldiers stepped back, and his smirk deepened as he anticipated the moment when the device would emit a single, long beep - signaling that the bombs in the city had been activated. Each long beep would activate one bomb at a time, detonating a tenth of the city.

The device's beeping quickened, becoming shorter and more rapid. Ko'mas' smirk widened as he observed. The beeping increased, resembling a heartbeat at an alarming 200 beats per minute. The device glowed red and the lights of Zeus city suddenly died. After a few seconds, the lights flickered back on.

Maka's grin faded when he didn't hear deafening explosions coming from the city. His face shifted from euphoria to incomprehension as he anxiously scanned the area. The guards were likewise confused, yelling out in Mondonii in a state of alarm. Suddenly, a guard's arm was detached and dropped to the ground. His agonizing screams echoed through the night as dark blood spurted from his amputated arm. One by one, the guards were butchered, their limbs, heads, and even torsos flying across the power plant. Most fell dead instantly, with only a few left howling in agony amidst the carnage.

General Ko'mas brandished his sword in every direction, unsure of where to strike. He felt a presence from behind and slashed furiously. He swung to the side, then forward. He swung and yelled multiple times, then paused to catch his breath. He stumbled back, seeing his guards sprawled in pools of black blood. Most were dead, the rest were moaning and teetering on the brink of death.

He began to retreat, his sword quivering in his grip. Then, with a single stroke, his blade was cleaved in two. Dropping his sword, he scrambled to his hip and pulled out a pistol-sized laser gun. In a desperate frenzy, he fired off a shot in front of him.

"Do you now feel like the helpless one?" He heard from his left side. He whirled around and fired the gun in the direction of the voice. "Like I told your subordinate, you don't know how ruthless I can be to protect the ones I love." The voice sounded exactly like Kam's.

Ko'mas was flabbergasted. His expression was one of utter astonishment. "You're dead!" He shouted, still shaking with fear as he pointed the gun in front of him. "There's no way you could have survived that!"

"How do you explain this?" Kam asked. "I might not have a rational explanation for your survival, but Axpherians don't heal that quickly, especially if the wounds are fatal. You are a walking anomaly. But I'll make sure you take your last breaths this time!" Ko'mas shouted as he continued to aim his gun in every direction. "You're not faster, stronger, or more perceptive than me!" Ko'mas exclaimed with shaky confidence.

"Your arrogance will be your downfall. Put the gun down. This is your only chance to surrender."

"Do you suppose you can impede me? Do you truly believe you are formidable enough to bring me to my knees!? I caution you, you will die in your attempt!" Ko'mas roared with such intensity that it caused his throat to ache.

"Your people took from us! They took our lives, our families - slaughtered by the millions!" Ko'mas roared. "And you think you can just take it all again?!"

"You have repeatedly decimated your own kind. And when they refused to accept your oppressive leadership, you tried to annihilate what you perceived as a weaker race. Wiping out planets will not bring peace to your people, but rather, an apocalypse for countless innocent species," Kam declared.

"Shut up!"

"Now you're furious because I threw a wrench in your plans," Kam remarked. "A pathetic Axpherian like me, that's what you call us, isn't it?"

"Shut up! Shut up!!" Ko'mas roared as he fired his gun wildly, hoping to find a fatal hit.

"You can't hide forever, Kam. Remember what I said, as good as dead." He pointed the gun in the direction of the dome-shaped metal structure, believing he spotted him there. Then he swung it around to the back, then the side again. Suddenly, the barrel of the gun was sliced in two, and Ko'mas let out an anguished cry, dropping the weapon. He frantically searched his surroundings, now defenseless. He gazed upon one of the deceased guards, finding a gun lying in a pool of blood. He lifted the weapon up, and it seemed to magically drift into his grasp.

The gun was massive, resembling a shotgun, but with an eerie red-glowing barrel and a white-glowing trigger. He narrowed one eye and steadied his aim. In the far distance, he spotted a figure cloaked in camouflage attempting to flee. His smirk widened as he targeted the figure. His aim was precise. His grin widened as he squeezed the trigger, the gun's barrel aimed unerringly at the camouflaged figure's head.

Ko'mas plummeted to the ground after firing the gun, as if the shot had ripped the life right out of him. He let out a gut-wrenching howl as he felt the laser penetrate his chest. His hand instinctively flew to his wound, a faint orange light glowing from his palm as he tried to heal the injury. To no avail, as the pain only intensified. His heart began to beat faster and faster, and he could feel the life slowly slipping away from him. He lay there, helpless and desperate, as the blood gushed from his body.

"See, I told you it would work!" He heard beside him as he tried to catch his breath. Suddenly, Kam, Bliss, and Orna materialized in front of him. Ko'mas was astonished and mortified at seeing Bliss and Orna still alive.

"Electric and bulletproof suits, came in pretty handy, didn't they?" Bliss asked, sounding proud of herself. Kam and Orna grinned at her knowingly. "But it was my idea to bring an extra Tonch," Kam retorted. "Yeah, yeah, but it was me and Orna who played dead and planted the last one."

"But it was me who designed the reverse shotgun," Kam replied. Bliss gave a subtle nod, her expression showing a hint of agreement. "You beat me there, I'll admit," She replied.

The reverse shotgun fired a massive amount of Viola poison directly into Ko'mas' body. He was immediately stripped of all his abilities, and it was certain death. Ko'mas was dumbfounded to have been outwitted. He felt every ounce of energy being drawn away from him, rendering him powerless to do anything but lay there, enduring the excruciating pain as his consciousness began to slowly leave him.

Kam, Bliss, and Orna encircled Ko'mas, who glared at Kam with a mix of anger and disbelief. His chest, still oozing blood, was a stark reminder of the moment he saw Kam seemingly take his last breath before his eyes. Yet, here he was, looking as alive as ever.

"I still don't know how you survived, but you won't be a survivor for long," He grunted as he struggled to stay conscious. Kam just grinned and shook his head. "So intelligent, yet so ignorant to how capable I am," He said as his eyes paused on a dying Ko'mas.

Ko'mas suddenly smirked, as if his victory was still assured. "Do you really think you've won?" he queried, his gaze now encompassing all three of them. "Well, we did, so..." Orna said as Bliss and Kam chuckled.

"Stupid, kids! You have no idea what's in store for you!" Ko'mas shouted arrogantly. Kam cast his eyes upon him, a part of him bearing empathy. Yet, another part of him was pleased to witness his affliction. "Just holding on to pride until the end. Unfortunately, pride won't heal your wound. Or stop what's coming to you," Kam said. Ko'mas surprisingly kept a smile on his face, then erupted into a hearty laugh as if he had won. This left Kam slightly perplexed.

"Should I shut him up or you?" Bliss asked menacingly as she trained her gun at Ko'mas' head. Kam silently took the gun from Bliss's grip and aimed, just as she had done, at the same spot above his right eyebrow.

"May the gods forgive your crimes," Kam uttered as he put Ko'mas out of his misery.

| 38 |

The final chapter

Maxine awoke to the rhythmic beat of a heart monitor. Her gaze swept over the hospital beds that lined either side of her own, and her skin crawled at the feel of the oxygen machine pressed against her face. She ripped the mask off, her heart racing as she cried out for her father. The nurse sprinted into the room, her shoes squeaking on the tiled floor, and with a strong grip, she pressed Maxine back into the bed. Her screams echoed in the room as she desperately called out for Tobias.

The nurse tried her best to contain her, but it was clear she was slightly delirious. "Ma'am, Ma'am! You're in good hands! You're still healing!" The nurse exclaimed. "Where am I? Where is dad?" Maxine screamed frantically.

"Miss, you're in the base camp hospital." Maxine looked confused. "Base camp?" "Axpherian base camp hospital," The nurse reiterated. Maxine suddenly relaxed, yet she still seemed lost. The nurse was breathtaking. Her chestnut complexion complimented her sunset-colored eyes.

The nurse informed Maxine of the Axpherian army's invasion of the herloid facility. Most of the herloid soldiers were slain, yet, the prisoners were saved, and were ferried to the base camps. The prisoners were provided medical attention, and they were administered a dose of antipoison. "Your supernatural abilities will take a few weeks before they're fully restored. Put your trust in the medical staff, and you should be back in optimal condition soon," the nurse stated as she smiled reassuringly before exiting through a set of automatic steel doors.

Maxine's body relaxed as she settled onto the hospital cot. Her thoughts turned to Kam, Ava, Tobias, and the others, praying they had all escaped unscathed.

Maxine awoke the following day to find Kincade and Ava hovering above her bed. "Hey, superwoman," Ava uttered in a raspy voice. Maxine noticed a long faint scar over her left eye. "Are you guys okay?" She asked.

"Physically, we're good, but emotionally…." Kincade gave a nervous laugh before continuing, "It's a character arc I'll trauma dump about in a less unusual circumstance." Maxine let out a joyful chuckle, pleased to see that Kincade's spirits had been restored. Ava, on the other hand, simply shook her head while grinning. "You're the epitome of bizarre," She said, half kidding. "Would I be Kincade if I wasn't?" He smiled. "Sadly, no," Ava replied into a slim chuckle.

Maxine's eyes suddenly lit up as she thought about Tobias. "Wait, where's dad?" "He's alive. Luckily, he doesn't remember being a herloid. Thank god. But he's over in recovery. Recovering and whatnot," Kincade said as Maxine and Ava shared a laugh.

"Well, we can hopefully keep the whole trying to end my life thing between us, then," Maxine said, sounding relieved. "Of course. We need this whole, trying to man up version of him intact. He might revert back to old ways territory, knowing him," Kincade said as Maxine grinned, and Ava held a chuckle.

Maxine thought about this. She wouldn't have been able to stand the over emotional love bombing or constant apologizing she would endure if he remembered what he had done. "Thank you," Maxine said with a heavy grin. "Yeah, whatever. We always got your back," Ava said. "Max!" Shouted a familiar voice.

Kam, Bliss, Orna, and Talo rushed to her side. Kincade was bewildered, never having seen these mysterious individuals with their almost perfect features and stunningly colored eyes. "Who's the team of unusually good-looking avengers?" Kincade asked. Maxine abruptly realized that this was Kincade's first encounter with them, and Ava's first encounter with Kam's sister and companions. Maxine rapidly presented them as they all exchanged handshakes.

"You never told me you had fourth-dimensional friends, sis," Kincade said after his initial introduction to the group. "Well not all of them are just friends," Ava slipped. Maxine was suddenly overcome with a wave of apprehension. She stared at Ava, as if she had said too much. Ava pulled a contrite expression and silently mouthed the word, "Sorry," to Maxine.

Kincade's brow furrowed in confusion. Then, comprehension dawned on him, and he cast his gaze upon Kam and his friends. "Okay Rogue, which one is Gamblet?" Kincade asked Maxine. All were perplexed, until Kam finally caught on and timidly lifted his left arm. Kincade beamed, asking, "Is he treating you no less than royalty?" Maxine nodded her head, a smile on her face.

Kincade sauntered up to Kam, who instinctively moved away slightly, as if he was being threatened. "No need to fear, brother," he said as he outstretched his arm and clasped his hand with Kam's. He then wrapped his other arm around Kam in an embrace. Kam, a bit awkwardly, returned the hug. "I'm gonna have to teach you how to greet like a brother, brother!" Kincade excitedly exclaimed as he gently planted his hand on Kam's shoulder. He leered in close and menacingly muttered, "Between me and you, you break her heart, I break your jaw like that shit was glass." With that, he stepped back.

Kam shrank back as Kincade cracked a smirk and gave him one more pat. "Welcome to our dysfunctional family," Ava said with a grin. "I'm already in one, so adjusting shouldn't be a pain," Orna shrugged. The group let out a collective, subtle laugh. "Yeah, I promise to try to go easier on you," Talo said to Maxine. "God, I hope so," Ava said, rolling her eyes. "You'll grow accustomed to her, we all had to," Bliss remarked as Talo gave her a playful tap on the chest, causing her to giggle. They were all in high spirits and bantering as if they had been friends for ages before they eventually headed off, allowing Maxine to get some rest.

Maxine lay still in her bed, reflecting on the events that had taken place. Her emotions fluctuated as she recalled the memories, ranging from laughter to tears. Though relieved that her loved ones were safe and sound, a sense of foreboding lingered in the pit of her stomach. She felt that something was amiss. Her intuition told her so, and her intuition was never wrong.

****

Kam and Bliss were taking in the scenic view of Zeus City from the top of a hill, outside of the base camp. "We almost lost them," Kam said. Bliss gazed downward as she processed this. "If I haven't told you already, I wouldn't know what to do without you," Kam said. "We rely on each other, bro. We did this together. All of us did," Bliss said. Kam smirked. "Makes me embrace this hero complex that's been halo-ing over my head this whole time," Kam said. "I still think your little complex is unbearable sometimes, but I wouldn't change a thing," Bliss said with a tight-lipped smile. Kam grinned in response.

Bliss then made a face, considering Kam's remarkable healing abil-ity. Even the most resilient Axpherians typically wouldn't bounce back so quickly. "How'd you do it?" Bliss inquired. Kam raised an eyebrow. "Not quite catching." "Your recovery was perplexing to say the least. I'd understand if it was Maxine or her siblings, because their species is known for their accelerated healing. But us, we heal fast, too, but you.." Bliss stopped herself in her tracks, not wanting to delve into the topic any further, worried it would spoil the atmosphere.

Kam had always been aware of his power, although he had kept it hidden. Even so, the full scope of it eluded him. "I can't explain miracles, sis. Maybe…" Kam trailed off, not sure how to explain the unexplainable. "Maybe it's just an ability hidden somewhere deep. I'm not sure," He said, coming up short of any other explanation. "Let's just be happy that you're here. Hero complex intact and all," Bliss beamed.

Kam grinned and stepped forward for a hug, squeezing Bliss a bit too tightly as usual. Bliss pretended not to notice, as she always did.

He quickly released his grip as they both glanced over and spotted Ala and Meeka. Fearful of what they might say, they both froze in place. "Thank the gods you two are alright!" Ala exclaimed as she and Meeka hastened to their side. Meeka let out a heavy sigh, "We apologize for not taking you both seriously before. We simply desire to shield you, so when we appear too strict, it is never out of malice. We love you too much, and it just makes us a bit overprotective sometimes." "And we promise to not keep so much from you guys in the future. We should've been more transparent from the start," Ala admitted.

Kam and Bliss beamed, elated that they didn't have to endure another scolding session from them. "You know we love you guys, regardless of your sometimes dictorian ways," Bliss smiled as they all shared a laugh. "I'm just glad you aren't keeping your distance for not believing you guys when you needed us most," Ala said. "And Kam, we'd love to know more of your late-night adventures Bliss keeps covering up for you," Ala said as Kam and Bliss glanced at each other, mortified. "We mean it. I was like you once. But we promise not to be restrictive, and to respect the fact that you both are growing up," Meeka said. "Thank you, dad." Kam said, relieved for his understanding. "We thought you were coming to execute us with your words," Bliss admitted.

Ala's lips curved into a sweet grin as did Meeka's. "We'll spare you this one time. Only because your little antics saved two civilizations," Meeka pointed out as Kam and Bliss shared a nervous chuckle. Kam's face lit up with joy as the group joined in a collective embrace. They chatted for a few more minutes before boarding their hovercraft and setting off for Axpherial. Everyone felt a sense of relief that the battle was finally over.

****

It had been six weeks since the fateful confrontation with the Herloids, and Maxine had made a full recovery. She and the others were returned to Zeus City, now protected on both sides by Axpherian and American soldiers. The anomaly test kits were no longer needed because the device the Axpherians had been perfecting had finally been completed, and the cure had been released into the atmosphere three weeks earlier, eradicating the viola poison for good.

Unfortunately, there was no way to bring back the deceased, but those who had been infected with the poison made a full recovery. Those who had been transformed into Herloids were restored to their pre-infected state with no recollection of the events. Maxine and her family were temporarily placed in a modest hotel in downtown Zeus City. Though not overly luxurious, the interior was pleasant with a renovated kitchen featuring stainless steel appliances, two king-size mattresses with memory foam, and a cozy couch equipped with cable TV and Wi-Fi. They were grateful for the accommodation since their home was close to being finished by the Axpherians.

Maxine and her family enjoyed a Chinese takeout dinner while playing Uno. Maxine was on a roll and won the majority of the rounds. Meanwhile, Tobias was glued to the TV, watching the latest news on the world's progressive recovery and reconstruction. "Uno, out!" Maxine exclaimed, slamming down a wild card. "You cheater, you held on to that!" Kincade exclaimed with a mouth full of orange chicken. "Say it, don't spray it, man!" Ava cringed as she saw bits of chicken fly from his mouth. "Can you think of an insult that's less, you know... cliché?" Kincade asked. "Well, dude, if the glass slipper fits," Ava replied, as Maxine stifled a giggle. Kincade wolfed down the chicken and playfully stuck his tongue out at her. Maxine and Ava burst into laughter, leaning into each other.

Suddenly, there was a subtle knock at the door that caught their attention. "I'll get it," Kincade declared as he opened it. Outside stood a remarkable figure with dark skin and ocean-blue eyes, draped in a white robe emblazoned with the symbol of Axpherial. The man handed Kincade a piece of paper, bowed his head, and silently departed. Kincade closed the door and read the message aloud. "Maxine Hewitt, Kincade Hewitt, and Ava Clark, you are hereby invited to be honored for your brave deeds in the Axpherian city of Elmana in a ceremony eleven days from now at the great strength. We thank you for safeguarding the lives of countless people. A hovercraft will arrive to pick you up at two o'clock. Regards, Soza, Lead Representative of Elmana."

Kincade gazed up, as did the others. Kincade grinned as he took in the reality of the situation. "I'm not sure about everyone else, but don't you all feel like main characters in some action-packed live-action hero movie?" Kincade asked. "More like the main characters in an action-packed book. Books, you know, are superior to films," Ava said. "Dude, that sounds exceptionally accurate," Maxine agreed. "Whatever, I just feel like we're going on a field trip to Wakanda or something," Kincade said. "Trust me, dude. It definitely looked like Wakanda in person," Maxine replied. "What are you guys talking about? It sounds very imaginative," Tobias asked, glancing over at them.

Everyone regarded him with a puzzled expression, having over-looked his obliviousness to all that had happened. "Should we tell him?" Ava asked. "Tell me what exactly?" Tobias asked. "Dad, we need you to unplug from the matrix of rationality for a minute if that's okay," Kincade uttered nervously. Tobias looked befuddled as the group assembled on the bed facing him. They all stared at him, uncertain of how to go about conveying what they knew. Eventually, after a brief pause, they began to explain everything. Well, almost everything.

Tobias was so bewildered; it felt like a dream when they informed him of their actual home, dimensions, supernatural abilities, the viola poison masquerading as a virus, and Axpherial. "It might need some time to marinate, pops. But trust me, it'll all make sense sooner or later," Kincade said, patting him on the shoulder. Tobias gazed at the floor and massaged his chin, still trying to ponder everything. Maxine seemed a bit worried as she saw his expression. "Dad?" She analyzed him further, "Dad, are you gonna say something?" Tobias still paused, not saying a word.

"Max, don't worry; he'll be fine," Ava said as they made their way back to the kitchen table. "Let's play a game of poker, I'll deal." "Why do you always deal?" Kincade asked. "Win a game, and I'll maybe let you shuffle the cards," Ava replied. "Max, you're gonna say some-thing?" Kincade asked kiddingly. "Something," Maxine gestured as they all laughed and sat down, continuing to joke and laugh amongst each other. Tobias still pondered, not yet recovering from the shock of the new information.

****

On the twenty-fifth floor in The Great Strength, a small arena fit-ting over a thousand citizens was filled to the brim. Kam, Bliss, Talo, Orna, Maxine, Kincade, and Ava were adorned in blue robes. Soza had them form a line, and as each one stepped up, he placed a hand on their shoulder and presented them with a black and white medal that had a small, gleaming golden sword implanted in its center. He proceeded to clasp it around their necks, and when they were all in a row, he made a heartfelt speech, expressing his gratitude for their efforts against the Herloids and their contribution to the preservation of Earth and Axpherial.

In the audience, Meeka, Ala, and Tobias, along with Orna's parents and his eight siblings, and Talo's parents and their incredibly handsome son, who was a few years older than Talo, were present. Everyone rose to their feet in applause after Soza's speech. The roar of applause continued for a while, with Soza making multiple attempts to ease the crowd. Kam, Maxine, and the others stood hand in hand, taking in the gratitude the crowd provided them.

Once the event concluded, they all stood in a circle outside the tower and discussed the accomplishment. Orna wiped a tear, feeling genuinely honored. He tried to conceal it, but Talo quickly took notice and grinned at him knowingly. "Don't start, Talo. Let me be a softie in peace," Orna uttered. "It's okay, I have nothing mean to say," Talo paused, then continued, "This time, anyway." Orna smiled and nodded, though perplexed that she was letting up. "This is an intriguing mo-ment of swift character development," Ava pointed out. Talo grinned. "I'm still working on said development, but thanks," Talo replied.

Kam and Maxine kept their hands intertwined, though they were trying to be subtle about it. "Peter and Mary Jane over there trying to duck behind their fancy robes," Kincade pointed out. "Who's hiding?" Maxine said as she grasped Kam's face and planted a soft kiss on his lips. Kam tensed up at first, but relaxed and let his lips get lost in hers. "Can you let them be mushy in peace? You already put him through the big brother hazing phase," Ava said, partly serious. "Nope," Kincade grinned.

She was referring to a few weeks earlier when Kincade interrogated Kam, sitting him down in a room for over an hour, giving him a rundown of all the consequences he'd face if he broke Maxine's heart in any way, shape, or form. He kept a cold attitude toward him until just recently when his attitude changed and he declared, "You passed!" after he had decided that he endured enough.

Orna gave Talo a mischievous glance, who responded with a nervous grimace. "Our turn?" Orna asked Talo. "Try to kiss me and I'll vaporize you," Talo snapped. "Oohh a challenge!" Orna replied with a hard grin. Talo shook her head and cringed as the group echoed a chorus of laughter.

Kam felt a sudden, familiar buzz in his hands. He quickly glanced around, catching everyone's bewildered stares. "What's with the wandering eyes, lover boy?" Bliss asked. Kam voiced his concern, "Something feels off." Everyone turned to him, sensing that he might be onto something. But none of them could put their finger on what it might be, nor could Kam.

Abruptly, a deafening engine sound reverberated from above. Glancing up, the onlookers widened their eyes as a silver, round-shaped object hovered a few hundred feet up in the air. A woman's voice suddenly emanated from the peculiar airship. "Citizens of Axpherial, heed this warning. We bring news of grave importance concerning the fate of your world." All eyes were upon the speaker, taken aback by the gravity of the proclamation.

She continued, "It is undeniable that our kind failed to conquer Earth, a planet we intended to annihilate and then reconstruct with our own race. However, your endeavors merely postponed the inevitable." Kam suddenly recalled Ko'mas's last words, "Stupid, kids! You have no idea what's in store for you!" Kam's heartbeat shot into overdrive as he grasped the reality of everything.

"We have succeeded in claiming another world for our ever-growing forces. We are now confident that our numbers are sufficient to overwhelm your population, governments, and military. Your military may be formidable, but it is no match for ours. We are now your sovereigns and you will accord us due respect. However, those who threaten to defy us shall be made examples of before we commence our reign," the voice from the hovercraft declared menacingly.

Suddenly, a holographic screen appeared before the hovercraft, displaying Kam and his companions in close-up. They stared in horror as they realized that the Axpherians would witness their demise in real time. "Defy not, for that would bring forth untold misery. Attempt not to flee, for you cannot elude us," The voice declared. "We are the Herloids! United in power, strengthened in numbers, and supreme in ruling! And this is a hostile takeover."

The final proclamation echoed ominously through the air as pandemonium erupted and they hastened to flee as the sounds of bombs began to go off. The horrified shrieks of the crowd filled the air as the bombs dropped from the sky, sending bodies flying and engulfing them in raging balls of fire. Many were left in disbelief, unable to comprehend the terror and destruction that had been unleashed.

Kam was hurled to the ground by the force of an explosion. Orna and Talo grabbed him and dragged him alongside them as they desperately tried to avoid the bombs. He spun around, searching for Maxine. He spotted her, running in the opposite direction, and he lunged forward, snatching her hand. They and their companions spotted a luminous orange portal beside them and dashed inside. The portal vanished in the same instant a bomb was dropped in its place, narrowly missing them.

To Be Continued..........

Book 1 of 3
Axpherial II: Demolition
Coming soon!!

ABOUT THE AUTHOR

Born in Las Vegas, NV, AJ Kelley's passion for writing ignited at a young age. From the tender age of 9, he started crafting stories, initially sharing them with family and friends. However, as he approached his late teens, his dedication to the craft intensified.

AJ began weaving beautiful poetry and spinning tales that captivated his readers for years. This dedication culminated in the publication of his debut book, "No Fairytale Allowed," when he was just 22 years old.

In 2022, AJ took a poetic turn with the release of "The Prayers Of A Black Sheep," a collection of poems inspired by the challenges of his own life journey. Now, he is putting out a trilogy of YA fiction books, inspired by ideas years in the making.

This is just the beginning of AJ Kelley's literary journey, and he has an exciting array of creative works in store for the near future. Stay tuned!